DE LINT
De Lint, Charles,
Triskell tales
:twenty-two years of c

Triskell
Tales

Triskell Tales

Twenty-two Years of Chapbooks

Charles de Lint

Subterranean Press ⅄ 2000

Deluxe Hardcover Edition
Second Printing
ISBN
1-892284-78-2

Trade Paperback Edition
ISBN
1-931081-83-2

Subterranean Press
P. O. Box 190106
Burton, MI 48519

email:
subpress@earthlink.net

web site:
www.subterraneanpress.com

author's web site:
www.charlesdelint.com

Contents:

Grateful acknowledgements are made to:

Kiya Heartwood for the use of a verse of "Wishing Well" from her album *True Frontiers*. Copyright © 1993 by Kiya Heartwood, Delta Boy Music/BMI, Outlaw Hill Music/BMI. Lyrics reprinted by permission. For more information about Kiya, her band Wishing Chair or her current label Terrakin Records, call 1-800-ROADDOG, or email terrakin@aol.com.

For MaryAnn

Foreword

You are about to have a unique experience. You are about to watch a young writer hone his craft. These stories mark Charles' development as a writer from the years 1977 to 1999. You'll see that he was a little awkward at the outset, but something very special stands out: he has always had a beautifully poetic quality to his writing.

Charles was twenty-five years old when he wrote that first Christmas chapbook for me. He was a way-cool, long-haired record store clerk with the most gorgeous, piercing green eyes imaginable. We were in the beginnings of what was to become a steadfast partnership. As with any new relationship, we had our unsteady moments. I was crazy about him, but I wondered whether I'd be able to sustain that feeling; I had a history of having fallen out of love with previous amours. I needn't have worried. I've never lost the intrigue I felt about him; that mysterious quality keeps me hooked these twenty-five years later, but more than that, he's the kindest person I know. Not a pushover, but genuinely thoughtful and caring. He's my beautiful lover and my very best friend.

Before we'd ever met, Charles sent me a handmade booklet of sweet little poems. Some were love poems. He'd taken my name and address off a cheque I'd written in the record store for a Donovan album. I couldn't set foot in the record store for a year after that. My intuition warned me that I would be too smitten, too out of control over this guy. But during that year my grandfather passed away, leaving me his 1912 Gibson mandolin, and I needed to find a music teacher. My friend Greg Torrington worked in the same record shop and he knew lots of players, so I gathered my courage and visited Greg to ask about possible teachers. I just about died when Greg promptly called across the store, "Charles, you play mandolin, don't you?"

We made a date for that first lesson, and as the hour approached I started to feel scared and nervous. I told my roomie to tell him I had a family emergency and fled. A couple of weeks later Charles called and asked whether I really wanted those lessons or not. This time I went through with it. My intuition was correct; I learned my first Celtic tune during that initial lesson and I also spent a very long time kissing the teacher.

⤙⤚⤙

Triskell Tales gathers twenty-two years of stories — a true labour of love, given that most of these works were written as very special Christmas gifts for me. There is poetry here, too. Considering that it was Charles' verse that first won my heart, it seemed fitting to share some of that with you, as well.

We've been approached at various times over the years to publish a collection of these chapbooks, and Charles has always been reluctant to do so. It took the right combination: a fine publisher, the arrival of the millennium, and a weak moment, to get Charles to agree to let Subterranean Press to gather these stories in one volume. I hope they give you a sense of the man behind the pen and the deep love that we share.

MaryAnn Harris

Introduction

I've told this story before, but it bears repeating here. And not simply because it shows my naiveté (which it does).

You see, I've always loved to write and tell stories; it just never occurred to me that one could make a living doing so. Oh, I was aware that there were authors, and they wrote the books I loved to read, but the idea of writing as a career option for myself never even entered the equation.

So from my mid-teens on I devoted myself to playing music, which was another passion. The trouble is, I chose the wrong kind of music. At the very beginning of the seventies there was no worldbeat, no Pogues, no cross-over artists. The traditional Celtic music that I loved was relegated to the same venues as the Irish American music of groups like the Irish Rovers: bars. In North America, or at least certainly in Ottawa, there were no pubs for quite some time, and even when they began to spring up, the patrons expected Celtic music to be Irish bar music.

(The one exception here in Ottawa was the Celt's Room above the Lido Restaurant on Queen Street, a haven of real traditional music in the mid-seventies run by the late Joe McFadden. But while the patrons were certainly appreciative and loyal, there simply wasn't enough business in the place to support a livelihood for the three rotating house bands of which my own Wickentree was one. We all needed outside work.)

Eventually I got tired of playing for drunks and quit performing for a few years, only playing music at sessions and in the kitchen, or on the front porch with MaryAnn and friends.

What does this have to do with writing?

Well, just as I backed off and kept my music at home, I'd always done that with my writing. I've been in love with words and story and character for as long as I can remember and from the mid-sixties on, never stopped writing. Mostly poetry and songs, endless pages of them that I'd make up into little handwritten books and give to friends and send to pen pals.

Much of it, particularly the fantasy-oriented material, was derivative. Much of the poetry and songs was inspired by British singers such as Donovan and the members of the Incredible String Band, though I used the work of Bob Dylan, Tom Rapp and Leonard Cohen as templates as well. Early stories were most heavily influenced by Lord Dunsany, though there came a period when I was writing what I thought of as spaghetti westerns in ancient settings, combining my appreciation of Louis L'Amour with heroic fantasy writers such as Robert E. Howard.

My first book-length work was a narrative poem in the style of William Morris, written in that bastard mock old English that he could do so well; coming from the pen of a teenage North American in the late sixties/early seventies, it was just silly, and certainly not marketable.

But I wasn't writing for a market. I was writing for the joy of it, something I still do today, though currently I'm lucky in that the things I want to write appear to have an audience.

Now, about the time that I took a hiatus from performing on stage, I was working in retail—record stores, to be precise, though I've done a bit of time in book stores too. I liked working on the floor (serving customers) and in the back (shipping/receiving), but when you stay anywhere for awhile, you eventually end up in management, and that I never liked at all.

The bookkeeping, hiring and firing of staff, the responsibilities…it takes all the fun out of working in a store. And also brings home what a dead-end job it can be. Once you're managing a store, the only place up that you can go is to open your own, and that creates a whole new mess of headaches.

But about the same time as the music stopped as a career option, I discovered that writing could be one. It was (and is) something I loved to do, and people will pay you money for it. Though when I started, I still had a lot to learn. Such as finding my own voice.

My first published novel was still derivative, this time of Tolkien, rather than those earlier fantasists mentioned above, but I was a quick learner and with the help of MaryAnn in particular, and later Terri Windling when she became my editor, I was able to improve at my craft and find my voice.

Which brings us to the stores and poems in hand.

Back in 1977, when earning a living as a writer was still as much a fantasy as the fiction I was writing, I decided that it would be fun to write a story for MaryAnn for Christmas. I wrote "The Three That Came" in secret, the story was just as secretly edited by my friend Charles Saunders, while another friend of ours, an artist named John Charette, provided a cover illustration for the package.

(These names will be familiar to you if you were involved in the fantasy small press during the late seventies, or ever picked up any of the magazines that the other Charles and I produced. Charles Saunders is now a well-respected and successful journalist living in Halifax who has been working on a wonderful African fantasy novel for the past few years. Unfortunately, I've lost touch with John, though I've heard from mutual friends that he's doing well.)

The finished chapbook (in an edition of one copy) was a great success on Christmas morning (though when you read it I'm sure you'll wonder, as I have when rereading it, why MaryAnn would have liked it; true love really must be blind). In fact it was enough of a success that I did another one the following year in 1978, incidentally the year of my first professional sale, a novella called "The Fane of the Grey Rose," which later became the novel *The Harp of the Grey Rose*, but that's a story for another time. Though I would like to mention here that this sale, and the story's subsequent appearance in *Swords Against Darkness IV* (Zebra Books, 1979) edited by Andrew J. Offutt, certainly helped me feel that the dream of writing for a living wasn't an impossible one—thanks Andy!

In 1979, the year of "The Oak King's Daughter," I decided to print up a hundred copies of the chapbook and send it out as a kind of Christmas card to friends, family and colleagues. Considering the time (pre-desktop publishing), it was a pretty spiffy presentation. Saddle-stitched, the pages trimmed, it featured an introduction by Charles Saunders and an intricate border design by Donna Gordon on the cover. (Though Donna didn't do every cover, this one was part of a long association with her that carried from my own magazines and chapbooks through to covers for the stories I wrote for Pulphouse Publishing in the eighties. For those curious, Donna now lives on a boat moored near Toronto and still does art.)

Better still, the characters in this third chapbook actually survived the end of the tale, and for the next nineteen years the chapbooks went out every year around Christmas, usually arriving in out-of-town mailboxes closer to New Year's Day.

In 1980's "The Moon Is a Meadow" I brought a different group of characters onto the stage, but the general consensus—quickly delivered by post and more quickly from those who lived locally—was that the stories should be about Meran and Cerin. And so, for the most part, they have been.

Probably the only other thing that needs to be noted about the characters is that, while I had already been writing novels in a contemporary setting for some time, these chapbooks continued to take place in some otherworld that never was. Nothing wrong with that, of course, and it allowed for some lovely covers by Donna and folks like Charles Vess, but as all my other fiction was more contemporary by now, I was itching to set the chapbooks in a more here-and-now as well. The trouble was, tradition had now decided that these were Meran and Cerin's stories and these two characters were decidedly not contemporary.

I thought about it for awhile, the consideration made more difficult by my being somewhat of a continuity freak, but then one day decided to simply set that year's story ("The Drowned Man's Reel," 1988) in the made-up beachtown of Santa Feliz. Meran and Cerin were in it, but rather than explain how they were suddenly in "the real world" and had come to base themselves in Newford, I simply ignored the question. They were now residents of the city along with Jilly and Geordie and the rest, and while I let characters in the stories wonder about their origins and how they came to arrive in the city, I simply carried on with the stories.

⅄ ⅄ ⅄

Now comes the apologia.

To be honest, I've argued against this collection for some time (MaryAnn being on the other side of the argument). I like the idea of it—collecting all the chapbooks under one cover—but the problem for me is that some of the earlier material reads so dreadfully to my ear that the very thought of it being made public (even within a specialty press book with a small print run) simply makes me cringe. There are reasons why some of an author's early work should remain unread, one of the main ones being that the early stories are usually crap and who wants to inflict that on anyone? (Though I hasten to add, and I'm sad to say, that at the time of their writing they were the best I could do. I wasn't *deliberately* writing crap.)

On the other hand, many of the stories and poems here are among my absolute favourites, especially pieces like "Meran's Stone," the poem cycle that makes up *Desert Moments* (every time I look at those poems I'm immediately transported back to our second trip to Tucson, Arizona, which, trust me, is a good feeling), or stories such as "Coyote Stories," "Crow Girls," and "Second Chances" that literally seemed to write themselves. Anyone involved in the creative arts will know what I mean when I speak of those rare occasions when one feels to be no more than a channel through which the stories come pouring out onto the page. It's always a great feeling to finish a story, but the ones that come as these gifts are pure magic.

Some of these favourites have never been reprinted and I'm delighted to have them find a larger audience.

There's another positive element about a collection such as this and that's how, through it, one can see the clear development of a writer, from year to year. What you get here is twenty-two years of the best story I could write towards the end of every year. I present them to you here, warts and all, with only typos corrected. Hopefully, you will find some improvement as you read from beginning to end.

⊱ ⊤ ⊰

And now, finally, some last notes about the additional material appearing here, some of which wasn't part of the Christmas chapbook series:

Under the headings of some years you'll find one or more poems following that year's story. These actually appeared as part of the chapbook for that year, hence their inclusion.

"My Ainsel'" is included here because otherwise it would be the only one of the early Songweaver stories that isn't in this collection.

"Humphrey's Christmas" is the only official collaboration between MaryAnn and myself. Although MaryAnn has a large input into my work (steering me towards work such as *Moonheart*, for instance, when she saw my interest lagging in secondary world fantasies, and certainly for all her astute editing suggestions over the years), this was the first time we actually worked on a story together. I can't remember who plotted or wrote what, though when it appeared in our local community newspaper in 1981, it was accompanied by a handful of lovely drawings by MaryAnn that I had no hand in whatsoever. Why's it reprinted here? Because I like it and it's one of the very few Christmas stories I've ever written, which is odd when you consider how the other stories are invariably referred to as the Christmas chapbooks.

"The Calendar of the Trees" is here because it's one of my favourite pieces of writing. It's one of those gifts of words that I have no memory of actually writing, the verses simply came through me. One day I hope to understand everything it has to say. And it was a chapbook, published in 1984 to coincide with the World Fantasy Convention held in Ottawa that year and as a showcase for Donna Gordon's artwork. She did a different illustration for each verse.

"The Three Plushketeers Meet Santy Claus" also appeared in our community newspaper, though it does have a bit more of a connection to the chapbooks than either of the above, since the year it appeared (1985) I produced two chapbooks: "The Badger in the Bag," which was business as usual, and "The Three Plushketeers and the Garden Slugs," which came out in an aedition of 26 copies that only went out to kids, or friends with kids.

"Mr. Truepenny's Book Emporium and Gallery," while strictly speaking wasn't one of my Triskell Press chapbooks, *was* a Christmas chapbook given out by the folks at Cheap Street.

"The Buffalo Man" is here because otherwise it would be the only story of mine to appear in chapbook form that wasn't collected here. Think how left out it would have felt.

➤ ➤ ◄

And there you have it. A garage sale of stories, as his own self Joe Lansdale likes to say. Some worth keeping, some you'll simply skip over. Some you might really like that no one else does, and vice versa.

I'd like to thank Bill Schafer (Mr. Subterranean Press) for taking on the task of publishing these stories, MaryAnn for inspiring them, and the folks who helped out in the production of the original chapbooks with artwork, introductions and sundry other kindnesses and goodwill: Charles R. Saunders, John Charette, Mike Ginies, Donna Gordon, Barry Blair, Galad Elflandsson, Sam Dixon, Stephen Peregrine, Jane Yolen, Charles Vess, Midori Snyder, Tim Powers, Sherwood Smith, Dean R. Koontz, James P. Blaylock, Terri Windling, Ellen Steiber, Frankie LeMonde-Meunier, the folks at Cheap Street, Kiya Heartwood and the folks at

⏵ Introduction ⏴

Allegra Print & Imaging who come through for me each year, even when I bring the chapbook in a day or two before Christmas.

And thank you, all of you reading this, for all your own kindnesses and support of my career so far. Perhaps we'll meet back here in another twenty-two years...

Charles de Lint
Spring, 2000

1974

Leaves for MaryAnn

(The booklet of poetry that Charles sent to MaryAnn in June 1974)

overtaken by
  the rain…i
  cupped my hands
and drank my fill

ㅅ

thunder
  and wind
in the face of motion
there is no change…

when anger
  is fulfilled
the gentle wind
blows still…

ㅅ

fire and thunder
  in the middle of the lake…

in the mouth of night
there is
  fulfillment

ㅅ

how
the wind
bends
the flowers

how
the flowers
drink
the sun

人

i will come
to your bower

  when
  the night
  is full

and the moon shines
fey and pale

  upon thee…

人

a twilight quest:
i journey forth
to rustle through the reeds
and cause ripples
in the quiet river
e'er i find my sleep

人

i am
whispering
you…

you hold
　the wind
in your hands…

touching me

⊁

o heed my call, Ladye Willoney
and thee, Mighty Tyrr:
keep my ladye in peace

and thee, o Celeste:
bless her dreams
and thee, Weaywd:
gather her in thy swift arms
and speed her home to me

ye Great Gods
and ye Lesser Gods
ye of the Earth
　and Skye and Sea
and ye of Fire and storm:
keep her safely for me

⊁

no regret
and no desire
only a slow
sadness
that lingers
changes
and softly
touches
all i am
with quick
glad hands

like leaves
falling
or like a
happy cloud
dreaming

人

give me a penny
  i'll sing you a song
bring me my supper
  i'll sing all night long

人

missing the ocean
  and all the magic
of stormy beaches
  i find the tide

warm in your eyes

人

i would love
  to remember
our bodies
  together
but silence
  bends our past
like wind on
  blades of grass
and so what never was
  can never last

人

o breasts that rise
  and fall so slow

your sleeping
seems to ease the skye

人

through my
sorrow and
none too soon…
six fine strings
and a happy
tune

人

when the wind
is gentle upon you
  remember me
and i will be near

Wendelessen

1977

The Three That Came

*...by dark of moon, the longstones lie
on broken heaths, neath shadowed sky
where brooding stars gaze down upon
the two that wend the hills and downs...*

from the Songweaver's Journeybook

On the eve of the waxing of the Snow Moon, Cerin Songweaver strode through the darkness that shrouded Eldwolde's golden woods. Northward he fared till he saw a small holding perched on a hill overlooking the Vales of Fortune. With a measured tread, he came to its door and knocked lightly thereon with his journey staff.

"Tyrr's blessing on all within," he said as the door opened and a grizzled carle peered out at him. "A weary traveller am I and it's lodgings for the night I seek. Have ye room?"

The carle smiled at his request and motioned him inside. His smile grew broader when he saw the harp that was slung over Cerin's shoulder.

"Enter, stranger," he said. "I am named Halwydd,"

He stood aside as Cerin stepped over the threshold. The harper had to duck his head under its low arch. By a crackling fire sat the carle's goodwife and a fair young maid who was surely his daughter.

"My wife, Goldwyn," the carle said, introducing his family. "And our daughter, Mishel."

Cerin gave them each a small bow. "I am named the Songweaver," he said.

"Will you sup with us?" the goodwife asked.

"If ye can spare the victuals, it would be my pleasure."

Cerin stood his staff against the wall by the door and slung his harp down from his shoulder, lying it by the foot of his staff. He was a lean, weathered figure, wrapped in a patched cloak which he doffed and laid by his harp. His shirt and trousers had been fine once, but now they were as worn as his cloak. His boots were scuffed and bore the signs of much travel.

But it was his face that held the attention of the carle and his family. Though the harper seemed no more than thirty, with long thin hair and a beard to match, his face was brown and time-wrinkled, and the eyes that gazed steadily upon them were a green-yellow with the weight of more years than a mortal's lifetime in them. It was a face of legends and secrets.

The meal was simple, yet ample and filling. No meat was there, but rather an abundance of vegetables, both cooked and raw, and great slabs of home-baked bread. For drink there was sweet milk. When the meal was done, Goldwyn set a large iron cauldron filled with water a-bubbling over the fire. By that fire, mother and daughter sat with their woolen shawls wrapped about them and soon had tea brewing in a clay teapot. Mishel poured four mugs of the freshly-steeped tea and spooned honey into each. Then Halwydd spoke.

"You have a harp with you, Songweaver. Will you play us a song?"

Cerin smiled. "A song? Aye, a song of sorts. There was a tale I heard, not long ago, and all the day as I walked it worried at my spirit and fingers. Mayhap one day I will set it to verse and tune. Still, the tale itself I can tell ye for now. Would that do?"

"Oh, aye," the carle said.

He settled with his family by the fire, eager for the telling. Cerin arose and fetched his harp, then sat with them. Running his fingers lightly over the strings, he stopped once or twice to tune one. And from the tuning, the notes subtly became the body of an air in a minor key and Cerin spoke over the music in a low quiet voice...

⅄ Ⲩ ⅄

Here is a tale, and a true tale I tell, of a witchwife who dwelt in the southern reaches of the Lodowick Forest, which lies in the land of Tamawain. She was named Meran and though she was old with untold years, her form was slim and like that of a young maid, and her face was very fair, with wide clear eyes and ruddy cheeks, all framed with dark tresses of tangly hair. Such a maid ye can scarcely imagine, so well-shaped and filled with beauty was she.

How long she dwelt there, the tale tells not, but in time there grew a cheaping burg anigh her dwelling place in the Lodowick Forest, and its folk named it Tinsmere.

Now the folk who dwelt in that town, and dwell there yet, were ever more concerned with gold and its garnering than aught else in the world. And for this reason they prospered, yet who can say that this is sooth when their souls were barren of kindness, save for the kindness that gold may buy. Still, they came to know of Meran and where she dwelt; of how she aided and healed the wild beasts of the wood and the commons without the wood, when the townsfolk would liefer have slain them all for the gold that their pelts could bring; of how she also helped the poor folk who dwelt anigh Tinsmere so that they need not fear the burg, nor pay the burg-healers' heavy fees. And the folk of Tinsmere were wroth with her, though they did naught to harm her, for they feared the powers they deemed she had; but rather they called her an old hag and shunned the woods by her dwelling, and this pleased Meran well.

Now the tale tells that on one summer's night, when the moon was full and the sky was clear and heavy-hung with stars, Meran fared forth upon the commons in search of herbs and healing plants and came upon a brecaln caught in a trap. Ye ken not a brecaln? Well, they are a small hill-cat, striped orange and white and standing perhaps as tall as a hound; very fierce are they and much favoured for their pelts among folk such as those of Tinsmere.

It was sore hurt and Meran took pity upon it so that she freed it from the iron jaws of the trap. But it could not walk and then needs must she bring it home with her that she might nurse it back to health. And the beast, though fierce as I have told ye, was exceedingly gentle with her. So then, did the days pass sweetly for these twain, for when the brecaln mended, it stayed with her and was a fair companion throughout that summer and the long winter nights that followed. And she named him Whythell.

Then came the stirring and, ere the snow was melted from neath the blossoming boughs of Lodowick Forest, there came a visitor to Meran's small cot and he was named Dougal, being the eldest son of Ranald who was a merchant of high-standing in Tinsmere. Tall and coarse was he, broad of chest and his eyes were as dark as his short-cropped hair and that was as black as the night.

He strode with a swagger to the door of her roughly-fashioned cottage and when Meran met him on the threshold, he said to her:

"Just as I thought: no old hag lives here and if ever there was one once, you are her daughter. Look, I have come for you, for you are to be my bride."

But Meran laughed at his words and bade him begone ere she set the brecaln upon him. As she spoke, Whythell came to her side and his ears were laid flat back along his head and his fur stood up along his neck and spine. But it was not for these that Dougal backed away, nor was it for the low growls that issued from the beast's throat. Nay, it was the hate that spat from Whythell's eyes and cut daggers into the merchant's son's heart and he was sore afraid.

He left then, vowing vengeance upon them, for he was a proud young man and he had been both scorned and made to flee. And alas! His vengeance was like a living thing and it struck them before the spring's end. So one moonless night, with Beltane Eve nigh upon the season, Dougal saw Meran and Whythell fare out onto the commons in search of herbs and he knew his time had come. With a half score of companions and a pack of baying hounds, he set the hunt upon them.

Ever cursed be Black Dougal, for throughout the night maid and brecaln fled before the pack until their breath tore at their chests and their feet became like leaden weights so that they could run no more. Then, just before dawn, they were trapped in the low hills that lie to the west of Tinsmere and, ere Dougal and his men could reach the site, the pack had torn the two to pieces and robbed Dougal of his sport. He was sorrowed then, but it was only the sorrow born from the loss of a possession, for no longer could he own the witch-wife as had been his will. And was he not a cruel man? For he gleaned great joy in that if he could not have Meran, then none would have her. As to the brecaln, he had hated it with a passion that was as dark as he himself was foul.

So the hunters returned to Tinsmere with many jests and they left their victims to the growing dawn as fare for the carrion fowl that haunt the commons. By the time they were at the town gates, the foremost thought in their minds was that it was a shame that the hounds had torn the carcass of the brecaln so badly, that its pelt could not be salvaged. Alas! Alas for poor Meran and her faithful companion, Whythell!

Yet now the tale tells of a strange thing that befell those hunters and it came to pass in but a week after their ill deed had been done. From the eaves of the Lodowick Forest, it was three that came and they approached the gates of Tinsmere with the twilight upon their fur. They were brecaln and this was their seeming: one was coloured with dappled stripes and he was named Pyber; one was orange and white, even as Whythell had been, and he was named Renkyas; and the third was small and grey in hue and she was named Favon. They were Meran's kith, Whythell's kin.

The folk of Tinsmere stared at the three with growing apprehension and fear, for from them came such an overwhelming sense of hate and dooming, that it fell upon the burg-folk like the waves of some merciless sea. Straight through the gates they came, for there had been no one who dared to bar their coming, and neither arrow nor spear, dagger nor sword, could halt them, though in the end the folk had tried. And when they kenned that this was so, the folk fled their homes in blind panic; yet the brecaln harmed them not.

Onward they paced through the town until they came to the hall of Ranald the merchant, all gilded were its inner walls with gold and precious gems, and therein the three entered. Aye, therein they entered and therein, huddled neath his father's great oaken supper table upon the dais, they came upon Dougal and he, knowing his death was upon him, whimpered for mercy as a child might. There came from the hall of Ranald the merchant one long shriek of despair and then the three brecaln stepped forth from its doorway. Neath the oaken table on the dais, they left all that remained of Black Dougal.

The tale tells further that the three brecaln fared throughout the burg of Tinsmere and slayed each and every one of those hunters and, aye, even the hounds were rent asunder in their kennels as the fury that raged through the three ran its course. Then they quit the town of Tinsmere, never to be seen again, and now here ends the tale of Meran and the Three That Came.

⊁ Υ ⊰

Cerin let the tune that he had plucked play on for a short while longer, though he was done speaking and the tale was full-told. Then he strummed a major chord and, as its notes rang out in sharp contrast to the tune he'd played before it, Cerin looked up at Halwydd and his family, and there was a sadness in his eyes.

"Poor Meran," said Mishel in a small voice. "That was a sad tale, Songweaver, yet it was fair-told."

There was a growing glisten in her eyes as she spoke and, when Cerin saw this, he smiled and said: "Be not over-sorrowed for Meran, Mishel, for the true sadness of my tale was that folk should be so cruel to each other. Fear not for her and Whythell, for though their ghosts do yet wend the commons nigh Lodowick Forest, their spirits were reborn into another land so that their tale might still continue." He paused for a moment, then added: "Here...I have thought now on a tune and have the verses for the ballad's ending. Shall I sing them for ye?"

As Mishel nodded, Cerin stroked his harp quietly and a bittersweet sound slipped from its strings. Then he sang:

> *...by dark of moon, the longstones lie*
> *on broken heaths, neath shadowed sky*
> *where brooding stars gaze down upon*
> *the two that wend the hills and downs*
>
> *on one's cloak, thorn and burr are caught*
> *the other's clad in fur and claw*
> *and gold their eyes, Tyrr! see them shine*
> *like glimmers from some Kowrie rhyme*
>
> *and though but shades of life they are*
> *as e'er they fare o'er rill and scar*
> *their souls are blessed, for true and hale*
> *they were reborn in other tales...*

"So now is that part of their tale done," said Cerin when the song ended. He stood and returned the harp to where it had lain by the door with his journey-staff.

"I am weary now," he said, "and would take my rest. May I sleep by the fire?"

"Aye," replied Halwydd.

Then Cerin stepped to where Mishel sat and he kissed her lightly on the brow, saying, "Sleep well."

He bowed to Halwydd and Goldwyn and lay down by the fire with his worn cloak wrapped about his thin shoulders. And soon, all within the hall were caught fast in slumber's embrace.

When Mishel awoke the next morn, the Songweaver was gone, but on the table there was a small curious carving of a wild hill-cat. A brecaln, she thought as she pored over it and though she pondered long, she could not tell from what stone it had been shaped. Slowly, she made her way to the door and, standing in the threshold, she sighed and looked out over the Vales of Fortune. Almost to herself, she whispered:

"Fare ever well, Songweaver…"

1978

My Ainsel'

The north wind leapt and roared across the long heaths of Lillowen, that land where the tinker-folk abide when they are not abroad plying their trade. Upon its back rode the rough weather of the season, for the swelling of winter was at hand and the snows were thick upon the meadows, choking the woods. In a small cottage by the Tenwyth Downs, not far from the circle of longstones that the local folk name Lanmeyn, Cerin Songweaver was guesting with Gram' Rose and her son's child Benj'n.

Out of the wild weather he had come with the night. His cloak was white with snow, the frost was hanging from his cap and leggings. Eyes that were both old and young peered from a brown wrinkled face as he shook the snow from himself, stamping his feet by the door. His journeystaff and harp he left at the threshold while, right merrily, he broke his fast with that grand old lady and her ward. The thick hot soup drove the chill from his bones. The spiced tea brought a twinkle to his eyes. Sitting back in his chair, he stretched his long legs out before him and sighed with contentment.

"I'd surely love to hear a tune," said young Benj'n to him.

He was not more than seven with dark curly hair and wide eyes. Before Cerin could make an answer, Gram' Rose said:

"The hour's late, Benj'n, and well past the hour when we should be abed."

"But, Gram'," he began.

She turned to Cerin with a questioning look. Cerin smiled and ran a hand through his long thin hair.

"I'd play for ye, sure enough," he said, "but the cold's cut to the marrow of my harp and I fear I'd be breaking more strings than I'd be playing tunes. Still…guesting here with ye this eve 'minds me of an old folk tale I was told when I was but young. Would ye care to know its telling?"

When they both nodded, Cerin sat up straighter to tell them the tale, And all the while he spoke, he tugged absently at his beard…

⊁ ⅄ ⊰

Here is the tale as I have it and propose to tell it. As to its truth, ye'll have to make up your own minds.

It's told that near the little village of Carnloth, in the land of Alba, there lived a widow and her son—and he was no older than ye, Benj'n. It was one winter's eve, when the wind howled without their cot as fiercely as it roars tonight, that the boy's mam called to him saying 'twas time for them to be abed. As she spoke, she lay down her mending and went to the little nook that lay just off the main room with its hearth to make ready their bed for the night.

"I'm not sleepy," said the lad.

Well, his mam was tired of the asking. Every night 'twas the same. She'd be long abed while he sat up, and neither sharp words nor a tanning would budge him.

"Ah, an' ye be sitting up all the nicht yer ainsel', the Good Folk will come an' take ye, mark my words," she said to him from the bed, repeating the words by rote and sleepily for she said the same every night and was well-weary of the saying.

The young lad laughed at that, and when his mam was long asleep, he was still sitting by the fire, his head full of dreams, and half-dreams, and all the fancies in between.

This night he was there longer than usual, watching the fire and savouring its cheery warmth, when there came a rustle and scuffle from the chimney. He stepped back, startled as ye might well imagine, to see a wee faery maid leap out of the fire and land on the hearth before him. She was no taller than he, with bright gold hair, cheeks as rosy as apples in winter, and little points on the tips of her ears. Fair as moonlight on a drowsy glen was she, and there was a gleam of the wild in her shining eyes that made the little fellow step back once more. She stood looking at him, hands upon her hips, and smiled so sweetly that she put all his fears to rest.

44

Ah, she's but a child her ainsel', he thought and asked her: "What do they ca' ye?"

"Ainsel," she answered, "an' wha' do they ca' *ye*?"

Fears rose up in the lad's heart once more. A child she might seem, yet she was still one of the Good Folk, filled with magic and all. Little though his youthful wisdom might be, he still knew enough not to give her his own name for fear she should then gain some power over him.

"My Ainsel'," he replied at last, meaning my own self, and they both laughed.

The ice was broken between them, as surely as the morning sun will melt the frost long before noon, and they began to play together, there on the hearth, like old friends. They played all manner of games, some he knew, and more she showed him. All went well until the fire began to dim. The young lad took up the poker to stir the flames back into life, and as he did, a hot cinder fell from the coals onto the foot of the faery maid. Her voice rose up in a great shriek of pain.

He dropped the poker and rushed to her, when there came a noise from the chimney. Who else could it be but the maid's kin? Sudden fear returned to envelop the lad and he had scarce the time to leap into bed with his sleeping mam, before he could hear another voice from the hearth. It was the wee maid's mam.

"Who's done it? Who's done it?" she cried, stamping her feet and roaring at her daughter.

I can tell ye, when the boy heard this, he lay very still beside his mam—who slept through the whole racket, I'm told—quivering and shaking in terror of his life. He was sure the faeries would take him away now. Never again would he see mam or home again. Aye, and when they had him, he wondered, trembling yet more, what would they do with him? But…

"It was My Ainsel'," answered the wee maid, for 'twas all the name she knew him by.

"Why then," said the old faery as she kicked her daughter up the chimney, "wha's a' the noise for? There's none but yer ainsel' tae blame!"

⊢ ⋎ ⊣

Little Benj'n clapped his hands with glee when the tale was done and scurried off to bed. Gram' Rose thanked the Songweaver kindly and was not long in following, leaving Cerin alone by the fire.

He sat and gazed into the flames awhile, half-expecting a little faery maid to come running down the chimney. Shaking his head, he chuckled, rolled himself up in his cloak, and settled down upon the hearth where he soon fell fast asleep as well.

Author's Note: The story the Songweaver tells here is based on Scots folklore.

Grymalkin

Were there not the Lady Meran,
nor the tales that let us know her,
the world would be a cheerless place—
and tale-telling the poorer.

from the Songweaver Journeybook

On a dark night at Lammas time, when the Wort moon was but a sliver of pale honey light high in the star-crowded sky, Cerin Songweaver walked the long heaths of Tulla. He came from the west, from the Hills of Bre, bound for a land that lay beyond the realms of man. His frame was spare, lean as a willow, his skin weathered; his hair and beard were autumn-long, wind-tangled. Yet in his worn face, midst the criss-crossing traces of age that webbed cheek and brow, his green eyes twinkled merrily, sparkling with youth.

He wore a threadbare cloak overtop patched shirt and trousers that day, and road-wise boots that were scuffed and thin with too much travel. Yet when he unslung the harp from his shoulder, loosening the thongs that held its leather bindings firm about it; when they saw the glorious harp, shaped from the heart-wood of the rowan tree, decorated with fabulous carvings that seemed to move, to breathe, so lifelike were they; when they saw the rose inset at the join of the harp's supports, fresh-petalled

47

and grey; when he laid the harp on his knee so that the grey rose rested against his cheek—they knew him for the Songweaver, and were content.

They were traders, the three travellers the Songweaver met, bound for the Southern Kingdoms. It was a long and wearying trek, league upon tiresome league they'd led their pack-ponies from Algarland far to the north, but one that promised a rich reward at journey's end. Still, they were worn of each other's company; they knew each other too well, or perhaps not well enough. Holder, the eldest of the three, the weight of his years reflected in the greying hairs at his temples, the paunch that strained against his belt, proffered a mug of tea, freshly-steeped. The Songweaver took it with a nod of thanks, nursed it in his hands, savoured its taste, its warmth, the heady hint of woodsmoke that hung in its vapour.

Silence padded soft-footed about the four. The traders waited patiently, stealing glances at the wondrous harp, at their guest who was more a myth to them than of the world they knew; the Songweaver sat quietly drinking, his gaze distant, resting upon some far-off, unseen thing. Then, like an indrawn breath slowly expended, the Songweaver smiled. He plucked a string on his harp to let the resulting note echo and ring. Rather than fading, it grew in strength, rebounding from the boughs of the sheltering oaks above, whispering across the nearby meadow, and as it did, the Songweaver seemed to grow in stature, his age falling from him like a discarded garment.

"Would ye a tale, then, to wear away the wearying hours till moonset?"

Kelten, the youngest of the three, his youth apparent in his downcast eyes, in the nervous folding and refolding of his hands upon his lap, nodded eagerly. "That we would, Songweaver. But would you not care to sup first?"

"Time enough when the tale is done. Tell me. Do ye ken the tale of the first of the mys-hudol, the talking beasts?"

The three shook their heads.

"Then I would tell ye of the brecaln Grymalkin and the Lady of the Fairstream Downs."

➤ ➤ ◄

Of the mys-hudol, Grymalkin was the first born, and so he was both the youngest of the brecaln that might speak, and the eldest of the hillcats so blessed. Jaalmar, the Lord of Secrets and Quiet Walking, sired him, and the Lady of the Even, Fayere, was his mother. Now this was many ages ago, countless years as men reckon time, years more numerous than the leaves of yon oak, than the blades of the grass beneath us. It was in the foothills of the Wall of the World, on the edge of the Woods of Auldwen, that Grymalkin was born, and it was there that the troubling came to him.

The Lady of the Fairstream Downs was young in those days, though the wisdom of an elder was hers. What was her seeming? She was slim, yet full-breasted; she was mortal, yet her beauty outshone that of elfin Kowrie or even Tuathan. Her hair was dark, the dark brown of twilight woods, falling in tangled curls over her slender shoulders and halfway down her freckled back. Her chin was firm, her lips full, her eyes two dark bottomless pools. Her voice was clear and sweet, like the woodlark in spring and thrice as melodious, its cadences musical and harmonious, though she did but speak. Should she lift that voice in song the very hills would pause in their slow thoughts and lift heather-backed hills high, the better to listen. Her name? Ah, and was it not Meran?

The tale tells that Meran fared nigh the Woods of Auldwen of a summer's day—though of what her errand was, it makes no mention—to come upon Grymalkin where he lay hid in a fold of the rocks. Orange and white are the brecaln, standing as tall as a Kohr hound. Pale green are their eyes, though his were reddened and brimmed with tears; stiff and curved their whiskers, though his drooped and hung sorrow-low; clean and well-groomed their fur, though his was knotted and unkempt.

"What ails you, hill brother?" she asked.

Grymalkin looked up. When he saw her he thought—as surely ye would have, had ye been there—that here was one of the Tuathan come forth from their fabled realm to walk the mortal lands.

Lady, he said. *My dame is slain and our young son with her.*

His voice echoed sadly in her mind, for the mys-hudol cannot shape words with their throats and so must needs mind-speak.

Meran frowned and her beauty took on a hard edge. "Who has done this thing?"

Lady, I know not. I returned from the hunt—it was yestereve—to find the entrance to our den burst asunder, as though a wind had risen and torn the very earth from the ground in its storming. Within...aie! Within they lay, Jennet and young Welne...

"And you do nothing? You hide here like a frightened hare and do nothing?"

The brecaln's lips drew back to bare his teeth and a low growl rumbled from his throat. *I do nothing? Have I not cast about for scent till I fell from the weariness? Was there not madness upon me? Did I not rage, tearing bark and brush, sod and even stone? What would you have me do? There is no foe that I may loose my anger on. There is nothing...save the dead.*

"My words were harsh." Meran bowed her head in repentance. "Let me make amends. Where do they lie? Have you built for them a cairn?"

Grymalkin held up a paw. *Without hands?*

"I will be your hands."

Wearily, the brecaln arose and led the way down slope. They took a branching gully that opened into a tiny glade, hilled on all sides; thorn and bramble below, oak and apple higher on the slopes. Once it would have been a fair place, but now there was a great hole in the hillside where the den had been, and all about lay the remnants of Grymalkin's rage: shredded brush and claw-cut trees, upturned sod, the rubble of an anger unappeased. Yet for all that the glade lay beggared of its beauty, there still grew one small stand of primroses neath a bramble bush high on the hillside. Scattered amongst the yellow blossoms and running up into the wild apples and oaks was a handful of white wood sorrel. Amidst them lay a hedgehog, curled into a spiky ball, fast asleep.

Meran entered the den and brought forth Grymalkin's dead, one at a time. As she lay them on the grass, she turned to look thoughtfully at the bramble. Crossing to it, she stooped to pluck a pair of primroses. One she placed between her lips and chewed, the other lay forgotten in the palm of her hand as she gazed to where the two bodies lay.

"Your child is not dead," she said softly. "Or if he is, not dead here."

What do you mean?

The look of puzzlement faded from Grymalkin's eyes as he ate a proffered blossom. *The humble primrose, do ye see? To eat of it dispells illusion.* Lying there, in the seeming of his son, was a dead coney, left as a changeling.

Who? Who would do this...?

Meran shook her head. "That I cannot tell. I tasted enchantment in the air, a glamour laid. Yet there is one here can tell. Urchin!"

Under his bramble, the hedgehog uncurled to stand upright on his hind legs, and lo! He was no beast, but rather a piskey, a little cousin of the muryan, the people of the moors.

"Why do you wake me, Bright Lady?" he piped up in a reedy voice.

Grymalkin lunged for the piskey, stopping in mid-stride at Meran's call.

"Hold, hill brother! Be not so swift to loose your anger lest it be your foe, in truth, that stands before you. Yon urchin has done us no harm, but he may do us great good. Sheath your claws. So. Come, urchin. Tell us what befell here, if you can. We will do you no harm."

The piskey eyed Grymalkin with undiminished alarm and stood stock-still, stiff with fright. Though he was shaped like a little man—and no more than a half foot high—he'd yet a hedgehog's spikes, and they rattled on his back as he trembled and shook. "I...I saw nothing."

"Nothing?"

The piskey began to back around the bramble bush. "Nothing save Koldar...the traal." With that he vanished behind the bush. By the time Grymalkin had bound to the spot where he'd stood, there was neither sight nor scent of the little man.

The brecaln paced stiff-legged back to where Meran stood, the fur on his back standing upright. The afternoon sun shone bright on that fur, turning orange to a tawny gold. *A traal? But why?*

"What does a traal do?" asked Meran rhetorically.

Hoards, spat Grymalkin. *Hoards treasure, jewels...gold.* Understanding dawned on him. So that was it. In the bright sunlight, a brecaln's fur shines like gold, finer than earth-delved metal, brighter than polished. What better thing for a traal to own than living gold? *I will seek him. I must...*

"Aye. We will seek him...together. But first we must build a cairn."

Grymalkin looked to where Jennet lay, cold and stiff in the summer sun, and tears brimmed his eyes once more. Hill-ramblings and wood-lopings ran through his mind; a thousand memories of joyful times shared, times that would be no more. Yet Welne, their son...there was a chance that he still lived. And if he lived, Grymalkin would find him.

Meran laboured all that day and on into the moonrise, raising a cairn for Grymalkin's dame. The stones chaffed her hands until they were blistered and bloodied; the stones awoke an aching in her arms and shoulders, in the base of her back, until she could scarce move for the pain. Yet, in time, her labour was done and Jennet's cairn rose from the hilltop to look out across the moors. As the last stone was laid, Meran could feel the dame's spirit touch her, blessing her for her labour. She turned then to face Grymalkin, lifting her hand to stop him as he tried to voice his thanks.

"No need to speak, hill brother. Your feelings are writ' in your eyes as plainly as sun-runes on a river's bed. But tell me this, how are you named?"

Grymalkin.

"And I am Meran. Now let us away, Grymalkin. Hours of hill-treading lie before us ere we will come to Koldar's holding."

You know where it lies?

"I can guess. Where the moon-roads cross neath Gilder Hill...I sensed a shadow fall upon the land there—it was not long ago—but I paid it little mind. Now though...the wind tells me, the heather whispers it, the moon points the way. Shall we be tardy?"

So they fared, maiden and hillcat, each pacing the other, north and north again. The hills passed beneath their tread, the stars rested on their shoulders, and ever the moon pointed the way. When at last they came to Gilder Hill, the moon was just beginning to set. Yet there was still enough of its light to show them where the two moon-roads—they were leys, do ye see?—where the two moon-roads met. Secreted in a cleft high on the hill, they peered downward. Aching legs joined Meran's aching back; bare feet were as bruised now as blistered hands. Grymalkin laid his head upon his paws for he, too, was weary.

Meran turned to him suddenly. "Aie! We are fools."

What is amiss?

"We have brought no weapon with us to slay the traal...no rowan or hazel wand, no cold iron...nothing. Save those, only the blood of an innocent child must slay him and that I would not spill were it my own life that be forfeit. We must fetch a weapon, aye, and return with it later."

Grymalkin's eyes burned with anger, yet he knew her words for wisdom. How to lay low the traal without a weapon? To face him defenseless would only mean throwing their lives away and what then of young Welne? With grieving hearts they turned to leave, but to their dismay, the traal was there behind them. He towered above them, blotting out the stars. He was huge; his coarse features were like roughly-chiselled granite; his eyes, two purple orbs of fire.

The brecaln moved to stand between Meran and the traal. He growled, baring his fangs, and paced forward. The traal's fist lashed out, striking Grymalkin with such force that he was thrown into the air for a dozen paces. When he landed, Meran heard his skull crack dully against an outcrop. The traal reached for her. She turned, gazed in horror at the brecaln's broken body, then back to the traal. Stark terror swept her soul, but there was nowhere she might run.

The same fist that had slain Grymalkin unclenched its fingers to grasp her. One-handedly he held her, shook her, glared at her with a greedy curiosity.

"What is this I have?" His voice boomed like thunder in Meran's ears. "What is this that is neither elf nor muryan, yet walks upright, moon-fleshed?"

Meran pummelled the creature's chest in desperation, knowing that her doom was upon her. Had they but stopped to think, to plan ahead. She tasted sourness rising up into her throat; the bitterness, the futility of this unequal struggle was like a nightmare scudding into wakefulness—impossible and unfair. The cuts on her hands broke open once more and...then a wonder.

Where her blood touched the traal, his flesh began to burn, to smoke and smolder. A harsh cry of pain broke from the creature's lips and he flung her from him so that she lay in the heather, her breath knocked from her. The traal moaned, beat at his smoldering flesh, but the burning spread. In the next moment he was consumed by flames, a bright pyre in the dark moor night, lighting the body of the slain brecaln, of the bruised Lady of the Fairstream Downs. She lay, her breasts heaving, her eyes wide with disbelief.

The blood of an innocent child, she thought, *or just the blood of an...innocent.*

The tale tells that Meran found the traal's cave where young Welne lay in a huddled, shaking bundle, mewing piteously. She took the kitten in her arms, clasped it tightly to her bosom, and returned to stand over Grymalkin's body. There would be another cairn to build. The tears streamed down her cheeks. Had she but known Grymalkin in another time, had she but shared some of his joy, rather than only his sorrow. She stroked the kitten as she wept, the kitten that she would raise as her own child.

"You that were Welne," she said softly. "I will name you for your father. Grymalkin...that will be your name." Laying the kitten in the heather, she fell to gathering stones once more.

So ends the tale of Grymalkin, first of the mys-hudol, and of Meran, the Lady of the Fairstream Downs.

⊱ ⊤ ⊰

The moon was setting as the last strains of the Songweaver's harp faded into a dying echo. The three travellers sat in silence, watching the Songweaver's age slip over him once more. The bittersweet sadness of the tale spread through their bodies, awaking tears in dry eyes, sending cold chills running up their spines.

Gahen, he that was neither the eldest nor the youngest, neither greying nor beardless, sighed. "That was a tale, Songweaver. One that I will remember for many's the day."

"It is a good tale to remember," said the Songweaver. "From that day on, ye see, there has always been a Grymalkin among the brecaln. The tale has been coarsened through the years, the edges worn from it. Aye, even the brecaln themselves no longer hold it in its fullness. Yet the eldest of them, their lord, is ever named the Grymalkin, and that title stems from that day."

"And Meran?" asked Kelten. "What became of her?"

"Was she not mortal? The Grymalkin Welne outlived her—for the lives of the mys-hudol are not reckoned as are the lives of mankind—yet they lived a long and merry life, the two of them, together. And after...she was reborn to live on in other tales, in other lands, even unto this day." The Songweaver smiled. "Now I would sup, and then to my rest."

The travellers gave him meat and drink in plenty—barley bannocks, rich stew and honey wine. When the meal was done, they slept; and when they awoke in the morning, the Songweaver was gone. But in the first chorus of birdsong that heralded the morning, they could still hear the resounding echoes of his harp, the tune that had held his tale; and where he had sat, there grew new a small rose bush, and amidst its thorns, one grey rose.

1979

The Oak King's Daughter

Do legends wane with aching sigh,
or yet wax strong,
when all the summer
of their years is spilled?
Could moon and twilight
seek another autumn song?
Ah, could the roseharp's strings
indeed be stilled?

from the Songweaver's Journeybook

The first days of autumn were striding across the Dales of Kettleley the afternoon that Luthorn met the old harper. Luthorn was a harper himself—self-taught, though none the less skilled for that. Youthful pride stirred in him when he remembered how this first summer of road-wending had gone for him.

He had followed the ways of the barden—the hedge-singers and traveling players—singing to the accompaniment of his roadharp, fashioning his own turns to well-known tunes, his own words to retell the old tales. Success of a sort had come to him—once the first nervous playings were borne through. The half-filled pouch with clinking coins weighting his belt was ample reminder.

That afternoon he was taking his ease under a stand of trembling aspen, on a hilltop where the Old Road turns in on itself before faring through the downs to Foxhold. With a small knife he busied himself, carving the semblance of a rose into the upper supports of his harp. Wood shavings were scattered in an untidy pile on his knees and his mind was far from his work.

With the coins in his pouch he need find no patron to tide him through the winter—not unless he himself desired it. He had enough, spent sparingly, to see him through both the autumn that was upon the land now and the bitter moons of winter still to come, with perhaps just enough left over to last until the roads cleared in the spring.

A step on the road below brought his thoughts tumbling back to the present. Looking down, he saw a stranger smiling up at him from the road. He was a lean and weather-worn man, his clothes dusty and shabby. Long salty grey hair fell in thin strands to his shoulders, bordering a face that was narrow and webbed with age-lines. A thin wisp of white beard fluttered at his chin.

But it was his eyes more than any other feature that drew Luthorn's gaze the most. Young and twinkling with all the merry wonder of the spring just past, they seemed out of place in a face so old. From the stranger's shoulder hung the unmistakable shape of a harpcase.

Luthorn sheathed his knife and laid aside his harp. "Greetings," he called down. "Would you care to share a warm cup?" He pointed to where a pot of herb tea was steeping by the fire.

The old harper nodded, his smile growing broader. "Greetings indeed, lad. Ye be well-met for the road's dusty and my throat's as dry as a tale's end."

He joined Luthorn by the fire. Above them, winds gusted through the aspens, stirring the leaves so that their naming rang true. Making himself comfortable, the stranger accepted a mug of tea, cupping his fingers around its warmth. He regarded the half-completed carving on the youth's harp with interest.

"Curious," he said at last.

"The carving?"

"Aye."

Luthorn smiled a little self-consciously. He tapped the toes of his boots together and looked off down the road. "Have you ever heard tell of a harper named the Songweaver?" he asked at length.

The old harper nodded. "And who has not?" He paused, looking at the carving in a new light. "I have it now," he said. "The Songweaver was said to have a harp with a rose—a grey rose—carved just so. Ye'd have the same?"

"Oh, yes," replied the youth. "For when was there such a harper in all the world as the Songweaver? Wild magic was in his harping and the tales he's said to have writ'…ah, his own life was his greatest tale of all. This," he added, touching the rose, "will 'mind me of him…that one day my own playing might be as renowned as his was during his own life-time."

"Surely ye're not saying he's dead?"

Luthorn looked oddly at his guest, then smiled condescendingly. "And how could he not be? Old he was when yon' oaks were still saplings."

The old harper's twinkling eyes followed Luthorn's gaze. Across the road stood three tall oaks—stately sentinels that were twice a hundred years old if they were a day.

"I have heard it said," murmured the stranger, "that he walks the roads still…and will till the ending of days."

"No," said Luthorn, shaking his head with the assurance of youth. "He was a great man—a legend, yes—but a man none the less. He died as all men must in time."

"There is a tale of his passing, then?"

"There is a tale," agreed Luthorn, taking his harp on his lap. He plucked a quiet chord and amidst its soft ringing, he began a simple air. "This is how I have it," he said, his voice taking on a storyteller's resonance. "It happened so…"

⊱ ⊤ ◅

They say only the moon remembers. It was in Abercorn, near the Worthingside Hills of Eldsdale, that the Songweaver came walking from moors so distant that the folk of Abercorn have no name for them. The twilight was upon his shoulders as he left the Dolking Downs and looked into the Vale of the Oak King. Many were the woods therein, but greatest of all were the large tracks of Ogwen Wood, the oak wood, where the oak king Ogwen claimed his holdings.

The Songweaver was weary. The weight of his years was a heavy mantle on his stooped shoulders. His hair appeared more white than brown, his face lined and creased. The world's roads he had wended, but now his bones grew too old and brittle for the wild places. He sought a quiet harbour to pass his remaining days.

A piteous figure he might have cut—ragged and bent—were it not for the shining wonder that still sang from his tarn-deep eyes. Another wonder was hidden in the battered harpcase that was slung from his shoulder: his instrument…the glorious harp of the Grey Rose.

The moon was rising, the twilight deepening into full night. The Songweaver paused to take a deep breath. His old eyes could see beyond the night, could pierce into the heart of the Vale. He was gladdened to see the summer rich in Ogwen Wood, the fields of Abercorn a lush green.

Here he must linger, he decided, drinking in its beauty. He let his harpcase slide from his shoulder to lie on the dewy grass, following suit with his own tired body.

The scent of sweet grasses, of clover and wildflowers, was rich and heady. Caught in their fragrances, his soul brimming with a deep peace, what could he do but take his harp from its case and let the full sound of that instrument echo the wonder he felt within? The Dolking Downs can be dreary, even in summer. Each hill became a reflection of the next, endlessly the same. Here the height of that same summer was a thousand myriad sensations. It responded to his harping and the night became filled with a breathless trembling.

There was always magic in the Songweaver's harping. His harp was a gift of the Tuathan—those bright, starry gods—and the Grey Harper himself had breathed power into the Songweaver's soul when white hair was a hazel brown and the weight of years was a burden yet to come. There was a fey beauty in his playing and the harp's sweet notes carried far. They echoed about him. They went rushing down the hillside. They flowed into Ogwen Wood itself.

Now in the heart of the wood—where secrets lie deep and riddles are born, where the sharp-tongued River Perriwern scolds the rushes—lies the hall of Ogwen, the oak king. It was a majestic oak, taller and older than any other in the wood. Within it, amidst the living timber and sap all flowing, was a fairer holding than ever the mind of man could imagine.

The people of the wood dwelt within the living trees, for their flesh was never so coarse as that of men. But in the great oak dwelt only the king and his family. His lady was like a spirit of the summer—having taken earthly form. She was rich and full, deep with honey secrets. Two tall sons he had, with beards that were green and brown and shoulders that spanned a man's reach. Three daughters he had, each fairer than the next. But the fairest of them all was she who was neither the youngest nor the eldest.

Her name was Meran and if ever there was a maid deserving the praise of the poets, it was she. She was like a star even amidst such splendor as filled the oak king's hall and, when he counted his treasures, he counted her foremost amongst them all.

Slender as a sapling she was, yet full as the boughs of an elder growth. Her face was a heart, her eyes the deep brown of the forest's marrow. Her hair was the hue of the oaks—the light of the boughs, the darkness in the lower bark, the sweet green of the leaves—all mingled and falling in tangled curls.

On the eve that the Songweaver came and played his harp, she was alone on the wood's borders, gathering dreams in the night's birth. Her heart was filled with a sadness that reached deep within her, twisted as a willow's roots. And it was a willow that cast sorrow's shadow across her heart; an old willow that walked when the night was its darkest, taking to it the babes of the oak people.

This night she sat huddled and small, pushing away the dark willow thoughts to grasp at the dreams that whispered about her. Hare thoughts were cozy and the little grey squirrels set laughing smiles trilling through her. But Old Badger had a deep thought that night. Not one hedgehog's curl did he unwind, passing them by, rather, to follow a deepness that ladled an old wisdom in his soul. Meran touched them all—well-known and warm—until the deepness that had touched Old Badger nudged the edge of her own mind and she wondered.

She listened more closely and felt the wood listen with her. The moon was full and that ever put a deepness into the wood-folk's thoughts. But this was another thing altogether. This was a wildness that trembled rather than raged; that smiled a bittersweet hallowing and made the soul sing with it. It was harping, she realized, and her heart caught in her throat. Where in all the Vale was there a harper?

She listened closer still. The shadow in her heart fell back a little. The tenseness in her shoulders loosened. She could feel a smile tremble on her lips—lips that had not smiled for a full mooning, but were formed just so to always smile.

Half-fearfully she rose. She took one step, then another, until the wood lay just behind her, tugging at her—for the wood-folk cannot fare far from their trees. The music swelled with a stinging beauty and as she followed it to its source, never pausing, her fear fled.

Strangely, though she neared the harper, the music never grew in volume. It sang and laughed, whispered sadly, then rose high and keening, skirling wilder yet never grew louder.

The moon was bright on the meadows. The wood was behind her—its pull was stronger, but not so relentless now, as though it too was soothed by the music. Slowly she walked up the hill, her feet scarce touching the grass, and then she saw him.

Old he was, his pale hair shining in the moonlight. But when he raised his face to her she saw the bright youth in his eyes and her heart sang. His fingers moved with a liquid grace over the harp's glistening strings.

Wondrous was the harp's workmanship—like a thing from the far elder days when it was said that the old gods still walked the world. Its decorative carvings seemed to live and most strange of all was the grey rose carved into its upper supports, for it bloomed as a true blossom might, for all that it too was carved from wood.

She sat before the harper, comfortable in the welcome she read in his eyes. He spoke never a word, but the music sang and danced through her, rushing and gently fierce. Not till the moon was lowering in the sky did the last chord ring from the harp. The harper smiled and set his instrument aside on the grass.

"The roads I have wended are countless," he said, "but for all I have seen, surely there was never a fairer vision than what these old eyes see now. Well met, fey lady, for mortal you could never be."

Like his harping, his voice had an otherworldly deepness to it. Quietly spoken, his words still carried clearly across the dozen or so feet that separated them. Meran could feel a blush warm her cheek. She bent her head so that her brown-green curls hid it.

"Are you a mortal?" she asked. There was in her the desire to ask him to guest in her father's hall. Her heart sank as she asked, for she feared that being mortal, he could not pass within.

The harper seemed to read her thoughts. "In part," he said. "Yet there is a feyness within me, no doubt of it. Undersea I have dwelt and within stone—for there are words I ken that hold my mortal blood at bay—yet never have I known a tree-hall from within."

"How could you know—" she began.

The harper smiled. "If the fairest oak could take mortal form, how else would it appear, save as you?"

The blush was hot on her cheeks now. Their eyes met and for a moment it seemed that their souls shared one shaping.

"Would you see a tree-hall, then?" she asked, surprised at her own boldness. "From within?"

"That I would. But only in your company."

This was a meeting from a barden's tale, thought Meran. From where came the sudden closeness that pushed fears aside, made boundaries nothing? The harping, the fair-speaking of the harper himself, her own boldness—all had the unreal quality of a dream unwinding before her. Such a one as this could hold her heart for all time. A sharp pang stabbed deep within her at that thought and she felt willow roots squeezing her soul...bitter roots that bespoke of a promise that must be fulfilled.

Across from her, the Songweaver's thoughts echoed hers. This was the long road's end. Then he sensed the power that touched the maid with its evil intent, saw the sudden fear start in her eyes.

He spoke a word that formed in the air to hang amber between them and the other presence was gone. Meran regarded him with growing wonder, all thoughts of willows and promises fled. The harper put away his harp and, shouldering his case, took Meran's hand. Together they fared into Ogwen Wood, walking till they came to the hall of the oak king, her father.

➤ ➤ ◄

The oak king greeted his daughter's guest with a guarded reserve. He read the joy in her, the peace that rested in the harper's eyes, but felt only sorrow. He knew love to see it. That it should come to her at such a time...He shook his head sadly.

The Songweaver stood silent before the old king. His eyes went from the hoary face and grizzled grey-green hair to scan the hall. The air was dry and sap-scented, the whole of the room seeming much larger from within than it might from outside the tree. The hall's furnishings were sparse and simple, growing from the oak itself. Impossibly-detailed carvings—that were shaped with thoughts rather than a knife—were a marvel to see. Untold riches sparkled and gleamed, dazzling the eye with a spellbinding wonder.

But for all that there was to see, the Songweaver's gaze returned to the face of the oak king and he waited. He sensed something like a sickness hanging over the hall, poisoning the mood of his hosts. He remembered the maid's fear and wondered anew. What held these folk in thrall to fear? What dire thing might this be? These were a hale folk, fey and mighty in their own right. What could dismay them so?

"I know you," said the oak king Ogwen at last. "They name you the Songweaver. They say you are old and wise—older and wiser even than I."

The Songweaver inclined his head respectfully. "Older perhaps. But wiser? The wisdom of the Dhruides is hoarded in your sap, wood-father. And yet...there is something else..."

Ogwen sighed heavily. He gave his daughter a look that asked how much their guest knew. When she shook her head, he sighed again. He drew the Songweaver to cushions fashioned from moss and leaf.

"There is something," he said slowly when they were seated. "The bane of the oak-people is at hand and twisted are his roots. Helgrim they name him. The Willowlord.

"This spring the fullness of his age came upon him and he was tree-bound—as all wood-folk must be in time. Yet his binding eats like a poison within him and—Piper have mercy!—he walks the land still. Three saplings has he slain...and the babes within. But what can we do?

"His tree walks. We, not yet tree-bound, have no strength against one such as he. This he knows and a bargain he has struck with us. One sapling to be his at Beltane and Samain. That and the hand of..." He looked pointedly at Meran. "The hand of my daughter," he finished sadly.

"And your magics?" asked the Songweaver.

The oak king's eyes filled with a stark fear. "No use," he said in a whisper. "Helgrim...he has a longrune."

The Songweaver nodded his head gravely. A longrune. Any who dealt in the fashioning of the old magics knew the horror of such. Few and few there were in all the many worlds. Once every hundred years, in the dark of the moon, one might come drifting through the silhonell—the spirit plane. Most were lost before ever they were found. Yet once or twice in each world's history it was said...ah. If this Willowlord held one, truly he held power.

A longrune could lay waste to the whole of the Vale and the land for leagues about it. The Songweaver looked at the oak king's clenched fists and the white face of his daughter. He felt a dull rage stir in him. There was a crackle of power within the oak-hall as the Songweaver touched his harp meaningfully.

"I think I will have a word with this Willowlord," he murmured.

Ogwen took his arm in a powerful grip. "No! Would you doom us all? I have said Helgrim is poisoned, not a fool. You carry your power about you like a mantle, Songweaver. Should he sense your coming..."

"I will lay a shape-shifting upon my harp and I—"

"And what good would that do? He will read your spirit's intent. Perhaps...ah, perhaps you could hide your purpose from him, but the harp. How can you hide its power that shines like a beacon for any with deepsight to see? He will speak the longrune and then..." There was no need for him to finish.

The Songweaver nodded thoughtfully. It struck him bitter that this fear lay upon these folk. And yet, what was there that could be done?

The very helplessness of their situation aided fear's growth. In turn, the fear blinded thought, stilled wisdom, until the folk were as they were now—cowering in their halls, willing to strike any bargain. It was the unknown that stole their courage, more than anything else. The madness of one of their own, unwilling to accept the natural course of the world's faring. That and the longrune.

The Songweaver regarded the folk in the hall and his heart went out to them. He put his hand over the oak king's where it lay on his arm and squeezed it reassuringly. Ogwen started at the touch, a strange calm filling him. The Songweaver set his harp on the floor and faced Meran.

"I felt my road's end here," he said. Suddenly he was grasping for words—he whose tongue was as glib as the wind's murmur, the river's babble. "Here, with you, I saw its end."

He stood and stepped forward. Taking her hands in his own, he drew her to her feet.

"My harp I will leave in your care; my magics I will lay aside. As a man I will go to face this Willowlord and do what I can. If I fail, there will be no trace of spellings to lead him back to you. I ask only...will you be here for...should I return..?"

Meran's heart was thudding in her breast. To lose what she had scarce tasted...to have him fall prey to the Willowlord..."I would wait," she said slowly. "But you...you cannot go. We are doomed as it is. Do not walk in our shadow."

"I will not allow it!" boomed her father in agreement. "We fail. No other will fall with us."

The Songweaver smiled sadly. Here was the courage—and so misguided. He was not the foe. He shook his head and spoke a silver word that bound the folk to their places. He kissed Meran softly on the cheek, ignoring the pleading in her eyes.

"I must try," he said simply and loosed her hands.
Turning, he left the hall.

➤ Υ ◄

Dawn was in the air when the Songweaver stepped outside. He set out, keeping to a steady pace. Each step echoed in his mind like the tolling of a distant bell, low and mournful. Road's end indeed, though not as he'd imagined.

At mid-day he came to a place where the land buckled like a wave. The wood dropped into a scar, the ridge of the wave's crest falling into a marshy hollow. The Songweaver sat on its edge and stared down. He felt a dooming in the air, a shadow flitting across his heart.

Below it was dark, though the sun was bright overhead. The darkness came from the shadow that touched the Songweaver's spirit. His loneliness fed it. When first he had left the hall of the oak people, an aged badger had followed him, keeping a companionable distance. He took the old beast for one of the mys-hudol, the talking beasts, for its size was greater than that of a normal beast and intelligence seemed to sparkle in its eyes. But when he spoke a word of greeting in the old tongue, the striped head faded into the undergrowth and he was alone.

The Songweaver stroked his beard as he thought on that. Alone. He had been alone this many's a year. Age had followed him at a slower pace than it did most mortal-born. Friends and lovers he had seen to their graves while he lived on. The road-wending, the long mystic paths of the traveling people, had become his life.

Yet just once he would be with one that could walk through the years with him and not become dust in the blink of an eye. So many years and so many roads, walking alone and never thinking of loneliness. Till now.

He remembered the oak-maid coming to him, drawn by the harping that was as filled with moon-magic as it was with his own twilight spirit. Within her he sensed a welcome and a promise of years that would be long and merry. Save for the threat that lay below, it could be so.

Sighing, the Songweaver looked into the hollow. The Willowlord dozed, his limbs gnarled and cracked with age. Twice lightning had bitten him—once recently, for a still unhealed scar stood out white. The Songweaver tried to imagine this mighty willow in motion—not the sway with the wind, but the roots stepping across the land.

It was a vision that could not be pictured easily. Almost, the old tree amidst its younger siblings, seemed a scene of idyllic peace…save for the subtle buffet against the Songweaver's spirit. The Willowlord dreamed dark dreams and their bitterness spread about him. Silent were the other willows and not one songbird lifted a throaty warble.

The Songweaver sighed once more. He stared at his adversary. Once he thought of building a fire, but the tree sensed his thoughts and stirred restlessly until the Songweaver quickly filled his mind with peaceful visions. The Willowlord settled in his sleep.

The sun crept across the sky, deepening the afternoon, and still the Songweaver sat in silence, still at a loss. Only when the first trickle of twilight slipped across the land did he stir with a new thought in hand. But then Helgrim, the Willowlord, awakened.

⤚ ⤙ ⤙

Meran struggled through the woods under the weight of the Songweaver's harp. When the sun had breathed its last breath for the day, the silver rune faded, its spelling done. Loosed from its grip, she had but one thought and that was to follow the pale-haired harper and bring him his instrument. Without it he was doomed. With it…only the moon could say what might befall.

Old Badger padded at her side, his large eyes brimmed with concern. They sped with the swiftness that only the folk of the wild places have. On and on they went, silent and quick. The harp on her shoulder began to murmur. It was the softest of melodies—peaceful and soothing—but Meran paused in alarm.

"Be still," she whispered. "Oh, be still."

But the harp played on. Soon its magic stilled the fear that pounded through her and as they fared on, they seemed to move swifter than ever before. Ahead in the darkness where she knew the Willowlord's lair lay, she thought she heard a sibilant counterpoint to the harp's tune, and it hissed: "Too late, too late…"

Meran strove to ignore the insistent words and raced on.

⤚ ⤙ ⤙

The Songweaver rose to his feet as the Willowlord awakened. In that moment between sleep and waking, he sensed an illness in Helgrim—a duality of his spirit as though there were two within the old willow, one a prisoner to the other. Waking sharpened into clarity. The Songweaver sensed hidden eyes opening within the tree, piercing him with their cold gaze.

Man, said an icy voice within the Songweaver's mind. *Man and yet more...*

The Songweaver left the ridge, slowly making his way down into the hollow until he stood before the ancient willow.

What brings you creeping with the dark...man?

The Songweaver watched the willows branches leaning towards him, the roots lifting like snakes and slithering across the marshy ground. His own boots sank with each step he took, squelching unpleasantly when he lifted them.

As the twilight had first woken, a thought had come to him. The icy voice that spoke in his mind reinforced that thought. At the first touch of the Willowlord's boughs—clutching him, binding him—that thought became a sure knowing. It was not the Willowlord that animated the tree, but rather the longrune itself. The longrune had its own sentience.

He let the boughs and roots grip him and stood still. He no longer feared the longrune's loosing. Being sentient, it must follow the first law of the worlds and that was self-preservation. Once loosed, the longrune itself would perish amidst the ensuing destruction. So...it sought to spread a shadow—its own shadow—and wax in strength until not the greatest Wysling, not even the Wild Lord himself, could use it.

Still care must be taken, for the power *was* there and it *would* be loosed in the end, were it not first bound. The Songweaver spoke a word and his body's coarseness became lighter and he drifted within the tree.

Man! cried the voice of ice, laced with anger. And there was another voice below that cry—that of the tree-bound Helgrim.

As the Willowlord's hall formed about him, images cascaded through the Songweaver's mind. He saw Helgrim, old and bent—but not evil—walking his domain. There was a longing in the Willowlord, for he knew the time of his tree-binding was at hand and there was yet so much he wished to do in the world.

It was the time of the dark of the moon and in his sadness Helgrim loosed his spirit into the silhonell. There the sorrow slipped back, for the beauty and wonder of that realm has the power to ease pains, heighten joys. And then...falling...falling from who knew what dark void...the longrune.

The Songweaver read Helgrim's surprise, read as well the longrune's quick summation of the Willowlord. The rune hovered before Helgrim. From it spread a promise of freedom from tree-binding…insistent, but oh so truthful-seeming…soul-piercingly bright.

The Willowlord hesitated, uncertain of what he beheld, then gave way to the pressure only to find himself trapped within his own tree and the longrune now become the Willowlord. The Songweaver shared Helgrim's bitter and futile struggle for freedom. He saw the longrune's power to hold, felt its bindings working into place about his own spirit and he knew true fear.

The longrune's power tightened about him with a numbing strength. Blind rage blossomed in the Songweaver that was futilely spent in one last attempt to free himself. Then the longrune's strength washed over him and he was bound as surely as Helgrim.

He cursed himself for a fool. He had guessed, but how to know? Hoof and Horn! A rune was a rune—a tool for the workings of magics, no more. That it had a life of its own…its own hopes and fears…ah, who could have known?

⤚ ⟊ ⤙

He felt as though he floated in the waters of a dark pool that was the longrune. Its twisted intent lapped about him, soaked him, stalking each hidden corner of his mind, delving deep into his spirit. Now it held both his own Twilight strength—his gift from the Wild Lord—and Helgrim's. Floating, unable to move, the Songweaver wept a bitter litany. Not so much for himself was his sadness, as for what was yet to come.

Already Helgrim was weakened with his confinement. The longrune sucked vitality like a leech. In the end, all that would remain of the Willowlord would be a husk. And so it would be with him. He could feel the depletion of his powers, the strengthening that grew in the longrune. How many more would fall?

This bargain struck with the oak people was no bargain at all—no more so than the bargain first struck with Helgrim in the silhonell. Where would it stop? In these days of peace, when the great powers had passed on to other realms, to other struggles, who remained that might prevail against such an alien thing?

A rune with a life of its own. Over and over the impossibility of it pounded through the Songweaver's mind. It became a chant, its very repetition driving home the deadly reality.

Devoid of all sensory perceptions, the Songweaver could only lie in the liquid darkness and listen to those voices in his mind. He strove to think of other things...the sweet oak-maid and her doomed folk...older memories...other friends...as close as kin...But always the voices, chanting discordantly, arose above and drowned it all out. All save the self-recrimination and the growing despair. And echoing frighteningly amidst this cacophony came the mad mutterings of Helgrim who—in his own binding—hated all things now.

How long he lay so, the Songweaver never knew. The voices grew too many, too insistent and strident for him, and he rose and fell on the waves of their chanting. Then amidst it all—like the sweet scent of a wildflower coming from a refuse heap—came a sound so familiar that his heart ached for the very memory of it. Faint it was, like a river's distant murmur, yet he knew it. His heart cried out to its fey beauty.

Telynros...ah, Telynros...

His heart's cry swept through him. The chanting voices began to flee before it, taking with them their soul-binding grief and doom-saying. It was Telynros, his harp. Named so in years agone. Telynros, the roseharp, the harp of the Grey Rose...

Telynros, he cried again.

The harping grew clearer. The wild wonder of the Moon-mother and the Horned Lord spoke in the ringing of its strings. How came the harp here? He gave way to that thought and called once more.

Telynros...Telynros...

In that dark place where he was, his fingers shaped chords, though he knew it not. The harping took on a deeper power. The Songweaver sensed the longrune's awareness. It had been there all along. He had simply not been aware of it, so filled with joy had he been to hear that harping, to be freed of the clamour of voices within him.

The longrune expanded and the Songweaver felt the draw on his strength. Helgrim's gibbering became a shadow sound at the back of his mind. He fought the longrune, sending his waning strengths into the harp. The music swelled, wove and rose like a living thing. The Songweaver could feel the longrune give way before the harp's magic.

This was the way of it, he thought. He should never have listened to Ogwen's fears. The harp had the power and what else but such power might best a thing like the longrune?

There was tremor in the willow. The Songweaver realized that he was no longer in that place of dark liquid. He lay in the hall of the Willowlord.

Helgrim lay beside him, broken and weeping. Impossibly, the harp's power swelled still more. The longrune no longer fought the harpmagic. It sought only to loose itself, that with its own passing, its tormentors might die as well.

The music was a deep veil now, encompassing all existence within the willow. One by one the bindings that held the Songweaver dropped away. Freed, he stood on shaky legs and saw the dark thing that was the longrune—a shape that would haunt his dreams for all the years to come. He sensed its living presence, the depth of its hatred. Then the harpmagic was all—a crescendo of sound that seemed to defy the laws of the world.

The Songweaver fell to the floor, hands over his ears to no avail. The peak of the harpmagic lasted an eternity. Long after it faded, his ears still rang and rang with its thunder. When at last he could stand, he knew himself to be alone within the Willowlord's hall.

On the floor beside him lay the husk of what had once been Helgrim. Before him, where the shape of the dark rune had pulsed with its power, was a black stain. A strange gibbering arose in the Songweaver's mind that died when he turned his gaze from the spot.

The roseharp had done its work well, though a shadow of the longrune would always remain—in that stain, in the Songweaver's own memories. The music had cut the rune's shape from it so that, unformed, it no longer had power, was no longer a threat.

The willow was creaking and groaning in its death-throes. Weakly, the Songweaver spoke a pale rune. He was hesitant to use such spellings, but knew no other way he might depart from this doomed hall. He stepped from the tree and a great weight lifted from his chest. He saw his harp before him, glowing amber amidst the surrounding night. And in its light he saw the oak-maid rocking back and forth, her eyes red from weeping. The striped face of a badger poked from around her skirts.

"Lady," he said softly.

She stiffened at the sound of his voice. Slowly she looked up. Disbelief took the place of sorrow until it gave way to a joy that spread across her face—a joy as deep as the night sky above.

"We can know peace now, my brave oakling," he said. Then she was in his arms and there was no need for other words.

► ▼ ◄

Luthorn paused in his playing. His last chord hung in the air, slowly fading. The old harper regarded him with respect in his eyes.

"And then?" he asked softly. "His passing?"

Luthorn sighed deeply. "They were wed and dwelled in an oak on the edge of Ogwen Wood, and many and full were the days of their loving. From time to time the Songweaver would still wend the world's roads with his harp on his shoulder, but never for long. Meran could not leave her wood, you see, and he could not be from her for long.

"Who can number the days of their peace? But there was a shadow still in the Willowlord's hollow...the bitter remains of Helgrim's hatred that had their birth in the longrune's binding and grew to encompass all things. It was the harp of the Songweaver that ended his thralldom, but that same harping destroyed his willow, and so destroyed him.

"There came a night—a clouded night in the dark of the moon—when the remains of Helgrim's hatred crept like willow-snakes from his hollow. They found the Songweaver on the banks of the River Perriwern—alone and deep-dreaming. His wife and his harp were in their oak some distance away.

"There Helgrim's hate-sendings found him. There too Meran found him when she went out in the morn looking for her husband. There were willow roots binding his limbs and one thick branch wrapped thrice about his neck. So the Willowlord's evil ended, but...so, too, came there an end to the tale of the Songweaver, he who carried Telynros, the harp of the Grey Rose."

A long silence followed Luthorn's last words. The afternoon had passed into evening and long shadows stalked the Old Road. Luthorn set his harp aside and the old harper spoke.

"Ye tell a tale, my friend, and tell it well. It has the ring of truth about it, but the...finality of its ending...ah, it sorrows me. Somehow, as I road-wended alone amidst the wild places, it warmed me to think that somewhere the Songweaver still told his tales, still walked the world. That perhaps the very roads my old feet trod along would know his step once more." He sighed. "But now..."

They shared a supper and more tea before making ready for bed. As the old harper spread out his blankets, he broke the silence again.

"Where did ye get that tale?"

Luthorn regarded him thoughtfully. "It came," he said slowly. "I was playing an old tune on my harp one day and the tale wended in amidst its turns."

"So come the best of them," said the old harper. He rolled himself up in his blankets and composed himself for sleep.

ꜱ ꓤ ꜱ

When Luthorn's breathing evened out, the old harper arose from his bedding and gathered his belongings into his pack. He shouldered it, then his harp. Looking down on the sleeping youth he smiled.

He remembered a night by a riverbank, how the quiet was broken with the sudden rush of living willow boughs. He remembered too the simple crimson rune spoken and the withering of those same boughs. But stronger and clearer in his mind—as ever it was—was the image of a woman: she with the pale oak-green still alive in her now-grey locks.

He smiled again. The Old Road below called to his feet and the oak tree at road's end called stronger, for she was awaiting him there. But first…He spoke a small amber rune and the half-finished carving on Luthorn's harp shifted in shape, taking on the semblance of a stem of blue and white forget-me-nots.

He smiled a third time. Then he turned and followed the Old Road's windings—an old harper on an old road, with the song of an oak-maid's love stirring in his heart.

1980

The Moon Is a Meadow

Mistress Moon, she has three aspects;
  one is old and mountain-strong,
cragged with years of weaving patterns,
  hoarding stone-thoughts, earthy strong.

One is mid-aged, tree truth riddled,
  forest-deep with secret spells,
when she whispers winds breathe wisdoms,
  longstones dance and seasons swell.

Lastly, one is young and merry,
  meadow-gentle, wise and small;
hers the heart that heals all hurts, and
  she I love the best of all.

Wendelessen

The town of Ganford straddles the mouth of the Clearwater River where it leaves the long hills of Donnering to mingle its fresh water with the salt tides of the Clun Sea. Its two-storied stone and wood buildings lean across narrow streets as though to whisper dark secrets to one another, while the townsfolk, never known for their hospitality, appear to take their dourness from the Darkwood to the south, or the grim moors that run north into the

Dales of fey Eorn. Or perhaps the town itself has stamped the unsmiling cast upon their features.

Tam was thinking of this as he approached the first outbuildings— Cotter's Mill, The Wolf's Eye Inn, Timmer's Stable. He could feel the town close in on itself, the nearer he got. And when his boots were scuffing the packed dirt of Ganford's streets, the buildings seemed to lean closer still, narrowing the way. He could feel a hundred eyes on his companion and himself—a communal and unpleasant staring that, had it a weight, could break his back.

"Won't be long now," he murmured.

Gurgi raised his head, green eyes glittering. He was curled in the crook of Tam's arm—a thin, bright-eyed cat the colour of marmalade. Tam himself was small and slender, a study of greys and browns. His wool jacket and trousers were grey with dust; his brown curls hung limp. But insignificant though his initial appearance might be, there was a look about him that demanded more than a cursory glance. His was merriment contained by a tightly-reined anger. His rich amber eyes were too bright in the darkening twilight; his rowan staff was too white.

He could sense, more than see, the townsfolk's scrutiny—the sly movement of curtains drawn back a few inches, the eyes of fishermen, merchants and gossips alike, burning with curiosity. And fear. For, watch him though they might from their distances, and for all their ill will, there was not one of them would raise a hand against him. Not with his eyes and that staff in his hand. Not unless their memories had failed them. It might have been a year since last he walked Ganford's streets, but they would remember him. Tam Tinkern. The hunchback's friend. And if she they'd meant to burn had no power, they knew that *he* did.

Tam let Gurgi pounce to the ground as they neared the squat stone building that housed Reeving, the town steward. He rapped on the door with his staff. Once. Twice. Gurgi cleaned a paw, feigning indifference. But his bright eyes stayed on the door.

"Open up, you toad," Tam muttered. "I know you're in."

He gave the door a third rap. This time the oaken beams smoldered for he'd woken the cold witchfire and the tip of his staff glowed red-white like an ember. The door creaked open on leather hinges. A face, ugly with hate, frightened, peered through the eight-inch crack. Tam pushed the door open wider.

"Where is she?" he asked quietly. At his feet, Gurgi stared unblinkingly at the steward's heavy-jowled face.

"Gone."

"Where?"

"Don't know."

Tam frowned. His forehead wrinkled and his brows dipped to form a 'v'. He reached forward with his staff so that its glowing tip was only inches from the steward's face. Reeving took a step back, his features strained and white with fear. His gaze darted up the street. And then Tam knew. She wasn't in the stone cellar under Meggan's that sometimes served as the town gaol. Nor in the back of the steward's house, chained in the pantry as he'd thought she might be. She was up the hill. In Crey's Caer.

Tam locked eyes with the steward. Silence hung between them, gravid with tension. Reeving licked his lips nervously. Full night had come.

"Did you think I'd never return?" Tam asked. He lowered his staff. The witchfire winked out.

"We...I..."

"Why?" Tam's question lashed whiplike across the steward's halting mumble.

"She...she raised a gale. Sunk Caffar's ship. Four-fourteen dead. She..."

Tam cut him off with an abrupt motion of his free hand.

"Liar! The truth'd be more that Caffar was sniffing around her cot again and wouldn't take no. And then Caffar got so drunk that he couldn't handle his own ship when a squall came up."

Reeving shook his head. "No—"

"I'll be back."

Tam's voice was edged with a cold promise. He looked down at Gurgi. The cat reached out and lovingly ran his claws along the base of the doorjamb. The wood smoldered under his touch. The steward stumbled back, eyes rolling. The thick stench of fear was on him, his face beaded with sweat.

"We never...knew..." he began.

"I'll wager you didn't," Tam said coldly. "That I'd be back. You'd better pray to whatever gods you hold dear that she's still unharmed."

"We..."

Tam spat in the dirt. "Did you ever stop to think that if she *was* the witch you were hoping her to be that she'd fry the whole town before she'd ever let you take her?"

"But..." The steward was shaking. "Her back...the hunch...it..."

"I know."

Tam turned and began the walk to Crey's Caer. Gurgi favoured the steward with a last slit-eyed stare, then padded swiftly after the small mage. Reeving leaned against his doorframe, wiping the perspiration from his face with the cuff of his shirt. He stared after the two until the darkness swallowed all but the sound of Tam's boots on the hard-packed dirt. It was only a whisper of sound but, to Reeving, it was as loud as the tolling of the dooming bell.

Up the street, Gurgi had resumed his position in the crook of Tam's arm. The mage stared straight ahead, his face an unreadable mask. And although he kept guard against possible attack, he found his thoughts dissolving into...

⊱ Υ ⊰

Mara.

Her hair was dark and as curly as his own, framing an oval face. There was a bittersweet quality about the greeting she gave him that day he first came to her cottage; her large otter-curious eyes were wary, her smile hesitant. She stood in the doorway of her cot, a voluminous cloak thrown over her slim shoulders, the orange cat at her feet. There was clay splattered on her shift under the cloak, on the cloak itself, caking her hands. And lifting from her back was the hump, bulking her cloak, giving her slender figure more of a squat look.

Tam smiled a greeting, neither ignoring nor paying overly much attention to the hump.

"Can...can I help you?" she asked. She picked at the clay on her hands without much success.

"You're a potter?"

"That I am." Her smile grew more sure. "Would you like to see my work?"

"Love to," Tam replied. "But I've not come to buy."

"Then...?"

"I'm thirsty." Tam grinned. "I was on the road—my name's Tam Tinkern and I'm a...traveller. I saw your well and stopped to ask if I could draw myself a drink."

"Oh."

"Do you mind, miss...?"

"Mara," she named herself. "No. I don't mind at all. But...would you rather have some tea?"

She offered him her hand.

"Now this is strange," Tam said.

"What is?"

"To find a friendly welcome in the Dales of Donnering."

He took her hand, marvelling at the feel of it—tiny, almost weightless; as though only the clay gave it substance. She pulled back suddenly.

"I've gotten clay all over your hands. I wasn't thinking..."

Tam shrugged and wiped it off on his trousers. But remembering the feel of her hand, his gaze went to her hump and his eyes narrowed. Understanding came to him in a flash and a sad smile settled on his lips.

"It seems a shame," he murmured.

"What does?" She watched him, nervous again.

"That you must bind your wings."

Her mouth shaped an 'o' before her near-weightless hand covered it. She backed away from him. The cat hissed at his feet. But Tam only nodded. She was hollow-boned. Had to be, if she'd ride the winds.

"I've not come here to hurt you," he said softly.

He knelt down and reached a hand out to the cat who quietened at his touch. In moments the small bundle of orange fur was purring and rubbing up against his hand. When he lifted his gaze to Mara, she was suddenly aware of the colour of his eyes—deep and amber. The eyes of a...

"Wizard," she said. "You—you're a wizard."

"Of sorts. More a witch, or a moonmage, for my power comes from the Goddess. Now...you can see that we're both strange, each in our own way. Can we be friends?"

"I..."

"After all. If the cat can be your friend—and what closer cousin to the Goddess is there?—why can't I?"

She faced him wordlessly, her shoulders tense, her limbs rigid—like a startled sparrow poised on the brink of sudden flight. Tam watched the play of emotions across her face. Hope mingled with fear; the need for companionship coupled to the hopeless resignation of never having a friend save her cat. Then something changed. She shivered. Slowly she let her cloak fall from her shoulders and he saw the white feathered tips above her shoulders. She spread her wings wide and Tam marvelled. A sigh escaped him. She was a vision, achingly beautiful. Then the wings were folded against her back once more, loosely now, and her hesitant smile returned.

"I'll put the water on," she said.

⊱ ⋎ ⊰

They left Ganford behind them. Now only the night and road were ahead and, further still, Crey's Caer. Tam hummed tunelessly to himself. He was caught between the warmth of his memories and the red cloud of his anger. Gurgi wriggled in his arms and he let the cat down to pace at his side.

The moon would be rising soon.

⊱ ⋎ ⊰

He stayed for the tea, then for dinner. The night lengthened into the following day, that day into a week, into a month. He helped her with her pottery, but his clumsy efforts generally made for more work than helped. More often than not, he simply sat with her, the whir of the wheel under-cutting their conversation, his eyes on the swift sure play of her hands as she worked the clay, Gurgi on his lap, purring.

Sometimes they spoke of weighty matters.

"What is this Goddess of yours, Tam?"

"She...She's everything. She's the corn growing. She's a hare, a wolf, a raven. She's the earth and the seeds lifting from her. She balances the seasons. Look to the night skies and you'll see Her—silvery and bright."

"You mean the moon?"

"Yes."

"But what's She like?"

"Like a mountain."

Mara shivered. "All stone and sharp edges?"

"Like a forest as well."

Mara thought of the Darkwood whose edge lay not far from the door of her cottage.

"All dark and shadowed?" she asked.

Tam smiled. "She's like a meadow, too. She's all three. Old and hard, wood-wise and full of secrets, young and merry."

"I like the meadow best of all," Mara said.

"I do too," Tam agreed. "Then She reminds me of you—winged and tangle-haired."

But other times they spoke of matters that concerned just the two of them, and then agreement was not so easy to come to...

"Why do you stay here?" Tam asked.

"This is my home. And I should walk the world with these?" A wing reached out and tickled his chin.

Tam sighed. "There are fairer places to live than the Dales of Donnering. There's still magic in the land, though it's far from these hills. Come away with me. We'll go north to where the old tales are histories, not myths, and the Moon's the Mistress of the land, not hard-hearted, penny-grasping lords."

"I can't."

"Why not?"

"I'm afraid."

"But I'll be with you. We'll go together—with Gurgi. The three of us. With the blessing of the Goddess my magics'll keep us safe."

But Mara only shook her head.

"One day I'll have to go on, Mara. You know that. These Dales wither my spirit. I..."

"I know, Tam. I understand."

"Come with me."

"I can't. But you'll come back...from time to time?"

"I'll be back."

And he did come back. Sometimes he stayed a week, sometimes a month. Their love grew deep and close except for the one thing that lay between them: that she would not go, and he would not stay.

⊁ Υ ⊰

The moon was up now.

Tam felt strengthened in Her light. He lifted his face to Hers. The colour of his eyes changed, matching Hers, and he felt Her presence warm in his heart. He took Gurgi up again, settling him in the crook of his arm, and strode on.

⊁ Υ ⊰

It was on a day in the middle of high summer that he last visited Mara. The fields were green, the barley swelling. The hedgerows were a riot of colour. The Darkwood's shadow withdrew and the wood's edge drowsed, sleepy and content in the summer sun. Tam followed the road, humming to himself, his cloak folded over one arm, his staff making dimples in the dust of the road.

As he neared the turn-off to Mara's cottage, he met a broad-shouldered fisherman. He was red-haired, red-bearded, with the dour look of a Ganforder about his thick features. Nodding a curt greeting to Tam, he frowned when he saw that they were both turning off at the same place.

"Where're you going?" the fisherman demanded.

"To see a friend."

Tam regarded the burly man warily, smelling trouble in the offing. The fisherman shook his head.

"Not today, you're not. It's three times in three weeks that the hunchback's been in town selling her grubbing pots, and three times she'd refused me. Well, I've a wager set with the lads in The Wolf's Eye and today I mean to see what it feels like gripping that hump when I'm riding her and bedamned to the man who stands in my way. Do you follow me, little man?"

Tam had a liquid temper—quick as a summer storm. It settled a red mist across his eyes.

"I follow you," he said quietly.

He let his cloak fall to the road and held his staff loose and ready in his hand.

The fisherman grinned. His features, so accustomed to their grim set, twisted with the expression. He took a step towards Mara's lane. Tam's staff came alive. One moment it rested at his side; the next he held it two-handedly, one knobby end whipping out. It struck the fisherman in the stomach, doubling him over. The other end of the staff whistled through the air, hitting the man's head with a loud crack. He toppled forward in the dirt.

Tam stepped back. The fisherman raised himself, shaking his head.

"You...shouldn't have tried that, little man."

He made to stand and the staff came whistling at him again. But for all his bulk, the fisherman moved quickly. He caught the staff in a huge meaty hand and shook it. Tam stumbled, losing his grip. The fisherman stood, the staff in his hand. With his hard eyes focused on Tam, he broke the staff in two. Then he moved forward.

Tam waited to meet him. His anger was dark, dark and bloody. He raised his magic, the deep power that slumbered inside him, but the fisherman was already upon him. Once, twice, the meaty fist connected with his face. His head rang with the blows. Again he was struck, the fisher-

man keeping him aloft with one hand, striking him with the other. Then he let Tam fall. As he tried to rise, the fisherman kicked him in the side. Pain exploded as ribs cracked, blood vessels burst.

Tam's magic was far from him now, buried under his pain. The fisherman kicked him again.

"Best be gone when I'm done with the hunchback, little man, or I'll finish the job."

With that he strode on up the path.

Tam lay for long moments, drawing in ragged gasps of air. Slowly, slowly, he fought his way to where his staff lay, broken in two. Eyes closed with the effort, he placed the broken ends together and struggled to find power, to raise it from the waves of pain that swallowed it. When it came, it was weak, hurting. But the staff grew whole, ragged edges joining, solidifying. Slower still, Tam used the staff to get to his feet.

His head spun. Bile was sour in his throat. Sky and earth fought for position in his gaze. Grimly he hung on, breathing deeply, ignoring as best he could the sharp rasp of pain that came with each breath. He looked up the lane. So near, but so far. Could he even make it up that short way? Then he heard the scream, and he cursed his limbs into motion.

The two hundred yards up from the road, past the well, through the trees, to where the cot lay, seemed to take a lifetime to lurch along. But the cry echoed and echoed across his pain, driving him on. He'd heard it once. Then nothing. Mara! Goddess! He prayed. Let me reach her before the brute hurts her more.

At the door of the cottage, he was too weak to go further. He fell across the threshold. From where he lay he could see them. The fisherman had ripped away Mara's cloak and the shift underneath it. Fighting the buffetting of her wings, he pinned her under him.

Goddess! Tam cried. Give me strength!

But he couldn't move. He could only stare numbly. He saw Gurgi launch himself at the fisherman's broad back. The man roared with pain as the cat's claws and teeth cut deep. He reached behind him, grabbed the scratching bundle of orange fur, and threw it against the far wall. Gurgi lay still. Then the fisherman saw Tam.

He left Mara where she lay and turned to Tam. Their eyes looked in a pitiless gaze. Hatred leapt between them.

"Couldn't wait to die, eh?" the fisherman mocked.

As he stepped forward, Tam drew on the last of his strength. He *pointed the rowan staff at the man and mouthed a word through swollen lips. He saw the fisherman's eyes widen as he saw the staff whole once more. He saw him step back as the tip of the staff glowed red-white with witchfire. He saw the fisherman's hair blaze—red still, but red now with a nimbus of flame. The stink of burning flesh choked the air. One long scream echoed through the small cot.*

Gasping for air, Tam fought his way to his feet. He leaned heavily on his staff and worked his way to where Mara lay. He ignored the crumpled heap that was the fisherman, the head that was a ruin of charred flesh and blackened bone. Beside Mara, Tam fell to his knees, holding back a cry as a shaft of pain lanced through him.

"Mara?"

"I—I'm all right." Her lips quivered. Her face was blanched, her eyes wide with shock. Loose feathers were strewn about the floor. "Tam...I...oh, Tam..."

He held her close.

Later...

His witcheries helped sustain him. The healing had already begun, but still he ached, still it was painful to breathe. He laid his hands on Gurgi, and brought the stunned cat to wakefullness. Gurgi's eyes watched him strangely, knowingly, the greens luminous. Together, Tam and Mara dragged the fisherman's corpse to the cliffs behind her cot and rolled him into the sea. They stood there a long while, gazing seaward. Mara was still pale, her cloak wrapped about her against the inner chill.

"Did you know him?"

She sighed. "His name was Hawrd—from the town. He and some others—Caffar, Trimm—have been...bothering me."

Tam nodded. "You'll not come with me now?"

"I..." She shook her head. "This is still my home, Tam."

Tam nodded again. "I'll have to go now—for a longer while. Until things die down. I'll try to forestall any questions that might come your way, but...Can someone else take your goods to town? For awhile, at least?"

"There's Tomasin. He lives on the next holding towards town. He and his family have been friendly."

Tam sighed. Did these Dales not wither his spirit, he'd stay. But if stay he couldn't, he'd make sure that no one would try to harm Mara again. He bent down and rubbed Gurgi's ears. The cat seemed none the worse for the fisherman's ill-treatment. Straightening, he hid the sudden pain in his side with a strained smile.

"I'll be going then," he said.

⊢ ⅄ ⊣

Crey's Caer was near. The moon was riding high now. Tam felt the Goddess inside him, heartening him. Her face was an old woman's strong and hard as a mountain's heart, old and powerful.

For the hundredth time, he berated himself for ever leaving Mara alone after the trouble. If he'd not gone, this new trouble would never have happened. Spirit-withering though these Dales might be, surely he could have lived in them. With Mara, could he not live anywhere? Aye. But the trouble that was come now—might it not have come all the sooner if the townsfolk knew that the witch-man lived near them, the witch that slew Hawrd and brought the red-white flames into Ganford?

⊢ ⅄ ⊣

The door of The Wolf's Eye Inn opened at his touch. Inside it was gloomy. Flickering candles burned on the tabletops, their wax running into the wood grain, hardening into lava-like patterns. There were a few men scattered the length of the room. The innkeeper behind the bar, polishing a tankard. A tinker sitting alone in a corner, nursing a mug of ale. Three merchants discussing cloth and slated-fish, and the road south.

And two fishermen.

Tam walked to their table, aware of the eyes on him. He knew what he looked like: face bruised and swollen, his breath ragged. He was weak, aye, but strong enough for this thing that must be done.

"Caffar?" he asked. "Trimm?"

At their nods, he continued before they could speak.

"You had a wager with a man named Hawrd. Well, you've won. But if you'd collect your coin, you'd best set to dragging the sea before the tide goes out."

Confusion ran across their faces. Then the bigger of the two stood, anger flooding his features as the beginnings of understanding came to him.

"What do you mean?" he demanded.

"I killed him," Tam replied in his quiet voice. "As I'll kill any who'd harm the folk that live along the south road. Do you understand me?"

"Why you—"

Tam had made the mistake once of trying to settle the trouble without magic. He would not make it again. His staff-end burst into flame—red-white flame, cold witchfire. The fisherman sat down, his face ashen, eyes fixed on the staff.

"I asked if you understood."

"I...yes." The big man exchanged a frightened glance with his companion. "We understand."

"Good. I'll be near. I'll be watching. Always. If you're lying now, remember that."

He left.

Nursing his wounds in the Darkwood, he kept his word. Once they came—five fishermen, one with a long-unused sword, a new edge ground onto it, the others with harpoons. Their weapons he slagged. In Ganford's harbour, he burnt one of their boats. Again, a lone man tried coming by sea. From the clifftops, stones toppled to smash the bottom from his boat. The man was left alive to carry back the tale, but that night a third of Ganford went up in flames—red-white flames of witchfire.

They didn't come again, though Tam waited a month.

⊢ ⋎ ⊣

Aye. They didn't come again. Not until at least a year had passed and their memories grew thin, grew weaker than their hate. And then they came. Caffar's boat, wrecked in a storm, and there was a reason for them. Witch-work. We did no harm, but still the witch persecutes us. So slay her—the hunchback. And where is her consort—the small man with the devil's eyes and the child's body? He with the white staff? Gone is where. Burned at a stake somewhere more than likely, as the hunchback should be. We'll wrap her with so many iron chains that she can't hardly breathe, little say move. For it's iron that binds them, eh? Iron and witchbane, plucked at noon and dried with a priest's blessing upon it.

Tam could almost hear the way their thoughts had run. And he could picture their faces when they tore the cloak from her to see her wings. Open-mouthed with fear, they'd've hung her slender frame with chains and tied the evil-smelling witchbane in her hair and around her waist, to either wrist and ankle, around her neck and between her legs. They'd drag her through the town, jeering and mocking, the iron weighing down her hollow-boned limbs.

Would they have bothered with a trial? No. It was straight to the Lord's Keep they would go, laughing and joking, though here and there one or two of them would make the sign of their god, smiling ruefully at their companions when they were seen.

But it was Tam Tinkern was the witch, not Mara. And he was *not* dead. No. He'd felt the need to come and so he'd come. He'd found the cottage empty and he'd known. He'd found Gurgi, the green eyes blazing with anger, and he'd filled the small orange cat with the power of the Goddess to temper his rage. Together they'd gone into Ganford. Now together they fared to Crey's Caer—the Lord's Keep.

Crey's Caer. When the Donnering Dales were young, it was a hill fort, set high and back from the sea. A gathering place for the tribes, where they'd herd their cattle and sheep and families when the sea-raiders came. But the sea-raiders settled south, and their warlike ways fell from them. And the tribes grew plentiful and soon *they* were braving the sea, fishing the deep waters, building their towns along the coasts.

But if they'd conquered their fear of the sea, there was another still left to them: the fear of those strange beings that they'd driven from the land with their own coming, so long ago that the doing of it was no longer even a memory amongst them. The older folk—the followers of the Goddess—and folk older still, those whose shapes were only partly a man's. Horned folk, scaled folk, winged folk.

In these days they were few, a withering race. Mostly they dwelt in the north, with the remnants of the Goddess's people. But some—like Mara—dwelt amongst men. *Their* blood was thinner still, for these were the products of a coupling between the elder folk and humans. And that was their curse. Like Mara, their bodies were the bodies of the elder folk, but their hearts belonged to mankind. They needed the proximity of what, to them, was their own kind. So they made their homes near towns and such. And how many were discovered and slain? As many as Tam's kin, those who followed the Goddess. Perhaps more.

Crey's Caer. Now it was here, before them. Tam looked at the low stone walls, his face so grim that it might never have tasted a smile. Gurgi rubbed once against his legs, then faded into the deeper shadows of the hedgerows.

Tam took the reins of his anger and held them tight. Slowly he paced up to the broad oaken doors of the keep. He placed the tip of his staff against them and spoke a word. The Goddess filled him. Mountain strong, forest deep. The doors burst inward with a crack like a thunderclap. Alone, Tam stood amidst the ruin, smoke wreathing his small form, his eyes glowing silver-bright, moon-bright. Alone, he stood and waited.

He heard cries of surprise and rage. He saw men running about in the courtyard—some still pulling on their trousers, others stark naked, but with their weapons to hand. The courtyard was small and it filled quickly, for the Lord of Crey's Caer kept a small retinue. No more than a dozen men-at-arms and a score or so of maids, cooks, stablehands, stewards and huntsmen.

The gathered people stopped when they saw Tam. Superstitious fears exploded in them as they looked to the broken gate-doors and his small figure standing in the smoke and ruin, eyes glowing, staff-tip alive with witchfire.

One guard threw his spear and it burst into flame before reaching the mage. Its ash drifted about Tam's feet, mingling with the charred timber of the doors. Others gathered their courage to attack, but fell back in frenzied fear as lines of witchfire erupted at their feet.

"Bring her to me," Tam said.

His quiet voice rang and echoed in the courtyard, growing stronger rather than dying down.

"Bring her out!"

Now his voice was like thunder. He placed the staff-tip on the ground and the flagstones of the courtyard buckled and cracked at his feet, spreading out like a spider's web.

Then she was there. In the doorway of the inner keep, chained and humbled, her curly tangles hanging flat, her head bowed, wings drooping, limbs hung with chains, the witchbane tied all over her so that she looked like a scarecrow. At her side was the Lord of the Keep, his face flushed with triumph. He held an iron dagger to Mara's throat.

"I knew," the Lord said. "I knew this would bring you. Move now, witch, and your winged lover dies. Did you think I'd do nothing? That I'd let a cursed thing like you terrorize my Dales? Did you think me power-less, witch? Drop your staff. Hold back your power. Let my men lay the iron to you, and the witchbane. And do it quick. This blade yearns for her demon blood."

Stalemate. Tam stared at the Lord. His rage flooded him. He could smell death in the air. Mara's, his own, the Lord's...many. So be it. Did this man think that life was a thing to barter? Moon on earth! Did he hold it in such low regard? Did he think that one life was all? Did he think that Tam feared death? The Goddess was in him. Mountain strong, forest deep. His blood ran hot with Her power.

His gaze flicked to Mara and she lifted her head. The power thrummed in Tam, but her humanity reached out to him. *No matter what they've done, what they do,* she seemed to stay, *how can I allow so many to die?* He read it plain. In her face. In her eyes. Then her features shimmered and he saw the Goddess there—Her maiden face, sweet and gentle as a meadow.

Tam hesitated. The word was there, in him, that spoken would lay the whole of the keep to waste. Mountain strong, forest deep. It hovered on the tip of his tongue. It raged through his veins. It throbbed in his temples. But he felt now an imbalance. He saw himself perpetuating the very evil he meant to destroy. He saw his own face mirrored in the Lord's and he shuddered. Slowly, he lowered his staff.

Tension lifted slightly in the courtyard. Weak smiles traced the lips of the Lord's people. They had him. The witch *and* his consort. There'd be a double burning for the gods on the morrow and the land would be cleansed of the foul witch-taint once more.

One man-at-arms stepped forward hesitantly, then with more assurance when the witchfire failed to blossom at his feet. Others followed. They saw their enemy as nothing more than a small man with smoldering eyes—scarcely bigger than a child of fourteen summers. *This* was the mighty witch?

A grin started on the face of the first man-at-arms. He turned to look back at his Lord. His companions were all around him, buoying his confidence. He felt a heady rush of pleasure at what they'd done this night. Then he froze. He stared wide-eyed at his Lord...saw the orange flash leap from the shadows, claws extended, witchfire crackling in the night air once more.

"No!" he cried.

Too late. Gurgi landed on the Lord. The power of the Goddess filled him, giving him the strength to send the Lord sprawling. The iron dagger clattered on the flagstones. Gurgi crouched between Mara and the Lord, green eyes blazing. The Lord mouthed an obscenity and lunged for the dagger. As he moved for Mara, Gurgi sprang to meet him. Again fires awoke from the cat's paws and this time the Lord blazed. He fell to the flagstones, a charred man-shape.

A cry of dismay went up from the crowd. As they began to move,

Tam's witchfires roared about them once more—holding them, not slaying. Tam paced forward and the people fell back from him. He walked the length of the courtyard and stood before Mara. Rage had fled. A deep sorrow swam across his senses.

"You," he said to a stableboy. "Loose her."

The proximity of the iron and witchbane struck daggers through him, but Tam stood close all the while, taking a hold of Mara's arm when she was freed. He turned to face the Lord's people. They shook under his gaze, knees knocking together. Many made the sign of their god. Tam dropped his gaze to Gurgi. The cat's green eyes watched him for a long moment. Then he began to clean a paw.

"Up you," Tam said, making a crook in his arm.

Gurgi leapt up, settling himself comfortably. Then Tam led the way back through the courtyard, staff before him, Mara walking at his side. Not one, man or woman, raised a hand to stop them.

⼂ 丫 ⼃

"One life for the evil done is not such an unfair bargain," Tam said. "Not when he began the bartering."

Mara shook her head. They were a mile north of the Crey's Caer, sitting on roadside stones. Gurgi was asleep, or feigning sleep, in Mara's lap.

"Thank you for sparing the others," she said. "I don't know. I should hate them, I suppose, but I can't. They're small-souled and spiteful and there's not much good can be said for them, but..."

"But your mother was one of them," Tam finished for her.

She nodded. "When I saw you there, the gates smoldering about you, the fury in your eyes, I finally understood what you meant about the Goddess being like a...mountain. Or the Darkwood. There was such power there...something so old and strong..."

"Aye. But to loose it, I would have been no better than those that took you." He held her hand and squeezed it gently. "What now, Mara?"

"I don't know. I can't go back to my cottage..."

"No," Tam agreed. "Will you come with me now? We'll build another cot—north, where the old ways still linger and the Goddess is remembered with love."

"Mountain. Forest." Mara smiled suddenly. The past troubles seemed to wash from her as though they'd never been. She looked Tam in the eye.

"Where the moon's a meadow?" she asked.

"Indeed," Tam replied, a smile tugging at his own lips.

"I'll come with you," she said. "Oh, yes, Tam." She scratched Gurgi behind the ear. "We'll both come."

Author's Note: Gurgi's name was taken from Lloyd Alexander's wonderful novel *The Book of Three*, and not simply for this story. We had an orange cat with that same name as a well-loved member of our family for many years.

1981

Humphrey's Christmas

Humphrey Oakmouse had been working hard all day in preparation for the big party. His house was a burrow nestled in amongst the roots of the old sentinel oak that overlooked the meadow separating the Forest from the Farm. Always a cheerful place, tonight Humphrey's house fairly bristled with colour and glitter, for this was Christmas Eve and, as the Oakmice had done for as long as there had been mice in the meadow, tonight he would host a marvelous Christmas party.

Whiskers a-quiver with excitement, Humphrey lit fat red candles and set them in the window nooks where they spilled their rosy light across the green and red holly, and out onto the white snow. He was an old mouse, with more grey than brown in his fur and a slight hobble in his walk, but still, when all was told and done, he thought that if anything, he'd truly outdone himself this year.

Apple logs burned in the hearth, giving off a sweet smell before the smoke went rushing up the chimney. The long table in the dining room was laden with every imaginable treat, from honey-sweetened corncakes topped with roasted apple seeds, to raspberry wine and elderberry pudding served in hollowed out walnut shells. In one corner a tall pine twig was festooned with tassles of coloured wool, tinsel and brightly-painted seed chains. There were ribbons on the backs of all the chairs and hung across the room. Smooth gleaming acorns waited in a basket for the traditional game of bowl-and-spill and earlier this afternoon Humphrey had balanced on a rickety ladder to hang a festive sprig of mistletoe above the doorway. The only thing missing was a merry wreath for above the hearth, but that was special. That was for the guests to bring.

"Yes, oh yes," he murmured to himself as he tapped his way across the floor with his cane. Sighing happily, he settled down in his favorite chair, put up his feet, and drifted off into that pleasant expectant state that comes just before the first guest arrives at any party.

And he waited. And he waited.

At first he didn't think too much of it. He got up to putter around, straightening that bowl and these mugs, making sure that the kettle was filled and ready to put on the fire when the first guest knocked at the door. He stirred the apple cider for the hundredth time, rearranged some of the decorations on the tree, peered out through the window, his breath frosting the glass, and waited some more.

Was no one going to come?

He hadn't sent out any invitations because they weren't needed. Every year there was a wonderful party at Oakmouse burrow. It was traditional. It was...well, it was expected. It simply was.

Feeling confused, Humphrey went to the front door and tugged it open to peer out. The meadow lay silky white in the starlight. And although he could smell snow on the wind, he knew the sky would remain clear for hours. So where was everybody? He stayed awhile longer, shivering in the doorway, looking this way and that, holding his tail in his paw so that it wouldn't catch a chill from the cold stones in the hall. At last his gaze roamed beyond the meadow, down the hill to where the Farm's windows peered yellow-eyed and square back at him. And then he knew where the others were. In the barn.

Humphrey closed the door and slowly made his way back to the sitting room. The trouble was that he was just too old. All his dearest friends had gone on by now. Old Tansel Tinker, Sam and Sara Stonemouse, Tilly Featherseed. They were all gone. And with them went the old ways. No one wanted to work when there was a barn full of grain just across the meadow. Why forage and risk the fox's hunt or the hungry owl, when you could make a home in the hay and grow fat and lazy with nothing more to worry about than a lazy old orange cat who was more inclined to blink and roll over than give chase?

Pouring himself some cider, Humphrey sat down once again in his comfy chair and looked around. The sitting room didn't feel quite as jolly anymore. It was as if the burrow itself knew that no one was coming. Almost ten o'clock and where, in other years, youngsters would have been shrieking at the acorn bowl-and-spill, tonight there was only Humphrey and he felt very lonely indeed. A large tear surfaced in the corner of his eye and slowly trickled down his nose. He snuffled it away, took a little sip of cider, then sighed heavily.

Perhaps they'd only forgotten? Without the old folk around to remind them, mightn't they have done just that? He could go down to the Farm and invite them up. He thought of the long walk. Now it occurred to him that he hadn't seen much of anyone for a long time. What if the tunnels in the meadow under the snow were blocked up from disuse or there were weasels using them? He thought about the long trek over the snow and shivered as he imagined the black shadow of a hunting owl dropping upon him. But if he didn't go, he'd only end up sitting here and being all alone on Christmas Eve.

Humphrey took a handkerchief from his pocket and blew his nose. Then, gathering his courage before it failed him altogether, he put on jacket, cap and boots, took up his cane, and left Oakmouse burrow to trundle down the hill. The tunnels were, as he'd feared, blocked from disuse. With no one to keep them up, the snow had simply settled down and flattened them. So, with many a look sideways and backwards and up, Humphrey set off across the snow. Near the bottom of the meadow, by the Farm's fence, he met a hare.

"Bad night for walking," said the hare, whose name was Brennan. "Snow's coming, for one thing, and the fox's been about. Once or twice I saw an owl—never heard anything, mind, just saw that awful shadow come drifting across the snow."

Humphrey leaned on his cane, legs trembling. Snow and fox and owl. The words went tumbling head over heels through his mind. He looked up but all he saw was the velvety night, sprinkled with stars. Owls scared him the most.

"Where're you going, anyway?" Brennan asked.

"Down to the barn."

The hare shrugged. "Well, that's good enough for some, I suppose, but not for the likes of me." He sniffed the wind and scratched behind a long ear. "Well, I'm off, Mister Oakmouse. Mustn't keep the missus waiting, it being Christmas and all. Have a nice time at the barn."

"Oh, I don't mean to stay there," Humphrey explained. "I've come to invite the others to my party."

"Party?" Brennan snorted. "Fat chance! Do you think they'd go on a trudge across the meadow for a party when they've got all they want right where they are? Not likely, Mister Oakmouse. Not hardly likely at all. But the best of luck to you. I must be off!"

And with that he was gone, leaving Humphrey standing alone in the snow. He looked uphill, but a hump in the slope hid his candle-lit windows from sight. Shaking his head, he continued on towards the barn, hoping the hare's words about the other mice weren't going to prove prophetic. Unfortunately they were.

"What?" Bonyface Withers cried when Humphrey finally reached the barn and had had his say. "Don't be silly, you old gaffer!"

"Why should we want to go all the way up to the hill?" Rhona Tupbottom demanded. She was very plump and munched on a handful of seeds while she spoke.

"But..." Humphrey looked around the ring of faces and realized that he knew very few of them, and the few he did know were the laziest of all that the meadow had to offer. "It's a tradition," he tried to explain. "It's when we give thanks for good foraging and ring in the new year. It's Christmas—a time of happiness..." His voice trailed off.

"Well, thank you very much," Bonyface said, "but no thanks. We're happy enough here and if we're to give thanks—why, what better place to do so than here in the barn?"

"But in the old days it was always—"

"These aren't the old days anymore, gaffer," Rhona said. "And besides. Here it's like having Christmas all year long. Plenty to eat and no need to work for it."

"But that's not what Christmas is all about," Humphrey said. At the back of the crowd a young mouse that he recognized as Tamsel Tinker's son was standing. "What about you?" he asked. "Don't you remember coming last year when your dad was still alive and I dandled you and your sister on my knee?"

Taffy Tinker looked like he wanted to melt into the floor.

"Well," he said, looking down at his feet. "We did have a very good time there—"

"Oh, shut up, Taffy!" Bonyface said. He turned back to Humphrey. "You're welcome to stay here if you want, only don't go filling impressionable heads with tall tales, see? There's nothing in the meadow for us but foxes and owls. Here we're safe. We don't even have to forage—the farmer does it for us!"

A chorus of "Here, here!" and laughter went up at his words.

"But it's not right," Humphrey said. "Never mind the party. Just think—"

"No," Bonyface said. "We won't think about it anymore and we won't listen. Be off with you, gaffer!"

Humphrey's lower lip began to quiver and he felt tears well up in his eyes, but he refused to break down in front of them. He looked around once again, trying to find even one friendly face, but those that didn't seem angry at his coming just looked bored. All except for Taffy Tinker, but he wouldn't meet Humphrey's eye. Slowly the old mouse turned and left the barn.

"Watch out for owls, old gaffer!" someone called after him.

"Why don't you invite them to your party?" someone else shouted to a round of laughter.

Shoulders hunched more against their jeering than the cold, Humphrey began the long trek back home.

By the time he reached the hedge that separated the meadow from the farmyard there was a bitter edge to the wind, driving before it the first crystals of a new snowfall. Humphrey drew his scarf tighter about him and blinked a large flake out of his eye. His whiskers were white with his frozen breath. He felt a nervous pin-prickle start up at the nape of his neck and looked anxiously around, sure he was being watched or…stalked. He thought of owls' talons and foxes' teeth and shivered. He tried to think of something else.

He wasn't quite sure if he was angry or sad about the way the other mice had brushed him off. It was to be expected, he supposed, though that didn't make him feel any better. They were a new generation and with so many of the old folk taken away (the image of an owl rose in his mind and he quickly pushed it down) the old traditions were being forgotten. But this was still Christmas and…well, they hadn't even decorated the barn. Too lazy for even that! He recalled Taffy Tinker's face and thought to himself that without the influence of others, like Bonyface and Rhona, he at least might have come. He tried to remember if he'd seen Taffy's sister in the crowd. It took him a moment just to come up with her name. Ellen.

By this time he was halfway across the meadow and far from shelter of any kind. His nervousness grew more pronounced the further on he went. The storm clouds were still building in the north, scudding nearer like dervishes on a wailing wind. Sprinkles of snow tumbled down and were caught in a whirling dance. Cane tapping the snowy crust, Humphrey hurried on, not caring anymore about the other mice or Christmas or anything. He just wanted to be safe at home and out of danger.

The sentinel oak at the top of the hill and his house in its roots seemed very far away still. His gaze darted left and right, searching out danger, but when it came, it came from above.

Humphrey felt a large shadow leap across him, a shadow cast from something flying in the sky just above him. Tiny heart thumping in his chest, he searched frantically for a place to hide, found nothing, and being desperate, began to run. He stumbled and fell headlong in the snow, cane tumbling out of his hand. Scrunching his eyes closed, he waited for the owl's pounce, too frightened and cold to try to escape anymore. Christmas, he thought. What a present. His little shoulders were tense with expectation, but the fierce grip of the owl's talons never came.

Above the growing howl of the wind, Humphrey thought he could hear a tinkling sound, like little bells. Trembling from head to toe, he slowly turned over and peeked up into a giant face that seemed to be all white beard, rosy cheeks and a pair of twinkling blue eyes that laughed merrily under bushy white eyebrows. A red and white hat with a fluffy pom-pom on its end pushed down a cloud of long thick and curly hair the colour of snow.

"Ho, ho!" the giant said. "What have we here?"

Wide-eyed, Humphrey could only stare. Beyond the big man in his red suit, the old mouse saw a sleigh and eight reindeer. St. Nick, he thought. Oh, my goodness! It's Santa Claus!

"Humphrey Oakmouse, I'd say," Old Nick murmured. He took off a mitt and gently lifted Humphrey up in his palm. "It's a cold and blustery night for a walk, Humphrey. Why aren't you inside with your friends? It's Christmas Eve!"

"I know. It's just...that is..." Humphrey stumbled over his words, but with some prompting and a big smile, St. Nick soon coaxed the tale out of him. Sadly Santa shook his head.

"I'm afraid there's nothing we can do for them, Humphrey," he said. "Either they care, or they don't. We can't make them be any different from what they choose to be."

"I know," Humphrey said mournfully. "But it doesn't seem right." And he was so lonely, but he didn't quite want to say that. Still, old Nick saw it in his eyes.

"I've need for a helper tonight," was what Santa said. "A small one. They make chimneys so small these days, when they have them at all! Do you think you could give me a hand? You can squeeze in and open the doors for me, for where's the house that can keep out a mouse?"

"*Me*? You want *me* to help *you*?"

Santa nodded. "It won't take long. I'll have you home by three at the latest."

Humphrey didn't care about going home. It was far too lonely there and all the party makings would just make him feel terrible.

"Oh, yes!" he said. "Please! I'd love to help!"

And so he did.

It was closer to three-thirty by the time Santa's sleigh finally let him off at his own front door, and what a time he'd had! He'd crept into all the big houses by the secret ways that only a mouse knows and unlatched a window or slipped a key under the door for St. Nick to come in. Then it was fill up the stockings (Humphrey got to fill the tiny dolls' stockings that hung in dolls' houses) and sample the cookies and milk left out for Santa.

That one night seemed like a whole lifetime. And everywhere there were Christmas trees blossoming with coloured lights in windows, laurels and wreaths hung from the doors, and a sense of goodwill and camaraderie that filled the old mouse from the tip of his nose to the end of his tail.

But now as he waved goodbye to Santa and looked at the door to his own home, a sort of wistful sadness crept through him. With "Ho, ho!" and tinkling sleigh bells still ringing in his ears, Humphrey straightened his back and went to his door. He'd go straight to bed and not bother to put everything away until tomorrow. He simply couldn't bear to do it tonight.

The door creaked open and he stepped in, shutting the winter and storm out as he closed it behind him. Hanging up his jacket and cap and kicking off his boots, he slowly made his way down the hall to his sitting room. He'd been determined to not even look around, to go right to his bedroom and face the world tomorrow morning, but he glanced up at the hearth and saw, hanging there all green and red and sparkling, the special guest wreath that had been missing earlier.

Where? How? But then his gaze was drawn downward and there, curled up in his favorite chair, were Taffy and Ellen Tinker, fast asleep. Hardly able to believe what he saw, Humphrey crossed the room and looked down at them. As he watched, Taffy cocked open a sleepy eye.

"We...I hope you don't mind..." the little mouse began shyly.

Humphrey grinned from ear to ear.

"No," he said in a soft and wondering voice. "I don't mind at all. You're welcome to stay as long as you like."

Taffy sighed and, curling up closer to his sister, drifted off again. Looking down at them, Humphrey felt tears start up in his eyes again, but they were tears of joy. Two little mice, braving the meadow and storm and all to come to Oakmouse burrow! He gathered them up, one at a time, and took them into his guest room where he tucked them into the big cozy bed there. Pausing in the doorway, Humphrey glanced back and smiled contentedly. What a Christmas it had turned out to be!

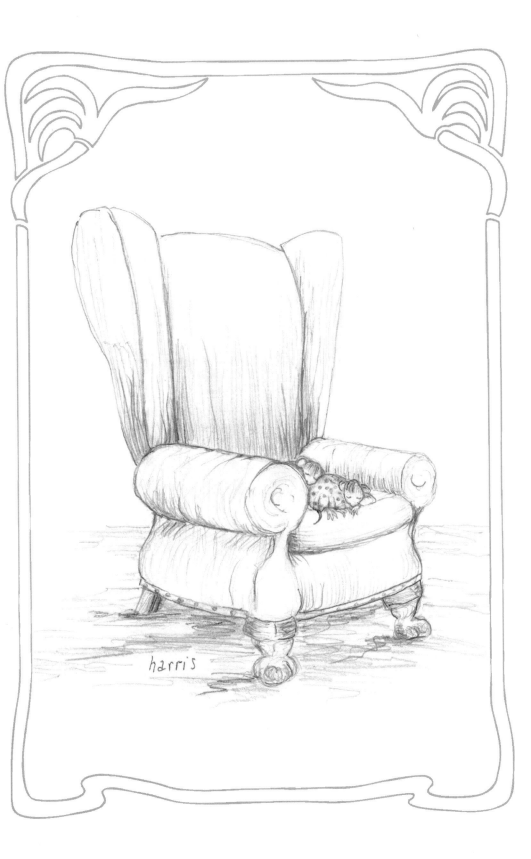

A Pattern of Silver Strings

Nagakaramu
Kokoro mo shirazu
Kurokami no
Midarete kesa wa
Mono wo koso omoe

Lady Horikawa

(Will he always love me?
I cannot read his heart.
This morning my thoughts
Are as disordered
As my hair.)

Meran Gwynder was the daughter of an oak king and the wife of a harper, though neither her royal green blood nor her marriage seemed very real to her just now. Loss filled her heart and she could find no way to deal with it. The sadness of what seemed a broken trust shared an uneasy rule with her unending questions. If she could know why...

"He left without a word," she said.

Bethowen the hillwife clicked her teeth in reply, though whether the sound was meant to be sympathetic or was only a habit remained debatable. They sat on a hilltop, under the guardianship of an old longstone, with the stars glimmering pale in the night skies above and the fire between them throwing strange shadows that seemed to echo the whisper of the wind as it braided the hill's grasses. Stirring the fire with a short stick, Bethowen looked through the glitter of sparks at her guest.

Meran had nut-brown skin and brown-green hair. She was slim, but strong-limbed. Her eyes were the liquid brown of an otter's. The hillwife could see none of this in the poor light. Those images she drew up from her memory. What she saw was a troubled woman, her features strained and wan in the firelight. At the oakmaid's knee the striped head of Old Badger looked up to meet the hillwife's eyes.

"Men will do that," Bethowen said at last. "It's not a new thing, my dear."

"Not him."

"What makes me wonder," the hillwife continued as though she'd never been interrupted, "is what brings one of the treefolk so far from her tree." Ogwen Wood was a good two hours south and west across the dark hills, a long distance for an oakmaid.

"My tree fell in a storm years ago—you never heard? I should— *would* have died but for him. As the green blood spilled, he drew me back. With his harpmagic. With his love."

"And you have no more need of your tree?"

"He made me charms. Three talismans."

Meran could see his quick sure hands working the oakwood as surely as though he were beside her now. First he made a pendant, shaped like an oak leaf, and that she wore under her tunic, close to her heart. Then a comb, fine-toothed and decorated with acorn-shapes, and that she wore in her hair to keep the unruly locks under control. Lastly a flute that she kept in a sheath hanging from her shoulder. Oak was not the best of woods for such an instrument, but his harpmagic had instilled in it a tone and timbre that the natural wood lacked.

"He built us a new home of sod and stone and thatch and there we lived as we had before. Until this morning..."

"When you awoke and found him gone," Bethowen finished for her. "But he journeys often, doesn't he, this husband of yours? Roadfaring and worldwalking from time to time. I have heard tales..."

"And well you might. But you don't understand. He left without a word. I woke and he was gone. Gone." She tugged at the edge of her cloak with unhappy fingers and looked up to meet the hillwife's bright eyes. "He left Telynros behind."

"Telynros?"

"His harp. The roseharp."

Telynros was a Tuathan gift, an enchanted instrument that plainly bore the touch of the old gods' workmanship. Silver-stringed and strangely carved, it had, growing from the wood where forepillar met the curving neck, a living blossom. A grey rose.

"Please," Meran asked. "Tell me where he has gone."

Bethowen nodded. "I can try, my dear. I can only try."

From the unrolled cloth that lay at her knee, she chose a pinch of flaked alder bark and tossed it into the flames with a soft-spoken word. The fire's hue changed from red-gold to blue. Muttering under her breath, she added a second pinch and the blue dissolved into violet.

"Look into the flames," she said. "Look and tell me what you see."

"Only flames. No. I see..."

An oak tree strained at its roots, green-leafed boughs reaching for...something. There was a sense of loss about that tree, an incompleteness reflected in the pattern of its boughs. Under the spread of its leafed canopy, half covered in autumn leaves, stood a harp.

"My tree," Meran whispered. "But it's..." She shook her head. "My tree standing in my father's wood as ever it did. And that is Telynros, his harp. Bethowen...?"

"It is the present you see," the hillwife replied. "But a view of it that we already know, not what you seek."

Sighing, Bethowen closed her eyes. Deep inside, where the herenow curled around her thoughts, she drew on the heart of her strength. Her taw, the inner silence that is the basis for all magic, rose sure and firm like a well-remembered tune. When she spoke a word, the air crackled about her and a pale green rune hovered in the air above the fire. Sinking, it slowly became a part of the flames.

Meran leaned closer to the fire. The scent of wildflowers was strong in the air. The vision in the flames remained. Only its perspective changed. First the harp grew large and larger still, until all she could see was the silvery glisten of its strings, then between them, amidst eddying rivers of mist that hid more than they showed, she saw him, saw his face. Her heart grew tight in her breast.

"Cerin," she breathed. There was both hope and loss in her voice.

He stood on the ramparts of an old ruined fortress, the grey stone-works stark against a spill of dusky hills and the tendrils of the mist. Beside him was a man clad all in black—tunic, trousers, boots and jacket. The man in black had a strange-shaped lute hanging from a shoulder strap. Its shining wood was of the darkest ebony. Even the strings were black. Meran shivered and looked away.

"Who is he with?" she asked.

Bethowen shrugged.

"Where are they, then?"

"In this world, but not."

Bethowen passed her hands above the fire and flames stirred the image into a new shape. The two men still stood on the ramparts, but now the fortress was changed. Gone were the ruined walls and tottering high towers. Stone was fashioned cunningly to stone, wall to towers to inner keep until the whole of it seemed the fashioning of master stoneworkers. Brave pennants fluttered in a breeze that blew across the sudden green hills.

"That is what he sees," the hillwife said.

She spoke a last word and the vision was lost in mists once more. Harpstrings, silver and taut, took shape amidst the swirl of mist, then a harp, half covered with leaves, and above it a yearning oak keeping watch. Then there was only the fire and its red-gold flames.

"Where is that keep?" Meran asked.

"North of Abercorn and far from your father's wood. Across the Dolking downs. Too far for an oakmaid. In the old days they named it Taencaer and it prospered. Now it is a nameless ruin where no one goes."

"I must go to him."

"Too far," Bethowen said.

"But still I must go." Meran bit at her lip, finding her next question, for all that it burned inside her, difficult to frame into words. It was not the question so much as what the answer to it might be.

"Is he...is he enspelled?" she asked.

Bethowen shrugged. "I have shown you all that the flames have to show, my dear. More I cannot do. For your sake, I hope..."

The hillwife shut her mouth and entwined her knobby fingers together on her lap. She hoped what? That all was well? If all was well the oak king's daughter would not be here asking her questions.

"You must take care," she began, but stopped again. Hers was only the gift of farseeing and a few remedial cures. Advice had never been her province. To each their own wisdom. But this oakmaid, so determined, as stubborn as the badger that bided by her knee, as much a part of the Middle Kingdom as the ensorcered keep she meant to visit...what advice had the hills for her? None, save caution and, to one so headstrong, that would only be so much mouthing in the wind.

"He is enspelled," Meran said.

He had to be. He would never just leave her. But the fear, once having risen whisperingly inside her, couldn't be shunted aside. Like a serpent's insidious hiss it worried at all she'd ever held as certainty.

Is our love such a frail thing that I should question it like this? she demanded of herself.

He left, the whisperer replied slyly. Without a word.

He was enspelled! she insisted. He'd never be gone otherwise.

Men will do that, the inner voice replied, repeating Bethowen's earlier words, but mockingly, without the sense of comfort that one woman might offer to another.

Fiercely Meran shook her head. She thought of the roseharp's strings and the dead leaves entwined amidst them. She turned her gaze northward and followed the line of the hills with her eyes.

"Thank you," she murmured to the hillwife, her thoughts already far away, already planning her journey.

Fighting down the draw of her dead oak that still called to her for all the charms she carried with her, she left the hilltop. Old Badger trailed at her heels.

"Luck go with you," Bethowen said, but there was no one left to answer. Only the night remained, with its voiceless stars and the crackle of the flames.

➤ ⸸ ◄

Those same stars looked down on what was once named Taencaer, the old ruined hillfort that straddled the border between Abercorn and Staynes. But where they saw the keep for the impoverished memory that it was, with leaning stone-cracked towers and debris rounding the once-straight planes of its walls, the two men who stood atop its ramparts saw it as it had been in longyears past—a bustling keep filled with the retainers of the old king's court, the last bastion of man before the grim wastes of the wild northlands. Where the hawk in the deserted west tower and the rodents that made their nests in the courtyards below heard only the wind and the stirrings of dead grasses as they rasped against the weathered stones, the two men heard music drifting lazily from the inner keep, the voices of stableboys and maids gossiping in the courtyard, horses stamping in the stables, the creak of a wooden wheel as water was drawn from the well, and the hundred other sounds of an occupied keep.

One of the men was a black-haired tinker, brown-skinned and dark-eyed. His name was Jeth Tewdol. He leaned against the old stone of the ramparts and eyed his prisoner with amusement, his lean fingers straying from time to time to the strings of his lute. The occasional snatch of music that answered had a sardonic quality to it that matched the dark cunning of his eyes for mood.

The other was Cerin called the Songweaver, the husband of Meran Gwynder and a harper, though he was far from his wife and had no instrument at hand to show his calling. There was more grey than brown in his beard and his braided hair was greyer still. He was thin and his face seemed a map of lines, like the many roads he'd journeyed, but where the tinker's dark eyes reflected without depth, his were clear and tarn-deep, more the eyes of a young man for all his body's apparent age.

Staring across the darkened hills, Cerin worried at the why and where of his situation. It was a strange thing to go abed in your own house, with your wife at your side, and wake in a strange keep, who knew where, a prisoner. The sun had arisen and set once since then, and still he was here. Try as he might, there was no way free of it. His captor's lutemagic bound him as surely as though he were chained, sapping his will, refusing him the chance to raise his own magics.

For he had magics, only they were denied him, here in this strangely familiar place. His taw, the inner quiet where his power had its birth, was silent, but silent with a silence of absence, not the silence that was like music, that was his strength. What he needed was his harp, but Telynros too was denied him.

Ordinarily there was a bond that joined them so that, no matter what the distance between them, he could call the roseharp to him, or him to it. But when he reached out to it, the lutemagic thickened about him and he heard no scatter of welcoming notes, no greeting. Nothing. With the roseharp in hand he could have surmounted his captor's spells, the clear notes cutting through his unseen fetters like an otter cutting through water. But as it was...

And Meran. What was she to think, waking and finding him gone?

As though reading Cerin's thoughts, Jeth Tewdol grinned. He pulled a flask from the pocket of his jacket and took a long swig before offering it to his prisoner.

Cerin shook his head. "I think not."

"Afraid it's a faery drink?" the tinker asked. "That if you take a sip you'll be bound here forever?"

"Something binds me already, tinker."

"Why, so it does."

Jeth Tewdol drew chords from his lute and Cerin's head swam with the sharp pains that came like dagger blows on the heels of the dark music. He staggered and leaned against the stonework for balance, his lips drawn back as he fought the pain.

"A reminder," the tinker said with a smile. His hands fell away from his instrument.

As the last note failed, Cerin's breath returned to him in ragged gasps. The pains faded into a dull ache and were gone. All save the memory of them.

"You've only the one more night of my company, Songweaver," Jeth Tewdol added. "And then?" He grinned. "Why, then you're free to go as you will, where you will. Home to your woman of wood, if you want. If she'll still have you."

For all that he controlled the situation, the tinker took a step back at the sudden fire in his prisoner's eyes.

"No," he said, holding his hands up in a disarming manner. "You mistake me. I haven't harmed her, nor will I." His moment of unease dissolved as though it had never been and he made himself comfortable on the stoneworks, enjoying himself again. "This is the why of it," he explained. "Have you heard in your travels of Taencaer, the old king's keep?"

Cerin looked around with a new insight. The sharp edges of the keep wavered for a moment, as though the deepseeing of his magic had returned to him. The sounds that rose up from the courtyard and inner keep were now like the wind playing through ruined stonework. Then that moment was gone and all was as it had been, except that Cerin knew now where he was: in ruined Taencaer, where ghosts were said to play with the wind and the spirits of the dead slept lightly if they slept at all. The hillfort had been brought back to a semblance of life through the tinker's lutemagic, the same lutemagic that kept him from gathering his taw and putting an end to his captivity. Recognizing the fort and the hills beyond, he wondered how many he would know amongst the ghosts that the tinker had woken.

"What of it?" he asked. Where he was, he now understood, but not the why.

"They had a contest here, in days long gone. Barden and musicians came from many lands to compete in it."

"I know," Cerin said. "Tasanin was the last to win it—a young fiddler from Yern."

The tinker regarded him strangely. Something in his prisoner's voice brought him up sharp, but Cerin, for all the furor of his thoughts, kept a bland expression on his face.

"How could you know that?" Jeth Tewldol asked.

"I was here that day."

"But that was…long ago."

Cerin smiled, enjoying the tinker's disconcertment. "I know. But still I was here and remember it."

"Songweaver," Jeth Tewdol said. "That's your name? Not a title?"

At Cerin's nod a queasy feeling went through the tinker. It had been one man through the centuries bearing that name, not wearing it as a title? For a long moment he said nothing, then a new gleam entered his eyes.

"This makes it even better," he said. "That contest will be held again tomorrow night—for the first time in many a year—and I mean to win it. It was for that reason that I raised the dead of Taencaer. I meant to win the contest and take the title of Songweaver from you. But now…now I take more than a title. I take your name and all the magic in it."

"Contests mean nothing," Cerin said. "They are for youths who have yet to prove something to themselves, not for men such as you and I. And my name, like the roseharp, was a gift of the Tuathan. You cannot take it from me."

Jeth Tewdol touched his lute and an eerie note sang forth. "You needn't sound so smug, Songweaver. I too have a god-gifted instrument, though mine was given to me by the Daketh."

Cerin looked from the lute that the tinker claimed came from the Tuathan's dark cousins, to the man's brown face.

"How so?" he asked. "Why were you gifted?"

"Through no special effort on my part," Jeth Tewdol said. "Would you know the tale? I can see by your eyes you would—for all that you shake your head. Then listen and marvel, you who have lived down through the longyears. We are more alike than I thought, for I see now that as you are, so must I be, for are we not both god-gifted?

"My instrument came to me in such a fashion: I was traveling through the Kierlands—do you know them? They're unfriendly dales in the best of times, but for a tinker there's none worse. It was winter and I sought lodgings, but was turned away from every inn until I took refuge in one place no man could, or would, deny me—a ruined fane in the north marches. There was little enough there, but the walls that remained were enough to shelter me from the wind's cold bite, and what with this and that—a stolen haunch of a wild fowl from the last inn I'd tried, a small fire that spluttered and spat more than it gave off heat, and a threadbare cloak—I made do. A piteous picture, don't you think?

"I gave no thought to ghosts or the like—knew nothing of them save from my own people's roadtales. I fell asleep knowing nothing of the history of those ruins. That I found out later. Once it was a Tuathan fane, desecrated in years long gone, and now a place of dark shadows where the Daketh's power was strong. I slept and dreamt that they came to me, those dark gods, came to me who was nothing. I remember cowering from them, yet accepting their presence as we will do in a dream. They saw something in me—my bitterness, perhaps?—and fanned it to life with promises.

"'What would you have?' they asked me.

"I remember thinking of the instrument my father had left me—a poor old flute that I sold for a week's lodgings and meals a year or so before. I'd never've done it, but I was desperate. The innkeeper had the city guard waiting at his door if I couldn't pay him something.

"Well, I thought of it, and remembered its warmth and comfort. You must know what I mean, Songweaver. When all's wrong in your world, a snatch of music can still lift your spirits. So I opened my mouth to ask for another like it, but when I spoke, all that came out was one word: 'Power'.

"The Daketh laughed—such a sound!

"'Then power you shall have,' they said and were gone.

"When I woke, my fire was gone out and the wind was howling. I recalled my dream and found, lying next to me, this." The tinker tapped his lute. "They left me this instrument and its magics, yes, and the skill to use both. Why? Who can say? On a whim, no doubt. It makes little difference to me, for I'll tell you this, Songweaver. Innkeepers no longer look at my darkened skin and bid me begone. With the lutemagic I could tumble their walls down about their ears and they know it. They see it in my eyes, sense the lute's power. Ah, isn't she a beauty?"

Cerin nodded obligingly.

"And it's with it that I'll take your name."

"I do not engage in contests," Cerin replied.

"Are you afraid to lose?"

"Win or lose, it means nothing. I take my music as I find it. Whether you are the better musician or not, does not invalidate my own skill. And my name is still my name."

"And yet there will be a contest and you will play in it. And when the king's barden name me the winner, I will be the Songweaver and you will be nothing."

Cerin shrugged. If the tinker wished a contest, so be it. If he named himself Songweaver, there was little he could do about that either. A name was only a name. It had power, as all names must, but only if it was a true name. The tinker deluded himself if he thought otherwise.

"I have no instrument," he said.

Jeth Tewdol smiled. "I have one for you. A harp—the like of which you've never seen before."

And indeed he hadn't.

When the tinker brought the harp to him, Cerin could only stare. The soundbox was cracked. The supports, forepillar and curving neck both, were warped. The tuning pins had no hold in them so that a string wouldn't stay in tune, while the strings themselves were discoloured with rust and buzzed when he tried one.

"Well?" the tinker asked.

Cerin looked from harp to man and answered softly, "A fine instrument, Jeth Tewdol, and I thank you for its use. If you will allow me to...accustom myself to it?"

"By all means," the tinker laughed. "I will leave you to your task. Only, Songweaver. Do us both a favour. Don't try to escape." He tapped his lute meaningfully, with all the subtlety of a bit actor in a mummer's play.

"I am yours to command," Cerin said.

"So you are. Why, so you are!"

Chuckling to himself, the tinker wandered off, plucking a tune from his lute. When he was gone, Cerin leaned against the stoneworks and eyed his borrowed harp for long moments. Then, sighing, he began to take out the tuning pins, one by one. Rubbing dust and stone powder onto them, he fitted each back into place, testing them for give and how they'd hold for tuning. Some still fitted so loosely that he had to add slivers of wood to achieve the desired tightness. When he was done with them, he polished the strings themselves, working every fleck of rust out of them until they gleamed as bright as his roseharp's. He ignored the warpage and the soundbox's cracks. There was nothing he could do for them except rub the wood until it regained some of its lost luster.

He thought of Meran as he worked and wished there was some way he could get word to her so that she'd not think he was hurt or dead, or worse, that he'd left her. What *would* she think? The shock of waking alone and finding him gone...Frowning, he rubbed the wood all the harder, trying not to think of it.

At last he was done and he could test the instrument. The tuning pins held, for what it was worth, but the tone was abysmal, without projection. The bass strings still buzzed, though they could perhaps be fixed. Holding the harp on his lap, he closed his eyes and concentrated on Telynros, hoping that the tinker's guard might have dropped or the lutemagic fallen away enough for him to reach the roseharp with his need, but it was no use. He called up the grey rose and silver strings, but only mists answered.

Weary, he went to find a place to sleep for the day. Finding it, he lay long awake, thinking of his wife and their home, and what the tinker would do with him when the contest was done. Surely he would not simply set him free? He would fear Cerin's reprisal, as well he might. But worry though he did, if there was a solution to his situation, Cerin couldn't see it.

► ʏ ◄

Dawn found Meran many leagues north of Ogwen Wood and the longstone where Bethowen the hillwife kept her seeing-flames. Her legs ached, from ankle to calf especially, and she longed to rest. But there was still so far to go. And when she got there...What if he wasn't there? What if he was, but he'd gone of his own volition?

"I'm tired," she said, kneeling in the coarse grass. "Ah, but I'm tired."

Old Badger rubbed up against her and she ruffled his thick neck fur. She watched the sun rise, saw the hills unfolding for bleak miles north. Her dead oak called to her, stronger than before, for she'd never been this far from her father's wood. Rubbing her pendant, feeling the oak grain between her fingers, she tried to ignore the insistent summons to return, but it stayed with her, a constant need that sapped her determination, weakening her when she needed all her strength.

"I don't know if I can run that far, Old Badger. I don't know if it's in me."

But it had to be. As surely as though she felt Cerin's arm around her shoulders, she knew he needed her. Or was it her own need that drove her? She frowned, not liking this turn her thoughts kept taking. He was enspelled, she told herself yet again, and wished that the voice inside her, whispering otherwise, would go away. She would continue. She'd run until her legs collapsed under her and then she'd run some more. Unless...

She smiled suddenly, wondering why she hadn't thought of it earlier. Drawing her flute from its sheath, she looked along its length, seeing Cerin's handiwork in its every carved inch. Then she lipped the instrument and, gazing skyward, began to play.

For a moment she thought she heard a harp answer, accompanying her as it had so many times before, then knew that it was only her need that heard it. She shook off the feeling and concentrated on her playing. Her fingers moved in a slow dance across the wood and clear notes rang in the air. For a long time it was the only sound the hills heard. Then, far off in the distance, there was an answer—a deep-throated whistling call. A black speck grew larger in the sky and larger still, until a greatowl dropped groundward on silent wings.

Like calls to like, the old tales say. So an oakmaid's playing drew one of her skykin to her. The greatowl's wingspread spanned sixteen feet and its torso was as long as a man's. Landing, he ruffled his feathers and became a man, tall and round-eyed, with feathers streaming down to his shoulders in place of hair. Meran drew her flute back from her lips and laid it across her knees.

"Thairn," she said in greeting, her voice warm. They were old friends, these two.

"Your song was sad enough to make the wind weep, Meran. Why did you call me?"

Listening to her reply, he cocked his head like the great bird in whose shape he was more comfortable.

"I can bear one of you," Thairn said, looking from her to Old Badger when she was done.

Meran sheathed her flute and bent down to kiss Old Badger's brow.

"That will be enough," she said.

Thairn nodded and took his skyshape again. He lowered his neck to help her get a better purchase and she mounted awkwardly, afraid to pull the feathers too hard lest they loosen and come away in her hand. Once she was settled, Thairn rose effortlessly into the morning air and hovered.

"Goodbye, Old Badger!" Meran called down. "Wish me luck!"

Thairn's long wings plied the air and they were off, swifter than ever Meran's legs could have taken her. Behind, Old Badger whined, looking this way and that. Then he set off, doggedly following the bird and its rider. When they were only a speck in the distance and finally gone from sight, still he followed, his short legs churning, his body moving in a strange flowing motion that looked for all the world like a furry carpet come to life and floating a few inches off the ground as it followed the contours of the terrain.

The distance sped by under Thairn's tireless flight. Burrowing her face in his soft neck feathers, Meran stared ahead, northward, until just before the coming of twilight she saw the fortress in the distance. By the time they reached its ruined walls, the night had fallen. Thairn coasted in and landed near the gates. Disembarking, Meran stretched, trying to work the stiffness out of her muscles.

"Thank you, Thairn," she said.

The greatowl took manshape again.

"I'll come with you," he said.

Meran shook her head. "Please. I have to go by myself."

She didn't want to have to explain about the whisper that had kept up its constant nagging the whole of the journey north. All she knew was that she wanted to see Cerin on her own in case...in case...

She bit at her lip and savagely pushed the thought away.

"You're certain?" Thairn asked.

"I'm certain."

She waited until he'd changed back to a greatowl and his wings had lifted him into the dark skies again before she turned to make for the gate. As she reached it, the whole fortress seemed to waver in her sight. She blinked and rubbed at her eyes. In place of the ruin were solid walls, rearing high, lit by torchlight. Where the gateway had been empty, two guards now stood.

"Your business?" one of them demanded.

"I..."

The guard looked at the flute sheath hanging from her shoulder. "Are you here for the musician's contest?"

"The...? Yes. Yes, I am!"

Musician's contest? Was it for this that her husband had left her? To take part in some mad contest? The whispering grew stronger in her mind and, feeling sick, she didn't have the strength to force it away.

"They're just finishing up," the guard said. "In the main hall. You'd better hurry."

Nodding her thanks, feeling more numb than real, Meran stepped through the gates and made her way across the inner courtyard. A musician's contest? Why had he come to it? Without his harp, even! As if he cared for such things in the first place. Contests were for people who needed titles, he'd told her often enough, not for anyone who cared about their music. Then she heard someone playing a harp, a strange harried sound as though the player were exhausted or drunk, and she recognized her husband's playing in the phrasing of the notes.

He *was* here! Part of this contest, and playing badly. Unsure if she were angry or sad, or perhaps some painful combination of the two emotions, she made for the door.

➤ ⲩ ◄

Disconcerting as the gathered dead were, what interested Cerin most was that there were more contestants than simply the tinker and himself. He wondered why. Long tables ran the length of the hall, except for the cleared space before the dais where the king and his retinue sat. And though he knew the people gathered here were only shades of the dead, he saw no mouldering corpses or gaunt boney shapes wrapped in their death palls. Instead they appeared as real as the tinker that walked at Cerin's side. They joined the other contestants, three men and a woman, at a table set aside for them to the left of the cleared space.

"The rules are simple," Jeth Tewdol told him. "Musicianship is judged by those three," he indicated the dais where the king's barden sat with fiddle, harp and flute respectively on their knees. Cerin didn't recognize any of them, though he knew the king. He looked away at the dead king's mocking smile. There had been no love between them when the king was alive.

"But the judging," the tinker was explaining, "is also measured on how well you appeal to the less tutored—those gathered here to listen. Thunderous applause is what you're seeking, Songweaver. If you wish to keep your name." He glanced down at Cerin's instrument and grinned. "I wish you the best of luck."

One by one the contestants played and, living or dead though they might be—Cerin was no longer sure—they were all skilled musicians. He found himself enjoying their strange tunes and tried to remember this flourish or that decoration for future reference. *If* Jeth Tewdol was going to allow him a future. Then it was the tinker's turn.

He bowed, first to the king's dais, then to the crowd that filled the hall to overflowing. Giving Cerin a wink, the tinker began to play. There was no doubting his skill. Why on top of that he needed to be named the best, Cerin couldn't understand. He played with a dark grace. Moody tunes grew out of his fey instrument that sent shivers up the spines of his listeners and their feet to tapping the weird rhythms. When his last note died away, a long silence filled the hall. Then it was shattered as the people roared, clapping their hands and stamping their feet. They banged their mugs on the tables, whistled shrilly and generally raised a hullabaloo. Beaming, the tinker returned to the contestants' table.

"Now it's your turn," he said.

Cerin nodded, rising as his name was called.

"Lastly, Cerin called the Songweaver. Harper from Ogwen Wood."

As Cerin took his place, settling the tinker's harp on his lap, a murmur went through the crowd. There were faces he knew amongst them— face of folk long dead—and they recognized him and his name, though there wasn't one that had a friendly smile for him. Looking down at his instrument, he sighed. It's not the harp, it's the player, he told himself. And it matters not whether you win or lose, just let it be done.

He was tempted to play badly, just to let the tinker win, but knew he couldn't. Whatever he might think of contests or his present situation, he had the pride of his art to consider as well. When he played, he always played his best, whether it be for a king in his court or a shepherd in his cot. Tonight could be no different else he'd lose his name in truth, though not in the way that the tinker meant he should lose it. Turning so that he could watch Jeth Tewdol, he began to play.

He started with a familiar air, fingers curled like a hawk's talons as they plucked sweet notes from the shabby instrument on his lap. It was a simple piece but, in his hands, for all the drawbacks of the instrument, he breathed new life into it; gave it a deepness so that for all that his listeners had heard it played a thousand times before, in his hands it sounded like a newly-composed piece. He grinned at Jeth Tewdol as he began another, enjoying despite himself the look on the tinker's face. But his amusement didn't last long.

Seven bars into the tune, he saw Jeth Tewdol caress a string of his lute and the harp Cerin played ran discordantly. He tried to remedy the turn his music had taken, but the more he tried, the worse it sounded. The damage was done. Titters started up at the back of the hall and his neck reddened, but try though he did, he could no longer control the instrument. For every true note he fingered, the lutemagic awoke a dozen discords. At last he let his hands fall from the strings and he bent his head under the laughter of the gathered dead. And laughing loudest of all was Jeth Tewdol.

"Ha!" he cried. "I've won! See him now, he who was once called the Songweaver!"

Cerin's face burned. He knew he could play better, knew the flaws heard by these people were none of his doing, but knew as well that as far as they were concerned, he was worse than a novice player. They had wanted to see him fail and cared not how that failure was brought about. He could hold the truth of his own skill in his heart, but it did little to diminish the weight of the ridicule he bore. This was like his worse nightmares as a fledgling harper come to life. How often hadn't he woken bolt upright in his bed, sticky with sweaty fear, the dregs of a dream thudding in his heart? He'd be before a crowd, playing his best, and then it would all go wrong, and instead of applause, he received jeering and laughter. Like now.

Slowly he rose to his feet and, clutching the harp tight against his chest, made his way back to his seat. There was no use protesting, no use in doing anything except to see this thing through to its end. And perhaps, in some measure, he deserved to be treated in this way, taken down a notch. He didn't believe in contests, no. But perhaps all his noble wordage as to why merely covered up the fact that he thought himself above them. Just as when he'd been playing and he'd mocked the tinker—something he'd never done to another musician no matter how good or bad his playing. Who was better? Was it because perhaps Jeth Tewdol *was* better? Why should it matter? It never had before. But just now, with the jeering and catcalls still loud in his ears and the tinker's grinning face so near his own, it seemed to matter more than anything else ever had before.

"We have little love for the living," the dead king said as the noise finally fell away. His voice boomed hollowly through the hall. "But, in truth, Jeth Tewdol, you have provided an entertainment this evening that we'll not soon forget. To see the Bright Gods' companion brought so low! Ha! Arise and accept from me now the winner's cup!"

"See?" the tinker said to Cerin. "It's done."

As he rose to collect his reward, Cerin caught at his arm.

"Am I free to go now?" he asked.

Jeth Tewdol shrugged. "Perhaps." He ran a finger along one of his lute's dark strings and Cerin shivered as the lutemagic bit at him. "There's still the matter of a name to settle between us. We can scarce have two Songweavers wandering the world, now can we?"

He laughed at the impotent rage in Cerin's eyes and turned away. Laying his instrument on the dais before the king, he went to where the king's harper held the winning cup. But before his hand touched it, the clear sound of flute-playing spoke across the hall.

As one, all heads turned to the door to see the woman with her green-brown hair and her cloak like leaves who lipped her flute. Her fingers fluttered across the holes of the instrument as though she were caressing a lover and there came forth such a sound! The low notes thrummed like a bear's honeyed breath, the high ones skirled and pierced the sky with sudden stars.

"Who?" the tinker cried, but none save Cerin and the king's harper heard him. The rest were too entranced by her playing to heed him.

"A last contestant it seems," the king's harper said.

"Meran!" the Songweaver cried.

Her playing was like the woods in summer, full and merry, deep with old tree secrets, yet held an underpinning sweet sorrow, for like music, the seasons change, summer to autumn to winter and round again to spring. Her music told the tale of that circle, now joyful, now sad. And, by the faces of those who listened, such a music had never been heard in that hall before.

Jeth Tewdol's features contorted with rage. He leapt for his lute to stop her music, but Cerin was there first. The harper's boot crushed the hellish instrument before ever the tinker could lay a hand on it. With the sound of a great wind, the glamour of Taencaer fled, ghosts and all. The three of them stood in a ruined hall, the stars showing through the roofless heights above them. And still Meran played. Jeth Tewdol spun away from Cerin's sudden grasp and made for her.

But as the tinker scrabbled across the rubble, he forgot who his prisoner was, the power Cerin wielded that had been denied him. Still seething from the ridicule he'd undergone, concerned for his wife, no longer restrained, Cerin reached out to Telynros, his thoughts leaping the distance between the ruins of Taencaer and the cottage where his roseharp awoke with music as it stood by the hearth, though no hand touched its strings. A moment it played on its own, then the harp was in Cerin's hands and its music rushed forward to accompany the sound of Meran's flute.

Across the ruined hall, harper and flute-player met each other's gaze. Meran brought her flute from her lips and held it at her side, her fingers whitening where she squeezed it. She tried to focus on her husband's face, but her vision swam.

She didn't know what had possessed her to play in the doorway as she had, unless it be that those people had mocked her love and she meant to show them that it was wrong to do so. She'd not played to be a part of the contest. Rather she'd only tried, through her music, to reach out and touch the audience, show them that ridicule was cruel, hoped to awaken some compassion in their dead hearts. Blinking now, she saw only the vision from Bethowen's seeing flames—the pattern of silver strings and the dead leaves that half covered the instrument, the mists aswirl, and then, at last, her husband's face.

The sly whisperer inside her was laid to rest at last as she looked into his eyes. But a new fear rose to take its place. He played Telynros savagely and the dark-clothed man that was between them jerked to the music, helpless as a marionette. Cerin's eyes were dark with a wild anger, as though he didn't know what he was doing, or worse, that he knew all too well.

"Cerin!" she cried. "Cerin!"

His anger seemed to blind him, for there was no flicker of recognition in his eyes when she called his name, no lessening of that terrible harping. She opened her mouth to call again, then lifted her flute to her lips and sent her own music skirling through the maelstrom of the roseharp's notes, weaving and binding them. As their musics joined, she came to understand what drove him. It was not so much his ordeal that burned in him, as what he'd found in himself.

A new tone entered her playing and it pierced his anger with its reason.

No one can be perfect, love, it seemed to say. Yet remember that he drove you to it and learn the lesson of it. Don't become what he is. Where is the gentle man I love? Where is the Songweaver amidst such anger?

Slowly his rage faded. Telynros's grim notes dissolved into echoes and Cerin slumped to his knees, hugging his roseharp to him. He stared at the tinker's still form, sick at what he'd done. But as he watched, Jeth

Tewdol raised himself painfully and sat up against a block of weather-roughened stonework, lifted, it seemed, by the flute music that still rang sweetly through the hall, healing all hurts. Then it too died and Meran picked her way across. She paused by the tinker and looked down at him.

"Why?" she asked. "By my father's Oak, why?"

Jeth Tewdol lifted his gaze. "I am a tinker," he said bitterly.

"That is not reason enough."

"The Dark Gods gave me an instrument that made me a prince of players—I who was nothing before they gifted me, a two-copper pretender of a musician, a tinker welcomed more often with a cuff in the face and a curse. The Daketh gave me power. They delight in torment, so should I not offer it to them in payment? Is that not reason enough? They..." He shook his head. "How could you understand?"

Meran regarded him silently for long moments, then handed him her flute.

"Then I gift you with this," she said. "Will you now take delight in bringing joy to people?"

"I..." The tinker looked at the flute, remembering its sweet tone when she'd played it. His fingers trembled as he took it in his hands, running his fingers along the smooth length of its wood. For long moments, he was silent. When he spoke again, his voice had a different tone to it. Gone was the mockery and self-assurance.

"I...I know it's the player, not the instrument that makes a musician. Your husband...even on that box with strings I gave him to use...he was still the better player. I can't accept this. I..." His eyes glistened with unshed tears. "I don't deserve it."

"Still you don't understand," Meran said softly. "It's the music that matters, not who's better or worse."

"But...I...What will you use?"

Meran looked to Cerin and smiled. "Perhaps my husband will make me another. There's still some of the old tree left."

Jeth Tewdol could find no more words. He simply leaned against the stone, holding the flute as though it were the greatest treasure the world had to offer. Watching them, hearing his wife speak, Cerin felt the tightness in his chest ease and he could breathe again. He thought to himself that he should still be angry, but searching inside, all he could find was pity. Shaking his head, he stood and then Meran came to him, lifting her face to be kissed.

"Such a spell you wove!" he said with a smile. "Who's the Songweaver now?"

She grinned. "You are, silly! Who else?"

"Perhaps," he said as he kissed her.

Meran looked at his harp and, remembering the pattern the strings had made in the seeing-flames, reached out to touch one. A tiny bell-like note rang forth.

"Maybe I'll take up the harp then," she said, "and maybe not. But right now there's an Old Badger stuck somewhere between here and home, and a night's sleep that we never saw completed."

"So there is." He looked over her shoulder to the tinker. Jeth Tewdol raised his gaze from the flute to meet Cerin's eyes.

"If I said I was sorry…" the tinker began, but Cerin shook his head.

"We both learned something tonight, Jeth. I as much as you. If you're ever 'round Ogwen Wood, visit us, will you? Only come when we're awake."

Cerin's smile awoke a tentative answer on the tinker's lips. "If you'll have me," he said slowly, "I'd be honoured to come."

"Good. Till then…"

Cerin set the roseharp to ringing with deep chords and an amber hue surrounded Meran and him.

"Thank you!" the tinker called.

From the amber glow he heard a chorus of farewells. When the harping died away and the amber hue was gone, Jeth Tewdol sat alone amidst the ruined stoneworks of Taencaer. Rising, he went to the ramparts to watch the dawn pink the sky above the eastern hills. He thought for a moment of the Daketh instrument that lay broken below him, then shook his head and lifted Meran's flute to his lips. He was out of practice, so the sound that came forth was awkward and breathy, but the tinker smiled.

Verses from the Songweaver's Journeybook:

Root of Horn

A moon like pale honey
rides the night
when Tywys hunts.

The hills are awake with wind
and the thunder of a stag's hooves;
sloe-skinned with shadows,
grey-bearded with sleeping stones;
older than oak;
fiercer than the knife-edge of memories
borne by willow bards,
reed-thin fingers on their silver strings,
circling song to ash
under the watchful eyes of the Great Bear
—five stars, point to point,
the sky-paws beckoning—
as voices lift on high the words
of forgotten rhymers
who, remembering,
forget;
while still the sea-harps glisten,
the old bone
wet with the tears

of waves and wonder,
of harpers harping undersea,
while Tywys hunts.

Then the riddle unwinds
in stately time,
measure for paced measure,
and I remember
those who ruled before,
who were Myrddin's forefathers:
the proud-browed treekings
and wizened woodwizards,
the erlkin and their seakin,
the hillmother in her hall of earth bone
and, deeper still,
the silent speech of stone to stone,
quartz-veined and waiting,
that tells of
the bearded hillwalker
—his horns like apple boughs,
hung with holly;
his hair like September fields
braided with dreams
of moons adrift in seas of shadow,
high on high;
of words the bards left unrhymed,
and lips never tasted;
of tunes that fingers never knew,
or tried;
of riddles unanswered,
but remembered;
of histories retold,
hide-bound with lies;
while still the stars turn above,
the seasons reach, one into the other,
winter sharp, and leaf-fey summer;
where the pack gathers
—fox-red wolves with grey eyes
who heed the horn

and follow with gruff-throated cries—
as Tywys hunts.

Howls haunt the moon
and tear the night
when Tywys hunts.

Meran's Stone

Darker still
and streaked with mica tears,
an old grey stone
'bides the solemn weaving
of the seasons;
  recalls the touch
of dark-skinned hands,
the rasp of deerskin,
click of bead and quill,
the fox light-stepping winter snow,
and summer bees,
and older still,
the dryads dancing,
tree to tree
—each footfall
drumming the hint of an alphabet
rooted in the world's lost languages;
 seeks again
the strain of wind-lipped flutes,
cut from time's reeds
—downhill,
where the stream meanders
riverlike, in miniature;
  stirs under druid branches,
finger-thin leaves
and braided grasses,
rough granite smoothed by starlight;
  gazes moonward,
with secret dreams
of silver hares and branch-browed moose,
and remembers the sea.

Withered Trickster

Wake now, withered trickster.
Hear the humming
Of bees a-meadowed
and the hedgerows thrilling to
the grey harping of the twilight.
Under the long shadow
of the shepherd hills,
where the herons fly in summer,
see the moon wreathe pale
the night clouds
and the Horned Bear dancing
bright behind them.
Old lord winter waits
the last days of autumn's edge
and yours the hand
that sets the seasons spinning.
Wake now and remember.

The Piper

Wild-eyed
the Piper is come
and 'bides in shadow.

His breath
is the wind of the west
and sets the woods a-tremble.

His movement
is the growth of the mountains
and the hidden whispers of the hill.

His blood
is the wash of a thousand tides
and the sigh of moonless oceans.

O his spirit
Is the Fire King's daughter
And the glory reborn in ashes.

Secret Stones, Hollow Hills

Whose the spirit, deft of old
shook the circle
cast the stone?
Whose the breath, the twilight will
that set a-dream
the hollow hills?
Where the wood, the well, or Weir?
The harvest laugh?
The winter tear?
Ah, those that 'bide the amberspell,
the secret ken,
but never tell...

Days of Fading

When depth is lost
  to timeless wills,
the fey withdraws,
  the spirit stills;
the ragged breath
  of darkness grows
upon the pattern,
  'pon the soul.

The wild eyes of
  Pan are missed,
as on we wander,
  shadow-kissed:
almost horned,
  in restless flight
almost gold,
  but never bright...

They Will Come Again

They will come again,
the Bright Gods who walked deep woods;
who held patterns amidst the dancing stones,
'woke a wild twilight with summer thoughts,
broke wave upon wave of wonder
across the backs of the hollow hills
and shared the impossible beauty of the moon
with the pale stars of winter.

They will come again,
loosing their magics to speed like arrows
swift and sure into the starry west,
where grey peaks poke holes in the clouds
and swans glide on dream wings;
spinning riddles, girdled with deeper dreams,
and sharing an untamed wonder
as clear and singing as the first chord
that ever a harp rang.

1982

Glass Eyes and Cotton Strings

Oh, Cerin. Do look."

The Harper laid down the tunebook he'd been studying and came to the table where his wife stood admiring a display of stuffed cloth dolls. There were all manner of beings represented on the table, from princesses in moon-pale gowns to gaping-mouthed gremlins, tiny dragonets to tatter-cloaked tinkers, willow-thin elfin kowrie folk to a fat town magistrate with a pipe in his mouth and a heavy coin sack at his belt. There was even a harper.

The workmanship was uncanny. The tiny faces were made of dyed cotton, so cunningly stitched that their features appeared almost real. Teased sheep's wool for hair, coloured glass eyes and an attention to detail in the various costumes completed the illusion.

"Beautiful," he murmured.

"They're perfect," Meran said. "Look at the face of this one."

She held aloft a gangly-limbed marsh kowrie for his inspection. Puffed cheeks and twinkling eyes gave the cloth sculpture a look of barely-contained mirth.

"His name is Rush Tongue," the woman behind the table said.

She was a cheerful, grey-haired dame, sixty if she was a day, with the exaggerated features of one of her own creations. Her eyes were small and sparkling, nose more long than short, mouth wide with a pronounced dimple in each corner of her smile.

"And she, good sir," she added, "is named Lorwyn—for she is a mistress of moon magic."

Cerin looked down at the doll in his hand. She wore a long blue robe with trailing sleeves and carried a small wooden staff with a horse's head carved at the top. Her hair was a waterfall of gold, the tiny eyes a deep sea-blue, her face gentle, with just a hint of the moon-power that spoke through her...The harper shook his head. Any moment he expected the eyes to blink, the mouth to open and speak to him.

"They are very true-to-life, Mistress..?"

"My name's Nonie, good sir."

"How do you make them seem so alive?" Meran asked.

They were a striking couple—the tangle-haired daughter of an oak king and her tall husband. She had nut-brown hair and otter-brown eyes, and a touch of green in her tousled locks. Further from her tree than an oakmaid might normally fare, she carried three talismans carved from the wood of her storm-fallen oak to sustain her. There was a leaf-shaped pendant that she wore under her green dress and a comb that she wore in her hair in an attempt to keep the unruly tangle somewhat subdued. The third was a flute that she carried in a sheath from her shoulder.

"Well, there's the thing," Nonie explained. "I do the faces first, you see, and it's the face that decides what sort of being it will become. There's a moment, though, when I'm halfway through the stitching of the features, that the doll seems to decide for itself what it will be. And then, no matter how I protest—and I've long since given up protesting—that is what the doll will be."

Cerin smiled. It was the same with all artists—whether they be a craftsperson or musician. Start them talking about their art and you had best set an hour or two aside for the listening. He was no different himself. Let him begin on tunes or old tales...He missed his harp then, missed the familiar weight of it on his shoulder, but the townsquare was too crowded to carry a harp today. Every foot of it was taken up with the stands and tables and plain assemblage of craftspersons, gypsies, musicians, poets, guildsfolk, tinkers and the folk who'd come to see and sample their wares. Once a year they gathered in Chappenderry for the Samhain Fair that roared all about them in full swing.

The harp he missed was a gift of the Tuathan. Telynros was its name, the roseharp, an enchanted instrument that bore the touch of the old gods' workmanship. Its strings were silver, the wood the same deep brown as Cerin's beard and braided hair. Growing from the joint, where forepillar met the curving neck, was a living blossom. A grey rose. Telynros awaited their return in their room at the Greyapple Inn—a habitual staying-house for musicians visiting Chappenderry, the whole of the year through as well as at fairtime.

"Take this one," Nonie was saying, lifting a wicked-looking goblin from the collection on her table. "It fair frightened me when that face was looking up at me—come from the work of my own hands, as it were. Yet the choice was not mine. I sewed the cloth, but this perverse little gobber decided who he would be. Not I. I call him Gally Grim—after the creature Nellie Tiggens said she saw one night on the way home from town..."

⊢ ⋎ ⊣

A few tables away, two men in mage's blue took notice of the pair at the dollmaker's table.

"There's the Songweaver," said the one with straw-yellow hair and a narrow chin. "The harper of Ogwen Wood himself."

"So it is," his portly companion replied. "What of it?"

"What say we play a joke on him, Berrimyn?"

"What for?"

"Why, for the sake of the joke itself!"

"Cauledd..." Berrimyn began.

The blond-haired mage shook his head. "A harmless prank—that's all. Watch."

He lifted a hand, fingers taut and moving curiously as he spoke three soft words. One was for the cloth, one for the glass eyes, one for the shape of the doll.

"There are so many tales," Cauledd murmured, "told about his great deeds. Surely there should be one in which he is played for the fool?"

He blew across his hand, loosing the spell.

⊢ ⋎ ⊣

Meran held the figure of Gally Grim in her hand and decided she didn't like it at all. Its skin was of a dark green felt rather than cotton, its eyes yellow. The rough tunic and trousers were made to seem like the leaves of trees and green moss that grew in some haunted forest.

"I could never have finished him—" she began, then froze.

The doll's right eye slowly winked at her.

"Cerin!"

"What is it?"

"It...the doll blinked!"

Nonie chuckled. "They play tricks on you," she said. "Often I think to myself, now did it move or—"

The doll's sewn mouth snapped open and two rows of sharp, yellowed teeth bit down on Meran's thumb. With a cry of pain, she tossed it to the table and took a step back. The bite left a circle of puncture marks on her thumb. An oakmaid's green blood oozed from the wound.

"I never—" The rest of Nonie's sentence stayed in her throat.

Cerin stepped close to his wife, then turned startled eyes to the table. In amongst the inanimate dolls, the green figure of Gally Grim rose hissing. Wickedness gleamed in its yellow eyes as it slowly surveyed the crowded square. Save for Nonie and her two customers, no one else was yet aware of it. No one, but the two blue-cloaked mages, three tables down. One had given it life. Only he could take that gift away again.

⊁ ⋎ ⋏

"You've gone too far!" Berrimyn cried. "Stop it now!"

"Can't," Cauledd whispered. "It's not what it was any more. The spell was for cloth and glass and a shape. I never thought…It is a creature now—and I need its name."

He took a step forward. The little goblin leapt from the table. Snatching a knife from the belt of a passerby, it flung the blade true, then vanished into the crowd before anyone could make a move to stop it. Cauledd fell forward, the knife buried to its hilt in his chest. His eyes lost their focus.

"Cauledd!" Berrimyn cried, trying to support his friend.

Words spilled from between his lips, a spell took shape, but he was too late to save the stricken mage. Slowly, he lowered Cauledd to the ground. Around him, the square was in an uproar as the word went about, exaggerated each time it was told.

"—came to life, it did!"

"Damnedest thing!"

"Where a gobber, it were. Three, maybe four feet high!"

"Killed a man with a look!"

Berrimyn looked up as a hand touched his shoulder. Cerin kneeled beside him.

"It was a prank," he told the harper. "No more than a prank. I swear!"

"What was?"

"He meant no real harm. But now he…he's dead."

"Your friend," Cerin asked gently as understanding came to him. "He brought the doll to life?"

Berrimyn nodded. He gripped the harper's arm.

"It's tasted murder," he said. "It won't stop now. It'll kill again. It must be stopped. But the spell to stop it…"

Cerin nodded grimly. "…died with your friend."

He stood up, glanced at Meran.

"How is your hand?" he asked.

She tried to smile. "Old Badger's nipped me worse in play. It was more the shock…"

He drew her close. "At least you're not harmed worse," he said. "But now…now we must find a way to stop it. The mage is right. Having killed once, it will kill again. Such is always the way when a thing that was never meant to live is given life." He scowled at Cauledd's body. "Damn the man for choosing to play the fool with his magics!"

"Good sir," Nonie began at his elbow. "I never meant…"

"It was never your fault, Mistress," the harper assured her.

⊢ ⊤ ⊣

By nightfall, there were five more dead: a guardsman, two weavers, a serving girl, and a young child—the son of the blacksmith in Gernsfedd. Reported sightings were too numerous to follow up.

"I put a shaft right through it," Meran overheard a young guardsman say as she and Cerin returned to their inn. "Damn gobber ran off with the arrow sticking out of its back like a third leg!"

The talk in the commonroom was more of the same. The town's guard was only five strong—less one of their number now. The town magistrates were at their wits' end. There was talk of ending the fair though it was only into its second of five days. Already many folk had departed. A sixth of the stalls in the square stood empty and the tent-town that sprang up outside of Chappenderry each year was shrinking. The blacksmith's son and one of the weavers had died there.

The oakmaid and her husband found room at a long table by the hearth and ordered up a dinner which neither had much stomach for. Zintal, a local potter who was a friend of Meran's, joined them as their food came. He ordered ale and sat quietly pulling at his moustache, listening to the talk.

"Bad business this," he said at length.

Cerin nodded. He had worked a seeking spell with his roseharp earlier in the afternoon, but Gally Grim had proved to be as cunning as it was murderous. Search though Cerin did, with his harpspell filling him and the instrument's rich notes resounding in the confines of their room, there was no trace of the wicked creature for miles about the town. Yet still it struck.

"It's a matter for magic," the harper said, "but there's no mage in town kens a workable spell. Berrimyn, whose friend was the one to start it all, has run through every one he can remember and not one of them works. Seekspells return barren. Castspells catch nothing."

"There must be something," Zintal said.

"It's a dark riddle," Cerin replied, "and I see no answer to it."

"Unless," Meran began. The two men looked to her. "It's a cloth creature, given life, is it not?"

"Yes. But..."

"Like calls to like," Meran said.

Zintal understood first. "We must animate another of the dolls to seek out the first."

"That could prove dangerous," Cerin said. "The risk—"

"Would not be great," Meran told him. "So long as we animated the proper doll. A wizard, say, or..."

Cerin flexed his fingers, already feeling the roseharp's strings under them.

"Or a harper," he said.

⊱ Y ⊰

A red-eyed Nonie met them at the door of her house—the three of them with Berrimyn in tow. That one of her creations, made with such love and to bring only joy, should be the cause of all the trouble was a hard thing for her to bear.

"I never liked that one," she said, repeating a sentiment she'd expressed earlier in the day. "When I saw its evil face leering up at me...I should have left it unmade. I know that now. I never meant for them to cause anyone grief. But now there are six dead, and Arn knows how many others must die..."

Meran took the dollmaker's hand and squeezed it gently.

"We know that, Nonie," she said. "It was ill-luck that set this whole day to follow its sad treading. May we come in?"

"Surely. I..." Nonie sniffed. "Where's my manners gone to?"

She set water to boil, then tea to steep. Gathered around her kitchen table, with steaming mugs before them and the room filled with Nonie's artistry in all its phases of completion, they told her their plan.

"I don't know," she said at last. "It seems...wrong somehow, to give life to another."

"Not if we choose well," Meran said.

"You want Dierin," Nonie said.

She glanced at the harper doll where he sat on the windowsill, an old rough hat holding down his woolly hair, his tiny wooden harp with its cotton strings on his lap. Cerin nodded.

"I had thought..." Nonie began, her gaze shifting to the blue-robed mannequin that she'd named Lorwyn, then she shrugged. "Dierin it is," she said and brought the sculptured harper to the table.

"Berrimyn?" Cerin asked.

"I still have my doubts as well," the mage replied with a sigh. "But I am ready. If you would begin the tune we agreed upon..."

Cerin brought Telynros up from the floor beside his chair and set it on his lap. Before coming to the dollmaker's house they had resolve to mix magecraft with a harpspell so that, if there was further trouble, there would be more than one able to deal with it. Zintal and Meran leaned forward as the first chords filled the room, the potter nodding his head. He never tired of hearing the roseharp played. Cerin closed his eyes, the better to concentrate, and Berrimyn called up three words, similar to those Cauledd had used before, but adding to them a fourth—the mannequin's name. Nonie's gaze went from the doll on the table to where Lorwyn stood, golden-haired and blue-robed. A far-off look stole into her eyes as she regarded the doll she would have chosen.

The harpspell and the mage's words met to work their enchantment. A low gasp escaped Zintal's lips as the tiny harper stirred and came to life, his fingers mimicking the movement of Cerin's on Telynros.

"We need your help," Meran said softly to the little figure.

The cloth fingers came away from the toy instrument and the small face turned to looked at her. All around the table breaths were drawn in and held. Had they erred, or would the doll help them? Had they brought another Gally Grim to life, or a being of a more gentle nature?

"Lady," the doll's voice piped. "How may I help you?"

Cerin and Berrimyn exchanged relieved glances.

⟩ ⟨ ⟨

Hours later the sound of harping stilled in Nonie's kitchen. Cerin lifted his head wearily, limbering stiff fingers. With watchspells he and the mage had followed the doll's progress as he searched the town for his wicked cousin, followed him over rooftops and through alleys and ditches, peered with him through windows and into barns and stables. Meran laid a hand on her husband's arm, a question in her eyes.

"Nothing," he said. "We found nothing."

The prolonged use of spell-working had taken its toll on both him and Berrimyn. Dully, they watched Zintal rise to open the kitchen door. The small bedraggled doll stepped inside. The bright cloth of his tunic and trousers was stained and torn, the gentle face was haggard.

"I am weary," he said in his high-pitched voice. "I would rest." He turned to Meran. "Lady, I am sorry."

Meran was touched by the little harper's loyalty.

"You did all you could," she said, "and for that we are grateful." She gathered the doll in her arms and brought him back to the windowsill. "Rest, now," she added.

Cerin touched tired fingers to his harp and brought the harpspell back to life. Berrimyn spoke the words, the name, and the doll returned to his previous inanimate state. The weariness remained etched in the cloth features. The glass eyes reflected the disappointment that filled the kitchen.

"We have done all we can tonight," Zintal said. "You need to rest, Cerin...Berrimyn. There is still tomorrow."

"Yes," Cerin said. "Tomorrow. Then we will make the attempt again." He glanced at Nonie. "If you are still willing, Mistress?"

"Surely," the dollmaker said.

Her voice was a touch distant, for she was trying to keep the tune of the harpspell fresh in her mind. She had already marked the words that Berrimyn had used. When her guests were gone, she sat for a long while at her kitchen table, regarding the small faces of her cloth charges. Time and again her gaze returned to the now tattered harper and the mistress of moon magic that stood beside him in her blue robes. At length she sighed.

"Tomorrow may be too late," she told her dolls. "How many more will have died before the night is done?"

The rows of silent mannequins made no reply. Nonie rose heavily from the table then and brought two dolls back with her. She sat down and, with her chin propped in her hands, regarded them with affection. Her little harper had proved to have as great as heart as she'd imagined he would. And Lorwyn...she had always been special.

"We can't wait," she told them.

She stilled the tumult in her mind and worked to recall Cerin's harpspell. It was a simple tune, easy to hum.

"My need is great," she said aloud. "O Moonmother Arn, surely you see that."

Her gaze went to the window where the moon shone outside. One by one, she called up the words the mage had spoken. Lastly, she named the tiny harper.

"Dierin. Awake once more. I have a last task for you."

Life returned to the glass eyes.

"Mother," the small voice piped. "Why do you call me?"

"You must speak the words for me," she told him. "You must set your cloth strings ringing and work the magic for me."

For a long moment the harper doll met her gaze. His eyes were sad.

"If you find it," he said, "and you...do not prevail. Who will care for us then? Who will shape our unborn cousins if you are gone?"

"There are others with my craft," she said.

"But not with your skill. Not with your love."

"Dierin. Please..."

A small sigh stirred in the harper's cloth chest. He lifted his tiny fingers and drew forth music from the cotton strings of his harp, played the Songweaver's harpspell that on his toy instrument was more a vague echo—a recalled memory of music, rather than sound itself. The high-pitched voice spoke the three words over the music. Last he put a name to the spell—one name that dissolved into another and...

Nonie blinked and stared up at the large body that had once housed her soul. She lifted the tiny staff with the horse's head on its one end in a salute.

"Thank you," she whispered to the harper.

"Mother. Be careful," Dierin said. His voice did not seem so shrill to her cloth ears.

"I will do what I must," Nonie said.

She made her way down from the table. A touch of the staff, and the kitchen door slipped open just wide enough for to go out into the night.

The moonlight was bright on Chappenderry's streets. Its presence set Nonie's heart to trembling.

"Bless you," she called up to the source of that light.

Strange stirrings awoke in her as the doll's moon magics rose to the fore. She saw the town, not only from a new perspective, but with a deeper insight. She could feel Gally Grim's presence somewhere in its shadowed streets. Raising the horse-headed staff before her, she set off, following the tug of the moonspells within, the moonspells that would lead her to the goblin. Like calls to like, she remembered the harper's wife saying. But that was where their likeness ended. For she could never be as wicked as that evil creature, and it could never understand what motivated her.

⊢ ⊤ ⊣

"What is it, Cerin?"

The harper turned from the window, a strange light in his eyes.

"Spells are stirring," he murmured. He caught up the roseharp. "Come," he added, moving to the door. "The dollmaker...Nonie. She's worked a magic on herself and's gone hunting."

"Oh, no!" Meran cried.

"Oh, yes."

Worry flickered deep in both of them as they left their room and ran down the stairs.

⊢ ⊤ ⊣

It will be here, Nonie thought as she came to the arbor in the garden of Hehir, who was a magistrate of Chappenderry. She would not have to seek her gobber now, for she could feel it stalking her. Here. She leaned on her staff, fingers entwined nervously around its wooden haft. It would be soon now. She was surprised to find that she wasn't frightened at this moment. There was too much rightness in what she did. Her only fear was that the gobber would escape her.

Something stirred in the shrubberies at the far end of the garden and she turned in that direction. A familiar shape came sidling out from under the bushes—yellow eyes gleaming with a feral light, a dagger in its hand that was like a sword to a being its size. It moved steadily towards her, gaze flicking left and right, gape-mouth grinning when it knew she was alone. Two feet apart, they faced each other in the moonlight.

"I made you," Nonie said. "So I can unmake you."

She raised her arm and the moonlight seemed to fill her until she glowed with a pale light. Gally Grim howled, dropping the blade and dancing back, but she moved too quickly for him. Stepping in close, she brought her hand down and the moonstrength flowed through her arm, through her hand, piercing the goblin to its wicked marrow. It gave one long wailing cry, then collapsed onto the grass before her.

For a long moment Nonie regarded the fallen doll. Sadness welled in her—both for what it had done and what it had forced her to do. She was a maker, not a destroyer. She raised her gaze to the moon and felt it call to her. A last thanks she whispered as she left the blue-robed cloth body behind and drifted upwards, reaching for the peace that Arn promised her in the heart of the moon's silver light.

⊢ ⊤ ⊣

The oakmaid and her husband arrived in time to see the spark flee the doll's body and leap up into the sky—a momentary star that flickered and spun before it was swallowed by the moon. The tiny blue-robed figure folded in upon itself and fell across the lifeless shape of Gally Grim.

"Too late!" Meran cried. "Oh, Cerin!"

The harper nodded, unable to speak. Slowly he moved to where the two dolls lay and knelt beside them on the grass. The horse-head staff was charred almost beyond recognition. There was a smile on the face of the blue-robed doll—a smile that, could they but see, was echoed on Nonie's peaceful face where she rested as though sleeping in her kitchen.

"She knew," Meran said. "She knew if she found Gally Grim, she wouldn't survive. Didn't she?"

Cerin nodded. "She was not a mage, but she knew there was a price to pay for what she did. Untrained, she paid with the only coin she had."

Holding each other, the harper and his wife wept.

⊢ ⊤ ⊣

In the dollmaker's kitchen, the tiny harper lifted his toy instrument onto his lap. The cotton strings trembled with the sad chords of his lamenting and tears, one by one, trickled from the corners of his glass eyes to soak the cloth of his cheeks.

1983

In Mask and Motley

The storm came out of the east, a rage of thunder and wind-driven rain that struck the Vale of the Oak King like a physical blow. The old giant trees of Ogwen Wood rocked and swayed, their heavy boughs dipping dangerously, their roots lifting from the dark earth. In the great tree that was the hall of Ogwen the Oak King, terror-struck wooderls shivered and rolled their eyes, looking to their grey-haired lord for comfort. But the winds howled and even the King's oak swayed and groaned under the blows of the storm's onslaught.

The King's gnarled hands were white-knuckled as he grasped the arms of his throne. He was a tall bear of a man with hoary features and a grey-green grizzle of a beard. His eyes were clouded with sadness. He did not fear the storm for himself—only for the damage it would leave in its wake: toppled oaks, the lifelines of the wooderls, lying broken and cracked, uprooted and dying as they were torn from the earth that sustained them. And with each tree that fell and died in Ogwen Wood, one of his people would die with it...severed from life as the storm ripped the boughs from the forest's trees and cast them down.

He looked at his people through a mist of tears. A storm like this came but once in a lifetime. How many would die? And his kin, flesh of his flesh, their lifetrees seeded from the King's oak...He had two sons and three daughters. They were all here...all save Meran. His grip tightened on the arms of his throne, knuckles so white they appeared like bone. Meran, newly wed to her harper whom men called the Songweaver...

ᚤ ᚣ ᚥ

Where the King's oak swayed back and forth like a great galleon riding the rough waves of a tempest, his daughter's lifetree was like a small coracle, lost and tossed upon savage seas. The tree groaned as the wind bent its boughs, roots lifted, torn from the earth to claw at the air. Lightning wracked the black skies—sheets of piercing light and forked barbs that licked the topmost boughs of the forest.

Inside the tree, Meran clung to her harper, numbed by the storm's fury, her dark eyes wide and glazed. Two things the wooderls feared above all else—fire and storm, and the one strode often hand in hand with the other, with death-white eyes, spitting flames and wind. A thunderclap cracked like a peal of doom, so close it shook the pair to their bones. The oak-maid cried out softly, her limbs trembling as though she was fevered.

The harper laid a steadying palm against her brow, stroked her tangled hair softly. The nut-brown locks were touched with green. Outside the storm continued to rage.

"Easy, my love." He spoke the words with lips pressed close to her ear so that he could be heard above the tumult of the elements. "It will pass."

This far from the lands held by men, the wooderls had no fear of axes. Here their fortunes were held in the hands of the Goddess. Yet those same soft hands Arn used to spin nights silvered with stars, or dappled glades heavy with mid-summer sun, became bone-thin and crone-like when they loosed the wildness of a storm's fury upon the world. It was no comfort to know that she meant no personal enmity—not when lifetrees cracked and dipped in the wind's fury, when rain lashed the sodden branches and the lightning leapt from the dark roiling clouds seeking the tall tops of the forest's heights.

"It will pass," the harper repeated as the tree shook under a new onslaught.

He was a tall thin man who appeared to grow younger with each passing moon rather than older. His beard and braided hair were a deep brown, his eyes a mingling of gold and green. His name was Cerin, but men called him the Songweaver for the harp he carried was a gift of the Tuathan, and his voice and harping skills were too fey for him to bear a name as other men did.

His harp had a name, too. It was called Telynros—the roseharp. An enchanted instrument that plainly bore the touch of the old gods' workmanship, it was silver-stringed and strangely-carved and had growing

from the wood where forepillar met the curving neck, a living blossom—
a grey rose.

Against his shoulder he could feel the oak-maid shake her head. Always so brave, only a storm such as this could steal her courage. If her
lifetree fell...

She spoke and he had to bend his ear to her mouth to hear what she
said above the thunder and raging winds.

"I was too happy with you, my love—happier than any erl or once-
born has a right to be. See how the storm punishes me? I will not survive
its fury..." Wild-eyed and despairing, she turned to him. "Oh, Cerin—
say you will not forget me."

"Hush," he replied.

Silently, he cursed the storm. He looked to his harp. He had already
tried its magic against the raging elements, but the fury would not abate.
The thunder swallowed the sound of its strings as well as the cry of his
voice raised loud in spellings. There were some powers that no magic
could touch.

The tree shook violently as though struck by a giant's hand. Meran
cried out and the harper knew a moment of dread premonition. They were
doomed.

The lightning bit deeply into the old oak's wood and his wife went
stiff in his arms. The tree toppled—striking the ground with a crash that
made the thunder seem quiet. The impact flung Cerin across the room,
tearing his wife from his arms. He struck his head, tried to rise, but a
black wave washed over him. He fell down again to sprawl senselessly,
with the sound of the thunder ringing in his ears and the wood of the dying
oak pressed against his cheek.

The tree itself lay joined with the earth, no longer root to soil, but
with the span of its trunk and boughs spread full length against the wet
ground like the splayed limbs of a dead man.

➤ ⊤ ◄

Ogwen went alone to his daughter's tree.

His heart was already heavy. Twelve trees were lost in the
storm...twelve of his people lay slain by the hand of the storm. And
now...

He bent his head in grief at the sight of his daughter's oak—the proud
boughs crushed and broken, its great length lying on the ground rather

than stretching for the sky. He walked slowly forward to lay his hand on the dead wood. He saw Old Badger snuffling mournfully at the cold bark, seeking his friend and mistress. And lying beside the ruin of branch and trunk, he saw his daughter's husband lying in a sprawl like a stringless marionette, a wound on his brow and his harp lying in a tangle of branches and wet leaves.

The Oak King could not move. Half-blinded with tears, he watched Old Badger approach the harper to push his striped head against the stricken man's shoulder. Only when Cerin stirred did Ogwen shake free enough from his sorrow to come to the harper's side. The first word on the Songweaver's lips was his wife's name.

"Meran..?"

The gold-green eyes searched the Oak King's sad features, read there what his heart already told him.

"She...she is gone from us..." Ogwen said.

"No." The harper's hand was weak as he touched the front of the King's shirt. "Say that you...lie..."

"No...lie..."

The words caught in Ogwen's throat. Despair filled Cerin's eyes. He turned his face to the sky.

"Sweet gods!" he cried. "How can you have taken her from me?"

When he turned again to look at Ogwen, the Oak King saw a fey light burning in the Songweaver's eyes, and his heart grew heavier still. His daughter was dead, and now her husband was gripped by madness...

"Come with me," he said softly to the harper. "Let me take you to the hall. You have hurts that need mending. We all share your grief and—"

"No."

"Cerin, please."

"No. I won't leave her. Why do you want me to leave her?"

"She is dead," Ogwen said.

He tried to pull the harper to his feet, but for all Cerin's leanness, there was a strength in him that would not let the Oak King move him. The muscles worked under Ogwen's tunic, but it was as though the harper had turned to stone. When the roseharp began to play of its own accord, in amongst the tangle of vegetation where it lay, the Oak King stepped back. Fresh tears started in his eyes as the sweet fey music sang its lament.

"I...I will return for you," he said softly. "When you are ready to come with me."

The harper gave no sign that he'd heard. He bowed his head, listening to the music that spilled from Telynros's strings, remembering the features of the one he loved, the sweet sound of her voice and the tilt of her head when she lifted her lips to be kissed...

"I will find her," he said, his voice no more than a whisper.

"She is dead," the Oak King said.

"Then I will win her back from death."

Ogwen shook his head slowly and left the harper there with only Old Badger and the heart-wrenching music of his harp for company. He would return with his sons to fetch him. The harper was kin—for all that the tie that bound them was slain. They would care for him in the great hall for as long as need be.

➤ ⅄ ⅃

While Old Badger watched and Telynros laid a glamour of harp-spells over them both, Cerin took a small knife from his belt. From the wood of his wife's dead oak he carved three talismans. First he shaped a fine-toothed comb, decorated with tiny acorns. This was for the body. Next he made a pendant, shaped like an oak leaf, and this was for the heart. And lastly, with sure and steady hands and the harp-magic cloaking him with its enchantment, he made a six-holed flute the length of his forearm. When it was done, he put his lips to it and played a soft air and Telynros answered with a spill of notes like a rush of tumbling water. This was for the soul.

The making of the talismans took him three days. And during this time, he neither slept, nor ate, nor drank. Ogwen came with his sons, but they couldn't talk him from his task. The eerie music of the harp that played with no one's fingers at the strings and the fey light in the harper's eyes when he looked at them kept them at bay. So they watched and they waited, one of them always near, until the end of the third day when Cerin lipped the flute. When he finally laid it down, twilight came stealing over the Oak King's wood and Telynros ceased to play. A stillness, deep and trembling, crept into the air and the Songweaver stood.

"Now I must go," he said.

"This is your home," Ogwen said. "*We* are your kin now."

"I will return—but only when I've found Meran."

"We share your grief," Targn, the eldest and tallest of the Oak King's sons said. "But Meran is lost to us now."

"I will find her."

"She is no longer of this world."

"I know," Cerin said.

Pendant and comb went into his pocket, the flute he thrust into his belt. He took Telynros from its green tangle and shouldered the harp so that it hung before him, the strings gleaming eerily in the half-light of the gloaming. When he touched the strings a throaty murmur came from them. The wind rose from the Dolking Downs in answer. Old Badger hid his striped face, but crept to the harper's feet. A faint amber glow touched the ground where they stood.

"Cerin," the Oak King pleaded. "Do not go..."

The harper would not be dissuaded. Ogwen and his sons watched the glamour grow about him, bathing harper and badger with a pulsing amber glow. They saw a doorway open in the air—a brightening in the air, oval in shape, and within it, watching them, watching the harper step close, was a masked face, eyes mocking in the slit eye-holes, a death's grin touching its thin white lips.

"Cerin!" Ogwen cried.

The face receded. The Oak King saw the motley garb that the masked figure wore—a jester's garb, patched and threadbare, the colours no longer bright, almost mingling as they'd faded. The Songweaver followed the macabre figure, Old Badger on his heels. The harp rang with a last chord, then the doorway closed and neither Cerin, the badger, nor the masked figure were to be seen. The dark of night swept over the woods and only the Oak King and his sons remained near the broken ruin that had been Meran's lifetree.

➤ ➤ ◄

The man facing Cerin was as lean as a child's stick-figure toy, his patchwork clothes hanging ragged from his limbs like a willow's dropping cloak. His mask covered the upper half of his face and appeared to be made of leather—thin and worked with designs that a priest of the Daketh might understand. But Cerin was no follower of the Dark Gods, and knew only repugnance as he looked upon the symbols. The strange man's hair was more white than grey and hung thin and uncombed to his shoulders, while his eyes, through the slit-holes of his mask, changed from jet black to a milky grey, then were black once more.

He bowed to the harper, caricaturing a jester's movements with his spindly limbs. Tiny bells on the ends of his sleeves and the curled tips of his boots tinkled when he moved. Cerin touched the strings of his harp to banish their disturbing sound, but Telynros was strangely muted in this place. At the harper's feet Old Badger made a low sound—somewhere between a growl and a whine.

"Who are you?" Cerin asked.

"It is not always so easy to remember names in this place," the other man said. His voice was high and mocking. "But you may call me Laughter, harper."

"And what place is this? Is it Death's realm?"

Laughter shrugged and waved his hand so that the bells sounded, but he made no verbal reply. Cerin gritted his teeth at their disquieting tinkle.

They stood in a forest glade with the dark shapes of leafless trees rearing skeletally on all sides. A moon, pale as a ghost, rode in a sky studded with unfamiliar constellations—unfamiliar even to a traveller such as the Songweaver who knew as many different worlds as there were strings on his harp, from the realms of men to those of the Middle Kingdom. A fetid smell hung in the glade—reeking like something spoiled and rotting. The air was close.

"I have come for my wife," Cerin said. "Her name is Meran Gwynder and she is the daughter of Ogwen, the Oak King of Abercorn."

Laughter laid a long thin finger along the side of his nose and flicked it at the harper.

"Indeed?" he asked in his high mocking voice. "And will you trade your harp for her? Will you trade your own life?"

"Gladly."

Laughter shook his head. "I think not. Neither your harp nor your life would be a bargain—you offer them too freely.

"Enough!" Cerin cried.

Old Badger, crouching at his feet, pressed close to his leg. Anger flickered in the harper's eyes. The mocking figure and his hellish bells pushed too far. The Songweaver pulled a sharp angry chord from his harp, wove a spell into its sounding to silence the jester, but all that issued forth was a muddy dissonant sound that was too reminiscent of Laughter's bells. Either the jester, or the dead forest itself, stole the richness from Telynros's tone, drew the harpmagic from its music.

"I think," Laughter said, "that it is time you slept, harper."

Cerin shook his head, but Laughter had already stepped close, lifting an arm. The bells tinkled and his bony fingers stroked the harper's brow.

A moment Cerin stood, swaying on his feet, then his legs gave way and he tumbled to the ground. Laughter caught the roseharp before it fell from his hands and laid it down by the craggy roots of a half-dead tree. He smiled his mocking smile as he returned to look down at the unconscious harper. Old Badger bared his teeth, but the jester shook his head.

"I mean him no harm," he said to the badger. "He brings his own harm with him."

Old Badger whined, uncertain. Laughter winked.

"Dream, harper," he said, his milky-grey gaze centred on the Songweaver's sleeping features. "Who knows what you might find...in dreams."

➤ ➤ ➤

It seemed to Cerin that the Goddess came to him in the guise of a harper while he slept. She sat enthroned in the branches of the world-tree, watching him with eyes that were sad and wise. Her fingers drew music from her instrument that eased the storm in the Songweaver's breast. Her hair hung long and unbound. Within a gap of the tree's hollowed trunk, Cerin could see the stars of a night sky, entrapped in miniature.

"Why do you strive against what is?" she asked.

Cerin lifted his head, his gaze steady on hers for all the awe that filled his heart.

"Why will you not take me in her place?" he asked, replying with a question.

The Goddess shook her head. "Your time is not come—but I did not take the oak-maid. Do you think I pick and choose who will live and who will die? Men—and the beings of the Middle Kingdom—are masters of their won destiny."

"Meran never chose to die."

"I did not say she did," the Goddess replied. "There is a pattern...The only goal for men is beauty, Songweaver. And that beauty can only be found in harmony."

Her harping underlaid the words, deep and resonant. Cerin shook his head. He didn't understand.

"Look for the pattern," she explained. "Within its harmony, all things can be. You who carry the harp of my twilight daughter—how can you have forgotten such a simple truth?"

"Losing my love," Cerin said, "all patterns have become frayed."

"Then you must weave them anew."

Cerin bowed his head.

"Lady," he said, "without her I see no pattern to mend—save restoring her."

He waited for her reply. When it didn't come, he looked up, but she was gone. Again he bowed his head. This time a darkness slipped over him. He saw the patterns of the night's constellations in its black web, heard the sound of the Moon's music, binding star to star in a perfect weave...

Weariness swept over him and he slept.

➤ ⅄ ◄

When he woke, he was alone in the forest of dead trees, except for Old Badger who lay beside Telynros, watching him. There was a tree standing in front of him that had not been there before—a tree like the one that had enthroned the Goddess, except in the bark of this tree he saw a shape raised from the wood, a face he knew, carved into the tree with her eyes closed as though she slept and the long hair falling in tangles to either side of her face.

"Meran," he breathed.

He stepped near, searching in his pocket for the talismans he'd shaped for her. Without these ties to her lifetree, there was no hope of reclaiming her from death. With them...

Softly he touched the carved cheek, his eyes misting. He took out the comb and worked it gently into the wooden hair that was so cunningly made that each strand was a separate carving of delicate woodwork. The pendant he laid against the slope of her breast, wedging its leaf-shaped end into the carved lift of her bodice. Lastly, he worked the flute into her hand, working slowly and carefully with the delicate fingers, that were pliable yet, for all their being carved from wood.

He brushed his lips against her stiff cheek, then fetched his harp and sat in front of the tree, Telynros on his lap. He ignored the gaunt limbs of the dead forest, the smell of rot in the air. Old Badger crept to his side, laid his striped head against his knee. Then closing his eyes, Cerin began to play.

He put all his heart and soul into his harping, filling the music with his love for her and the magic that leapt between them that was stronger than any spell he might draw from the harp on his own. But for all his playing, Telynros's strings rang falsely. Their clear tone was dulled and they entrapped his fingers so that he played like a novice. Despair cut through him and he looked up to the tree. The carving's eyes opened and it was Meran looking back at him through those wooden orbs.

My love, she said. He heard her voice in his mind—gentle and familiar. *Why are you here? This is no place for the living.*

"How can I go on without you?"

You must go back, she said.

The eyes closed once more. And the sense of her presence inside his mind faded.

"Meran!" he cried.

He made as if to rise, to set his harp aside and go to her, but the sound of bells came to his ears and he turned to find the jester watching him with his sardonic eyes.

"Your charms were well-crafted," Laughter said, "and your harping is skilled. A pity the air of this realm does not lend itself to an instrument such as yours. Still..." He tapped his chest, setting up a new jangling of the tiny bells. "It touched me here—your music."

"Release her!" Cerin cried.

"Why should I? This is her home now. She is content, harper. She has accepted what must be—and so should you."

Anger, dark and red, rose in the harper.

"Why do the living rail so against their passing?" the jester asked him. "This is not all there is to the hereafter. It is but a waystop—a resting place—until the soul forgets the turbulence that was life and grows tranquil enough to journey on."

Cerin looked into Laughter's mocking eyes. The constant ringing of the bells fed his rage. The mockery and the bells, his own unappeased sorrow—they combined to stir a storm inside him. The fey light in his eyes blazed. He brought his hands up to Telynros's strings to wake a great magic—a magic that would destroy him as it took the life of the sly mocking figure that stood before him.

He felt the pressure of Meran's presence at his back—locked in wood, not as a wooderl, a living breathing part of her tree, but imprisoned, tauntingly joined to the dead wood without release from the cruel pressure of its constricting grain. His hands curled like claws as they neared the strings. He focused all his rage and despair into the one chord that would tear asunder the very fabric of the land wherein they stood. He drew up that power, touched finger to string—

Then paused.

There was a look in the masked figure's eyes. Behind the mockery lay a sadness that Cerin had been blinded to. His hands hovered near the strings. He remembered the jester saying...

You may call me Laughter...

And the Goddess. When he'd told her that all the patterns had become frayed...

Then you must weave them anew...

Not destroy—but remake them. Understanding came over him in a rush that took his breath away.

He touched fingers to strings and woke not destruction, but a music that rejoiced. It sprayed from his instrument as though nothing had ever muddied its sound: a jig as light as the morning's sun on a robin's wing as it lifted its head in song...a scatter of notes as gay as a spring breeze tipping the heads of newly-bloomed flowers to spill their pollen into the air...warmth and joy and the tenderness of...

You may call me...

—laughter that rang for sheer pleasure. He buried his anger and his despair. He brought to mind not Meran's loss, but what time they'd had together. He opened himself to the joy that life held, no longer ignoring the reverse side of the coin, for there was no difference in the pattern it presented. They were one and the same, two parts of one whole.

The jester smiled and clapped his hands together. Now the bells tinkled merrily to Cerin's ear—a happy sound. In wonder, he watched the masked figure's garb become less threadbare. The cloth mended itself, colour returned until Laughter stood before the harper in a wild profusion of yellows and reds and greens—his motley as brilliant as that of any jester in a high king's court.

The scent in the air grew clean and a fresh wind blew. Buds sprang to life on the limbs of the dead trees and grass grew thick and green underfoot. The buds became leaves. The air hummed with the sounds of insects and birds. And all the while Telynros played under the Songweaver's sure fingers—a music that lifted and sang.

In the fresh-green grass, the jester capered and danced. His bells jingled and the thin-lipped smile no longer held its mocking cast. He pulled off his mask and threw it into the air, revealing a plain but kind face, with clear eyes.

"Sing, hey!" the jester cried to him.

Cerin nodded back. His anger was gone. Only the sadness remained—hidden from his music, but touching the harper to his very marrow.

When he first heard a flute's low notes sound across the dancing spell of his harping, he cocked his head, nodding at the sureness of its tone and the easy roll of the player's grace notes. Then he paused, hands falling from his strings, and slowly turned. The sound of flute and bells continued, but Cerin's arms hung limp at his sides.

"Meran?" he said softly, wonderingly.

The carved figure of his wife looked at him over the flute. Her eyes smiled and she stepped from the tree, her tangled hair falling free except for where the comb held it, the wooden limbs become flesh, with the leaf-shaped pendant lying against her breast. She lowered the flute and regarded it with wonder.

"I never played a flute before," she said.

She looked from the harper to the jester and then about the glade.

"Cerin? Where are we? What is this place?"

She had no memory of the storm, the falling oak, her death...

He turned from her to confront the jester, the question plain in his eyes. Was this an illusion? Was this some new torment?

As the doubt touched him, he caught a glimpse of frayed and threadbare apparel, a masked face, a mocking glint in pale eyes. For a moment, the trees wavered in their greenery and bare limbs showed.

"This place is only what you make it," Laughter said softly. "It is what you bring to it in your heart."

And he'd come, Cerin thought, bringing sorrow and death. His face cleared and the moment of doubt was gone. He set aside his harp and took the oak-maid in his arms. The press of her body against him with no illusion. The quick tilt of her face for a kiss was so familiar, his heart ached with it. He kissed her, faced the jester with an arm about her shoulders.

"What now?" he asked.

Laughter shrugged. "Go home," he said. "I will allow you your respite. Few enough come to me with joy—fewer still allow joy to lift above their despair. Your talismans have freed your wife from her need for her lifetree. Go forth into the world and prosper, harper. One day I will call for you—and then we will be merry again."

"What does he mean?" Meran asked.

She held her flute in one hand, held Cerin's tightly with the other.

"I'll tell you later," he said.

He fetched Telynros, returned to his wife. Old Badger got underfoot, joyful with the return of his mistress and friend.

"When next we meet," the jester asked, "will you fight me still?"

Cerin looked about himself, tested the strange wonder he felt in his heart. He met Laughter's gaze.

"Life is sweet as well," he said. "How can I make that promise?"

"Good!" the jester cried, a hint of mockery returning to his eyes. "I dislike promises. Go home, harper."

The glade wavered in the Songweaver's sight. He held Meran's hand tightly as they were swept away with a rush of spinning wind. Ground shaped underfoot and Meran stumbled. The harper caught her arm, steadied her, looked up to see the shocked, but happy faces of the Oak King and his sons. Meran caught sight of her lifetree and clutched at her breast, understanding where it was they they'd been. Old Badger nudged her leg playfully. Her father stepped close, wrapped his big arms about her, tears in his eyes.

"Bless you, Songweaver," he said over her shoulder, wonder plain in his features.

Cerin nodded. His heart sang, too. He glanced at the fallen ruin of Meran's tree, but saw instead an image of a jester in his mask and motley.

"Were you Death itself, or but a wise fool?" he asked softly.

From far away he heard the jester's high and mocking voice in his mind.

It is not always so easy to remember names in this place...

Cerin sighed. He joined Meran and, arms entwined, they went with her father and brothers to the great hall. Old Badger followed, capering on his short legs.

Verses from the Songweaver's Journeybook:

Blood to Blood

Blood to blood
the gift flows.
From the grave-fire,
from the raised stones,
from underhill,
from the Summer Country
—the voices of our kin
still reach
to weave a pattern
in the flesh we wear.

Telynros, the Roseharp

As the moon is silver in the twilight
and the green fire burns hill to hill
so roots run deep and boughs reach high
and the rose itself is a grey sea of riddles.

For such a harp could court the summer stars
each of its strings is a mystery
and each tune played is a promised wisdom
but the knowing lies only in the harper's hand.

Alken's Song

This is the way I will go:
underhill, a-barrowed.
I will be bones
in that place of stone.
I will be a wind
that howls on the hills at dusk.
I will be the tears
in a harper's eyes
when he sings of who I was.
I will be a ghost
  —a shape without a crown,
  a name without a form.
I will be gone.

The Mysteries

Which is more secret:
the moon in the sky
or her silver light
reflected in the waters below?
Some riddles have no answer
save that which is hidden
in the hazel grove
where a horned wind plays
the twig-strings of the trees
and the grey-eyed harpers
listen.

Root Truths

When I was young
I caught riddles
that had no voice
save that of the wind,
and I stored them
in the fingering of strings.

Their names
were the names of the trees
that calendar the years,
and as season follows season,
I can still remember
their tune,
while the mystery
ever deepens.

Four Seasons and the First Day of the Year

Silver fir am I and I   the year begin
I am the womb   of every holt
the summer sun grows   from my winter hours
my candles consecrate   those new-born

Furze am I and I   blaze on every hill
the first bees seek   my flames and
hill to hill and   point to point
my green waves   frighten witches

Heather am I and I   restore luck
I am the queen   of every hive
reddening the mountains   in midsummer
stag and stone   revere my harping

White poplar am I and I   bind the brows
of heroes for I am   the shield for every head
my shifting leaves   remind the dead
that the end of life   is not the end

Yew am I and I   am the death tree
my roots spread to   the mouth of every corpse
I coffin the vine   and fill the circle
I am the tomb   to every hope

1984

Laughter in the Leaves

*...but the wind was always
laughter in the leaves to me.*

Wendelessen,
from *An Fear Glas.*

Listen," Meran said.

By the hearth, her husband laid his hand across the strings of his harp to still them and cocked his head. "I don't hear a thing," he said. "Only the wind."

"That's just it," Meran replied. "It's on the wind. Laughter. Giggles. I tell you, he's out there again."

Cerin laid his instrument aside. "I'll go see," he said.

Outside, the long grey skies of autumn were draining into night. The wind that came down from the heaths was gusting through the forest, rattling the leaves, gathering them up in eddying whirls and rushing them between the trees in a swirling dance. The moon was just starting to top the eastern horizon, but there was no one out there. Only Old Badger, lying in his special spot between the cottage and the rose bushes, who lifted his striped head and made a questioning sort of noise at the harper standing in the doorway.

"Did you see him?" Cerin asked.

The badger regarded him for a few moments, then laid his head back down on his crossed forepaws.

"I've only seen him once myself," Meran said, joining Cerin at the door. "But I know he's out there. He knows you're going tomorrow and is letting me know that he means to pull a trick or two while you're gone."

"Then I won't go."

"Don't be silly. You have to go. You promised."

"Then you must come. You were invited."

"I think I'd prefer to put up with our bodach's tricks to listening to the dry talk of harpers for two whole nights and the day in between too, I'll wager."

Cerin sighed. "It won't be all talk..."

"Oh, no," Meran replied with a smile. "There'll be fifteen versions of the same tune, all played in a row, and then a discussion as to which of twenty titles is the oldest for this particular tune. Wonderfully interesting stuff, I don't doubt, but it's not for me. And besides," she added after stooping down to give Old Badger a quick pat and then closing the door, "I mean to have a trick or two ready for our little bodach myself this time."

Cerin sighed again. He believed there was a bodach, even though neither he nor anyone but Meran had ever seen it—and even then only in passing from the corner of her eye. But sometimes he had to wonder if every bit of mischief that took place around the cottage could all be blamed on it. Whether it was a broken mug or a misplaced needle, it was always the bodach this and the bodach that.

"I don't know if it's such a wise idea to go playing tricks on a bodach," he said as he made his way back to the hearth. "They're quick to anger and—"

"So am I!" Meran interrupted. "No, Cerin. You go to your Harper's Meet and don't worry about me. One way or another, we'll have come to an agreement while you're gone. Now play me a tune before we go to bed. He's gone now—I can tell. Do you hear the wind?"

Cerin nodded. But it sounded no different to him now than it had before.

"The smile's gone from it," Meran explained. "That's how you can tell that he's gone."

"I don't know why you don't just let me catch him with a harpspell."

Meran shook her head. "Oh, no. I'll best this little fellow with my wits, or not at all. I made that bargain with myself the first time he tripped me in the woods. Now come. Where's that tune you promised me."

Cerin brought Telynros up onto his lap and soon the cottage rang with the music that spilled from the roseharp's strings. Outside, Old Badger listened and the wind continued to make a dance of the leaves between the trees and only Meran could have said if the smile returned to its voice or not, but she would speak no more of bodachs that night.

⊢ ⋎ ⊣

The morning Cerin left, Meran's favorite mug fell from the shelf where it was perched and shattered on the stone floor, her hair when she woke was a tangle of elfknots that she didn't even bother to comb out, and the porridge boiled over for all that she stood over it and stirred and watched and took the best of care. She stamped her foot, but neither she nor Cerin made any comment. She saw him to the road with a smile, gave him a kiss and a jaunty wave along his way, and watched him go. Not until he was lost from sight, up the track and over the hill, with the sun in his eyes and the wind at his back, did she turn and face the woods, arms akimbo, to give the trees a long considering look.

"Now we'll see," she said.

She returned to the cottage, Old Badger at her heels.

The morning passed with her pretending to ignore the presence she knew was watching her from the forest. She combed out her hair, unravelling each knot that the little gnarled fingers of an elfman had tied in it last night. She picked up the shards of her mug, cleaned the burnt porridge from the stove, then straightened the kindling pile that had toppled over with a clatter and spill while she was busy inside the cottage. The smile on her lips was a little thin, but it never faltered.

She hummed to herself and it seemed that the wind in the trees put words to the tune:

> *Catch me, snatch me,*
> *Catch me if you can!*
> *You'll never put the fetters*
> *On a little kowrie man!*

"That's as may be," Meran said as she got the last of the kindling stacked once more. She tied it in place with knots that only an Oakmaid would know, for she was the daughter of the Oak King of Ogwen Wood and knew a spell or two of her own. "But still we'll see."

When she went back inside, she could hear the kindling sticks rattle about a bit, but her knots held firm. And so it went through the day. She rearranged everything in the cottage, laying tiny holding spells here, there and everywhere. She hung fetishes over each window—tiny bundles made up of dried oak leaves and acorns to represent herself, wren's feathers for Cerin, a lock of bristly badger hair for Old Badger, and rowan sprigs for their magic to seal the spell. Only the door she left untouched. By then twilight was at hand, stealing softfooted across the wood, so she pulled up a chair to face the door and sat down to wait.

And the night went by.

The wind made its teasing sounds around the cottage, Old Badger slept under her chair. She stayed awake, watching the door, firmly resolved to stay up the whole night if that was what it took. But as the hours crept by after midnight, she began to nod, blinked awake, nodded again, and finally slept. When she woke in the morning, the door stood ajar, her hair was a crow's nest of tangles, and there was a small mocking stick figure drawn with charcoal on the floor at her feet, one arm lifted and a wide grin almost making two halves of the head.

The wind gusted in through the door as soon as she was awake, sending a great spill of leaves that rattled like laughter across the floor. Stiff from an uncomfortable night spent in a chair, Meran made herself some tea and went outside to sit on the stoop. She refused to show even a tad of the frustration she felt. Instead she calmly drank her tea, pulled loose the new night's worth of tangles, then went inside to sweep the leaves and other debris from the cottage. The stick figure she left where it had been drawn to remind her of last night's failure.

"Well," she said to Old Badger as she went to set down a bowl of food for him. "And what did you see?"

The striped head lifted, eyes mournful, until the bowl was on the floor. And then he was too busy to reply—even if he'd had a voice with which to do so.

Meran knew she should get some rest for the next night, but she was too busy trying to think up a new way to stay awake to be able to sleep. It was self-contradictory, and she knew it, but it couldn't be helped. A half year of the bodach's tricks was too long. Five minutes worth would be too long. As it drew near the supper hour, she finally gave up trying to rest and went to the well for water. A footfall on the road startled her as she was drawing the bucket up. She turned, losing her grip on the well's rope. The bucket went rattling down the well until it hit the bottom with a heavy splash. But she didn't hear it. Her attention was on the figure that stood on the track.

It was an old man that was standing there, an old travelling man in a tattered blue coat and yellow breeches, with his tinker's pack on his back and his face brown as a nut and lined with age. He regarded her with a smile, blue eyes twinkling.

"Evening, ma'am," he said. "It's been an awfully dry road I've been wending, no doubt about that. Could you see yourself clear to sparing me a drink from that well of yours?"

It's the bodach, Meran thought. Oh, you mischief-maker, I have you now.

"Of course," she replied, smiling sweetly. "And you'll stay for supper, won't you?"

"Oh, no, ma'am. I wouldn't want to put you to any trouble."

"It's no trouble at all."

"That's kind of you."

Meran drew the bucket up once more. "Come along to the house and we'll brew up some tea—it'll do more for your thirst than just water."

"Oh, it does that," the old man agreed as he followed her back to the cottage.

Meran watched him with many a sidelong glance as they entered the cottage. He gave the chair facing the door an odd look, and the charcoal drawing an even odder one, but said nothing. Playing the part of an old tinker man, she supposed the bodach meant to stay in character. A tinker would know better than to make remarks about whatever oddities his hostess might have in her house. He laid his pack by the door and Meran put the kettle on.

"Have you been travelling far?" she asked.

"Oh, far enough for these old bones. I'm bound for Matchtem—by the sea, you know. My son has a wagon there and we winter a little further down the coast near Applewater."

Meran nodded. "Do have a seat," she said.

The old man looked around. She was busy at the table where the other chair was, so he sat down gingerly in the one facing the door. No sooner was he sitting, than Meran slipped up behind him and tossed a chain with tiny iron links over him, tying it quickly to the chair. Oh, the links were small and a boy could have easily broken free of them, but anything with iron in it bound a bodach or one of the kowrie folk. Everyone knew that. Meran danced around in front of the chair.

"Now I have you!" she cried. "Oh, you wicked bodach! I'll teach you to play your tricks on me."

"I *am* an old man," the tinker said, eyeing her carefully, "but I've played no tricks on you, ma'am—or at least none that I know of. My name's Yocky John, and I'm just a plain travelling man."

Meran smiled at the name, for she knew a word or two in the old tinker language. Clever John, the bodach might call himself, but he wasn't clever enough for her.

"Oh?" she asked. "You didn't tangle my hair, nor break my crockery, nor play a hundred other little mischiefs and tricks on me? And who was it then?"

"Is it trouble with the little folk you're having?" Yocky John asked.

"Just one. You. And I have you now."

"But you don't. All you've caught is an old tinker, too tired to even get up out of this chair now that he's sitting. But I can help you with your bodach, I surely can. Yocky John's got a trick or two for them."

Outside the wind made the leaves laugh as they rushed in a rattling spray against the walls of the cottage. Meran listened, then looked uncertainly at the tinker. Had she made a mistake, or was this just another of the bodach's mischiefs?

"What sort of tricks?" she asked.

"Well, first I must know how you've gained the little fellow's ill-will."

"I don't know. There's no reason for it—save his nature."

"Oh, no," Yocky John said. "They always have a reason." He looked slowly around the room. "It's a snug place you have here—but it's not so old, is it?"

Meran shook her head. It was just a year now since she'd lost her tree—the tree that a wooderl needs to survive. It was only through Cerin and the spells of his roseharp that she was able to live without it and in this cottage that they'd built where her tree had once stood.

"A very snug place," the old man said. "Magicked, too, I'd say."

"My husband's a harper."

"Ah. That explains it. Harp magic's heady stuff. A bodach can't live in a harper's home—not without an invitation."

"Still he comes and goes as he pleases," Meran said. "He breaks things and disrupts things and generally causes no end of mischief. Who'd *want* to have a bodach living with them?"

"Well, it's cold in the winter," Yocky John said. "Out in the woods, with no shelter but a cloak of leaves, maybe, or a rickety lean-to that the wind howls through. The winds of winter aren't a bodach's friends—not like the winds of summer are. And I know cold, too. Why do you think I winter with my son? Only a fool tries to sleep in the snow."

Meran sighed. She pictured a little kowrie man, huddled in a bare-limbed winter tree, shivering in the cold, denied the warmth of a cottage because of a harper's magics.

"Well, if he felt that way," she said, "why didn't he come to us? Surely he'd have seen that we never turn a guest away. Are we ogres?"

"Well, you know bodachs," Yocky John said. "He'd be too proud and too shy. They like to creep into a place, all secret like, and hide out in the rafters or wherever, paying for their way with the odd good turn or two. It's the winter that's hard on them—even magical kowrie folk like they are. The summer's not so bad—for then even an old man like myself can sleep out-of-doors. But in the winter..."

Meran sighed again. "I never thought of it like that," she said. She studied the tinker, a smile twinkling in her eyes. "Well, Yocky John the bodach. You're welcome to stay in our rafters through the winter—but mind you leave my husband and I some privacy. Do you hear? And no more tricks. Or this time I'll let his roseharp play a spell."

"I'm not a bodach," Yocky John said. "At least not as you mean it."

"Yes, I know. A bodach's an old man too—or it was in the old days."

"Do I look like a kowrie man to you?"

Meran grinned. "Who knows what a kowrie man would look like? It all depends on the shape he chooses to wear when you see him, don't you think? And I see you're still sitting there with that wee bit of iron chain wrapped around you."

"That's only because I'm too tired to get up."

"Have it your way."

She removed the chain then and went back to making supper. When she called him to the table, Yocky John rose very slowly to his feet and made his way over to the table. Meran laughed, thinking, oh, yes, play the part to the hilt, you old trickster, and went and fetched his chair for him. They ate and talked awhile, then Meran went to bed, leaving the old man to sleep on the mound of blankets that she'd readied for him in front of the hearth. When she woke in the morning, he was gone. And so was the charcoal drawing on the floor.

⊁ ⊤ ⊰

"So," Cerin said when he came home that night. "How went the great war between the fierce mistress of the oak wood and the equally fierce bodach that challenged her?"

Meran looked up towards the rafters where a small round face peered down at her for a moment, then quickly popped out of sight. It didn't looked at all like the old tinker man she'd guested last night, but who could know what was what or who was who when it came to mischief-makers like a bodach? And was a tinker all that different really? They were as much tricksters themselves. So whether Yocky John and the bodach were one and the same, or merely similar, she supposed she'd never know.

"Oh, we made our peace," she said.

An Fear Glas

Green was I
and Grey,
it was all the same to me.

My woods were
a tangle of poetry
—brambled words
and hoary rhymes
roots that dug the deep earth
  for wisdom,
  for legend,
but the wind was always
laughter in the leaves to me.

A trick well-turned
I'd try,
or a riddle,
or a history as wise
as the stuff of legend,
it was all the same to me.

And in winter,
when all was drear,
the blackthorn frost rimmed thick
and nights were long,
I was the bodach looking
  for summer,
  for green,
for death was still a lie to me.

A Green Man,
a Grey Man,
it was all the same to me.

Author's Note: *An Fear Glas* is Gaelic for "the Green Man," or "the Grey Man"—*glas* meaning either green or grey. *Bodach* meant old man, or sage, but the word degenerated in time to mean a hobgoblin sprite in the Scots Highlands.

The Calendar of the Trees

Reed am I and I   the calendar begin
the river sound and sea   shape my fires
hill to hill and   wave to wave
burns the wood and   the old stones listen

Elder am I and I   my fruit keep
to cradle the water-witch   my wood speaks
to the unhewn stones   and ill-luck brings
to all save those   who ride me

Birch am I and I   give birth to
the seven-tined stag   and new-leafed
speak moon-words   to those that arm themselves
twig and bough by   the Green Man's corn

Rowan am I and I   am sister to the Red Man
my berries are guarded   by dreamless dragons
my wood charms   the spells from witches
and in the wide plain   my floods quicken

Ash am I and I   like a wind on the sea
ride the white horses   wave to wave and
hill to hill for   my roots strangle
all save the wizard's   pale spiraled wand

Alder am I and I   hoard the sun
in my tears and   resurrect the dead
the crimson-stained heroes   my colours wear
and my music   pipes the sidhe from sleep

Willow am I and I   am the answer
to the riddles   the wry-neck speaks
wicker I yielded   to the Brown Man and
like a hawk on a cliff   the moon owns me

Hawthorn am I and I   was a giant
unlucky in my new clothes   till the horn bloomed
fair among flowers yet   thorned and scathed
gifting only those who   follow the White Track

Oak am I and I   burn green in midsummer
I speak in smoke   hill to hill and
wave to wave to   court the summer storms
my roots run as deep   as my boughs reach high

Holly am I and I   run with the deer
my blooms are summer's   I greet the winter
green and growing   my spears are as true
as the staff the   Brown Man bears

Hazel am I and I   hoard knowledge
like a salmon in   a sheltered pool
my nuts remain   unshelled and when
you seek me I   am not to be seen

Vine am I and I   flower like words
on a hill of poetry   brambled and berried
wave to wave and   point to point
only the sidhe partake   of my heady fruit

Ivy am I and I   rush wildly like
a ruthless boar   yellow-berried and
secret with the fire   of toadstools
my harvest is the   gold wren's nest

1985

The Three Plushketeers
Meet Santy Claus

There was an old man going through the garbage can on the corner. He pulled out this, then that, studied it, put it down again, then rooted about some more. He had dirty white hair and a dirty white beard and was wearing a lumberjack's checked shirt and green workman's trousers that bagged on his skinny frame. Against the cold, he also wore a brown corduroy jacket.

Standing across the street, waiting for the light to change, Morty Moose watched him. He scratched one antler, then the other, and thought about all the sorts of people that Sam had warned him to be careful of. There were those who wanted you to take a ride in their car or offered you candy—they had to be avoided. But, he decided as the light changed, Sam hadn't said anything about people going through the garbage. He crossed the street and stepped up to where the old man was still busily rooting about.

"Hi," he said.

The old man looked up with a frown. "Go away, kid."

"What are you doing?"

"What does it look like I'm doing? I'm Santa Claus, looking for presents to give away on Christmas Eve."

"Santy Claus?" Morty Moose cried happily, then his face fell. "You don't look like Santy Claus."

The old man leaned on the lip of the garbage can. "What do you mean?"

"Well, you're too thin."

"I've been on a diet."

"You haven't got a red suit."

The old man opened his shirt to reveal a red undershirt. "I'm in disguise."

"Well, where's your sleigh?"

"I left it at home."

"How about your reindeer? Santy Claus never goes anywhere without his reindeer."

"They're on strike."

"Oh." Morty Moose thought about that for a moment or so, trying to figure out what the man meant. Finally he gave up. "Is this where you *really* get your presents?"

"What do you think, kid?"

"I thought elves made them."

"Yeah, well, production's down—you know what I mean?"

"Not really." Morty Moose sighed. This man didn't look at all like the jolly Santy Claus he'd met last Christmas at the Billings Bridge Shopping Plaza.

"Look, I'm really busy, kid. Why don't you get out of my face?"

"My name's Morty Moose—I'm one of the Three Plushketeers."

"Plushketeers?"

"You know: All for fun and fun for all."

"I think you mean Musketeers." He stood back to regard Morty for a moment. "Or maybe I should say Mouseketeer."

"I'm a moose, not a mouse."

"And the big difference is? No. Never mind." The man abruptly shook his head. "What am I talking to you for, anyway? Beat it, kid or you won't get any presents for Christmas. Maybe I'll just *cancel* Christmas."

Morty Moose backed away, wishing he'd never talked to the man. Sam should have warned him about people going through the garbage as well.

"Go on!"

Dejected, Morty Moose hurried off home. The old man watched him go, then shook his head and went back to his garbage can.

Ⱡ Ƴ ⱡ

Scott and Darby, the other two Plushketeers, were making Christmas cards at the kitchen table when Morty Moose came home. Scott had glue stuck all over his paws and bristly terrier whiskers, while Darby had accidentally glued his Derby hat to the card he was working on. The bear made grumbly noises as he tried to pull his hat free without tearing the card. They both looked up as Morty Moose came in, slammed the door, and went running down to his room in the basement.

"What do you think that was all about?" Scott asked.

Darby shrugged and went back to working on his hat.

Scott watched him for a moment, absently pulling at his whiskers which was how the glue got transferred from his paws to them in the first place. "I think I'll go see," he said.

He found Morty Moose lying on his bed, crying into his pillow.

"Hey, Mort, old sport," he said, sitting down on the bed. "What's the matter?"

"Nothing," Morty Moose sniffed.

"Oh. Want to come upstairs and make Christmas cards with us?"

"No. There's not going to be any Christmas this year."

"What do you mean? Who told you that?"

"I met Santy Claus coming home and he's a horrible man and I don't care and who needs Christmas anyway."

He began to cry again. Scott patted him on the shoulder, gave him a Kleenex and pried the story out of him. At the end of it, Morty Moose started to cry all over again. Scott tried to comfort him, but it was no use. Eventually he left the little moose lying there and went up to talk to Darby. A little while later they both came down.

"I'll cheer him up," Darby said. "You'll see. Hey, Morty," he added as he plonked himself down on the bed. "What's red and white and black all over?"

"Don't care."

"A newspaper—wait a sec. I think I got that mixed up."

Morty Moose began to wail louder, so loud, in fact, that the typing that had been going on all the while in the next room came to an abrupt halt.

"Now you've done it," Scott muttered.

"What's going on *now*?"

Sam the Monkey stood in the doorway, eyeing the three with suspicion. Of all the plush toys in the house, they were the most mischievous, always getting into trouble, while Sam was the cleverest, and usually the one that had to get them out of trouble.

He was only a quarter the size of any one of the Plushketeers, but that didn't stop them from being nervous around him. His white fur was quite worn—"It just means I've been well-loved," he liked to say—he had an ink stain on one shoulder, and he'd been all over the world. He was also a writer, selling regularly to magazines like *The Winter Duck Times*, *Badgerweek*, and *ASKEW* (All Silly Kinds of Entertaining Whimsey—the local community newspaper). He was also the author of the book *The Adventures of Sam the Monkey* that made it to number one on the *New Goose Times* bestseller list.

"It's Morty," Scott explained. "Somebody told him that Christmas is going to be cancelled this year."

"It can't be cancelled," Sam said. "I'm just in the middle of a special Christmas story for *ASKEW*. Who told him that anyway?"

"S—santy Claus...did..." Morty Moose said through his sniffles.

Sam sighed and sat down on the end of the bed. "I think I'd better hear the whole story."

So Morty Moose told it all over again, breaking down into heavier sniffles before the end so that Scott had to finish it for him.

"That wasn't Santy Claus," Sam said at the end. "That was just a bum being mean."

"He...he had a red suit on...under his clothes. He opened his shirt and...and showed me."

"Well, if he *was* a Santy," Sam said, "he was just like the Santys they have in shopping malls—like the one you saw last year."

Morty Moose started to wail again.

"That's not the real Santy Claus," Sam told him. "There's only one real Santy Claus and he can't be everywhere, so he gets his friends to dress up as him and help him out at shopping malls and for parades and things."

"It's like pies," Darby explained.

Morty Moose's ears pricked up a little at the sound of food. "What...what do you mean?"

"Well, they can't all be lemon meringue," Darby explained.

"*That*," Sam said, "doesn't make any sense."

Morty Moose's snuffling got louder.

"I'll tell you what," Sam said quickly. "We'll get Santy Claus himself to tell you that there'll still be a Christmas this year—okay?"

"You...you will?" Morty Moose asked in a small voice.

"You *will?*" Darby and Scott said together.

Sam nodded. "And you two are going to help, so let's go upstairs and talk about it." Sam patted Morty Moose on the shoulder. "Everything will be just fine, Morty. You'll see."

"We *will?*" Darby and Scott said.

Sam frowned fiercely at them and went upstairs. Exchanging glances, the terrier and bear followed him, scratching their heads.

"How are you going to manage this?" Scott asked when they were all sitting around the kitchen table.

"I don't know," Sam said. "I'm still thinking."

"I've got a plan," Darby said.

Sam and Scott groaned, knowing Darby's plans all too well.

"We'll build a huge papier mâché Santy Claus," Darby said, "and we'll put Sam in its head and Sam will talk to Morty and explain everything and everything will be all right again. What do you think?"

The other two shook their heads.

"Maybe we could find the bum," Scott said, "and get him to tell Morty that he was lying."

Sam and Darby thought about that for a moment, then *they* shook their heads.

"Well, we'd better think of something," Scott said. "Christmas is only a week away, but a week of Morty's sulking will spoil Christmas for everyone. Besides, I hate to see him feeling so bad."

Glum nods agreed with that.

"I've got another plan," Darby said. "We'll have a big party on Christmas Eve and invite Santy Claus to it and *he* can tell Morty."

"That's not a half-bad idea," Sam admitted.

Scott shook his head. "That's Santy's busiest night. He won't have time to come to a party. And how would we get in touch with him anyway?"

"We'll write to the North Pole," Darby said.

"No, that won't work," Sam said. "What we'll do is get someone to dress up as Santy Claus at the party."

"Now that could work," Scott said.

"And Morty will stop feeling bad if he's got a party to look forward to," Darby added. "Now who will we get to dress up as Santy Claus?"

They all looked at each other.

"Oh no," Sam said. "I'm too small."

"Well, it can't be either one of us," the Plushketeers said. "We have to be there with Morty or he'll suspect."

"I know," Sam said. "I'll ask Gurgi to do it for us."

⊁ ⅄ ⊰

"Absolutely not," Gurgi said. He was the large marmalade tomcat that lived in the house. Like most cats, his life consisted of eating, sleeping and ranging around the neighbourhood—in that order of importance.

"But it's really important," Sam said.

"It'd never work and I'd look like a fool."

"No one would know who you were—they'd all think you were Santy Claus."

"I'm going to another party that night."

"You don't have to come to ours until it's late."

"I'm going to two parties that night—one early and one late."

"I'll buy you some cat treats."

The cat's eyes sparkled at the thought.

"*And* a catnip mouse," Sam added.

"Well, it *is* Christmas," Gurgi said slowly.

"Will you do it?"

"Can you throw in some of those dried fishy things? You know, the ones that crunch like little tiny bones?"

A dreamy look came over the cat and Sam shivered. He hoped that Gurgi realized that plush toy monkeys didn't have any bones, tiny or otherwise.

"Sure," Sam said. "Cat treats, a catnip mouse and some fishy things. Is it a deal?"

Gurgi held out a paw to seal the bargain.

⊁ ⅄ ⊰

Morty Moose moped around a bit for most of the week, but by the time Christmas Eve approached, with the party in the offing, even he couldn't hold back his excitement. The house had been festooned with Christmas decorations, all sparkling and bright, green and red streamers, a wonderful Christmas tree that reached right up to the ceiling, and more fizzy pop and treats than a plush toy could imagine.

The guests started to arrive about an hour before the party was supposed to start. By the time it *did* officially start, the house was crowded with plush toys of every size and description, all admiring the decorations and tree, shaking the gifts under it, eating the treats and getting silly on fizzy pop.

Sam and the two Plushketeers in on the Santy Claus secret bustled about, enjoying themselves, but keeping their eyes on the clock at the same time. Christmas carols were being sung with great gusto, everything from tender renditions of "Silent Night" to Joan Jett's rock'n'roll version of "The Little Drummer Boy" with Badger and a wooly scarecrow making buzzing electric guitar sounds for accompaniment with combs and tissue paper.

It was a fine party, but as the hours rolled by, Morty Moose sat down in a corner by himself and started to feel sad again. It didn't seem that Santy Claus was going to come after all and that meant, party or no party, there wouldn't be a real Christmas. He tried bravely not to cry, but first one tear trickled down his cheek, and then another. He gave a great long sigh and a third tear rolled down.

Oh, dear, Sam thought. *Where* was Gurgi? He went outside to look around, getting Scott and Darby to help him, but the marmalade cat wasn't to be found.

Inside, the party rollicked on. The fizzy pop was disappearing in alarming proportions. The treat bowls were getting empty. The clock struck midnight and everybody began shouting "Merry Christmas!" to each other, hugging and laughing—all except for Morty Moose who sat in his corner, weeping in earnest now.

"I'm going to kill that cat," Sam hissed to Scott.

The little terrier nodded. But just then there was a knock at the door. Darby rushed over and flung it open, and there was Santy Claus, all decked out in his red and white suit, with a bag of toys over one shoulder, his breath frosty in the night air and a twinkle in his eyes.

"Ho! Ho! Ho!" he boomed. "Merry Christmas, everyone!"

Morty Moose sat up in his corner, wiped his eyes and just stared. As did everyone else.

"Gurgi's missed his calling," Sam whispered to Scott. "He should be in Hollywood."

Scott nodded. "He's *good*," he whispered back.

Santy Claus sat down in the big easy chair by the window and plonked his bag of toys down on the floor beside it. All the little plush toys crowded around him and, one by one, they got up on his knee and talked to Santy. He gave them their toys, his voice booming with laughter and goodwill.

"Where did he get the toys?" Darby asked Sam.

Sam shrugged. "I don't know, but I'm not complaining. What a great end to the party! We should have bought Gurgi more treats than we did."

The last to get up on Santy's knee was Morty Moose, his lower lip still all quivery and his eyes watery, but that was from happiness now.

"And this is the little fellow who thought Christmas was being cancelled this year," Santy said. "Do you still think that, Morty?"

Morty Moose shook his head, clutching the present that Santy had given him close to his chest.

"But you know, Morty," Santy continued. "Christmas isn't just presents. It's not just Wodan's winter solstice, nor the Roman Saturnalia, nor Christ's birth. It's much older than any of that and it can never be cancelled. People have made it holy to their beliefs over the ages, but what it really is is a time for all creatures to come together and be peaceful for at least one time in the year.

"It's the time when one year turns into the next, and we should all pray that perhaps this will be the year that the goodwill carries through until the next Christmas, as once it did, so very long ago. Wouldn't that be fine, Morty, to feel this good about everyone for every day of the year?"

Morty Moose regarded Santy with wide eyes. Although he didn't understand some of the references Santy had made, he did understand the general meaning of what Santy was saying.

"He's laying it on a bit thick, don't you think?" Darby muttered.

"Shush!" Sam whispered. "It's beautiful."

"Sure. But it's just Gurgi who's—"

"Shush!"

"So don't let anyone ever tell you that Christmas is cancelled again," Santy said. "As long as you believe in it, it'll be there for you, Morty— every day of the year, if you'll have it."

"Oh, I will," Morty Moose whispered. "I really will."

Santy beamed down at him. "Ho, ho, ho! There's the lad, Morty. And now it's time for me to be going. I've got lots of places still to visit tonight, and the reindeer are getting restless. Hear them jingle their harnesses!"

Everyone in the room cocked their heads and thought they really could hear a jingle.

"How'd he do that?" Scott whispered.

"He probably has some friends outside with bells," Sam whispered back.

Santy said his goodbyes then and after that the party began to wind down, with everyone saying what a fine party it had been, how it had been the very best of parties, how there couldn't ever be a better one, how they must do it all again next year, how it would be even better next year, and so on.

"Oh, thank you, Sam," Morty said, eyes beaming as he went to bed.

"Merry Christmas, Morty," Sam said.

A little later, the other two Plushketeers having toddled off to bed as well, Sam stood alone in the messy room, a very warm feeling inside. He didn't even mind being left to clean up the mess. In fact, he thought, he wouldn't clean it up until tomorrow morning. He started for bed himself when a very bleary-eyed Gurgi came in the back door and laid his head down on the kitchen table, paws on either side of his head. He reeked of catnip.

"I'm *so* sorry, Sam," he mumbled.

"What for? You did marvelously. You were the best Santy I ever saw!"

The cat lifted his head to give Sam a look somewhere between surprise and suspicion. "I *was*?"

"Oh, yes. I didn't know you had it in you."

"Neither did I. Run it by me again, Sam. I'm feeling a little befuddled. Exactly how did it go?"

"You went out to that second party after all—didn't you?" Sam asked with a grin.

"Yes, well...Sam, what are you talking about?"

So Sam told him about how it had looked from where he'd stood, that Gurgi had made a very real Santy—"Stuffed that costume with a *lot* of pillows, didn't you?"—had the voice and the "ho, hos" down just right, how he'd made a speech about Christmas, how happy Morty had been.

"It was perfect, Gurgi. And that bit with the reindeers' bells—that was the perfect ending touch. You had a friend waiting outside, right?"

"Sure. Bells. Right. I guess it all went over pretty good then, didn't it?"

"Just perfect. Merry Christmas, Gurgi. I'll see you in the morning."

"Right. Merry Christmas."

Gurgi watched the little monkey go and slowly shook his head. He didn't know *what* had happened here tonight, but he certainly wasn't going to tell Sam or the Three Plushketeers that he'd forgotten all about playing Santy Claus until just before he'd come home a few moments ago. But if it hadn't been him, then who could it have been? He thought about that for a moment, still woozy from too much catnip at two different parties.

Like a far-off echo, he heard a faint jingle of bells then, and a distant "Ho, ho, ho."

"No," he said, shaking his head. "It couldn't have been."

The Badger in the Bag

This is what happens:
there is a magic made.

Wendelessen,
from "The Old Tunes."

They travelled in a tinker wagon that year, up hill and down. By the time they rolled into summer they were a long way from Abercorn and the Vale of the Oak King, roaming through Whistlederry now, and into the downs of Dunmadden.

The wagon belonged to Jen Kelledy who was a niece of Old Tess, Cerin's foster-mother, making her a cousin of sorts. She was a thin reed of a woman with a thatch of nutbrown hair as tangled as Meran's, but without the strands of oakmaid green that streaked Meran's brown curls. Among the tinkerfolk she was known as Tulo Jen—Fat Jen—because she was so thin.

The road had called to them that spring—to Meran who was no longer bound to her tree, and to her husband the harper—so they packed the cottage up tight when Tulo Jen's wagon pulled into their yard one fine morning and, before the first tulip bloomed, they were away, looking like the three tinkers that one of them was, following the road to wherever it led. They left Old Badger behind, for he was never one to travel, but they carried a badger all the same.

Tulo Jen had a fiddle with a boar's striped head carved into the scroll.

She called it her badger and kept it in a bag that hung from the cluttered wall inside the wagon, just above the spot where Cerin's harp was tied in place. There wasn't a tune that, once heard, Tulo Jen couldn't play on her fiddle.

"There's a trick to it," she explained to Meran who played the flute. Meran could pick up a tune quicker than most, but she still felt like a plodding turtle compared to the tinker.

"There's a trick to anything," Cerin said.

Tulo Jen gave him a mock frown. "Aye—just like there's a trick to listening when someone else is talking and not adding your own two pennies every few words like some kind of bodach."

"Oh, don't talk about bodachs," Meran said. "I've had my fill of them this winter."

Having let one stay in their rafters over the winter, she and Cerin had found themselves with the dubious honour of guesting up to a half-dozen of the little pranksters some nights.

"Part of the trick," Tulo Jen went on as though she hadn't been interrupted, "is to give your instrument the right sort of a name. Now a badger knows his tricks and, what's more, he never lets go, so when Whizzy Fettle explained this thing about names to me, I knew straight-off what to call my fiddle."

Meran looked down at her flute. "I don't know," she said. "This looks more like a snake to me. I don't much like snakes—at least I can't imagine putting one up to my mouth."

"And besides," Cerin added. "You already had the scroll carved into a badger's head. How could you *not* call it that?"

"What did I say about listening? Broom and heather, it's like I'm talking to the wind. First off—" Tulo Jen, bristling, made a show of counting on her fingers "—the badger's head came after, but that's another story. Secondly, it has to be the right sort of a name and you'll *know* when it comes to you and not before. And thirdly, the second thing I was going to say was that one should listen, *really* listen—"

"Thirdly, the second thing?" Cerin asked.

"I'm getting confused," Meran added. "Does the name come first or..."

Tulo Jen looked straight ahead and stiffly concentrated on keeping the horses on the road—make-work, really, for they were too well-trained to stray. She said nothing, letting the clatter of the wooden wheels on the road fill the place left by her lack of words.

"I was only teasing," Cerin said after a few moments of her silence.

"Oh, aye."

"It was a joke."

"And a grand one, too."

"I really do want to learn the trick," Meran added.

"Oh, hear me laugh."

"That's the trouble with Kelledys," Cerin said to his wife. "They don't like to get bogged down with all sorts of silly things like facts and the like when they're telling a story. So when you ask them to explain something, well..." He shrugged, smiling before giving Tulo Jen a quick glance.

The tinker tried to keep a straight face, but it was no use. "You're a hundred times worse than Uncle Finan," she said at last, "and Ballan knows, *he* could drive a soul to the whiskey sack without even trying."

"You were talking about Whizzy Fettle's advice," Cerin reminded her. "Something about tricking a name out of an instrument."

"You're the one to talk—with that roseharp of yours sitting in the back. Do you mean to tell me that *its* name means nothing?"

"Well, no..."

Telynros was a gift from the Tuathan, an enchanted harp that bore the touch of the Old Gods in its workmanship. Silver-stringed, with deeply resonating wood, it bore a living rose in the joint where the forepillar met the curving neck. A rose the colour of twilight skies.

"Well then, listen to what I have to say, or at least let me tell Meran without all your interruptions—would that be possible?"

There was an obvious glint of humour in her fierce gaze and Cerin nodded solemnly in acquiescence. Tulo Jen cleared her throat.

"As I was saying," she said, looking at Meran, "the name comes first. But that alone would never be enough. So..."

The road wound on and Cerin closed his eyes, listening to the rise and fall of the tinker's voice. The summer air was thick with the scent of hedgerow flowers and weeds. He was soon nodding. The sound of the wheels and the horse's hooves, the buzz of Tulo Jen's voice, all faded and he fell asleep with his head on Meran's shoulder. The two women exchanged smiles and continued their talk.

⊱ ⊤ ⊰

That night they camped in a field, close by a stream. They had a fire for their supper, but let the coals die down after they made a last pot of tea, for the night was warm. When they finally went to their beds, they rolled out their blankets on the grass and slept under the stars. All except for Meran.

She couldn't sleep, so she lay staring up at the night sky, tracing the constellations and remembering the tales her mother had told her of how they came to be. After awhile, she got up and dressed, then went to sit on the flat stones by the stream. The horses snorted at her as she went by and she gave them both a quick pat.

By the stream the night seemed quieter still. The water moved too slowly to make a sound, the wind had died away. She took her flute from its bag at her belt and turned it over in her hands.

A name, she thought.

Her husband had carved the flute for her, carved it from the wood of her own lifetree when it came down in a storm. With three charms carved from its wood, he'd drawn her back from the realm of the dead—a haircomb, an oak leaf shaped pendant, and the flute. Three charms and his love had set her free from the need of an oakmaid's lifetree.

The flute was very plain, but it had a lovely tone for all that it was carved from an oak. Something of a harpspell from Telynros gave its music its rich flavour.

Shall I call you roseflute? she thought with a grin, imagining Cerin's face when she told him. How he'd frown. Oakrose, maybe? Roseoak? The flute was so slender, perhaps she should call it Tulo Fluto.

She stifled a giggle and looked back at the camp, then froze. Something moved close to the ground, creeping towards the sleeping figures of Tulo Jen and her husband. She was about to call out a warning to them when she recognized the shape for what it was by its striped head.

It was a badger—like Old Badger whom they'd left back in Abercorn. Meran knew the look of a badger by night. She'd seen it often enough, traipsing through the woods with Old Badger. But this badger looked small. A babe separated from a sow, Meran guessed.

She rose quietly so as not to startle it and padded softly back to the wagon. When she reached the camp she was just in time to see the little badger crawl into Tulo Jen's fiddle bag.

Oh, no, you mustn't, Meran thought.

She hurried over and knelt by the bag, but when she touched its side, all she could feel was the shape of the fiddle and the bow inside. Slowly she drew the instrument out and studied it under the starlight. It looked the same as it had when Tulo Jen had been playing it this evening. The wood had a hue somewhere between chestnut and amber and the carved badger's head on the scroll regarded her with a half-smile in its eyes. Meran admired the workmanship of the carving for a moment, then set the fiddle aside. She reached into the bag again, took out the bow and shook the bag, half-expecting a baby badger to tumble out, for all that the weight was wrong.

There was nothing inside.

She was letting the night fill her head with an impossibility, Meran thought. Too many tinker's stories and harper's tall tales—that was the trouble. She replaced the fiddle and bow in their bag and laid down on her own blankets beside Cerin. She'd say nothing about this in the morning, she decided, but tomorrow night, oh, she'd be watching. Never have a doubt about that.

⤚ ⋎ ⤙

She watched the next night, and the night after that, and the third night as well, but all there was in Tulo Jen's bag was a fiddle and a bow. She gave up after the fourth night and put it down to her imagination and perhaps missing Old Badger. But she had to wonder. If she called her flute a snake, would it slither out of its bag one night and go adventuring? If she called it an oakrose, would the scent of acorns and roses spill out of the bag?

She meant to talk to the others about it the next day, but by the time she woke, she'd forgotten, and when she did remember, she was a little embarrassed about the whole affair. The teasing she'd get from that pair—tinkers were bad enough and Cerin was always twice as bad in their company. So she kept it to herself, but did wonder about a name for her flute. She'd finger it through its bag during the day, listen to its tone when she played tunes with the others around the fire in the evening, and late at night, she'd sit up sometimes, looking at its wooden gleam in the moonlight and under the stars.

⤚ ⋎ ⤙

Two weeks later they were camping in a hollow, with hills on one side, rolling off into gorse-thick downs, and dunes on the other, shifting to the sea. They all stayed up late that night, drinking a little too much of

Tulo Jen's heather whiskey. Eventually, Cerin and the tinker fell asleep, but the strong drink just made Meran feel too awake. She got up and wandered down by the water to see if she could make out what the tide was saying to the shore.

There was something hypnotic about the lap of the waves as they came to land. If she didn't love her father's wood so much, she could easily live by the sea, forever and a day. She came upon an outfall not far from the camp, a brook that ran down to the water from the gorse-backed hills. Seabirds stood by it, settled down for the night. A black and white oyster-catcher, as big as a duck, took to flight when she came too near, its wings beating rapidly as it flew off along the shore, sounding its high piping alarm call. But the gulls stayed put and watched her.

She backed away, not wanting to disturb them as well, and made a slow circuit back towards the camp. Standing on the highest dune, the one that overlooked the camp, she held her breath as a small greyish shape with a striped head crept away from where Tulo Jen and Cerin lay sleeping. Meran slipped out of sight behind the dune and then followed the little shape, her heart beating fast in her breast. She gave herself a pinch at one point, just to make absolutely sure that she wasn't dreaming, then realized that she could just as easily be drunk.

The little badger led her a good distance away from the camp before it finally paused and crouched down amongst driftwood and drying seaweed to gaze out to sea. It began to sing then, a low mournful song that sounded for all the world like a fiddle's strings when the bow pulled a slow air from them.

Oh, this can't be, Meran thought, who'd seen marvels in her time, but nothing like this. Not ever anything like this.

But the little badger stayed there by the edge of the sea and sang, sometimes jaunty tunes and sometimes sad airs. The jigs and reels made Meran want to get up and dance in the wet sand, to feel it press up between her toes as she stomped about to the music. The slower tunes made her want to weep. Then her fingers crept to the bag that held her flute and she caressed the wood through the cloth, wanting to play along with the badger, but not daring to break the spell.

There were more sad tunes than happy ones. And after awhile, there were no more happy ones. What could make it feel such hurt? Meran wondered. When the little badger finally fell quiet, Meran's eyes were brimmed with tears as salty as the briny water that lapped against the sand.

"Don't go!" she called softly as the little beast began to leave.

The badger froze and met her gaze with eyes that seemed to hold their own inner light.

"Who are you?" Meran asked. "What makes you so sad? Why were you singing?"

Her head was filled with a hundred questions and they all came out in a jumble when all she really wanted to ask was, how can I ease your hurt?

I sing the music that was never played on me, the little badger replied. His voice was like fiddle notes resounding in her head, staccato notes played on the high strings. Not unpleasant, just strange sounding. *The music that never had a chance to live. If I leave it unsounded, it builds up in me until I can no longer bear it. It becomes a pain that...hurts.*

"Are you sad?" she asked, coming nearer.

The badger held its ground, watching her. *No. Not sad. Just...*Its grey shoulders lifted and fell and a long note came from it, filling her head. It wasn't a word, just a bittersweet sound.

"Do...do all instruments feel that way?"

It was perhaps the whiskey that made her take this all so seriously, a part of her decided.

No, the badger replied. *Just those with names.*

Meran thought about that. She imagined Cerin's harp taking a walk to play some music for itself, then realized that there were times when she woke, late at night, and thought she heard it playing, thought it was just a dream...

Instruments with names. She touched her flute.

"Would you rather not have been named?" she asked.

Without a name, how could I live? And besides, what instrument sounds so sweet as one that has been loved and given a name?

"But..." Meran began, yet between one blink and the next, the badger had scurried away.

By the time she returned to the camp, she was still feeling woozy from the drinks and the walk, but tired enough to sleep. Before she lay down, she took the time to touch Tulo Jen's bag. There was a fiddle inside, and a bow—wood and gut strings and horsehair. No live badger. Meran went to sleep, holding her flute, and dreamed of an orchestra of instruments that changed into animals as they sounded, leapt from their player's hands and capered about, still making music. She smiled in her sleep.

⤛ Υ ⤙

It was a week after that, as they were traveling through the wooded vales of Osterwen, the tag end of the summer in the air now, that Tulo Jen asked Meran if she'd thought of a name for her flute yet.

"Well, I'm not sure," Meran replied. "I don't know if it wants a name."

"Everything wants a name," Tulo Jen said, and then she echoed the little badger's words. "How else can it live?"

Meran had been thinking about that, wondering if an instrument did want to live in such a way, but she hadn't been able to come up with an answer that satisfied her. So she told Tulo Jen about what she'd seen happen to the tinker's own fiddle.

"Broom and heather," Tulo Jen said when Meran was done. "Now there's a marvel!" She never doubted the tale for a moment and for that, Meran was relieved.

"I've heard that tale before," Cerin said, "only it was a set of bagpipes and they set up such a wail every night at the stroke of midnight that—"

"Oh, do be still!" Tulo Jen told him.

Cerin bit back the joking retort that was on the tip of his tongue when he saw that the pair of them were serious.

"Did you know about it?" Meran asked the tinker. "About the little badger and all?"

"No. But Ballan knows, it makes sense in a lovely sort of a way, don't you think?"

"I suppose. But now you can see why I'm not sure what I should do. What if the flute doesn't want a name? What if I give it the wrong one?"

"You couldn't do that," Cerin said, all jokes aside.

"But how's one supposed to know?"

Tulo Jen and the harper exchanged glances. It was Cerin who answered. "Because when the name comes to you, it will come from the instrument. It's the same as Old Badger. We don't call him Duffer or Stripes or anything but Old Badger, because that's who he is. You'll just *know*."

"Oh, it's easy for you to say. You're a harper."

"I didn't name Old Badger."

"Well, he's always been Old Badger," Meran said. "Ever since I can remember."

But as she spoke, she could remember the first time the name had come to her. She was tousling with the old fellow, back in a time before she'd met Cerin, when she'd still been tied to her tree. She could remember the exact instant that the name had formed in her mind and then sounded in the air for the first time. She'd called him many things before that moment, but when that name came, she'd just *known* it was the right one.

"I see," she said slowly.

"So will you name your flute?" Tulo Jen asked. "Because that's the first part of the trick, you know. And then it's just listening."

Meran thought of badgers in bags that were fiddles sometimes and other times were not. She touched her flute, then drew it from *its* bag and studied it in the sunlight. The wood gleamed, its grain rich with spiraling curlicues.

Badgers were tricksters, she remembered Tulo Jen telling her, and she could see that, considering the mischief Old Badger could get into. And there was a trick to learning tunes quickly. And like it or not, the image of the little brown man who lived in their rafters came to mind and, looking at her flute and thinking of him, she knew she had no choice.

Oh, but it was just making trouble for Cerin and herself, for now they'd have a pair of them in their rafters every night, not just the odd night when their gnarled little bodach had his friends over.

"I'll have to call it Bodach," she said, "because that's its name."

Cerin looked at her with raised eyebrows, but Tulo Jen nodded her head.

"That's a good name," she said.

Meran thought she heard a laugh in the wind that blew through the branches of the trees overhead and wondered if she'd been tricked into the whole thing. She sighed and pushed the flute back into its bag. As she put it away, she thought it moved in her hands, but perhaps it was just the way it had rolled between her fingers.

"Just you remember," she told it. "Your tricks are supposed to *help* me."

This time she was sure she heard a laugh on the wind.

The Old Tunes

This is what happens
every time a wooden case
is cracked open and the pipes are
lifted
from the soft cloth inside;
a drumskin is tightened,
held close to a fire;
a whistle is raised to catch
the quick breath of a lung-wind;
a fiddle is loosed
from the sett of its bag;
a harp knows the pluck
of a poet's fingers…

This is what happens:
there is a magic made.

The voices of the dead
can sing in it
—not mournful and dole,
but with a glad reckoning,
like moonlight
flickering in a drop of midnight dew,
or the glow of fireflies
in the deep meadows of summer.

And such a music can be made
though only one instrument plays
or many
—flute and drum, and skirling pipes;
fiddles rattling out their tunes
to the rhythm of clacking bones;

and the harps...the harps
making sounds
like the scent of apple blossoms,
like the rumble of stones
turning deep underground,
the two tones entwined.

Fast and glad, sad and slow,
this is what happens:
there is a magic made.

The Three Plushketeers
and the Garden Slugs

There were slugs in the garden, dining on the tomatoes and peas with bibs under their chins, but the Three Plushketeers were too busy drinking fizzy pop and eating sticky buns in the kitchen to pay them any mind.

"All for buns and buns for all!" Morty Moose cried, licking the sticky part of the sticky buns from his fingers. His antlers nodded in time as he bobbed his head to an improvised version of "Toys Just Want to Have Fun" that Darby and Scott were singing across the table from him.

Darby was a bearish sort of a fellow, in a striped bow tie and a Derby hat, while Scott's bluish-grey fur was offset by the beige box of terrier whiskers that bristled around his sticky bun-stained mouth. They took turns trading verses on the song, passing the last bottle of fizzy pop back and forth with shouts of "Huzzah!" whenever one of them thought of a particularly good line.

They were in the middle of another chorus when Sam the Monkey came into the kitchen. He was a quarter the size of any one of the Plushketeers, with an inky stain on one white shoulder where someone had carried both him and a leaky pen around in the same pocket.

"There are slugs in the garden," he announced.

Morty Moose pulled a face. "Ugh! What a thing to say when we're eating."

"Bird poop," Darby said wisely. "That's what they look like—slimy bird poop."

"I don't like slime," Scott said.

"They're eating our veggies," Sam told them.

"Well, *I* don't like veggies," Morty Moose said, lifting another bun to his mouth. "They can have them."

Darby nodded. "Let them eat kale."

"Oh, that's good," Scott said. "They can have their kale and eat it, too."

"Lettuce drink to that!" Morty Moose cried, not wanting to be outdone. He made a grab for the fizzy pop bottle but Scott got to it first.

Sam sighed and turned away, knowing there was no point in talking to them at a time like this. Plush toys shouldn't drink fizzy pop—it just made them silly.

"Beer!" Darby called after him.

Morty Moose wagged a finger at the bear. "You should say 'excuse me' when you burp."

"I wasn't burping. I was saying 'beer'."

"It sounded like a burp to me."

"What about beer?" Sam asked.

"I've heard," Darby said, "that if you put saucers of beer in the garden, the slugs will crawl into them and drown."

"Oh, that's nice," Scott said.

Darby giggled. "Dead bird poop in a saucer," he sang in an off-key falsetto.

Sam shook his head, but he'd heard that story too. Fetching a saucer and some beer from the fridge, he went out to the garden to a rousing chorus of "A-Hunting Slugs We'll Go" from the Three Plushketeers who elected to stay in the kitchen. Sam didn't harbour any particular ill-feelings towards slugs in general, but after putting a lot of work into the garden, he wasn't about to let it degenerate into a gastropodic salad bar.

By the time he returned inside, Morty Moose had fallen asleep on the floor with a sticky bun stuck to one antler, while Darby and Scott were half-heartedly rummaging through the fridge, looking for more fizzy pop, but finding only tomato juice and milk. They both looked a little sick.

Serves 'em right, Sam thought.

He left them there and went off to bed only to be woken a few hours later by a raucous hooting and singing. Now *this* was taking things a bit too far!

He got up out of bed, determined to really give the Three Plushketeers a piece of his mind. When he entered the kitchen, however, he saw that the three of them were passed out in a row on the floor by the fridge, the fridge door standing wide open. The noise was coming from outside.

Sam closed the fridge and peeked out the back door, blinking with surprise at what he saw there. The slugs were having a party.

They had hung Chinese lanterns on strands between the rhubarb and tomato plants. Under them, drunken slugs were dancing and singing, using the saucer of beer as a punch bowl at which they freshened their glasses whenever they got low. Around the bowl, as will happen at many parties, a number of slugs were leaning against each other, shouting out the choruses to old Beatles songs. Some of them had party hats, others had balloons. There were streamers and noisemakers and rattles and one old slug with a wisp of a slimy beard and a ukulele whose "Yes, Sir, That's My Baby" was being thoroughly drowned out by a dozen or so high-pitched voices raised in a surprisingly tuneful rendition of "Hey, Jude".

"I can't stand it," Sam muttered. He turned to go back inside and bumped into Morty Moose who'd also been woken by the row.

"Gosharooty," Morty Moose said. "That looks like fun."

"Never dance with bird poop," Darby warned, coming up behind him.

Scott, the last to arrive, nodded in agreement. "The slime gets all over you."

"I'm moving," Sam said. "I'm going to pack up my things and hitch a ride on a goose and get as far away from here as I can. I've had it!"

The Plushketeers regarded him with alarm.

"You can't!" Scott cried.

"Oh, no!" Morty Moose wailed.

"I have a plan," Darby said.

Sam shook his head. "I don't want to hear it—look where your last idea got us. Things were better off before I put out the beer. At least I could sleep then."

Darby patted Sam on the shoulder. "Go to bed," he said. "We'll handle this. That's what Plushketeers are for. To protect the innocent against vicious bird poop!"

The fizzy pop, Sam decided, had completely befuddled Darby and there was no point in arguing. So he simply nodded and went downstairs to pack.

"Do you really think he'll go?" Scott asked after Sam had left.

Darby shook his head. "Not a chance. Now here's my plan." He leaned towards them and whispered it in a low voice. Scott began to grin. Morty Moose rubbed his hands together. "Right then," Darby finished. "Let's get to it!"

And off they went.

Scott found some paper and made up the signs they would need using coloured magic markers. Darby got a cardboard box and painted it up in jolly blue and yellow and red stripes. Morty Moose went next door and borrowed Evan's wagon. Evan was asleep—after all, it was late at night by now, and he was just a toddler—but the Plushketeers didn't think he'd mind. It was all for the sake of justice, thank you kindly.

A half hour later, with Sam downstairs still muttering and packing, they went out into the back yard to put their plan into motion. Very carefully, they wheeled the wagon onto the lawn. The painted box sat in its bed with a little ramp leading up to a door cut in one side. The signs hung from the box, held in place by sticky tape. When the wagon was set in the right spot, its ramp straightened one last time by a fussing Darby, they all raced back into the house and watched through the window to see what would happen.

The slug playing the ukulele was the first to notice. He nudged a neighbour, who nudged someone else, and soon they were all gathered around the wagon. ""RIDE TO THE BINGO" one sign read. "FREE BEER" read another. "FREE SALAD BAR" read a third. "NO ADMISSION CHARGE FOR BIRD PO SLUGS" read the last.

An excited murmur went through the crowd. Cries of "Bingo!" and "Free!" got louder and louder until they had all worked themselves up into a frenzy. In a great rush they all piled up the ramp, onto the wagon and through the little door marked "ENTRANCE" on the side of the cardboard box.

The Plushketeers had been waiting with growing impatience, but finally the last slug was inside. Now they tiptoed out, Darby in the lead with a piece of cardboard in his hand. Sneaking up to the wagon, where the slugs were all singing Bingo songs and yelling "Wahoo!", he slapped the pieces of cardboard across the door and taped it in place.

"There!" he cried and turned to the others with a pleased grin on his face. "Now let's be quick!"

Down the road they ran, pulling the wagon after them, making a general racket with its clattering wheels, and not stopping until they reached the Bingo Hall a few blocks away. They deposited the box on its doorstep, then hurried home again, giggling and laughing all the way.

"Free ride!" Scott snickered.

"Free beer!" Morty Moose added.

"Bingo!" Darby cried. He was very pleased with himself for having remembered that if there was one thing in this world that slugs like better than chewing up a garden, it was playing Bingo.

They had just returned Evan's wagon and were trooping inside when they met Sam struggling up the stairs with his typewriter under one arm, a fat suitcase precariously balanced under the other, and two more in both hands. He dropped the suitcases in a heap at the top of the stairs and put the typewriter down.

"What have you done *now*?" he demanded, taking in the pleased smirks on their faces.

"Listen," Morty Moose said.

Sam did. He didn't hear anything.

"I don't hear anyth—" he began, then stopped, listening again, and rushed to the window. "The slugs! They're gone! How did you do it?"

"Trade secret," Darby said, puffing up his chest a little. "Just remember this: We dauntless Plushketeer types are always there when you need a helping hand."

"Though not with vacuuming," Scott said.

"Or washing windows," Morty Moose added.

"Just with life-and-death matters," Darby said.

Sam shook his head slowly. "I owe you all an apology," he said. "You've really done a wonderful job—and you don't even like veggies!"

Morty Moose pulled a face at the word, but Darby gave him a quick poke in the ribs with his elbow. "It's thirsty work, this rescuing gardens business," Darby said.

Sam looked from face to hopeful face, then sighed. "I suppose you've earned it," he said.

He took some money out of his wallet and the Three Plushketeers raced out of the house to the 24-hour Seven-Eleven store for fizzy pop and treats, leaving Sam to carry his suitcases and typewriter downstairs by himself. But he didn't really mind. He hadn't really wanted to move away. Much as they could infuriate him, he would have missed the Plushketeers too much. He started to unpack, then kicked a suitcase.

"This can wait!" he cried.

Leaving the suitcases where they lay, he hurried out of the house to catch up with the Plushketeers and have a treat himself.

Ⲏ Ⲏ Ⲏ

You might be wondering, as I was, if the slugs came back the next night, once they realized the trick that had been played on them; or if they didn't come back, why it was that they didn't. Well, it seems that they all fell asleep from the beer they'd been drinking and didn't wake up until the Bingo Hall opened the next day. Convincing Betty Bingo—a star player, if ever there was one, and first in line at the door—to lend them some money, they played Bingo, won the jackpot, and moved to Florida on their winnings.

You might think that a Bingo jackpot wouldn't be enough for a whole troop of slugs to live on, but don't forget that slugs are very small, and there are plenty of gardens in Florida. They only needed money to pay the rent on their condo and to play more Bingo.

Author's Note: Thanks to MaryAnn for introducing me to the Plushketeers and to Midori Snyder for the sotted slugs.

1986

And the Rafters Were Ringing

She'll have to be young," Yocky John said. "Otherwise she won't believe."

Wee Jack, skinny as a stick figure, nodded his narrow little head. "And pretty, too."

"Pretty's not so important," Yocky John said with a frown. "What good's pretty? But weight's important. Furey's already carrying Peadin and you and me—he'll want her to be thin."

Wee Jack hugged his knobby knees and rocked back and forth. He almost fell from the rafter, but Yocky John caught hold of his jacket and pulled him back into place.

"Hsst!" he said with a sharp breath. "Keep it down."

Wee Jack stared from their perch on the rafter to the bed below. The couple lying there appeared to be asleep. Then he caught the gleam of an eye and knew that Meran, at least, was awake and watching. He ducked quickly back out of sight.

They were bodachs these two, a pair of tricksters hiding up in the rafters of a harper's stone cottage. Yocky John was the older of the pair, a grizzled gnome of a bodach who took his name from an old tinker man he'd once befriended and whose shape he could wear if the fancy took him. But usually he looked like the bodach he was—bearded and brown with thick brows like tufts of grass over a pair of glittering eyes, slight of figure, though not so skinny as his companion.

Wee Jack had a pair of shapes, too. There was the one he wore now, and the one he wore when Meran put her lips to her flute. For then he *was* her flute, given life after she named him Bodach. Yocky John didn't much

223

care to call him Bodach. To his mind, that was like the pair below calling each other Man and Woman, instead of by their given names. So he called the younger bodach Wee Jack. Soon enough all the kowrie folk, from Furey, who lived in the river to the ravens who nested in the Oak King's Wood, were doing the same.

"The Mistress spied me," Wee Jack told Yocky John.

"I'm not surprised," the older bodach replied, "what with the way you carry on. I swear, if there's something to trip on, you will."

"Maybe so," Wee Jack said. "But all the same, I know someone's who's young and thin and pretty, too."

"You don't."

"I do. Hather the shepherd's youngest daughter Liane."

A wide grin beamed across Yocky John's face. "I never thought of her." He leaned closer to his companion. "We'll snatch her at moonrise and won't that be a night for her! She'll remember it until she's wizened and old, and still she won't forget."

"Maybe I should be called Yocky Jack," Wee Jack said, puffing up his chest, "because I've gone all clever." Yocky was a tinker word that meant just that. "And you can be Wee John, because your brain's gone all small on you."

Yocky John aimed a cuff at the younger bodach, who backed quickly away and lost his balance again. Yocky John snatched him out of the air by his collar before he could fall.

"Whose brain is wee?" he asked.

"Not yours," Wee Jack said quickly.

➤ ⋎ ◄

Down below, Meran stared up at what she could see of the pair in the rafters. "They're up to no good," she whispered to her husband.

Cerin turned onto his back and looked up. "You're always saying that. How can you tell this time?"

"I can feel it. Besides, they're bodachs and bodachs are always up to no good."

"It wasn't I who invited the one to live here and named the other," Cerin said.

Meran gave him a poke in the ribs with her elbow.

"Still," Cerin amended. "It wouldn't hurt to keep an eye on them, now would it?"

"Just what I was thinking," Meran said.

Cerin rolled over again and went back to sleep, but his wife stayed awake a long time, staring up into the rafters and straining to hear what the two little pranksters were talking about.

⤚ ⥿ ⤙

The next morning, while Cerin was transcribing some tunes that he'd recently picked up from one of his tinker cousins, Meran kept a sharp eye out for Yocky John. When he slipped away from the cottage at mid-morning, she followed, keeping well back as he made his way through the oak wood that was the holding of the Oak King Ogwen, Meran's father. Old Badger tramped at Meran's heels, his broad striped head almost directly underfoot. As the hour drew closer to noon, Yocky John emerged from the forest and clambered up a short hill. A reed-thin figure was waiting for him there by a rough cairn of old grey stones.

Meran recognized the figure easily enough. It was Peadin the hillhob. His skin was as dark as the earth of his hills, his hair a dull red thatch. Eyes like small saucers predominated his features. With his brown jacket and trousers, and skin darker still, he could be almost invisible, even when standing just a few feet away. Meran had spied him from time to time on her midnight rambles with Old Badger, so she knew him by sight and by the rumours of his prankish nature, but not to talk to.

Leaving Old Badger at the foot of the hill, she crept up the slope, bent low in the gorse, but close as she got, she only made out a few words.

Spree...snatch...Liane...

That was enough. Before she was spotted, she hurried back to where Old Badger was waiting and the pair of them disappeared into her father's wood. The badger regarded her quizzically.

"I knew it," she told him. "I knew he was up to no good. Cerin can tease me all he wants, but I know what I know."

And what she knew at this moment was that the tricksters meant to kidnap Hather's daughter for who knew what purpose. She turned her steps now towards that part of the moors where the shepherd's cot looked out over the Dolking Downs. Old Badger followed dutifully on her heels.

⤚ ⥿ ⤙

Liane was at home in her father's cot, carding wool. She was a slender red-haired girl, the red a bright flame rather that the dull burn of Peadin's unruly locks. Seeing that hair, Meran understood why the bodachs had chosen her. Red was the colour of poets and bards and the colour kowrie folk liked best in their humans. Liane rose from her work with a smile when she saw Meran approaching.

"It's not often the Oak King's daughter herself comes to visit," she said as she set about readying tea for them both.

Liane lived alone with her father. Her mother had died and her two older sisters were married now and lived in other parts of Abercorn.

"I've come with a warning," Meran said. She sat down on a chair by the hearth, Old Badger stretched out by her feet.

"A warning?" Liane's eyebrows rose questioningly.

Meran told her of what she'd overheard and explained her suspicions.

Liane smiled. "Oh, the hobs would never hurt me," she said. "They tease a bit, but we put out their bowl of cream every night and sometimes they even leave behind a fairy cake in exchange." At the look that came into Meran's eyes at that, Liane's smile widened and she added, "Oh, we take care not to thank them for it. We might live a simple life, but we're not simple people."

The kettle began to whistle over the fire and Liane busied herself with steeping them each a strong cup of tea. She served oatmeal cookies when the tea was ready, and talked readily about whatever came to hand, but she took no more notice of Meran's warnings at the end of the visit, than she had when Meran had first arrived. Finally Meran gave up and returned home across the downs.

➤ ⋎ ⋪

She found Cerin by the river where he was still worrying over the transcriptions of his harp tunes. She talked to him there, rather than at home where Yocky John might be able to listen in on their conversation if the bodach had already returned.

"She just wouldn't listen," Meran said, obviously frustrated. "It's hard when even a fourteen-year-old human won't take you seriously."

An oakmaid such as Meran lived a long life—as long as her tree. She had green blood running in her veins and green tints in her curly nut-brown hair. She no longer had a lifetree, but her husband's harp magics had drawn her back from the veil that separates the world of the living from that of the dead.

"Maybe *you're* taking it too seriously," Cerin tried, keeping the tone of his voice as diplomatic as possible.

"Oh, really!" Meran replied, tapping her foot with a dangerous gleam in her eyes. "And when her father wakes tomorrow morning and finds she's been snatched by a rowdy band of tricksters? Will you still think I'm taking it all too seriously?"

"The bodachs never hurt anyone," Cerin protested. "They have a bit of fun, I'll admit, and they can be wearying at times, but they're not going to hurt anyone."

Meran sighed. "I wish they'd snatch you," she muttered and returned to their cottage to leave him sitting there, the roseharp on his knee, his gaze following the stiff set of her back.

He didn't like seeing her so upset, but when it came to bodachs she had a stubborn streak three field-lengths wide and there was simply no shifting her once she had her mind set that they were up to mischief. He considered finishing up his work early, but when he heard the clank and rattle of pots and pans being knocked about, he thought better of it. Glancing down at the music he'd just written out, he ran through the passage that was giving him difficulty again.

⊱ ⋎ ⊰

That night, as soon as Yocky John was sure that Meran and Cerin were asleep, he gave a low whistle. In its bag, Meran's flute changed into a little bodach and Wee Jack crawled out from the cloth folds, rubbing his hands together and dancing on the spot, hardly able to keep quiet for excitement. Before he could wake the sleeping pair, Yocky John swung down from the rafters and, grabbing Wee Jack by his jacket collar, steered him outside.

"Oh, won't this be fun," Wee Jack said. "Won't it *just.*"

Yocky John looked up into the night skies, deep with stars, and nodded. "Oh, it's a grand night for a spree," he said. "Now come along and do be quiet."

He set off for the riverbank where a black horse shape rose from the water and pranced onto land. The kelpie shook his coat and water sprayed all about, glinting in the starlight.

"Ho there, Furey!" Yocky John called softly. "Are you still in the mood for a night of drink and dance?"

The kelpie shimmered in the darkness until he stood there in a bulky manlike shape. Water and weeds dripped from his clothes. His black hair lay flat against his head. Dark eyes gleamed with good humour.

"What do you think?" a new voice asked, and then Peadin was stepping out from between the trees.

"Time to ride," Furey said in a deep voice. His shape shimmered again and the black horse was back. The hillhob and bodachs clambered up onto his tall back and with a shout from Wee Jack, they were off.

⊱ ⊤ ⊰

Meran rose as soon as the bodachs left the house. She didn't follow them to the riverbank, but made straightway for Hather's cot on the downs. But by the time she arrived it was only to see Peadin and Yocky John carrying the shepherd's daughter out of the cot. Peadin leapt nimbly onto Furey's back, then he and Wee Jack reached down to take the weight of the girl from Yocky John. The older bodach took his place behind Liane as soon as she was hoisted from his arms. Before Meran could call out, they were off again with the girl seated between Yocky John and the hillhob and Wee Jack at the fore clinging to Furey's mane.

Meran followed at a run—the quick distance-eating gait that only kowrie folk can maintain, all night if need be. But quick though she was, the kelpie was quicker, burdened down and all. Across the downs he galloped, the gorse and heather disappearing underhoof with a blur. Meran could only follow as best she could, trying to keep them in sight. When they reached the stone formation known as the Five Auld Maids, she was still a hill and a half away.

She could see Furey encircle the stones. Once. Oh, there's a spell brewing, she thought, and put on more speed. Furey circled the stones a second time, hooves drumming hollowly on the sod. An amber glow sprang up around the hill. Meran's heart was fit to burst and a pain stitched her side. Furey completed the third circuit, then leapt into the center of the standing stones with a high belling cry. Meran covered the remaining distance at a desperate gait and threw herself in amongst them as well, just as the kelpie's spell took hold, and then they were all spirited away.

A moment later, the hill top stood empty, except for five old stones.

⊱ Υ ⊰

Cerin stirred restlessly in his sleep. He threw out an arm across the bed, but there was no oakmaid there to snuggle close to. His hand hung over the edge of the bed. He woke when Old Badger gave it a lick with his rough tongue.

Sitting up, Cerin stared around the darkened cottage. "Meran?" he called.

When there was no answer, he looked up to the rafters. There was no one there either.

"Why don't I listen to her?" he asked Old Badger as he hurriedly threw on his clothes. Slinging his roseharp across his shoulder, he set off for Hather's cot at a quick walk.

⊱ Υ ⊰

The room was smoky, especially up in the rafters where Meran found herself precariously balanced and about to fall until she clutched a support beam. She wrapped both arms around it, took a few quick breaths to steady herself, then looked around.

Further along the rafter, she spied the kowrie folk with Liane's bright red-haired head lifting above the other four. They didn't seem to be aware of Meran's presence. Below them was the commonroom of an inn. Music was playing—two fiddlers and a piper, with an old man sitting off to one side rattling a pair of bones in time to the tune. Meran recognized it as a reel that Cerin played sometimes called "The Pinch of Snuff". There were a half a dozen other mortals in the crowd—a pair dancing, three by the hearth, and the landlord on a chair by the kitchen door, tapping a foot to the music.

It was one of those rambling houses, Meran realized. A place where the local folk gathered for music and stories and songs, with the tunes and the drink and the dance going on until late in the night. No one ever knew how a certain place came to be known as the local rambling house. It was never planned. It might be a cobbler's kitchen or a farmer's barn, as soon as an inn. The best of such places simply happened. Meran had been in any number of them, for Cerin and his tinker cousins seemed to sniff them out no matter where they happened to be.

It was not a place for a girl of fourteen, Meran thought. She wondered why on earth the kowrie folk needed Liane here. She turned her attention back to them.

"Now do you remember the words we taught you?" Yocky John was asking Liane in a low voice that Meran could only just make out.

The shepherd girl nodded. Her face was flushed and there was a sparkle of excitement in her eyes. She cleared her throat and leaned over the rafter.

"Liane, don't!" Meran called to her, pitching her voice as low as Yocky John's.

Five heads turned as one towards her.

"Oh-oh," Wee Jack said nervously.

"Have you lost your senses?" Meran demanded. "What are you doing to the poor girl?"

"No harm, that's for sure," Yocky John retorted. "Broom and heather, Mistress, what do you take us for?"

"Incorrigible mischief makers. Kidnappers. Troublemakers. That child you've stolen—she's just fourteen."

"We needed her young," Yocky John said. "We needed a human to speak the charm that will let us join the spree below without the folk knowing we've come, and we needed her young because it's the young humans that still believe enough to make a kowrie spell work from their lips."

Meran left her perch and edged carefully along the rafter towards them. "Well, she's coming straight home with me and you can speak your own spells."

"Oh, please," Wee Jack said. He stood up and came towards her. "Don't spoil the fun. I've never been to a spree."

"You move aside, or I'll—"

Meran never finished her threat. Wee Jack, swaying on the rafter, lost his balance and fell.

Yocky John grabbed for his collar and missed.

Meran grabbed as well, but her fingers closed only on air.

Horrified, they watched Wee Jack fall, wailing and cartwheeling his limbs. But when he hit the floor, it was a flute that struck the hardwood boards and broke in two with a snap.

Utter silence fell like a leaden weight across the commonroom. Six humans looked from the broken instrument lying on the floor, up to the rafters where they all clung, staring down.

"Oh, no." Meran was sure her heart had stopped. Tears welled in her eyes.

"You've killed him," Yocky John said flatly.

"Hey!" the inn's landlord called up in an angry voice. "What are you doing up there?"

"Take us away," Peadin said to Furey.

"Can't," the kelpie replied. "Wee Jack was a part of the coming spell, so he's got to be a part of the going back one as well."

The landlord got a big axe from behind his kitchen door and waved it in their direction. A couple of the other men ranked themselves beside him, stout canes in hand.

"Get down here!" the landlord cried. "I'll have your skins for sneaking about in my rafters."

"It's looking ugly," Furey said softly to Yocky John. "Best we get down there and I'll give them a taste of a kelpie's hooves. We'll see how well they can shout while they're choking on their own teeth."

Meran barely heard what any of them were saying. She stared down at the broken flute through a blur of tears. She couldn't believe that the little bodach was dead. And that was not all...The flute was one of the three charms that Cerin had made from her lifetree to call her back from the realm of the dead. A comb and a pendant were the other two. She had them still, but it needed all three for the harper's spell to work. Already she could feel the dead lands calling to her.

"Mistress?" Yocky John called softly to her. She looked so pale and wan.

"I did kill him," she said hoarsely. "And now I'm dying, too."

Below them, the bones player and one of the fiddlers had fetched a ladder and leaned it up against the rafters.

"If you don't come down, then," the landlord cried, "I'll come up and throw you all down."

"That man has too many unpleasant words stored away in him," Furey said. "He needs to be thrashed."

"Don't make it worse than it is," Peadin said. "We'll have to pay for our trespass."

Yocky John nodded glumly. "Though we've already paid too dear a price," he said, looking down at what was left of his friend. And Meran...She appeared to be losing her substance now as the grip of the dead lands grew stronger on her.

"Take a hold of your anger!" Peadin called to the men below. "We're coming down."

One by one they descended the ladder. Last to come was Meran, who ignored the men and went to the broken flute. Sitting on the floor, she took the broken pieces onto her lap and held them tightly.

"I didn't mean to hurt you," she whispered. "I've cheated death once, so every day I've had since then has been a gift. But you—I named you. You were meant to live a long and merry life..."

"They're kowries," the landlord said, staring at them. Here and there, some of the men made the Sign of Horns to ward themselves against evil. "Look at the green in that one's hair and the strange faces of the others."

"She's no kowrie," the piper said, pointing to Liane.

The landlord nodded. "Come here, girl. We'll rescue you."

"I don't want to be rescued," Liane told them.

"They'll have gold hidden somewhere," one of the landlord's customers said greedily. "Make them give us their gold, or we'll take it out of their skins."

The landlord didn't seem so certain anymore. Now that the little bedraggled company was standing in front of him, his anger ran from him. It was wonder he felt at this moment, that he should see such magical folk.

"I have an old flute some traveller left behind," he said to Meran. "Would you like that to replace the one that broke?"

"You don't give kowries gifts," the other man protested. "You take their gold, Oarn." He hefted his cane. "Or you lather their backs with a few sharp blows—just to keep them in line."

He took a step forward with upraised cane, but at that moment the front door of the inn was flung open and a tall figure stood outlined in the doorway. He had long braided hair, and a long beard, and there was a fey light glimmering in his eyes. A harp was slung over his shoulder.

"Whose back do you mean to lather?" he asked in a grim voice.

"Mind your own business," the man said.

"This is my business," the harper replied. "That's my wife you mean to beat. My neighbour's child. My friends."

"Then perhaps you should pay their coin," the man said, taking a step towards the harper with his upraised cane.

"No!" the landlord cried. "No fighting!"

But he need not have spoken. Cerin brought his harp around in front of him and drew a sharp angry chord from its strings. The harp was named Telynros, a gift from the Tuathan, the Bright Gods, and it played spells as well as music. That first chord shattered the man's cane. The second loosed all the stitches in his clothing so that shirt, tunic and trousers fell away from him and he stood bare-assed naked in front of them all. The third woke a wind and propelled the man out the door. Cerin stood aside as he went by and gave him a kick on his backside to help him on his way.

"Good Master," the landlord began as Cerin turned back to face him. "We never meant—"

"They trespassed," Cerin said, "so you had reason to be angry."

"Yes, but—"

"Please," the harper said. "I have a more pressing concern."

He crossed the room to where not much more than a ghost of his wife sat, holding the two broken halves of her flute on her lap.

"Oh, Cerin," she said, looking up at him. "I've made such a botch of things." Her voice was like a whisper now, as though she spoke a great distance away.

"You meant well."

"But I did wrong all the same, and now I have to pay the price."

Cerin shook his head. "What was broken can be mended," he said.

He sat on the floor beside her and took Telynros upon his lap. Music spilled from the roseharp's strings, a soft, healing music. Meran grew more solid and colour returned to her cheeks. The two halves of the flute joined and the wood knitted until, by the time the tune was finished, there was no sign that there had ever been a break. As Cerin took his hands from the roseharp's strings, the flute shimmered and Wee Jack lay there in Meran's lap.

"I...I think I fell," he said.

"You did," Meran told him with a smile that was warm with relief.

"I was in such a cold place. Did you catch me?"

Meran shook her head. "Cerin did."

Wee Jack looked around at the circle of faces peering down at them. Yocky John had a broad grin that almost split his face in two.

"Did I miss the spree?" Wee Jack asked.

"Is that why you came?" the landlord asked. "Because you wanted a bit of craic? Well, you're welcome to stay the night—you and all your friends."

So Cerin joined the other musicians and Meran joined him, playing the flute that the landlord had offered her earlier so that Wee Jack could caper and dance with the others. The jigs and reels sprang from their instruments until the rafters were ringing. Liane drank cider and giggled a great deal. The bodachs and Peadin stamped about the wooden floors with human partners. Furey sat in a corner with the landlord, drinking ale, swapping tales and playing endless games of sticks-a-penny. When they finally left, dawn was cracking in the eastern skies.

"You're welcome back, whenever you're by," the landlord told them, and he spoke the words from the pleasure he'd had with their company, rather than out of fear because they were kowrie folk.

"Watch what you promise bodachs," Cerin said before he spelled the roseharp and took them all home the way he'd come—on the strains of his music.

Meran held a sleepy Wee Jack in her arms. "Oh, they mean well," she said.

Behind her, Yocky John and the others laughed to hear her change her tune.

Author's Note: "And the Rafters Were Ringing" completes the *Meran & the Bodachs* trio of stories that began with "Laughter in the Leaves" and "The Badger in the Bag." While I wasn't aware that these stories would continue as they have when I began the first, they've certainly grown, one out of the other, all the same. But isn't that part of the pleasure of writing in general—how stories grow out of each other, seeded by the words that went before?

1987

The Lark in the Morning

Mostly it was Jen Kelledy who held the reins while the other two sat, one on either side of her on the driver's seat. The horses plodded ahead of them, manes festooned with ribbons and silvery bells that tinkled as the tinker wagon was pulled through the summer dales, up hill and down. The wooden wheels clattered in the ruts of the road, the bells sounded, joined from time to time by the soft murmur of the riders' voices raised in desultory conversation.

For the last few summers, Meran and her husband had taken to travelling with the tinkerwoman for a month or two, satisfying the itch that grew throughout the winter. By spring they were eagerly watching the road for the arrival of the wagon and its driver, her features browned and friendly, her tongue as sharp as only a tinker's can be, making you smile for all its grumbling.

She was a bony-thin woman, with hair as brown and tangled as Meran's, but without the strands of oakmaid green that streaked Meran's nutbrown curls. She was known as Tulo Jen among the tinkers—Fat Jen— because she was so thin. At nights around the campfire, with the flames crackling merrily as they threw a flickering light, she played a fiddle with the head of a badger carved into its scroll.

Because it was Named, that fiddle awoke when Tulo Jen slept. It became a badger and wandered the night, singing the music that was never played on it.

Meran's instrument was a flute that was one of three charms made for her by her husband from the wood of her lifetree when it came down in a storm. He carved a flute, a haircomb and an oak leaf-shaped pendant to draw her back from the realm of the dead. Three charms and his love had set her free from an oakmaid's need for her lifetree. She called the flute Bodach after the trickster bodach Yocky John who lived in the rafters of the cottage she shared with her husband; Yocky John called the flute Wee Jack for reasons of his own.

Because it, too, was Named, it became a bodach at night when Meran slept, but the little twig-thin figure was more likely to get into mischief when it was awake, rather than singing unplayed music.

Meran's husband was Cerin, known as the Songweaver, and his instrument was the harp. Its name was Telynros, the roseharp, an enchanted gift from the Tuathan that bore the touch of those Old Gods in each part of its workmanship. Silver-stringed, with deeply resonating wood, it had a living rose growing in the joint where the forepillar met the curving neck. A rose the colour of twilight skies.

Although it was Named as well, it had only the one shape. Its enchantments were less earthly, and far more potent, and were closely tied to that of the harper himself, rather than individual.

They blended well these three—instruments and players, whether making music, or simply enjoying each other's company. Some nights they played alone, harp and fiddle and flute wandering through the old tunes, one or two following the melody, the third awaking a counterpoint harmony. But other nights the woods and fields around their camped wagon would come alive.

There were revels those nights as they were joined by small shy shapes creeping out from between a forest's trees or soft-stepping from the hedges. Some lipped their whistles and flutes, following the rhythm on skin drums, tiny fiddles soaring on the high notes. Others simply sat and listened, or danced in rounds, singly or in couples.

Kowrie folk. Thin-featured and gangly-limbed, some; others with round heads and tubby bodies. Waist-high, or the height of a thumb. Ears pointed or hidden under unruly thatches of hair, thick as brambly briars. Wise-eyed and merry. Some nights the trees themselves seemed to lean down and sway to the music. One night they camped under a fairy thorn, standing alone in a field, and Meran was sure that its gnarled limbs were directing the players as though they were an orchestra and it their conductor.

Whether a night of revels or not, there was always an enchantment when they played. For those three musicians and their instruments made a magic with their music, and like calls to like. It always has; always will.

But not all magics are kindly.

⅄ ⅄ ⅄

"You see?" Tulo Jen said. "I told you. You already know this tune."

She and Meran were sitting on kegs by the spoked wheels of the wagon, instruments in hand—Tulo Jen with her badger-headed fiddle and the oakmaid with her flute. Cerin was by the fire, busying himself with their dinner, still humming the tune that they'd just finished playing.

"Sometimes I just go blank," Meran said. "As soon as I hear a tune, I'm all right, but I can never remember which ones I know. Not from their names, anyway. I can sit for an hour trying to think of one to play and nothing, but then all someone has to do is whistle up a few bars and I'm away."

"Off into a world of her own," Cerin remarked. "When she's like that you have to rap a knuckle against her head and ask, 'Is there anybody home?' if you want to have any sort of a conversation with her."

Meran laughed. "He can be so sweet, can't he?"

"So can wine, before it turns to vinegar," Tulo Jen said.

"Now that hurts," Cerin said, clutching a hand to his chest.

"This is musician's talk," Tulo Jen told him. "Not cook's talk. See to your pots, cook."

Cerin gave his wife a wink, before he returned to chopping up greens. Ignoring him, Tulo Jen put her fiddle back up under her chin.

"See if you know this one," she said as she began a reel known as "The Nine Blind Harpers".

Meran cocked her head for a moment, listening, then lipped her flute and joined in as the tinker began the repeat of the first part of the tune. By the cookfire, Cerin hummed along under his breath, cutting the greens in time to the four-four rhythm.

⅄ ⅄ ⅄

"This is what I like best about taking my turn at the cooking," Cerin said as he watched the two women cleaning up after the meal.

He sat at his ease, Telynros on his lap, his fingers idly plucking a melody from the roseharp's strings. The tune was in a minor key and seemed to settle into the growing dusk as though it were an inevitable part of the evening, as though twilight had been waiting for that music to sound, before it soft-stepped across the land.

These were haunted hills they travelled through, a fey borderland between Dunmadden's rolling downs and the coasts of Pye, where they were bound. The forests were thick with mystery here; the hills rounded with age and topped with stoneworks that were gateways between the fields of man and the Middle Kingdom, between this world and otherworlds. A place where kowrie folk wandered the night.

When the meal was cleaned up and the horses settled for the night, Meran and Tulo Jen joined the harper where he was lounging by the fire. They each had mugs of steaming tea, laced with the tinker's heather whiskey, sitting by their knees. Tulo Jen brought her fiddle from its bag, Meran her flute.

"Do you know 'The Road to Lee' then, cook?" the tinker asked Cerin.

"I heard it was washed out in a storm last winter."

Tulo Jen gave him a fierce frown at his teasing. "The tune," she said, in a tone she reserved for fools and stubborn animals.

Cerin returned her frown with an innocent smile. "Oh—the tune," he said. But his fingers were already plucking the first few bars from the roseharp's strings.

"Broom and heather, I don't know how you put up with him," Tulo Jen said to Meran. "I really don't."

She brought her fiddle up under her chin, her eyes twinkling in the firelight.

"It's just a matter of steering him in the right direction," Meran said.

"I'd sooner steer a mule through a fen."

"Or a rope through the eye of a needle?" Cerin asked, abruptly changing the tune to "The Tailor's Twist".

Tulo Jen let him play the whole of it through, she and Meran playing along. Then as the tune came to an end, she gave a quick nod to Meran and they both launched back into "The Road to Lee". The tinker had to laugh when Cerin didn't miss a beat.

They let the music flow then, one or the other taking the lead as a new tune came to them. They had extra mugs set out in case of company, tea warming by the fire, leather sacks of heather whiskey and a platter of oat cakes nearby. In these haunted hills they expected to be heard and eventually joined by kowrie musicians, but the evening wound on, and while the music had as much magic as ever it did, they played just the three of them, for only the three of them.

Until midnight came.

In a break in the music, Cerin cocked an ear. "Listen," he said.

Clouds rolled across the moon, deepening shadows in their camp until they moved on. For one moment the night appeared to hold its breath, the chorusing sound of the insects stilling. In that sudden quiet, Meran and Tulo Jen could hear it too. Fiddling. Drifting down from the surrounding hills.

"I mislike that sound," Tulo Jen said.

No teasing quick retort came to Cerin's lips, for the music troubled him too. There was something in the air. Not just the fiddling, but a scent of enchantment. He touched a finger to the roseharp's strings, but no sound came forth. His gaze lifted to meet Tulo Jen's.

"What is it?" Meran asked.

She looked from one face to the other, growing nervous at the seriousness of their expressions.

"The fiddling has muted our instruments," Cerin said.

Though he did not voice the concern, Meran heard what he left unsaid. With Telynros mute, their own magics had been stolen away.

Tulo Jen plucked a fiddle string, but her instrument was as silent as the roseharp.

"It was so slyly done," Cerin said, "that I never felt it coming."

"But why?" Meran asked.

"Because you trespass," a voice answered from beyond the light of their campfire. "Because you play an enchanted music in a land where only our music may rule. Because the strains of your music undo the bindings we have set upon these hills."

Cerin rose to his feet as a tall figure stepped into the firelight. He was stork-thin and dressed all in black—boots, trousers, shirt and jacket, with a wide-brimmed hat that hid his eyes. The fiddle he held in the crook of his arm gleamed like polished ebony. The stick of the bow he held loosely between the fingers of his right hand was made of the same dark wood.

"We saw no *patteran* forbidding music," Cerin said.

Patteran were the signs that tinkers and kowrie used as messages that they left for each other. Stones set in a certain pattern. A stick with a piece of cloth tied about it. Symbols scratched into the face of a rock. Each with a meaning for those who could read them.

"These are our hills," the stranger said. "We have no need of *patteran* here, for none are welcome here. We allow the road, we allow travellers to cross the hills by it, but we allow no music."

"But how could we know that?" Meran asked.

The stranger turned to look at her. From her sitting position, she could look up under the brim of his hat. The cold fire of his eyes made her shiver.

"It makes no difference," he said. "Your instruments are forfeit."

"I think not," Cerin said.

He took a step forward, pausing when the stranger lifted his fiddle to his chin.

"This is not a matter for discussion," the stranger said. "You have trespassed—now you must pay the price."

With her own fiddle lying across her lap, Tulo Jen studied the stranger. Their instruments were forfeit? That was too dear a price for a simple evening of music. A Tuathan harp, an oakmaid's lifeline, her badger-headed fiddle with its own small enchantment. It was far too dear a price.

Out of the stranger's view, her left hand drifted towards the hilt of the foot-long tinker blade that was sheathed at her belt.

"Don't," Cerin told her, his voice mild.

She glanced at him, but he didn't seem to have taken his gaze from the stranger's face.

"You won't find taking our instruments such an easy task," he said. "We meant no harm. Now that we've been warned, we'll bow to your wishes and keep silent."

"Too late for that. Already secrets, slumbering for ages in the hills, begin to stir."

"Taking our instruments won't change that. Will you not reconsider?"

The stranger shook his head.

"So be it," Cerin said. "You've stilled our instruments, but warned as we are now of your magic, you won't find stilling us as easy a task."

The stranger raised the hand holding his bow to tip back the brim of his hat. He regarded the harper for a long moment.

"I see," he said slowly. "There is old blood—in you and that woman." He nodded towards Meran. "Very well. For the sake of that blood, we will have a contest. Do you win, you are free to go. Do I win, you must still go, but you will leave your instruments behind. Agreed?"

Cerin remembered an old king's holding, the ruined keep of Taencaer, and another contest. He sighed. Contests meant nothing. Whether one was a better player than another, did nothing to invalidate the loser's skill. But though he loathed such displays, he saw that here they had no choice.

"Agreed," he said. "Who is to judge?"

The stranger shook his head. "Not a contest of skill, harper, but a contest such as was held of old. We will merely trade tunes, each in turn, neither repeating one that the other has already played, until one or the other has no more music. The last to play will be the winner."

"Very well."

Cerin went to fetch Telynros from where he had left it, but the stranger stopped him.

"The contest is not between you and I, harper," he said. "Nor between the tinker and I." He pointed the end of his bow at Meran. "But between us."

Meran shook her head. "Oh, no. I couldn't..."

"There will be no more discussion," the stranger said. "You will either play, or your instruments are forfeit now."

Meran's knuckles whitened as she gripped her flute. "Cerin," she began. "I can't..."

"You must," Cerin said softly.

Meran read the sympathy in his eyes. The stranger had known immediately who to choose—the one with the least head for remembering tunes. Perhaps he had overheard her earlier conversation with Tulo Jen, perhaps he simply *knew*, but however he came to know which of the three of them to pick, it was too late now for anything to be done about it except see the thing through to its end.

⋏ ⋎ ⋋

It was simple at first.

Certain though she was that she'd come up without a single bar once the pressure was upon her, Meran found the tunes bubbling up in her. Each time it was her turn, she had one ready. A jig or a reel, a clog dance or a hornpipe, an air or a set dance. But the stranger matched her one for one, sometimes playing the next tune she had ready as though he were stealing it directly from her mind, other times playing his own strange and doleful tunes.

Cerin and Tulo Jen sat silently, listening and watching. If they hadn't been so worried for Meran's sake, they would have marvelled at that night's music. In the same way that the tinker stored her maps in her mind, a part of Cerin was cataloguing and filing away the stranger's music, but mostly his attention was on his wife, lending her what support he could though it was nothing more than a smile, or an encouraging nod.

As the night progressed, each of the contestants needed more and more time between tunes to find a new piece to play. The blankness Meran had feared filled her mind now. Whenever her turn came, she sat for long silent moments, hopelessly uninspired, until finally her gaze alit on Tulo Jen's battered old kettle and she played "The Tinker's Black Kettle" jig, or she found herself staring at the soles of Cerin's shoes and remembered "The Hole in the Boot" reel. But the moments between the stranger ending his turn and those sudden inspirations, seemed endless.

Dawn was just approaching when the stranger, having taken the longest time of either of them yet, finally stopped his pacing back and forth between the wagon and the cold coals of their fire to lift his fiddle to his chin. The tune he played was an oddity, jumping between key signatures in each of its three parts. When he was done, he laid his instrument on his lap.

"That is it," he said. "I have no more music."

Meran could have cried. All she needed was one more tune and she'd win, but she couldn't think of one. The more she looked around the camp, the more depressed she became. Nothing inspired her. Every tune she could think of she or the stranger had already played. There simply *were* no more tunes. At least none that she knew.

She thought of trying to make something up on the spot, but at this moment she could hardly think straight, little say compose. Besides, the making of music had always been Cerin's gift, not hers.

It was hopeless. She had come so far, only to lose it all.

Dawn turned the horizon pink and still she had nothing. Bird song arose from the trees around the campsite. Meran lifted her head. The morning chorus. The clear song of a lark snagged at her thoughts. It reminded her of—

No. She'd already played both "The Bird's Chorus" and "The Lark's March", while the stranger had rendered an astonishingly good version of "The Blackbird". But she still felt that she was forgetting something.

She looked at Cerin, but except for an encouraging look, his features were schooled to give no hint of a tune to her for fear that the stranger would claim foul. If she could just remember...

And then she had it. The bird song reminded her of a story that Cerin had got from an old piper, a story of a piper's contest much like their own. When the hero ran out of tunes, he walked out in the morning, searching for inspiration, and didn't he hear the lark's song in the morning? To this day, when he was performing, Cerin used that story to introduce the tune, just as the old piper had.

Grinning, she lipped her flute and played through all four parts of

"The Lark in the Morning", and then played them through once again, just for good measure.

The stranger gave her a sour look, but he nodded his head in acquiescence. "Congratulations," he said.

Cerin jumped up from where he'd been sitting and embraced his wife. "Oh, well done!" he told her.

Even Tulo Jen was grinning. Cerin gave Meran a final hug before turning to face the stranger.

"And now?" he asked.

"You have won back your instruments," the stranger said.

Cerin nodded. "You spoke of secrets loosed in the hills," he went on. "Would you have me bind them for you?"

"You...?"

The stranger had long since removed his wide-brimmed hat. His brow was wrinkled now, his gaze puzzled.

"To set right what we inadvertently let loose," Cerin went on. "I can feel them—gate guardians unsettled, eager to leave their duties behind if they can; the shades of dead kings, stirring in their barrows; night haunts loosed from their hills."

As he spoke he went to the roseharp, touched fingers to its strings. Its sound was still muted. At a look from the harper, the stranger played a few bars on his black fiddle. When next Cerin touched a string, its clear bell-like tone rang forth, unfettered and free.

"Who are you?" the stranger asked.

"He is the Songweaver," Meran said, not a little proudly.

"The Songweaver," the stranger repeated slowly, recognizing the name. There were few in the Middle Kingdom who hadn't heard of the travelling bard with his roseharp. "Old blood, indeed." He glanced at Cerin's instrument again, seeing the living rose growing from its wood as though he saw it for the first time. "I should have recognized you..."

"No real harm done," Cerin said. "What's your name?"

"Pol O'Tanger. It seems I owe you all an apology—"

Cerin shook his head. "It's we who were thoughtless. We should have taken time to judge the lay of the land, *patteran* or no *patteran*." He shouldered his harp. "Come then, Pol. Shall we to the hills and see what we can set right?"

The black clad man rose to his feet, fiddle cradled under his arm. "I'd be honoured," he said.

Cerin looked back at his companions. "We won't be long," he told them.

The two women watched them go.

"Ballan!" Tulo Jen muttered. "He could have saved us all a lot of bother if he'd only named himself from the start."

"You know that's not his way," Meran replied.

"Well, then you could have."

"It never occurred to me."

Tulo Jen shook her head. "It wouldn't. Not to either of you. Broom and heather, what a pair." She gave Meran a considering look. "Are you worn out, then?"

"Completely."

"So was it worth it?"

Now that the pressure was gone, with the glow of winning still making her cheeks ruddy and putting a sparkle to her eye, Meran nodded.

"Well, at least we heard some good music," Tulo Jen grumbled. "Though I could have done without the contest. My nerves are all on edge and I wasn't even playing."

Meran only grinned.

"Oh, come on, with you," Tulo Jen said. "I'll get you some breakfast. And you'll have to teach me that tune, the one that goes like..."

She hummed a couple of bars until Meran nodded, remembering it. She gave the tinker a hug, just for the joy of it, then the two of them set about building up the fire again and making breakfast.

In the trees around them, the forest rang with bird song, that of the lark rising above them all. But sweeter still was the sound of a distant harp and a fiddle that drifted down from the hills around them.

Bones

Bones

grey as granite
ribs of weathered wood
  once knew
the echo of work boot
and clog dance
bones

and older still

world marrow
grey as aged barn wood
  rising like slow thoughts
  from field
  and forest loom
has a voice
a tale to tell
bones

I remember

  old tunes
secrets forgotten
lost histories
entwined in

bones

1988

The Drowned Man's Reel

*No one ever keeps a secret so well
as a child.*

Victor Hugo

1

The ghost wasn't always a drowned man haunting the pool.

When Courtney McNair was six, it was a little brass man who lived in the abandoned cast iron stove on her grandparents' patio, though she didn't know it was a ghost then.

On certain nights, when the moon hung low and she was sure that her mother and her grandparents were asleep, she would creep down the stairs and out into the night. The sea air would be sharp with a salty tang, the sound of the rollers a comforting murmur, the deserted beach haunted with low-hanging fog. She would pull a plastic deck chair carefully across the cracked stones of the patio and sit beside the stove, rapping small knuckles on its salt-encrusted belly.

"Widden, are you there?"

Widden wasn't his real name, the brass man confided to her the first night they met, but it was the only name that belonged to him now. He had great parcels of history stored up in his head, burry tales and odd little stories that ranged from the beach town of Santa Feliz itself to a place he called only the Old Country—some place in England, perhaps, or in Continental Europe, Courtney decided when she was older.

He had every sort of story to tell. But nothing that related to himself.

"Widden?"

Names have meaning, he told her, even when they change. To name a thing is to know it, but the name he went by now only meant "wild," for that was what he was: a small lost wild thing, cast adrift from his past.

"Widden."

Three times lucky was more than a superstition, he told her, for charms work best when they're summoned by threes.

On the third call of his name, a soft light would spill from the griddle, which was always canted to one side, slightly askew, and out he'd come, pulling himself slowly up onto the rusty stove top.

He was no bigger than Courtney's hand—the size it was then, when she was six—a dapper little fellow with a slightly rounded belly, a hat that sat on his head as crookedly as the griddle fit on the stove top, cheeks round as apples and eyes bright as coals. A tiny man, made all of brass, who could move as easily as though he were flesh and bone. He had the look of his odd little home: a stout round stove of a tiny man who, in the eyes of a six-year-old, was all the magic of every fairy tale she'd ever been told come to life.

Sometimes his stories were sad, but mostly he would make her laugh— so hard that she had to bite at the sleeve of her nightgown to keep from waking the sleeping adults inside the house.

But he wasn't always there.

He wasn't there in the daylight, when the harsh California sun made shadows stark on the patio and Courtney brought her mother or one of her grandparents out to meet the funny little man who lived in the stove that Grandpa had always meant to have hauled away, but never quite got around to. And he wasn't there when she tried to show him to her friends. That was because he was a secret, he explained to her. Her secret.

But he was there on those certain nights—nights when Courtney woke to see the moon hanging low, where the dark ocean met the darker night skies, and simply *knew* he'd be there. The warm glow of his stories would warm her then, better than any stove, for they warmed the inside of her, the places that the night sometimes chilled with bad dreams and that nothing else could ease.

It wasn't until she was older that she realized he was a ghost.

It wasn't until he haunted the pool.

And then he looked like a drowned man and *he* became the chill that the night left inside her.

2

The Kelledys were playing at The Fisherman's Wharf—the restaurant at the end of the Santa Feliz pier that, after nine on Friday and Saturday nights, was transformed into a folk club by the simple expediency of removing a couple of tables near the southwest windows to make room for the musicians and PA system. They were a husband and wife duo that Courtney remembered from her college days when she attended Butler U., out east in Newford. The pair used to make a regular spring and fall circuit of the college clubs back then and Courtney had heard them enough times to know most of their repertoire by heart.

The thought of seeing them, across the continent in her old home-town, left her feeling a little odd—not quite nostalgic, but wistful all the same, remembering lost pieces of her past.

Things had changed for Courtney since her student days.

The glow of making her own way in the world, with all the responsi-bilities it inevitably entails, had worn a little thin for her over the past ten years. She worked in administration at the university in nearby Long Beach and it was a good job, but she couldn't quite shake that sense of, is this it? Is this all there is?

Lately, she'd realized that some essential spark was missing—the absence of which habit and the unvarying routine of work had cleverly hidden from her until one day, while leafing through a tattered file folder of childhood scribblings and sketches, it had simply occurred to her to wonder what had happened to that boundless sense of whimsy that had once been so much a part of her. The realization of how thoroughly it had been eliminated from her life disturbed her.

Thinking about it, she could see how it had gone. Over the years, that elusive component of her youthful makeup that had let her believe that anything was possible had simply faded away through disuse. And she could still remember when it finally let go, that last moment of true magi-cal wonder that she could recall: a moonless night, walking the narrow

streets of Crowsea, that part of Newford that was like a little slice of
Europe, tucked away from the glitter and neon of a New World's chrome
and steel city. A night when anything was possible, like those nights when
Widden came to her on her grandparents' patio.

When anything was possible.

That night was the last time she'd sensed peculiar movement in her
peripheral vision. Odd snatches of nonsense verse carried on the wind—
almost, but not quite heard. Whimsy bubbling like a cauldron between
her ears, tossing out a half-dozen fancies in as many minutes. What if that
lamppost grew spindly-thin arms and legs and stepped away from its
curbside duty to go adventuring, across the river, off through the broad
lawns of Butler U. and beyond? Or if that bookstore sign acquired mem-
branous skin, inflated like a helium balloon, and launched itself skyward
as though it were some outdated dirigible, a goblin captain at its helm?

If she squinted slightly, cocked her head to one side and looked out of
the corner of her eye, she could almost see it all happening.

But that was then.

When anything was possible.

Now the spark that connected her to that province of possibilities was
truant.

Once she realized it was gone, she tried to recall it. But the spark was
elusive, depending not so much on belief as on a simple unquestioning
faith which seemed next to impossible to regain. She felt that it was like
innocence—once spent, it was gone forever. But she tried all the same.

And got a drowned man's ghost haunting her landlord's swimming
pool for her trouble.

⊁ Υ ⊀

The Fisherman's Wharf was half full by the time Courtney arrived
there that Friday night. The restaurant didn't seat more than forty to begin
with and, since many of those already there were out-of-towners—tourists, people up from Orange, or down from Santa Monica—she took a seat
by herself at the bar. Having only recently moved back to Santa Feliz, she
still hadn't had time to look up old friends, or make many new ones. The
rent was steeper here than it had been in the little apartment she'd been
renting just off campus in Long Beach, but the move had seemed worth it
at the time that she made her decision.

Magic had been real here, once, so what better place to try to find it again?

It took an effort to keep her ghost's drowned features at bay.

She looked out the window. The ocean was choppy as the sun went down, but that didn't stop the diehard surfers from squeezing their last few runs out of the waves. On the beach in front of the house that her grandparents had owned, a couple was strolling the sand, the man kicking refuse out of his path with lazy arcs of his foot. Come morning, the beach would echo to the rumbles of the cleaning equipment that swept the sand every morning.

Turning back to the bar, she ordered a glass of the house white and waited for the band to come on. When they took the stage, promptly at nine, she was surprised at how little they'd changed over the years, at how well she remembered them, right down to their smallest details.

Seeing them brought back the feel of Butler U.'s Carter Hall—a rush of memory, sight and sound and smell, so strong that for one moment she forgot that she was half a continent away from her old campus. The restaurant vanished from around her and she was back there again, one student amongst a hundred or so others, sitting in the hardbacked seats that rose in tiers from the stage. Cigarette and marijuana smoke filled the air. A cheap bottle of French wine passed back and forth between herself and friends on either side. Stabbing the darkness from behind them, twin spotlights cut through the smoke to capture and track the two figures ambling onto the stage.

They sat on low stools, center stage, he drawing his harp up into a playing position. His hair hung in a long braid down his back, his bearded cheek lay close against the harp as he tested the tuning of its strings. There was a small grey rose on the head of the instrument, so cunningly carved that it seemed to be alive, while the strings glittered like spun silver in the spotlights.

She had dark brown hair, dyed with streaks of green, and liquid eyes, reminiscent of shadows pooling in deep woods. A simple Laura Ashley-styled flower-print dress left her shoulders bare, while its hemline fell to mid-calf. She laid her wooden flute on the cloth covered instrument case by her stool so that she could take up a bodhrán—a round goatskin drum, played with a small double-headed drumstick called a tipple.

It was she who called up the rhythm, an ancient wild sound that was both undeveloped and complex, all at once. A four/four beat, like the drum of hooves on hollowed hills, with the accent on the first note of each measure; a pulsing sound that seemed more primitive still, for all that it was captured by the modern technology of a PA and sent booming throughout the hall.

And then the harp ringing its notes overtop that hoofbeat rhythm, playing a lilting reel that must have been old when the world was still young. It was the kind of music that could romance a cynic, or even wake the dead.

Courtney blinked and the memory was gone, but not the music. The Fisherman's Wharf rang with that ancient reel, or one very like it, harp notes dancing against the simple rhythm, carrying her, and the audience, away with it.

They hadn't changed at all, she thought.

Never mind how they looked exactly the same after all these years. The magic was still there as well. She could tell that, in them, the abstract holes she sensed within herself had never emptied, but were filled instead with wonderful mysteries.

The child in them danced hand in hand with the adult.

At that moment the woman looked up from her instrument to meet Courtney's gaze with a smile of recognition, before she closed her eyes again, body swaying to the rhythm, the hand holding the tipple performing its intricate patterns as the double-headed drumstick danced against the bodhrán's skin.

She remembers me, too, Courtney thought. After all these years, she remembers five minutes of standing outside Carter Hall, half a continent away, with a kid whose tongue was too tied to say anything more than, "I...uh...really like what you do."

The tune ended and the woman put down the drum to play a slow air on her flute. As the breathy sound drifted from the speakers, her partner began to recite verses, interspersed with chords from his own instrument, and Courtney put away thoughts of things lost, and things past, and just let herself be taken away again.

3

Courtney leaned against the railing and looked down at the dark waters that washed against the pier's foundations. The evening's music was still thrumming inside her and she was too wound up to go home; too touched by magic to face the thing in the pool behind her landlord's house. She heard a footstep on the wooden planking behind her and found herself joined by Meran Kelledy.

"When you think too much," Meran said, "it goes away."

Courtney blinked. "What does?"

"What your eyes say you have lost."

"You mean my imagination?"

Meran shrugged. "If that's what you want to call it."

Courtney could see the mystery living in her companion's eyes— dark and hidden, full of promise. What lived there was more than imagination.

"Magic," she said softly.

Meran leaned against the railing and looked out over the ocean. In the distance the lights of the oil rigs took on an enchantment, glittering like fireflies. Sea fog hung low on the waves.

"Tell me about it," Meran said.

She didn't turn to look at her, but Courtney could sense she had her companion's undivided attention.

"It'll just sound stupid," she said.

"Humour me all the same."

So Courtney did. She talked about Widden and lost whimsies, about how her search to recapture those wonders had only resulted in the horror of finding the ghost of a dead man in the swimming pool behind her apartment.

"Wonder never dies," a voice said when she was done. "But it can be mislaid."

Courtney turned to find Meran's husband Cerin leaning against the railing at her other elbow. There was a curious buzzing at the back of her head—a lightness to her thoughts that left her completely unsurprised at the attention of the two musicians. This, she thought, was what it must be like when people fell in with the fairy folk—like in the story Cerin had told on stage earlier to introduce a tune called "The Golden Ring". All bewitchy and tingling.

"That's easy for you to say," she told them. "You're both magic."

Cerin shook his head. "It's a matter of perception."

"I know all about perception," Courtney said. "I took Professor Dapple's course on conceptual reality when I went to Butler. 'Things are what they are because we all agree that's what they are. Anomalies come about when someone with a strong will perceives a different reality from the one that we've all gotten into the habit of agreeing to.'"

"I've never accepted that," Meran said. "Not completely."

"Everything *is*," Cerin added with a nod. "Whether or not we agree to something or not, it still is. But *what* it is depends on our various perceptions of it."

"That's just semantics," Courtney said.

Meran nodded. "But all language is semantics. If it wasn't, we'd all find it easier to communicate with one another."

"I can speak of a handsome man," Cerin said, "but both you and my wife will probably visualize vastly different men."

Courtney didn't say anything for a long moment. She watched an empty Coke can bob on the waves below her.

"What are you saying?" she asked finally. "That my childhood magics have become a drowned ghost just because my perceptions have changed?"

"Earlier," Meran said, "you said we were magic. But that magic is your perception of us—of our music, the tunes and the tales, and of how we present them."

"But you don't age. You look exactly the same as you did ten years ago. And it's not as though you've become static—more like you're timeless."

"Perception," Cerin said.

"But—"

"Your Widden," Meran said, "whether he's a little brass man or the ghost of a drowned man, is trying to get your attention."

"But why the change? I used to like him—but now he just scares me."

"Most people, when they get older, find it easier to believe in horrors than in the fancies they delighted in as children."

"Okay. Say I go along with that."

But, word by word, she found it harder to take this conversation seriously. The light-headedness she'd been feeling was fading, the residual glow from the concert's magic dimming into an all too familiar mundaneness. The Kelledys didn't appear so much enchanted now as a couple of holdovers from the old Haight Ashbury days. The fireflies flickering out on the horizon were just oil rigs once more.

Perception, she told herself. Nothing's changing—it's only how you're perceiving it.

"What does he want from me?" she asked.

Meran smiled. "Why don't you ask him?"

4

They came home with her—for moral support, Courtney realized, as much as for the bribe of some freshly-brewed herb tea that she'd offered them. She kept them in her little kitchen, squeezed around a table in a nook meant to seat no more than two, for as long as she could. She talked about the cardboard boxes that were stacked in the hallway that she hadn't gotten around to unpacking yet. She offered them more tea, another slice of pound cake.

"Why don't you introduce us to Widden," Cerin said mildly.

Courtney sighed. Right. Introduce them to her ghost.

Neither of them looked in the least bit magical at the moment— just a long-haired, bearded harper and a flute-player who seemed to have stepped out of a Burne-Jones painting. How could they help her?

Even worse—what if the ghost wasn't there? Magic was one thing; hallucinations something else again. Did she really want to let these two well-meaning, but—let's face it, she told herself— just plain folks, in on her own little corner of dementia?

"Maybe later," she began.

But Cerin had already squeezed himself out from the nook and was heading for the back door. It opened out onto a small balcony, which in turn, had a small cast iron stairway that led down into the garden. Where the pool was.

Sighing again, Courtney followed with Meran in tow.

"What do you see?" Meran asked when they stood at the edge of the pool.

"I..."

The corpse floated there in the chlorinated water—features white and swollen, body bobbing gently. Its eyes looked straight at her.

"Courtney?"

But Courtney wasn't listening. She heard, instead, what Meran had said earlier.

Why don't you ask him?

She'd never thought of that. Not when he lived in her grandparent's stove. Not now when he lay floating in the pool.

"Widden," she said.

She repeated his name once more. Then again. For didn't charms work when they were summoned by threes?

"Hello, Courtney."

The dead white flesh moved, swollen lips forming the words. The voice was a muted rasp.

"What do you want from me?" she asked softly.

"Sing me to sleep. Let me go to my final rest."

Courtney looked at the man and woman who stood to either side of her. What were they seeing? What did they hear?

"How..." She cleared her throat. "Uh...what happened to you?"

"I was a...travelling man," the corpse said. "I fell asleep under the pier one night and a storm came up and took my body away. But it lies restless in the deep. It needs a song from one such as you with the gift of the kindlight to rest in peace."

"Kindlight?"

"It's an old word," Meran said softly from beside her. "The travellers used it to describe those with second sight."

"I don't have second sight."

"You have something," Cerin said.

Meran nodded. "If you give it to him, his spirit will sleep in peace."

But that's what I've been looking for, Courtney wanted to say. That lost magic. I don't want to give it away.

"The choice is yours," Cerin said, as though she'd spoken the thought aloud.

Courtney looked down at the corpse, floating in the water. Her skin crawled, but she forced herself to really look at it, to see beyond the swollen features to find those of the little man who'd come to her from the belly of a stove to give her stories and comfort when she was young.

How could she not give him what he needed? It hurt to know for certain that the magic was real, but she must give it away; that she would never have it again, but always remember that it had been real. Still how could she withhold it?

She turned to look at Meran. "How...how do I do it?" She shifted her gaze to Cerin. "I can't hold a tune. I don't know the words to what he wants me to sing."

The low rumble of a bodhrán crept across the stillness. Courtney shifted her gaze to find Meran playing the drum. A four/four rhythm woke from its skin.

But they hadn't brought their instruments with them, Courtney thought. So how…?

From the other side of her, a quiet harping started up.

How? Magic was how. Like the kindlight inside her that told her she didn't need words to sing. She just had to hum with the tune that Cerin was playing. She just had to…give the kindlight away.

She knelt by the edge of the pool, singing now, a wordless lilt, soft and throaty. The body floated closer and she held out her hands to it, not even shrinking when the corpse reached out to take hold of her hands. A soft gold light haloed her body, then sped down to fill the corpse until it glowed, bright and stately as moonlight.

The light held for one long moment to the shape of the corpse, then, slowly, it faded. The body was gone. The waters lay empty. Drum and harp were quiet now. She looked up from where she knelt to see the Kelledys standing empty-handed on either side of her.

The magic was gone.

Taken away with the kindlight, swallowed by a drowned man's reel.

"That was fairly done," Cerin said.

Meran helped her to her feet. The two of them led her back to her apartment and put her to bed.

"Sleep now," Meran said, brushing the hair from Courtney's brow.

And Courtney did, deep and dreamlessly.

5

In the morning, it all seemed like a dream.

But she looked out the window to the pool below and for the first time since she'd seen the body, the pool was empty. In the kitchen, the cups and plates that she and her guests had used were washed and sitting dry in the drainer.

Everything's normal again, she realized. The magic well and truly gone now.

She went down the back stairs to stand by the pool. The sun was bright overhead, the morning fog already burned off. And what was this?

Bending down she picked a small brass figurine from the tiles by the edge of the pool and rubbed her thumb across its fat little belly.

She was never sure if it winked at her then, just once, or if it had only been a glancing ray of the sun against the brass as she turned the figurine about in her hands.

She thought of lost things, found and freely given away. And of how sometimes that was the only way that they could truly be regained.

Smiling, she went back into the apartment.

1989

The Stone Drum

*There is no question that there
is an unseen world. The problem
is how far is it from midtown and
how late is it open?*

attributed to Woody Allen

It was Jilly Coppercorn who found the stone drum, late one afternoon.

She brought it around to Professor Dapple's rambling Tudor-styled house in the old quarter of Lower Crowsea that same evening, wrapped up in folds of brown paper and tied with twine. She rapped sharply on the Professor's door with the little brass lion's head knocker that always seemed to stare too intently at her, then stepped back as Olaf Goonasekara, Dapple's odd little housekeeper, flung the door open and glowered out at where she stood on the rickety porch.

"You," he grumbled.

"Me," she agreed, amicably. "Is Bramley in?"

"I'll see," he replied and shut the door.

Jilly sighed and sat down on one of the two worn rattan chairs that stood to the left of the door, her package bundled on her knee. A black and orange cat regarded her incuriously from the seat of the other chair, then turned to watch the progress of a woman walking her dachshund down the street.

Professor Dapple still taught a few classes at Butler U., but he wasn't nearly as involved with the curriculum as he had been when Jilly attended the university. There'd been some kind of a scandal— something about a Bishop, some old coins and the daughter of a Tarot reader—but Jilly had never quite got the story straight. The Professor was a jolly fellow— wizened like an old apple, but more active than many who were only half his apparent sixty years of age. He could talk and joke all night, incessantly polishing his wire-rimmed spectacles for which he didn't even have a prescription.

What he was doing with someone like Olaf Goonasekara as a house-keeper Jilly didn't know. It was true that Goon looked comical enough, what with his protruding stomach and puffed cheeks, the halo of unruly hair and his thin little arms and legs, reminding her of nothing so much as a pumpkin with twig limbs, or a monkey. His usual striped trousers, organ grinder's jacket and the little green and yellow cap he liked to wear, didn't help. Nor did the fact that he was barely four feet tall and that the Professor claimed he was a goblin and just called him Goon.

It didn't seem to allow Goon much dignity and Jilly would have understood his grumpiness, if she didn't know that he himself insisted on being called Goon and his wardrobe was entirely of his own choosing. Bramley hated Goon's sense of fashion—or rather, his lack thereof.

The door was flung open again and Jilly stood up to find Goon glowering at her once more.

"He's in," he said.

Jilly smiled. As if he'd actually had to go in and check.

They both stood there, Jilly on the porch and he in the doorway, until Jilly finally asked, "Can he see me?"

Giving an exaggerated sigh, Goon stepped aside to let her in.

"I suppose you'll want something to drink?" he asked as he followed her to the door of the Professor's study.

"Tea would be lovely."

"Hrumph."

Jilly watched him stalk off, then tapped a knuckle on the study's door and stepped into the room. Bramley lifted his gaze from a desk littered with tottering stacks of books and papers and grinned at her from between a gap in the towers of paper.

"I've been doing some research since you called," he said. He poked a finger at a book that Jilly couldn't see, then began to clean his glasses. "Fascinating stuff."

"And hello to you, too," Jilly said.

"Yes, of course. Did you know that the Kickaha had legends of a little people long before the Europeans ever settled this area?"

Jilly could never quite get used to Bramley's habit of starting conversations in the middle. She removed some magazines from a club chair and perched on the edge of its seat, her package clutched to her chest.

"What's that got to do with anything?" she asked.

Bramley looked surprised. "Why everything. We *are* still looking into the origins of this artifact of yours, aren't we?"

Jilly nodded. From her new position of vantage she could make out the book he'd been reading. *Underhill and Deeper Still*, a short story collection by Christy Riddell. Riddell made a living of retelling the odd stories that lie just under the skin of any large city. This particular one was a collection of urban legends of Old City and other subterranean fancies—not exactly the factual reference source she'd been hoping for.

Old City was real enough; that was where she'd found the drum this afternoon. But as for the rest of it—albino crocodile subway conductors, schools of dog-sized intelligent goldfish in the sewers, mutant rat debating societies and the like...

Old City was the original heart of Newford. It lay deep underneath the subway tunnels—dropped there in the late eighteen hundreds during the Great Quake. The present city, including its sewers and underground transportation tunnels, had been built above the ruins of the old one. There'd been talk in the early seventies of renovating the ruins as a tourist attraction—as had been done in Seattle—but Old City lay too far underground for easy access. After numerous studies on the project, the city council had decided that it simply wouldn't be cost efficient.

With that decision. Old City had rapidly gone from a potential tourist attraction to a home for skells—winos, bagladies and the other homeless. Not to mention, if one was to believe Bramley and Riddell, bands of ill-mannered goblin-like creatures that Riddell called skookin—a word he'd stolen from old Scots which meant, variously, ugly, furtive and sullen.

Which, Jilly realized once when she thought about it, made it entirely appropriate that Bramley should claim Goon was related to them.

"You're not going to tell me it's a skookin artifact are you?" she asked Bramley now.

"Too soon to say," he replied. He nodded at her parcel. "Can I see it?"

Jilly got up and brought it over to the desk where Bramley made a great show of cutting the twine and unwrapping the paper. Jilly couldn't decide if he was pretending it was the unveiling of a new piece at the museum or his birthday. But then the drum was sitting on the desk, the mica and quartz veins in its stone catching the light from Bramley's desk lamp in a magical glitter, and she was swallowed up in the wonder of it again.

It was tube-shaped, standing about a foot high, with a seven inch diameter at the top and five inches at the bottom. The top was smooth as the skin head of a drum. On the sides were what appeared to be the remnants of a bewildering flurry of designs. But what was most marvelous about it was that the stone was hollow. It weighed about the same as a fat hardcover book.

"Listen," Jilly said and gave the top of the drum a rap-a-tap- tap.

The stone responded with a quiet rhythm that resonated eerily in the study. Unfortunately, Goon chose that moment to arrive in the doorway with a tray laden with tea mugs, teapot and a platter of his homemade biscuits. At the sound of the drum, the tray fell from his hands. It hit the floor with a crash, spraying tea, milk, sugar, biscuits and bits of crockery every which way.

Jilly turned, her heartbeat double-timing in her chest, just in time to see an indescribable look cross over Goon's features. It might have been surprise, it might have been laughter, but it was gone too quickly for her to properly note. He merely stood in the doorway now, his usual glowering look on his face, and all Jilly was left with was a feeling of unaccountable guilt.

"I didn't mean..." Jilly began, but her voice trailed off.

"Bit of a mess," Bramley said.

"I'll get right to it," Goon said.

His small dark eyes centered their gaze on Jilly for too long a moment, then he turned away to fetch a broom and dustpan. When Jilly turned back to the desk, she found Bramley rubbing his hands together, face pressed close to the stone drum. He looked up at her over his glasses, grinning.

"Did you see?" he said. "Goon recognized it for what it is, straight off. It has to be a skookin artifact. Didn't like you meddling around with it either."

That was hardly the conclusion that Jilly would have come to on her own. It was the sudden and unexpected sound that had more than likely startled Goon—as it might have startled anyone who wasn't expecting it. That was the reasonable explanation, but she knew well enough that reasonable didn't necessarily always mean right. When she thought of that look that had passed over Goon's features, like a trough of surprise or mocking humour between two cresting glowers, she didn't know what to think, so she let herself get taken away by the Professor's enthusiasm, because...well, just what if...?

By all of Christy Riddell's accounts, there wasn't a better candidate for skookin-dom than Bramley's housekeeper.

"What does it mean?" she asked.

Bramley shrugged and began to polish his glasses. Jilly was about to nudge him into making at least the pretense of a theory, but then she realized that the Professor had simply fallen silent because Goon was back to clean up the mess. She waited until Goon had made his retreat with the promise of putting on another pot of tea, before she leaned over Bramley's desk.

"Well?" she asked.

"Found it in Old City, did you?" he replied.

Jilly nodded.

"You know what they say about skookin treasure...?"

"They" meaning he and Riddell, Jilly thought, but she obligingly tried to remember that particular story from *Underhill and Deeper Still*. She had it after a moment. It was the one called "The Man With the Monkey" and had something to do with a stolen apple that was withered and moldy in Old City but became solid gold when it was brought above ground. At the end of the story, the man who'd stolen it from the skookin was found in little pieces scattered all over Fitzhenry Park...

Jilly shivered.

"Now I remember why I don't always like to read Christy's stuff," she said. "He can be so sweet on one page, and then on the next he's taking you on a tour through an abattoir."

"Just like life," Bramley said.

"Wonderful. So what are you saying?"

"They'll be wanting it back," Bramley said.

➤ ⲩ ◄

Jilly woke some time after midnight with the Professor's words ringing in her ears.

They'll be wanting it back.

She glanced at the stone drum where it sat on a crate by the window of her Yoors Street loft in Foxville. From where she lay on her Murphy bed, the streetlights coming in the window woke a haloing effect around the stone artifact. The drum glimmered with magic—or at least with a potential for magic. And there was something else in the air. A humming sound, like barely audible strains of music. The notes seemed disconnected, drifting randomly through the melody like dust motes dancing in a beam of sunlight, but there was still a melody present.

She sat up slowly. Pushing the quilt aside, she padded barefoot across the room. When she reached the drum, the change in perspective made the streetlight halo slide away; the drum's magic fled. It was just an odd stone artifact once more. She ran her finger along the smoothed indentations that covered the sides of the artifact, but didn't touch the top. It was still marvelous enough—a hollow stone, a mystery, a puzzle. But...

She remembered the odd almost-but-not-quite music she'd heard when she first woke and cocked her ear, listening for it.

Nothing.

Outside, a light drizzle had wet the pavement, making Yoors Street glisten and sparkle with its sheen. She knelt down by the windowsill and leaned forward, looking out, feeling lonely. It'd be nice if Geordie were here, even if his brother did write those books that had the Professor so enamoured, but Geordie was out of town this week. Maybe she should get a cat or a dog—just something to keep her company when she got into one of these odd funks—but the problem with pets was that they tied you down. No more gallivanting about whenever and wherever you pleased. Not when the cat needed to be fed. Or the dog had to be walked.

Sighing, she started to turn from the window, then paused. A flicker of uneasiness stole up her spine as she looked more closely at what had caught her attention—there, across the street. Time dissolved into a pattern as random as that faint music she'd heard when she woke earlier. Minutes and seconds marched sideways; the hands of the old Coors clock on her wall stood still.

A figure leaned against the wall, there, just to one side of the display window of the Chinese grocerteria across the street, a figure as much a patchwork as the disarray in the shop's window. Pumpkin head under a wide-brimmed hat. A larger pumpkin for the body with what looked like straw spilling out from between the buttons of its too-small jacket. Arms and legs as thin as broom handles. A wide slit for a mouth; eyes like the sharp yellow slits of a Jack o'Lantern with a candle burning inside.

A Halloween creature. And not alone.

There was another, there, in the mouth of that alleyway. A third clinging to the wall of the brownstone beside the grocerteria. Four more on the rooftop directly across the street—pumpkinheads lined up along the parapet, all in a row.

Skookin, Jilly thought and she shivered with fear, remembering Christy's story.

Damn Christy for tracking that story down, and damn the Professor for reminding her of it. And damn the job that had sent her down into Old City in the first place to take photos for the background of the painting she was currently working on.

Because there shouldn't be any such thing as skookin. Because...

She blinked, then rubbed her eyes. Her gaze darted left and right, up and down, raking the street and the faces of buildings across the way.

Nothing.

No pumpkin goblins watching her loft.

The sound of her clock ticking the seconds away was suddenly loud in her ears. A taxi went by on the street below, spraying a fine sheet of water from its wheels. She waited for it to pass, then studied the street again.

There were no skookin.

Of course there wouldn't be, she told herself, trying to laugh at how she'd let her imagination run away with itself, but she couldn't muster up even the first hint of a smile. She looked at the drum, reached a hand towards it, then let her hand fall to her lap, the drum untouched. She turned her attention back to the street, watching it for long moments before she finally had to accept that there was nothing out there, that she had only peopled it with her own night fears.

Pushing herself up from the sill, she returned to bed and lay down again. The palm of her right hand itched a little, right where she'd managed to poke herself on a small nail or wood sliver while she was down in Old City. She scratched her hand and stared up at the ceiling, trying to go to sleep, but not expecting to have much luck. Surprisingly, she drifted off in moments.

And dreamed.

Of Bramley's study. Except the Professor wasn't ensconced behind his desk as usual. Instead, he was setting out a serving of tea for her and Goon who had taken the Professor's place behind the tottering stacks of papers and books on the desk.

"Skookin," Goon said, when the Professor had finished serving them their tea and left the room. "They've never existed, of course."

Jilly nodded in agreement.

"Though in some ways," Goon went on, "they've always existed. In here—" He tapped his temple with a gnarly, very skookin-like finger. "In our imaginations."

"But—" Jilly began, wanting to tell him how she'd seen skookin, right out there on her very own street tonight, but Goon wasn't finished.

"And that's what makes them real," he said.

His head suddenly looked very much like a pumpkin. He leaned forward, eyes glittering as though a candle was burning there inside his head, flickering in the wind.

"And if they're real," he said.

His voice wound down alarmingly, as though it came from the spiraling groove of a spoken word album that someone had slowed by dragging their finger along on the vinyl.

"Then. You're. In. A. Lot. Of—"

Jilly awoke with a start to find herself backed up against the frame of the head of her bed, her hands worrying and tangling her quilt into knots.

Just a dream. Cast off thoughts, tossed up by her subconscious. Nothing to worry about. Except...

She could finish the dream-Goon's statement.

If they were real...

Never mind being in trouble. If they were real, then she was doomed.

She didn't get any more sleep that night, and first thing the next morning, she went looking for help.

⤙ ⲑ ⤚

"Skookin," Meran said, trying hard not to laugh.

"Oh, I know what it sounds like," Jilly said, "but what can you do? Christy's books are Bramley's pet blind spot and if you listen to him long enough, he'll have you believing anything."

"But skookin," Meran repeated and this time she did giggle.

Jilly couldn't help but laugh with her.

Everything felt very different in the morning light—especially when she had someone to talk it over with whose head wasn't filled with Christy's stories.

They were sitting in Kathryn's Cafe—an hour or so after Jilly had found Meran Kelledy down by the Lake, sitting on the Pier and watching the early morning joggers run across the sand—yuppies from downtown, health-conscious gentry from the Beaches.

It was a short walk up Battersfield Road to where Kathryn's was nestled in the heart of Lower Crowsea. Like the area itself, with its narrow streets and old stone buildings, the cafe had an old world feel about it—from the dark wood paneling and hand-carved chair backs to the small round tables, with checkered tablecloths, fat glass condiment containers and straw-wrapped wine bottles used as candleholders. The music piped in over the house sound system was mostly along the lines of Telemann and Vivaldi, Kitaro and old Bob James albums. The waitresses wore cream-coloured pinafores over flowerprint dresses.

But if the atmosphere was old world, the clientele were definitely contemporary. Situated so close to Butler U., Kathryn's had been a favorite haunt of the university's students since it first opened its doors in the mid-sixties as a coffee house. Though much had changed from those early days, there was still music played on its small stage on Friday and Saturday nights, as well as poetry recitations on Wednesdays, and Sunday morning storytelling sessions.

Jilly and Meran sat by a window, coffee and homemade banana muffins set out on the table in front of them.

"Whatever were you *doing* down there anyway?" Meran asked. "It's not exactly the safest place to be wandering about."

Jilly nodded. The skells in Old City weren't all thin and wasted. Some were big and mean-looking, capable of anything—not really the sort of people Jilly should be around, because if something went wrong...well, she was the kind of woman for whom the word petite had been coined. She was small and slender—her tiny size only accentuated by the oversized clothing she tended to wear. Her brown hair was a thick tangle, her eyes the electric blue of sapphires.

She was too pretty and too small to be wandering about in places like Old City on her own.

"You know the band, No Nuns Here?" Jilly asked.

Meran nodded.

"I'm doing the cover painting for their first album," Jilly explained. "They wanted something moody for the background—sort of like the Tombs, but darker and grimmer—and I thought Old City would be the perfect place to get some reference shots."

"But to go there on your own..."

Jilly just shrugged. She was known to wander anywhere and everywhere, at any time of the night or day, camera or sketchbook in hand, often both.

Meran shook her head. Like most of Jilly's friends, she'd long since given up trying to point out the dangers of carrying on the way Jilly did.

"So you found this drum," she said.

Jilly nodded. She looked down at the little scab on the palm of her hand. It itched like crazy, but she was determined not to open it again by scratching it.

"And now you want to...?"

Jilly looked up. "Take it back. Only I'm scared to go there on my own. I thought maybe Cerin would come with me—for moral support, you know?"

"He's out of town," Meran said.

Meran and her husband made up the two halves of the Kelledys, a local traditional music duo that played coffee houses, festivals and colleges from one coast to the other. For years now, however, Newford had been their home base.

"He's teaching another of those harp workshops," Meran added.

Jilly did her best to hide her disappointment.

What she'd told Meran about "moral support" was only partly the reason she'd wanted their help because, more so than either Christy's stories, or Bramley's askewed theories, the Kelledys were the closest thing to real magic that she could think of in Newford. There was an otherwordly air about the two of them that went beyond the glamour that seemed to always gather around people who became successful in their creative endeavours.

It wasn't something Jilly could put her finger on. It wasn't as though they went on and on about this sort of thing at the drop of a hat the way that Bramley did. Nor that they were responsible for anything more mysterious than the enchantment they awoke on stage when they were playing their instruments. It was just there. Something that gave the impression that they were aware of what lay beyond the here and now. That they could see things others couldn't; knew things that remained secret to anyone else.

Nobody even knew where they had come from; they'd just arrived in Newford a few years ago, speaking with accents that had rapidly vanished, and here they'd pretty well stayed ever since. Jilly had always privately supposed that if there was a place called Faerie, then that was from where they'd come, so when she woke up this morning, deciding she needed magical help, she'd gone looking for one or the other and found Meran. But now...

"Oh," she said.

Meran smiled.

"But that doesn't mean I can't try to help," she said.

Jilly sighed. Help with what? she had to ask herself. The more she thought about it, the sillier it all seemed. Skookin. Right. Maybe they held debating contests with Christy's mutant rats.

"I think maybe I'm nuts," she said finally. "I mean, goblins living under the city...?"

"I believe in the little people," Meran said. "We called them bodachs where I come from."

Jilly just looked at her.

"But you laughed when I talked about them," she said finally.

"I know—and I shouldn't have. It's just that whenever I hear that name that Christy's given them, I can't help myself. It's so silly."

"What I saw last night didn't feel silly," Jilly said.

If she'd actually seen anything. By this point—even with Meran's apparent belief—she wasn't sure what to think anymore.

"No," Meran said. "I suppose not. But—you're taking the drum back, so why are you so nervous?"

"The man in Christy's story returned the apple he stole," Jilly said, "and you know what happened to him..."

"That's true," Meran said, frowning.

"I thought maybe Cerin could..." Jilly's voice trailed off.

A small smile touched Meran's lips. "Could do what?"

"Well, this is going to sound even sillier," Jilly admitted, "but I've always pictured him as sort of a wizard type."

Meran laughed. "He'd love to hear that. And what about me? Have I acquired wizardly status as well?"

"Not exactly. You always struck me as being an earth spirit—like you stepped out of an oak tree or something." Jilly blushed, feeling as though she was making even more of a fool of herself than ever, but now that she'd started, she felt she had to finish. "It's sort of like he learned magic, while you just are magic."

She glanced at her companion, looking for laughter, but Meran was regarding her gravely. And she did look like dryad, Jilly thought, what with the green streaks in the long, nut-brown ringlets of her hair and her fey sort of Pre-Raphaelite beauty. Her eyes seemed to provide their own light, rather than take it in.

"Maybe I did step out of a tree one day," Meran said.

Jilly could feel her mouth forming a surprised "O", but then Meran laughed again.

"But probably I didn't," she said. Before Jilly could ask her about that "probably," Meran went on: "We'll need some sort of protection against them."

Jilly made her mind shift gears, from Meran's origins to the problem at hand.

"Like holy water or a cross?" she asked.

Her head filled with the plots of a hundred bad horror films, each of them clamoring for attention.

"No," Meran said. "Religious artifacts and trappings require faith—a belief in their potency that the skookin undoubtedly don't have. The only thing I know for certain that they can't abide is the truth."

"The truth?"

Meran nodded. "Tell them the truth—even if it's only historical facts and trivia—and they'll shun you as though you were carrying a plague."

"But what about after?" Jilly said. "After we've delivered the drum and they come looking for me? Do I have to walk around carrying a cassette machine spouting dates and facts for the rest of my life?"

"I hope not."

"But—"

"Patience," Meran replied. "Let me think about it for awhile."

Jilly sighed. She regarded her companion curiously as Meran took a sip of her coffee.

"You really believe in this stuff, don't you?" she said finally.

"Don't you?"

Jilly had to think about that for a moment.

"Last night I was scared," she said, "and I'm returning the drum because I'd rather be safe than sorry, but I'm still not sure."

Meran nodded understandingly, but, "Your coffee's getting cold," was all she had to say.

► ⋎ ◄

Meran let Jilly stay with her that night in the rambling old house where she and Cerin lived. Straddling the border between Lower Crowsea and Chinatown, it was a tall, gabled building surrounded by giant oak trees. There was a rounded tower in the front, to the right of a long screen-enclosed porch, stables around the back and a garden along the west side of the house that seemed to have been plucked straight from a postcard of the English countryside.

Jilly loved this area. The Kelledys' house was the easternmost of the stately estates that stood, row on row, along McKennitt Street, between Lee and Yoors. Whenever Jilly walked along this part of McKennitt, late at night when the streetcars were tucked away in their downtown station and there was next to no other traffic, she found it easy to imagine that the years had wound back to a bygone age when time moved at a different pace, when Newford's streets were cobblestoned and the vehicles that traversed them were horse-drawn, rather than horse-powered.

"You'll wear a hole in the glass if you keep staring through it so intently."

Jilly started. She turned long enough to acknowledge her hostess's presence, then her gaze was dragged back to the window, to the shadows cast by the oaks as twilight stretched them across the lawn, to the long low wall that bordered the lawn, to the street beyond.

Still no skookin. Did that mean they didn't exist, or that they hadn't come out yet? Or maybe they just hadn't tracked her here to the Kelledys' house.

She started again as Meran laid a hand on her shoulder and gently turned her from the window.

"Who knows what you'll call to us, staring so," Meran said.

Her voice held the same light tone as it had when she'd made her earlier comment, but this time a certain sense of caution lay behind the words.

"If they come, I want to see them," Jilly said.

Meran nodded. "I understand. But remember this: the night's a magical time. The moon rules her hours, not the sun."

"What does that mean?"

"The moon likes secrets," Meran said. "And secret things. She lets mysteries bleed into her shadows and leaves us to ask whether they originated from otherworlds, or from our own imaginations."

"You're beginning to sound like Bramley," Jilly said. "Or Christy."

"Remember your Shakespeare," Meran said. "'This fellow's wise enough to play the fool'. Did you ever think that perhaps their studied eccentricity protects them from sharper ridicule?"

"You mean all those things Christy writes about are true?"

"I didn't say that."

Jilly shook her head. "No. But you're talking in riddles just like a wizard out of some fairy tale. I never understood why they couldn't talk plainly."

"That's because some things can only be approached from the side. Secretively. Peripherally."

Whatever Jilly was about to say next, died stillborn. She pointed out the window to where the lawn was almost swallowed by shadows.

"Do..." She swallowed thickly, then tried again. "Do you see them?"

They were out there, flitting between the wall that bordered the Kelledys' property and those tall oaks that stood closer to the house. Shadow shapes. Fat, pumpkin-bodied and twig-limbed. There were more of them than there'd been last night. And they were bolder. Creeping right up towards the house. Threats burning in their candle-flicker eyes. Wide mouths open in Jack o'Lantern grins, revealing rows of pointed teeth.

One came sidling right up to the window, its face monstrous at such close proximity. Jilly couldn't move, couldn't even breathe. She remembered what Meran had said earlier—

they can't abide the truth

—but she couldn't frame a sentence, never mind a word, and her mind was filled with only a wild unreasoning panic. The creature reached out a hand towards the glass, clawed fingers extended. Jilly could feel a scream building up, deep inside her. In a moment that hand would come crashing through the window, shattering glass, clawing at her throat. And she couldn't move. All she could do was stare, stare as the claws reached for the glass, stare as it drew back to—

Something fell between the creature and the house—a swooping, shapeless thing. The creature danced back, saw that it was only the bough of one of the oak trees and was about to begin its approach once more, but the cries of its companions distracted it. Not until it turned its horrible gaze from her, did Jilly feel able to lift her own head.

She stared at the oaks. A sudden wind had sprung up, lashing the boughs about so that the tall trees appeared to be giants, flailing about their many-limbed arms like monstrous, agitated octopi. The creatures in the yard scattered and in moments they were gone—each and every one of them. The wind died down; the animated giants became just oak trees once more.

Jilly turned slowly from the window to find Meran pressed close beside her.

"Ugly, furtive and sullen," Meran said. "Perhaps Christy wasn't so far off in naming them."

"They...they're real, aren't they?" Jilly asked in a small voice.

Meran nodded. "And not at all like the bodachs of my homeland. Bodachs are mischievous and prone to trouble, but not like this. Those creatures were weaned on malevolence."

Jilly leaned weakly against the windowsill.

"What are we going to do?" she asked.

She scratched at her palm—the itch was worse than ever. Meran caught her hand, pulled it away. There was an unhappy look in her eyes when she lifted her gaze from the mark on Jilly's palm.

"Where did you get that?" she asked.

Jilly looked down at her palm. The scab was gone, but the skin was all dark around the puncture wound now—an ugly black discolouration that was twice the size of the original scab.

"I scratched myself," she said. "Down in Old City."

Meran shook her head. "No," she said. "They've marked you. "

Jilly suddenly felt weak. Skookin were real. Mysterious winds rose to animate trees. And now she was marked?

She wasn't even sure what that meant, but she didn't like the sound of it. Not for a moment.

Her gaze went to the stone drum where it stood on Meran's mantel. She didn't think she'd ever hated an inanimate object so much before.

"Marked...me...?" she asked.

"I've heard of this before," Meran said, her voice apologetic. She touched the mark on Jilly's palm. "This is like a...bounty."

"They really want to kill me, don't they?"

Jilly was surprised that her voice sounded as calm as it did. Inside she felt as though she was crumbling to little bits all over the place.

"Skookin are real," she went on, "and they're going to tear me up into little pieces—just like they did to the man in Christy's stupid story."

Meran gave her a sympathetic look.

"We have to go now," she said. "We have to go and confront them now, before..."

"Before what?"

Jilly's control over her voice was slipping. Her last word went shrieking up in pitch.

"Before they send something worse," Meran said.

Oh great, Jilly thought as she waited for Meran to change into clothing more suitable for the underground trek to Old City. Not only were skookin real, but there were worse things than those pumpkinhead creatures living down there under the city.

She slouched in one of the chairs by the mantelpiece, her back to the stone drum, and pretended that her nerves weren't all scraped raw, that she was just over visiting a friend for the evening and everything was just peachy, thank you. Surprisingly, by the time Meran returned, wearing jeans, sturdy walking shoes and a thick woolen shirt under a denim jacket, she did feel better.

"The bit with the trees," she asked as she rose from her chair. "Did you do that?"

Meran shook her head.

"But the wind likes me," she said. "Maybe it's because I play the flute."

And maybe its because you're a dryad, Jilly thought, and the wind's got a thing about oak trees, but she let the thought go unspoken.

Meran fetched the long, narrow bag that held her flute and slung it over her shoulder.

"Ready?" she asked.

"No," Jilly said.

But she went and took the drum from the mantelpiece and joined Meran by the front door. Meran stuck a flashlight in the pocket of her jacket and handed another to Jilly who thrust it into the pocket of the coat Meran was lending her. It was at least two sizes too big for her, which suited Jilly just fine.

Naturally, just to make the night complete, it started to rain before they got halfway down the walkway to McKennitt Street.

＞ Υ ＜

For safety's sake, city work crews had sealed up all the entrances to Old City in the mid-seventies—all the entrances of which the city was aware, at any rate. The street people of Newford's back lanes and alleys knew of anywhere from a half-dozen to twenty others that could still be used, the number depending only on who was doing the bragging. The entrance to which Jilly led Meran was the mostly commonly known and used—a steel maintenance door that was situated two hundred yards or so down the east tracks of the Grasso Street subway station.

The door led into the city's sewer maintenance tunnels, but had long since been abandoned. Skells had broken the locking mechanism and the door stood continually ajar. Inside, time and weathering had worn down a connecting wall between the maintenance tunnels and what had once been the top floor of one of Old City's proud skyscrapers— an office complex that had towered some four stories above the city's streets before the quake dropped it into its present subterranean setting.

It was a good fifteen minute walk from the Kelledys' house to the Grasso Street station and Jilly plodded miserably through the rain at Meran's side for every block of it. Her sneakers were soaked and her hair plastered against her scalp. She carried the stone drum tucked under one arm and was very tempted to simply pitch it in front of a bus.

"This is crazy," Jilly said. "We're just giving ourselves up to them."

Meran shook her head. "No. We're confronting them of our own free will—there's a difference."

"That's just semantics. There won't be a difference in the results."

"That's where you're wrong."

They both turned at the sound of a new voice to find Goon standing in the doorway of a closed antique shop. His eyes glittered oddly in the poor light, reminding Jilly all too much of the skookin, and he didn't seem to be the least bit wet.

"What are you doing here?" Jilly demanded.

"You must always confront your fears," Goon said as though she hadn't spoke. "Then skulking monsters become merely unfamiliar shadows, thrown by a tree bough. Whispering voices are just the wind. The wild flare of panic is merely a burst of emotion, not a terror spell cast by some evil witch."

Meran nodded. "That's what Cerin would say. And that's what I mean to do. Confront them with a truth so bright that they won't dare come near us again."

Jilly held up her hand. The discolouration was spreading. It had grown from its pinprick inception, first to the size of a dime, now to that of a silver dollar.

"What about this?" she asked.

"There's always a price for meddling," Goon agreed. "Sometimes it's the simple curse of knowledge."

"There's always a price," Meran agreed.

Everybody always seemed to know more than she did these days, Jilly thought unhappily.

"You still haven't told me what you're doing here," she told Goon. "Skulking about and following us."

Goon smiled. "It seems to me, that you came upon me."

"You know what I mean."

"I have my own business in Old City tonight," he said. "And since we all have the same destination in mind, I thought perhaps you would appreciate the company."

Everything was wrong about this, Jilly thought. Goon was never nice to her. Goon was never nice to anyone.

"Yeah, well, you can just—" she began.

Meran laid a hand on Jilly's arm. "It's bad luck to turn away help when it's freely offered."

"But you don't know what he's like," Jilly said.

"Olaf and I have met before," Meran said.

Jilly caught the grimace on Goon's face at the use of his given name. It made him seem more himself, which, while not exactly comforting, was at least familiar. Then she looked at Meran. She thought of the wind outside the musician's house, driving away the skookin, the mystery that cloaked her which ran even deeper, perhaps, than that which Goon wore so easily...

"Sometimes you just have to trust in people," Meran said, as though reading Jilly's mind.

Jilly sighed. She rubbed her itchy palm against her thigh, shifted the drum into a more comfortable position.

"Okay," she said. "So what're we waiting for?"

► Υ ◄

The few times Jilly had come down to Old City, she'd been cautious, perhaps even a little nervous, but never frightened. Tonight was different. It was always dark in Old City, but the darkness had never seemed so...so watchful before. There were always odd little sounds, but they had never seemed so furtive. Even with her companions—maybe because of them, she thought, thinking mostly of Goon—she felt very much alone in the eerie darkness.

Goon didn't appear to need the wobbly light of their flashlights to see his way and though he seemed content enough to simply follow them,

Jilly couldn't shake the feeling that he was actually leading the way. They were soon in a part of the subterranean city that she'd never seen before.

There was less dust and dirt here. No litter, nor the remains of the skells' fires. No broken bottles, nor the piles of newspapers and ratty blanketing that served the skells as bedding. The buildings seemed in better repair. The air had a clean, dry smell to it, rather than the close, musty reek of refuse and human wastes that it carried closer to the entrance.

And there were no people.

From when they'd first stepped through the steel door in Grasso Street station's east tunnel, she hadn't seen a baglady or wino or any kind of skell, and that in itself was odd because they were always down here. But there was something sharing the darkness with them. Something watched them, marked their progress, followed with a barely discernible pad of sly footsteps in their wake and on either side.

The drum seemed warm against the skin of her hand. The blemish on her other palm prickled with itchiness. Her shoulder muscles were stiff with tension.

"Not far now," Goon said softly and Jilly suddenly understood what it meant to jump out of one's skin.

The beam of her flashlight made a wild arc across the faces of the buildings on either side of her as she started. Her heartbeat jumped into second gear.

"What do you see?" Meran asked, her voice calm.

The beam of her flashlight turned towards Goon and he pointed ahead.

"Turn off your flashlights," he said.

Oh sure, Jilly thought. Easy for you to say.

But she did so a moment after Meran had. The sudden darkness was so abrupt, that Jilly thought she'd gone blind. But then she realized that it wasn't as black as it should be. Looking ahead to where Goon had pointed, she could see a faint glow seeping onto the street ahead of them. It was a little less than a half block away, the source of the light hidden behind the squatting bulk of a half-tumbled down building.

"What could it...?" Jilly started to say, but then the sounds began, and the rest of her words dried up in her throat.

It was supposed to be music, she realized after a few moments, but there was no discernible rhythm and while the sounds were blown or rasped or plucked from instruments, they searched in vain for a melody.

"It begins," Goon said.

He took the lead, hurrying them up to the corner of the street.

"What does?" Jilly wanted to know.

"The king appears—as he must once a moon. It's that or lose his throne."

Jilly wanted to know what he was talking about—better yet, *how* he knew what he was talking about—but she didn't have a chance. The discordant not-music scraped and squealed to a kind of crescendo. Suddenly they were surrounded by the capering forms of dozens of skookin that bumped them, thin long fingers tugging at their clothing. Jilly shrieked at the first touch. One of them tried to snatch the drum from her grip. She regained control of her nerves at the same time as she pulled the artifact free from the grasping fingers.

"1789," she said. "That's when the Bastille was stormed and the French Revolution began. Uh, 1807, slave trade was abolished in the British Empire. 1776, the Declaration of Independence was signed."

The skookin backed away from her, as did the others, hissing and spitting. The not-music continued, but its tones were softened.

"Let me see," Jilly went on. "Uh, 1981, the Argentines invade—I can't keep this up, Meran—the Falklands. 1715...that was the year of the first Jacobite uprising."

She'd always been good with historical trivia—having a head for dates—but the more she concentrated on them right now, the further they seemed to slip away. The skookin were regarding her with malevolence, just waiting for her to falter.

"1978," she said. "Sandy Denny died, falling down some stairs..."

She'd got that one from Geordie. The skookin took another step back and she stepped towards them, into the light, her eyes widening with shock. There was a small park there, vegetation dead, trees leafless and skeletal, shadows dancing from the light cast by a fire at either end of the open space. And it was teeming with skookin.

There seemed to be hundreds of the creatures. She could see some of the musicians who were making that awful din—holding their instruments as though they'd never played them before. They were gathered in a semi-circle around a dais made from slabs of pavement and building rubble. Standing on it, was the weirdest looking skookin she'd seen yet. He was kind of withered and stood stiffly. His eyes flashed with a dead, cold light. He had the grimmest look about him that she'd seen on any of them yet.

There was no way her little bits of history were going to be enough to keep back this crew. She turned to look at her companions. She couldn't see Goon, but Meran was tugging her flute free from its carrying bag.

What good was that going to do? Jilly wondered.

"It's another kind of truth," Meran said as she brought the instrument up to her lips.

The flute's clear tones echoed breathily along the street, cutting through the jangle of not-music like a glass knife through muddy water. Jilly held her breath. The music was so beautiful. The skookin cowered where they stood. Their cacophonic noise-making faltered, then fell silent.

No one moved.

For long moments, there was just the clear sound of Meran's flute, breathing a slow plaintive air that echoed and sang down the street, winding from one end of the park to the other.

Another kind of truth, Jilly remembered Meran saying just before she began to play. That's exactly what this music was, she realized. A kind of truth.

The flute playing finally came to an achingly sweet finale and a hush fell in Old City. And then there was movement. Goon stepped from behind Jilly and walked through the still crowd of skookin to the dais where their king stood. He clambered up over the rubble until he was beside the king. He pulled a large clasp knife from the pocket of his coat. As he opened the blade, the skookin king made a jerky motion to get away, but Goon's knife hand moved to quickly.

He slashed and cut.

Now he's bloody done it, Jilly thought as the skookin king tumbled to the stones. But then she realized that Goon hadn't cut the king. He'd cut the air above the king. He'd cut the...the realization only confused her more...strings holding him?

"What...?" she said.

"Come," Meran said.

She tucked her flute under her arm and led Jilly towards the dais.

"This is your king," Goon was saying.

He reached down and pulled the limp form up by the fine-webbed strings that were attached to the king's arms and shoulders. The king dangled loosely under his strong grip—a broken marionette. A murmur rose from the crowd of skookin—part ugly, part wondering.

"The king is dead," Goon said. "He's been dead for moons. I wondered why Old City was closed to me this past half year, and now I know."

There was movement at the far end of the park—a fleeing figure. It had been the king's councilor, Goon told Jilly and Meran later. Some of the skookin made to chase him, but Goon called them back.

"Let him go," he said. "He won't return. We have other business at hand."

Meran had drawn Jilly right up to the foot of the dais and was gently pushing her forward.

"Go on," she said.

"Is he the king now?" Jilly asked.

Meran smiled and gave her another gentle push.

Jilly looked up. Goon seemed just like he always did when she saw him at Bramley's—grumpy and out of sorts. Maybe it's just his face, she told herself, trying to give herself courage. There's people who look grumpy no matter how happy they are. But the thought didn't help contain her shaking much as she slowly made her way up to where Goon stood.

"You have something of ours," Goon said.

His voice was grim. Christy's story lay all too clearly in Jilly's head. She swallowed dryly.

"Uh, I never meant..." she began, then simply handed over the drum.

Goon took it reverently, then snatched her other hand before she could draw away. Her palm flared with sharp pain—all the skin, from the base of her hand to the ends of her fingers was black.

The curse, she thought. It's going to make my hand fall right off. I'm never going to paint again...

Goon spat on her palm and the pain died as though it had never been. With wondering eyes, Jilly watched the blackness dry up and begin to flake away. Goon gave her hand a shake and the blemish scattered to fall to the ground. Her hand was completely unmarked.

"But...the curse," she said. "The bounty on my head. What about Christy's story...?"

"Your curse is knowledge," Goon said.

"But...?"

He turned away to face the crowd, drum in hand. As Jilly made her careful descent back to where Meran was waiting for her, Goon tapped his fingers against the head of the drum. An eerie rhythm started up—a real rhythm. When the skookin musicians began to play, they held their instruments properly and called up a sweet stately music to march across the back of the rhythm. It was a rich tapestry of sound, as different from

Meran's solo flute as sunlight is from twilight, but it held its own power. It's own magic.

Goon led the playing with the rhythm he called up from the stone drum, led the music as though he'd always led it.

"He's really the king, isn't he?" Jilly whispered to her companion.

Meran nodded.

"So then what was he doing working for Bramley?"

"I don't know," Meran replied. "I suppose a king—or a king's son—can do pretty well what he wants just so long as he comes back here once a moon to fulfill his obligation as ruler."

"Do you think he'll go back to work for Bramley?"

"I know he will," Meran replied.

Jilly looked out at the crowd of skookin. They didn't seem at all threatening anymore. They just looked like little men—comical, with their tubby bodies and round heads and their little broomstick limbs—but men all the same. She listened to the music, felt its trueness and had to ask Meran why it didn't hurt them.

"Because it's their truth," Meran replied.

"But truth's just truth," Jilly protested. "Something's either true or its not."

Meran just put her arm around Jilly's shoulder. A touch of a smile came to the corners of her mouth.

"It's time we went home," she said.

"I got off pretty lightly, didn't I?" Jilly said as they started back the way they'd come. "I mean, with the curse and all."

"Knowledge can be a terrible burden," Meran replied. "It's what some believe cast Adam and Eve from Eden."

"But that was a good thing, wasn't it?"

Meran nodded. "I think so. But it brought pain with it—pain we still feel to this day."

"I suppose."

"Come on," Meran said, as Jilly lagged a little to look back at the park.

Jilly quickened her step, but she carried the scene away with her. Goon and the stone drum. The crowd of skookin. The flickering light of their fires as it cast shadows over the Old City buildings.

And the music played on.

► ▼ ◄

Professor Dapple had listened patiently to the story he'd been told, managing to keep from interrupting through at least half of the telling. Leaning back in his chair when it was done, he took off his glasses and began to needlessly polish them.

"It's going to be very good," he said finally.

Christy Riddell grinned from the club chair where he was sitting.

"But Jilly's not going to like it," Bramley went on. "You know how she feels about your stories."

"But she's the one who told me this one," Christy said.

Bramley rearranged his features to give the impression that he'd known this all along.

"Doesn't seem like much of a curse," he said, changing tack.

Christy raised his eyebrows. "What? To know that it's all real? To have to seriously consider every time she hears about some seemingly preposterous thing, that it might very well be true? To have to keep on guard with what she says so that people won't think she's gone off the deep end?"

"Is that how people look at us?" Bramley asked.

"What do you think?" Christy replied with a laugh.

Bramley harrumphed. He fidgeted with the papers on his desk, making more of a mess of them, rather than less.

"But Goon," he said, finally coming to the heart of what bothered him with what he'd been told. "It's like some retelling of 'The King of the Cats,' isn't it? Are you really going to put that bit in?"

Christy nodded. "It's part of the story."

"I can't see Goon as a king of anything," Bramley said. "And if he *is* a king, then what's he doing still working for me?"

"Which do you think would be better," Christy asked. "To be a king below, or a man above?"

Bramley didn't have an answer for that.

1990

Ghosts of Wind and Shadow

*There may be great and undreamed of possibilities
awaiting mankind; but because of our line of descent
there are also queer limitations.*

Clarence Day,
from *This Simian World*

Tuesday and Thursday afternoons, from two to four, Meran Kelledy
gave flute lessons at the Old Firehall on Lee Street which served as Lower
Crowsea's community centre. A small room in the basement was set aside
for her at those times. The rest of the week it served as an office for the
editor of *The Crowsea Times*, the monthly community newspaper.

The room always had a bit of a damp smell about it. The walls were
bare except for two old posters: one sponsored a community rummage
sale, now long past; the other was an advertisement for a Jilly Coppercorn
one-woman show at The Green Man Gallery featuring a reproduction of
the firehall that had been taken from the artist's *In Lower Crowsea* series
of street scenes. It, too, was long out of date.

Much of the room was taken up by a sturdy oak desk. A computer sat
on its broad surface, always surrounded by a clutter of manuscripts waiting to be put on diskette, spot art, advertisements, sheets of Lettraset,
glue sticks, pens, pencils, scratch pads and the like. Its printer was relegated to an apple crate on the floor. A large cork board in easy reach of
the desk held a bewildering array of pinned-up slips of paper with almost

indecipherable notes and appointments jotted on them. Post-its laureled the frame of the cork board and the sides of the computer like festive yellow decorations. A battered metal filing cabinet held back-issues of the newspaper. On top of it was a vase with dried flowers—not so much an arrangement, as a forgotten bouquet. One week of the month, the entire desk was covered with the current issue in progress in its various stages of layout.

It was not a room that appeared conducive to music, despite the presence of two small music stands taken from their storage spot behind the filing cabinet and set out in the open space between the desk and door along with a pair of straight-backed wooden chairs, salvaged twice a week from a closet down the hall. But music has its own enchantment and the first few notes of an old tune are all that it requires to transform any site into a place of magic, even if that location is no more than a windowless office cubicle in the Old Firehall's basement.

Meran taught an old style of flute-playing. Her instrument of choice was that enduring cousin of the silver transverse orchestral flute: a simpler wooden instrument, side-blown as well, though it lacked a lip plate to help direct the airstream; keyless with only six holes. It was popularly referred to as an Irish flute since it was used for the playing of traditional Irish and Scottish dance music and the plaintive slow airs native to those same countries, but it had relatives in most countries of the world as well as in baroque orchestras.

In one form or another, it was one of the first implements created by ancient people to give voice to the mysteries that words cannot encompass, but that they had a need to express; only the drum was older.

With her last student of the day just out the door, Meran began the ritual of cleaning her instrument in preparation to packing it away and going home herself. She separated the flute into its three parts, swabbing dry the inside of each piece with a piece of soft cotton attached to a flute-rod. As she was putting instrument away in its case, she realized that there was a woman standing in the doorway, a hesitant presence, reluctant to disturb the ritual until Meran was ready to notice her.

"Mrs. Batterberry," Meran said. "I'm sorry. I didn't realize you were there."

The mother of her last student was in her late thirties, a striking, well-dressed woman whose attractiveness was undermined by an obvious lack of self-esteem.

"I hope I'm not intruding...?"

"Not at all; I'm just packing up. Please have a seat."

Meran indicated the second chair which Mrs. Batterberry's daughter had so recently vacated. The woman walked gingerly into the room and perched on the edge of the chair, handbag clutched in both hands. She looked for all the world like a bird that was ready at any moment to erupt into flight and be gone.

"How can I help you, Mrs. Batterberry?" Meran asked.

"Please, call me Anna."

"Anna it is."

Meran waited expectantly.

"I...it's about Lesli," Mrs. Batterberry finally began.

Meran nodded encouragingly. "She's doing very well. I think she has a real gift."

"Here perhaps, but...well, look at this."

Drawing a handful of folded papers from her handbag, she passed them over to Meran. There were about five sheets of neat, closely-written lines of what appeared to be a school essay. Meran recognized the handwriting as Lesli's. She read the teacher's remarks, written in red ink at the top of the first page—"Well written and imaginative, but the next time, please stick to the assigned topic"—then quickly scanned through the pages. The last two paragraphs bore rereading:

"The old gods and their magics did not dwindle away into murky memories of brownies and little fairies more at home in a Disney cartoon; rather, they changed. The coming of Christ and Christians actually freed them. They were no longer bound to people's expectations but could now become anything that they could imagine themselves to be.

"They are still here, walking among us. We just don't recognize them anymore."

Meran looked up from the paper. "It's quite evocative."

"The essay was supposed to be on one of the ethnic minorities of Newford," Mrs. Batterberry said.

"Then, to a believer in Faerie," Meran said with a smile, "Lesli's essay would seem most apropos."

"I'm sorry," Mrs. Batterberry said, "but I can't find any humour in this situation. This—" she indicated the essay "—it just makes me uncomfortable."

"No, I'm the one who's sorry," Meran said. "I didn't mean to make light of your worries, but I'm also afraid that I don't understand them."

Mrs. Batterberry looked more uncomfortable than ever. "It...it just seems so obvious. She must be involved with the occult, or drugs. Perhaps both."

"Just because of this essay?" Meran asked. She only just managed to keep the incredulity from her voice.

"Fairies and magic are all she ever talks about—or did talk about, I should say. We don't seem to have much luck communicating anymore."

Mrs. Batterberry fell silent then. Meran looked down at the essay, reading more of it as she waited for Lesli's mother to go on. After a few moments, she looked up to find Mrs. Batterberry regarding her hopefully.

Meran cleared her throat. "I'm not exactly sure why it is that you've come to me," she said finally.

"I was hoping you'd talk to her—to Lesli. She adores you. I'm sure she'd listen to you."

"And tell her what?"

"That this sort of thinking—" Mrs. Batterberry waved a hand in the general direction of the essay that Meran was holding "—is wrong."

"I'm not sure that I can—"

Before Meran could complete her sentence with "do that," Mrs. Batterberry reached over and gripped her hand.

"Please," the woman said. "I don't know where else to turn. She's going to be sixteen in a few days. Legally, she can live on her own then and I'm afraid she's just going to leave home if we can't get this settled. I won't have drugs or...or occult things in my house. But I..." Her eyes were suddenly brimming with unshed tears. "I don't want to lose her..."

She drew back. From her handbag, she fished out a handkerchief which she used to dab at her eyes.

Meran sighed. "All right," she said. "Lesli has another lesson with me on Thursday—a make-up one for having missed one last week. I'll talk to her then, but I can't promise you anything."

Mrs. Batterberry looked embarrassed, but relieved. "I'm sure you'll be able to help."

Meran had no such assurances, but Lesli's mother was already on her feet and heading for the door, forestalling any attempt Meran might have tried to muster to back out of the situation. Mrs. Batterberry paused in the doorway and looked back.

"Thank you so much," she said, and then she was gone.

Meran stared sourly at the space Mrs. Batterberry had occupied.

"Well, isn't this just wonderful," she said.

≻ Υ ≺

From Lesli's diary, entry dated October 12th:

I saw another one today! It wasn't at all the same as the one I spied on the Common last week. That one was more like a wizened little monkey, dressed up like an Arthur Rackham leprechaun. If I'd told anybody about him, they'd say that it <u>was</u> just a dressed-up monkey, but we know better, don't we?

This is just so wonderful. I've always known they were there, of course. All around. But they were just hints, things I'd see out of the corner of my eye, snatches of music or conversation that I'd hear in a park or the backyard, when no one else was around. But ever since Midsummer's Eve, I've actually been able to see them.

I feel like a birder, noting each new separate species I spot down here on your pages, but was there ever a birdwatcher that could claim to have seen the marvels I have? It's like, all of a sudden, I've finally learned how to <u>see</u>.

This one was at the Old Firehall of all places. I was having my weekly lesson with Meran - I get two this week because she was out of town last week. Anyway, we were playing my new tune - the one with the arpeggio bit in the second part that I'm supposed to be practicing but can't quite get the hang of. It's easy when Meran's playing along with me, but when I try to do it on my own, my fingers get all fumbly and I keep muddling up the middle D.

I seem to have gotten sidetracked. Where was I? Oh yes. We were playing "Touch Me If You Dare" and it really sounded nice with both of us playing. Meran just seemed to pull my playing along with hers until it got lost in her music and you couldn't tell which instrument was which, or even how many there were playing.

It was one of those perfect moments. I felt like I was in a trance or something. I had my eyes closed, but then I felt the air getting all thick. There was this weird sort of pressure on my skin, as though gravity had just doubled or something. I kept on playing, but I opened my eyes and that's when I saw her— hovering up behind Meran's shoulders.

She was the neatest thing I've ever seen - just the tiniest little faerie, ever so pretty, with gossamer wings that moved so quickly to keep her aloft that they were just a blur. They moved like a hummingbird's wings. She looked just like the faeries on a pair of earrings I got a few years ago at a stall in the Market - sort of a Mucha design and all delicate and airy. But she wasn't two dimensional or just one colour.

Her wings were like a rainbow blaze. Her hair was like honey, her skin a soft-burnished gold. She was wearing - now don't blush, diary - nothing at all on top and just a gauzy skirt that seemed to be made of little leaves that kept changing colour, now sort of pink, now mauve, now bluish.

I was so surprised that I almost dropped my flute. I didn't - wouldn't that give Mom something to yell at me for if I broke it! - but I did muddle the tune. As soon as the music faltered - just like that, as though the only thing that was keeping her in this world was that tune - she disappeared.

I didn't pay a whole lot of attention to what Meran was saying for the rest of the lesson, but I don't think she noticed. I couldn't get the faerie out of my mind. I still can't. I wish Mom had been there to see her, or stupid old Mr. Allen. They couldn't say it was just my imagination then!

Of course they probably wouldn't have been able to see her

anyway. That's the thing with magic. You've got to know it's still here, all around us, or it just stays invisible for you.

After my lesson, Mom went in to talk to Meran and made me wait in the car. She wouldn't say what they'd talked about, but she seemed to be in a way better mood than usual when she got back. God, I wish she wouldn't get so uptight.

⤙ Υ ⅄

"So," Cerin said finally, setting aside his book. Meran had been moping about the house for the whole of the hour since she'd gotten home from the Firehall. "Do you want to talk about it?"

"You'll just say I told you so."

"Told you so how?"

Meran sighed. "Oh, you know. How did you put it? 'The problem with teaching children is that you have to put up with their parents.' It was something like that."

Cerin joined her in the windowseat where she'd been staring out at the garden. He looked out at the giant old oaks that surrounded the house and said nothing for a long moment. In the fading afternoon light, he could see little brown men scurrying about in the leaves like so many monkeys.

"But the kids are worth it," he said finally.

"I don't see you teaching children."

"There's just not many parents that can afford a harp for their prodigies."

"But still..."

"Still," he agreed. "You're perfectly right. I don't like dealing with their parents; never did. When I see children put into little boxes, their enthusiasms stifled...Everything gets regimented into what's proper and what's not, into recitals and passing examinations instead of just playing—" he began to mimic a hoity-toity voice "—I don't care if you want to play in a rock band, you'll learn what I tell you to learn..."

His voice trailed off. In the back of his eyes, a dark light gleamed—not quite anger, more frustration.

"It makes you want to give them a good whack," Meran said.

"Exactly. So did you?"

Meran shook her head. "It wasn't like that, but it was almost as bad. No, maybe it was worse."

She told her husband about what Lesli's mother had asked of her, handing over the English essay when she was done so that he could read it for himself.

"This is quite good, isn't it?" he said when he reached the end.

Meran nodded. "But how can I tell Lesli that none of it's true when I know it is?"

"You can't."

Cerin laid the essay down on the windowsill and looked out at the oaks again. The twilight had crept up on the garden while they were talking. All the trees wore thick mantles of shadow now—poor recompense for the glorious cloaks of leaves that the season had stolen from them over the past few weeks. At the base of one fat trunk, the little monkey men were roasting skewers of mushrooms and acorns over a small, almost smokeless fire.

"What about Anna Batterberry herself?" he asked. "Does she remember anything?"

Meran shook her head. "I don't think she even realizes that we've met before, that she changed but we never did. She's like most people; if it doesn't make sense, she'd rather convince herself that it simply never happened."

Cerin turned from the window to regard his wife.

"Perhaps the solution would be to remind her, then," he said.

"I don't think that's such a good idea. It'd probably do more harm than good. She's just not the right sort of person..."

Meran sighed again.

"But she could have been," Cerin said.

"Oh yes," Meran said, remembering. "She could have been. But it's too late for her now."

Cerin shook his head. "It's never too late."

⊢ ⊤ ⊣

From Lesli's diary, addendum to the entry dated October 12th:

I hate living in this house! I just hate it! How could she do this to me? It's bad enough that she never lets me so much as

breathe without standing there behind me to determine that I'm not making a vulgar display of myself in the process, but this really isn't fair.

I suppose you're wondering what I'm talking about. Well, remember that essay I did on ethnic minorities for Mr. Allen? Mom got her hands on it and it's convinced her that I've turned into a Satan-worshipping drug fiend. The worst thing is that she gave it to Meran and now Meran's supposed to "have a talk with me to set me straight" on Thursday.

I just hate this. She had no right to do that. And how am I supposed to go to my lesson now? It's so embarrassing. Not to mention disappointing. I thought Meran would understand. I never thought she'd take Mom's side - not on something like this.

Meran's always seemed so special. It's not just that she wears all those funky clothes and doesn't talk down to me and looks just like one of those Pre-Raphaelite women, except that she's got those really neat green streaks in her hair. She's just a great person. She makes playing music seem so effortlessly magical and she's got all these really great stories about the origins of the tunes. When she talks about things like where "The Gold Ring" came from, it's like she really believes it was the faeries that gave that piper the tune in exchange for the lost ring he returned to them. The way she tells it, it's like she was there when it happened.

I feel like I've always known her. From the first time I saw her, I felt like I was meeting an old friend. Sometimes I think that she's magic herself - a kind of oak-tree faerie princess who's just spending a few years living in the Fields We Know before she goes back home to the magic place where she really lives.

Why would someone like that involve themselves in my mother's crusade against Faerie?

I guess I was just being naïve. She's probably no different from Mom or Mr. Allen and everybody else who doesn't believe. Well, I'm not going to any more stupid flute lessons, that's for sure.

I hate living here. Anything'd be better.

Oh, why couldn't I just have been stolen by the faeries when I was a baby? Then I'd <u>be</u> there and there'd just be some changeling living here in my place. Mom could turn <u>it</u> into a good little robot instead. Because that's all she wants. She doesn't want a daughter who can think on her own, but a boring, closed-minded junior model of herself. She should have gotten a dog instead of having a kid. Dogs are easy to train and they like being led around on a leash.

I wish Granny Nell was still alive. She would never, ever have tried to tell me that I had to grow up and stop imagining things. Everything seemed magic when she was around. It was like she was magic - just like Meran. Sometimes when Meran's playing her flute, I almost feel as though Granny Nell's sitting there with us, just listening to the music with that sad wise smile of hers.

I know I was only five when she died, but lots of the time she seems more real to me that any of my relatives that are still alive.

If she was still alive, I could be living with her right now and everything'd be really great.

Jeez, I miss her.

⅃ Y ⅄

Anna Batterberry was in an anxious state when she pulled up in front of the Kelledy house on McKennitt Street. She checked the street number that hung beside the wrought-iron gate where the walkway met the sidewalk and compared it against the address she'd hurriedly scribbled down on a scrap of paper before leaving home. When she was sure that they were the same, she slipped out of the car and approached the gate.

Walking up to the house, the sound of her heels was loud on the walkway's flagstones. She frowned at the thick carpet of fallen oak leaves that covered the lawn. The Kelledys had better hurry in cleaning them up, she thought. The city work crews would only be collecting leaves for one more week and they had to be neatly bagged and sitting at the curb for them to do so. It was a shame that such a pretty estate wasn't treated better.

When she reached the porch, she spent a disorienting moment trying to find a doorbell, then realized that there was only the small brass door knocker in the middle of the door. It was shaped like a Cornish piskie.

The sight of it gave her a queer feeling. Where had she seen that before? In one of Lesli's books, she supposed.

Lesli.

At the thought of her daughter, she quickly reached for the knocker, but the door swung open before she could use it. Lesli's flute teacher stood in the open doorway and regarded her with a puzzled look.

"Mrs. Batterberry," Meran said, her voice betraying her surprise. "Whatever are you—"

"It's Lesli," Anna said, interrupting. "She's...she..."

Her voice trailed off as what she could see of the house's interior behind Meran registered. A strange dissonance built up in her mind at the sight of the long hallway, paneled in dark wood, the thick Oriental carpet on the hardwood floor, the old photographs and prints that hung from the walls. It was when she focused on the burnished metal umbrella stand, which was, itself, in the shape of a partially-opened umbrella, and the sidetable on which stood a cast-iron, grinning gargoyle bereft of its roof gutter home, that the curious sense of familiarity she felt delved deep into the secret recesses of her mind and connected with a swell of long-forgotten memories.

She put out a hand against the doorjamb to steady herself as the flood rose up inside her. She saw her mother-in-law standing in that hallway with a kind of glow around her head. She was older than she'd been when Anna had married Peter, years older, her body wreathed in a golden

Botticelli nimbus, that beatific smile on her lips, Meran Kelledy standing beside her, the two of them sharing some private joke, and all around them...presences seemed to slip and slide across one's vision.

No, she told herself. None of that was real. Not the golden glow, nor the flickering twig-thin figures that teased the mind from the corner of the eye.

But she'd thought she'd seen them. Once. More than once. Many times. Whenever she was with Helen Batterberry...

Walking in her mother-in-law's garden and hearing music, turning the corner of the house to see a trio of what she first took to be children, then realized were midgets, playing fiddle and flute and drum, the figures slipping away as they approached, winking out of existence, the music fading, but its echoes lingering on. In the mind. In memory. In dreams.

"Faerie," her mother-in-law explained to her, matter-of-factly.

Lesli as a toddler, playing with her invisible friends that could actually be *seen* when Helen Batterberry was in the room.

No. None of that was possible.

That was when she and Peter were going through a rough period in their marriage. Those sights, those strange ethereal beings, music played on absent instruments, they were all part and parcel of what she later realized had been a nervous breakdown. Her analyst had agreed.

But they'd seemed so real.

In the hospital room where her mother-in-law lay dying, her bed a clutter of strange creatures, tiny wizened men, small perfect women, all of them flickering in and out of sight, the wonder of their presences, the music of their voices, Lesli sitting wide-eyed by the bed as the courts of Faerie came to bid farewell to an old friend.

"Say you're going to live forever," Lesli had said to her grandmother.

"I will," the old woman replied. "But you have to remember me. You have to promise never to close your awareness to the Otherworld around you. If you do that, I'll never be far."

All nonsense.

But there in the hospital room, with the scratchy sound of the IVAC pump, the clean white walls, the incessant beep of the heart monitor, the antiseptic sting in the air, Anna could only shake her head.

"None...none of this is real..." she said.

Her mother-in-law turned her head to look at her, an infinite sadness in her dark eyes.

"Maybe not for you," she said sadly, "but for those who will see, it will always be there."

And later, with Lesli at home, when just she and Peter were there, she remembered Meran coming into that hospital room, Meran and her husband, neither of them having aged since the first time Anna had seen them at her mother-in-law's house, years, oh now years ago. The four of them were there when Helen Batterberry died. She and Peter had bent their heads over the body at the moment of death, but the other two, the unaging musicians who claimed Faerie more silently, but as surely and subtly as ever Helen Batterberry had, stood at the window and watched the twilight grow across the hospital lawn as though they could see the old woman's spirit walking off into the night.

They didn't come to the funeral.

They—

She tried to push the memories aside, just as she had when the events had first occurred, but the flood was too strong. And worse, she knew they were true memories. Not the clouded rantings of a stressful mind suffering a mild breakdown.

Meran was speaking to her, but Anna couldn't hear what she was saying. She heard a vague, disturbing music that seemed to come from the ground underfoot. Small figures seemed to caper and dance in the corner of her eye, humming and buzzing like summer bees. Vertigo gripped her and she could feel herself falling. She realized that Meran was stepping forward to catch her, but by then the darkness had grown too seductive and she simply let herself fall into its welcoming depths.

⊢ ⋎ ⋏

From Lesli's diary, entry dated October 13th:

I've well and truly done it. I got up this morning and instead of my school books, I packed my flute and some clothes and you, of course, in my knapsack; and then I just left. I couldn't live there anymore. I just couldn't.

Nobody's going to miss me. Daddy's never home anyway and Mom won't be looking for me - she'll be looking for her idea of me and that person doesn't exist. The city's so big that they'll never find me.

I was kind of worried about where I was going to stay tonight, especially with the sky getting more and more overcast all day long, but I met this really neat girl in Fitzhenry Park this morning. Her name's Susan and even though she's just a year older than me, she lives with this guy in an apartment in Chinatown. She's gone to ask him if I can stay with them for a couple of days. His name's Paul. Susan says he's in his late twenties, but he doesn't act at all like an old guy. He's really neat and treats her like she's an adult, not a kid. She's his girlfriend!

I'm sitting in the park waiting for her to come back as I write this. I hope she doesn't take too long because there's some weird looking people around here. This one guy sitting over by the War Memorial keeps giving me the eye like he's going to hit on me or something. He really gives me the creeps. He's got this kind of dark aura that flickers around him so I know he's bad news.

I know it's only been one morning since I left home, but I already feel different. It's like I was dragging around this huge weight and all of a sudden it's gone. I feel light as a feather. Of course, we all know what that weight was: neuro-mother.

Once I get settled in at Susan and Paul's, I'm going to go look for a job. Susan says Paul can get me some fake ID so that I can work in a club or something and make some real money. That's what Susan does. She said that there's been times when she's made fifty bucks in tips in just one night!

I've never met anyone like her before. It's hard to believe she's almost my age. When I compare the girls at school to her, *they just seem like a bunch of kids. Susan dresses so cool, like she just stepped out of an MTV video. She's got short funky black hair, a leather jacket and jeans so tight I don't know how she gets into them. Her T-shirt's got this really cool picture of a Brian Froud faery on it that I'd never seen before.*

When I asked her if she believes in Faerie, she just gave me this big grin and said, "I'll tell you, Lesli, I'll believe in any-thing that makes me feel good."

I think I'm going to like living with her.

⊢ Ƴ ⊣

When Anna Batterberry regained consciousness, it was to find herself inside that disturbingly familiar house. She lay on a soft, overstuffed sofa, surrounded by the crouching presences of far more pieces of comfortable-looking furniture than the room was really meant to hold. The room simply had a too-full look about it, aided and abetted by a bewildering array of knick-knacks that ranged from dozens of tiny porcelain miniatures on the mantle, each depicting some anthropomorphized woodland creature playing a harp or a fiddle or a flute, to a life-sized fabric maché sculpture of a grizzly bear in top hat and tails that reared up in one corner of the room.

Every square inch of wall space appeared to be taken up with posters, framed photographs, prints and paintings. Old-fashioned curtains—the print was large dusky roses on a black background—stood guard on either side of a window seat. Underfoot was a thick carpet that had been woven into a semblance of the heavily-leafed yard outside.

The more she looked around herself, the more familiar it all looked. And the more her mind filled with memories that she'd spent so many years denying.

The sound of a footstep had her sitting up and half-turning to look behind the sofa at who—or maybe even, what—was approaching. It was only Meran. The movement brought back the vertigo and she lay down once more. Meran sat down on an ottoman that had been pulled up beside the sofa and laid a deliciously cool damp cloth against Anna's brow.

"You gave me a bit of a start," Meran said, "collapsing on my porch like that."

Anna had lost her ability to be polite. Forsaking small-talk, she went straight for the heart of the matter.

"I've been here before," she said.

Meran nodded.

"With my mother-in-law—Helen Batterberry."

"Nell," Meran agreed. "She was a good friend."

"But why haven't *I* remembered that I'd met you before until today?"

Meran shrugged. "These things happen."

"No," Anna said. "People forget things, yes, but not like this. I didn't just meet you in passing, I knew you for years—from my last year in college when Peter first began dating me. You were at his parents' house the first time he took me home. I remember thinking how odd that you and Helen were such good friends, considering how much younger you were than her."

"Should age make a difference?" Meran asked.

"No. It's just...you haven't changed at all. You're still the same age."

"I know," Meran said.

"But..." Anna's bewilderment accentuated her nervous bird temperament. "How can that be possible?"

"You said something about Lesli when you first arrived," Meran said, changing the subject.

That was probably the only thing that could have drawn Anna away from the quagmire puzzle of agelessness and hidden music and twitchy shapes moving just beyond the grasp of her vision.

"She's run away from home," Anna said. "I went into her room to get something and found that she'd left all her schoolbooks just sitting on her desk. Then when I called the school, they told me that she'd never arrived. They were about to call me to ask if she was ill. Lesli never misses school, you know."

Meran nodded. She hadn't, but it fit with the image of the relationship between Lesli and her mother that was growing in her mind.

"Have you called the police?" she asked.

"As soon as I got off the phone. They told me it was a little early to start worrying—can you imagine that? The detective I spoke to said that he'd put out her description so that his officers would keep an eye out for her, but basically he told me that she must just be skipping school. Lesli would *never* do that."

"What does your husband say?"

"Peter doesn't know yet. He's on a business trip out east and I won't be able to talk to him until he calls me tonight. I don't even know what hotel he'll be staying in until he calls." Anna reached out with a bird-thin hand and gripped Meran's arm. "What am I going to do?"

"We could go looking for her ourselves."

Anna nodded eagerly at the suggestion, but then the futility of that course of action hit home.

"The city's so big," she said. "It's too big. How would we ever find her?"

"There is another way," Cerin said.

Anna started at the new voice. Meran removed the damp cloth from Anna's brow and moved back from the sofa so that Anna could sit up once more. She looked at the tall figure standing in the doorway, recognizing him as Meran's husband. She didn't remember him seeming quite so intimidating before.

"What...what way is that?" Anna said.

"You could ask for help from Faerie," Cerin told her.

⊢ Υ ⊣

"So—you're gonna be one of Paulie's girls?"

Lesli looked up from writing in her diary to find that the creepy guy by the War Memorial had sauntered over to stand beside her bench. Up close, he seemed even tougher than he had from a distance. His hair was slicked back on top, long at the back. He had three earrings in his left earlobe, one in the right. Dirty jeans were tucked into tall black cowboy boots, his white shirt was half open under his jean jacket. There was an oily look in his eyes that made her shiver.

She quickly shut the diary, keeping her place with a finger, and looked around hopefully to see if Susan was on her way back, but there was no sign of her new friend. Taking a deep breath, she gave him what she hoped was a look of appropriate streetwise bravado.

"I...I don't know what you're talking about," she said.

"I saw you talking to Susie," he said, sitting down beside her on the bench. "She's Paulie's recruiter."

Lesli started to get a bad feeling right about then. It wasn't just that this guy was so awful, but that she might have made a terrible misjudgment when it came to Susan.

"I think I should go," she said.

She started to get up, but he grabbed her arm. Off balance, she fell back onto the bench.

"Hey, look," he said. "I'm doing you a favour. Paulie's got ten or twelve girls in his string and he works them like they're dogs. You look like a nice kid. Do you really want to spend the next ten years peddling your ass for some homeboy who's gonna have you hooked on junk before the week's out?"

"I—"

"See, I run a clean shop. No drugs, nice clothes for the girls, nice apartment that you're gonna share with just one other girl, not a half dozen the way Paulie runs his biz. My girls turn maybe two, three tricks a night and that's it. Paulie'll have you on the street nine, ten hours a pop, easy."

His voice was calm, easygoing, but Lesli had never been so scared before in her life.

"Please," she said. "You're making a mistake. I really have to go."

She tried to rise again, but he kept a hand on her shoulder so that she couldn't get up. His voice, so mild before, went hard.

"You go anywhere, babe, you're going with me," he said. "There are no other options. End of conversation."

He stood up and hauled her to her feet. His hand held her in a bruising grip. Her diary fell from her grip, and he let her pick it up and stuff it into her knapsack, but then he pulled her roughly away from the bench.

"You're hurting me!" she cried.

He leaned close to her, his mouth only inches from her ear.

"Keep that up," he warned her, "and you're really gonna find out what pain's all about. Now make nice. You're working for me now."

"I..."

"Repeat after me, sweet stuff: I'm Cutter's girl."

Tears welled in Lesli's eyes. She looked around the park, but nobody was paying any attention to what was happening to her. Cutter gave her a painful shake that made her teeth rattle.

"C'mon," he told her. "Say it."

He glared at her with the promise of worse to come in his eyes if she didn't start doing what he said. His grip tightened on her shoulder, fingers digging into the soft flesh of her upper arm.

"Say it!"

"I...I'm Cutter's...girl."

"See? That wasn't so hard."

He gave her another shove to start her moving again. She wanted desperately to break free of his hand and just run, but as he marched her across the park, she discovered that she was too scared to do anything but let him lead her away.

She'd never felt so helpless or alone in all her life. It made her feel ashamed.

⅄ Υ ⅄

"Please don't joke about this," Anna said in response to Cerin's suggestion that they turn to Faerie for help in finding Lesli.

"Yes," Meran agreed, though she wasn't speaking of jokes. "This isn't the time."

Cerin shook his head. "This seems a particularly appropriate time to me." He turned to Anna. "I don't like to involve myself in private quarrels, but since it's you that's come to us, I feel I have the right to ask you this: Why is it, do you think, that Lesli ran away in the first place?"

"What are you insinuating? That I'm not a good mother?"

"Hardly. I no longer know you well enough to make that sort of a judgment. Besides, it's not really any of my business, is it?"

"Cerin, please," Meran said.

A headache was starting up between Anna's temples.

"I don't understand," Anna said. "What is it that you're saying?"

"Meran and I loved Nell Batterberry," Cerin said. "I don't doubt that you held some affection for her as well, but I do know that you thought her a bit of a daft old woman. She told me once that after her husband—after Philip—died, you tried to convince Peter that she should be put in a home. Not in a home for the elderly, but for the, shall we say, gently mad?"

"But she—"

"Was full of stories that made no sense to you," Cerin said. "She heard and saw what others couldn't, though she had the gift that would allow such people to see into the invisible world of Faerie when they were in her presence. You saw into that world once, Anna. I don't think you ever forgave her for showing it to you."

"It...it wasn't real."

Cerin shrugged. "That's not really important at this moment. What's important is that, if I understand the situation correctly, you've been living in the fear that Lesli would grow up just as fey as her grandmother.

And if this is so, your denying her belief in Faerie lies at the root of the troubles that the two of you share."

Anna looked to Meran for support, but Meran knew her husband too well and kept her own council. Having begun, Cerin wouldn't stop until he said everything he meant to.

"Why are you doing this to me?" Anna asked. "My daughter's run away. All of...all of this..." She waved a hand that was perhaps meant to take in just the conversation, perhaps the whole room. "It's not real. Little people and fairies and all the things my mother-in-law reveled in discussing just aren't real. She could make them *seem* real, I'll grant you that, but they could never exist."

"In your world," Cerin said.

"In the real world."

"They're not one and the same," Cerin told her.

Anna began to rise from the sofa. "I don't have to listen to any of this," she said. "My daughter's run away and I thought you might be able to help me. I didn't come here to be mocked."

"The only reason I've said anything at all," Cerin told her, "is for Lesli's sake. Meran talks about her all the time. She sounds like a wonderful, gifted child."

"She is."

"I hate the thought of her being forced into a box that doesn't fit her. Of having her wings cut off, her sight blinded, her hearing muted, her voice stilled."

"I'm not doing any such thing!" Anna cried.

"You just don't realize what you're doing," Cerin replied.

His voice was mild, but dark lights in the back of his eyes were flashing.

Meran realized it was time to intervene. She stepped between the two. Putting her back to her husband, she turned to face Anna.

"We'll find Lesli," she said.

"How? With *magic*?"

"It doesn't matter how. Just trust that we will. What you have to think of is of what you were telling me yesterday: her birthday's coming up in just a few days. Once she turns sixteen, so long as she can prove that she's capable of supporting herself, she can legally leave home and nothing you might do or say then can stop her."

"It's you, isn't it?" Anna cried. "You're the one who's been filling up her head with all these horrible fairy tales. I should never have let her take those lessons."

Her voice rose ever higher in pitch as she lunged forward, arms flailing. Meran slipped to one side, then reached out one quick hand. She pinched a nerve in Anna's neck and the woman suddenly went limp. Cerin caught her before she could fall and carried her back to the sofa.

"Now do you see what I mean about parents?" he said as he laid Anna down.

Meran gave him a mock-serious cuff on the back of his head.

"Go find Lesli," she said.

"But—"

"Or would you rather stay with Anna and continue your silly attempt at converting her when she wakes up again?"

"I'm on my way," Cerin told her and was out the door before she could change her mind.

⊢ ⊤ ⊣

Thunder cracked almost directly overhead as Cutter dragged Lesli into a brownstone just off Palm Street. The building stood in the heart of what was known as Newford's Combat Zone, a few square blocks of night clubs, strip joints and bars. It was a tough part of town with hookers on every corner, bikers cruising the streets on chopped-down Harleys, bums sleeping in doorways, winos sitting on the curbs, drinking cheap booze from bottles vaguely hidden in paper bags.

Cutter had an apartment on the top floor of the brownstone, three stories up from the street. If he hadn't told her that he lived here, Lesli would have thought that he'd taken her into an abandoned building. There was no furniture except a vinyl-topped table and two chairs in the dirty kitchen. A few mangy pillows were piled up against the wall in what she assumed was the living room.

He led her down to the room at the end of the long hall that ran the length of the apartment and pushed her inside. She lost her balance and went sprawling onto the mattress that lay in the middle of the floor. It smelled of mildew and, vaguely, of old urine. She scrambled away from it and crouched up against the far wall, clutching her knapsack against her chest.

"Now, you just relax, sweet stuff," Cutter told her. "Take things easy. I'm going out for a little while to find you a nice guy to ease you into the trade. I'd do it myself, but there's guys that want to be first with a kid as young and pretty as you are and I sure could use the bread they're willing to pay for the privilege."

Lesli was prepared to beg him to let her go, but her throat was so tight she couldn't make a sound.

"Don't go away now," Cutter told her.

He chuckled at his own wit, then closed the door and locked it. Lesli didn't think she'd ever heard anything so final as the sound of that lock catching. She listened to Cutter's footsteps as they crossed the apartment, the sound of the front door closing, his footsteps receding on the stairs.

As soon as she was sure he was far enough away, she got up and ran to the door, trying it, just in case, but it really was locked and far too solid for her to have any hope of breaking through its panels. Of course there was no phone. She crossed the room to the window and forced it open. The window looked out on the side of another building, with an alleyway below. There was no fire escape outside the window and she was far too high up to think of trying to get down to the alley.

Thunder rumbled again, not quite overhead now, and it started to rain. She leaned by the window, resting her head on its sill. Tears sprang up in her eyes again.

"Please," she sniffed. "Please, somebody help me..."

The rain coming in the window mingled with the tears that streaked her cheek.

ᚦ Y ᚼ

Cerin began his search at the Batterberry house which was in Ferryside, across the Stanton Street Bridge on the west side of the Kickaha river. As Anna Batterberry had remarked, the city was large. To find one teenage girl, hiding somewhere in the confounding labyrinth of its thousands of crisscrossing streets and avenues, was a daunting task, but Cerin was depending on help.

To anyone watching him, he must have appeared to be slightly mad. He wandered back and forth across the streets of Ferryside, stopping under trees to look up into their bare branches, hunkering down at the mouths of alleys or alongside hedges, apparently talking to himself. In truth, he was looking for the city's gossips:

Magpies and crows, sparrows and pigeons saw everything, but listening to their litanies of the day's events was like looking something up in an encyclopedia that was merely a confusing heap of loose pages, gathered together in a basket. All the information you wanted was there, but finding it would take more hours than there were in a day.

Cats were little better. They liked to keep most of what they knew to themselves, so what they did offer him was usually cryptic and sometimes even pointedly unhelpful. Cerin couldn't blame them; they were by nature secretive and like much of Faerie, capricious.

The most ready to give him a hand were those little sprites commonly known as the flower faeries. They were the little winged spirits of the various trees and bushes, flowers and weeds, that grew tidily in parks and gardens, rioting only in the odd empty lot or wild place, such as the riverbanks that ran down under the Stanton Street Bridge to meet the water. Years ago, Cicely Mary Barker had catalogued any number of them in a loving series of books; more recently the Boston artist, Terri Windling, had taken up the task, specializing in the urban relations of those Barker had already noted.

It was late in the year for the little folk. Most of them were already tucked away in Faerie, sleeping through the winter, or else too busy with their harvests and other seasonal preoccupations to have paid any attention at all to what went on beyond the task at hand. But a few had seen the young girl who could sometimes see them. Meran's cousins were the most helpful. Their small pointed faces would regard Cerin gravely from under acorn caps as they pointed this way down one street, or that way down another.

It took time. The sky grew darker, and then still darker as the clouds thickened with an approaching storm, but slowly and surely, Cerin traced Lesli's passage over the Stanton Street Bridge all the way across town to Fitzhenry Park. It was just as he reached the bench where she'd been sitting that it began to rain.

There, from two of the wizened little monkey-like bodachs that lived in the park, he got the tale of how she'd been accosted and taken away.

"She didn't want to go, sir" said the one, adjusting the brim of his little cap against the rain.

All faerie knew Cerin, but it wasn't just for his bardic harping that they paid him the respect that they did. He was the husband of the oak king's daughter, she who could match them trick for trick and then some, and they'd long since learned to treat her, and those under her protection, with a wary deference.

"No sir, she didn't," added the other, "but he led her off all the same."

Cerin hunkered down beside the bench so that he wasn't towering over them.

"Where did he take her?" he asked.

The first bodach pointed to where two men were standing by the War Memorial, shoulders hunched against the rain, heads bent together as they spoke. One wore a thin raincoat over a suit; the other was dressed in denim jacket, jeans and cowboy boots. They appeared to be discussing a business transaction.

"You could ask him for yourself," the bodach said. "He's the one all in blue."

Cerin's gaze went to the pair and a hard look came over his features. If Meran had been there, she might have laid a hand on his arm, or spoken a calming word, to bank the dangerous fire that grew in behind his eyes. But she was at home, too far away for her quieting influence to be felt.

The bodachs scampered away as Cerin rose to his feet. By the War Memorial, the two men seemed to come to an agreement and left the park together. Cerin fell in behind them, the rain that slicked the pavement underfoot muffling his footsteps. His fingers twitched at his side, as though striking a harp's strings.

From the branches of the tree where they'd taken sanctuary, the bodachs thought they could hear the sound of a harp, its music echoing softly against the rhythm of the rain.

⋋ Ƴ ⋏

Anna came to once more just as Meran was returning from the kitchen with a pot of herb tea and a pair of mugs. Meran set the mugs and pot down on the table by the sofa and sat down beside Lesli's mother.

"How are you feeling?" she asked as she adjusted the cool cloth she'd laid upon Anna's brow earlier.

Anna's gaze flicked from left to right, over Meran's shoulder and down to the floor, as though tracking invisible presences. Meran tried to shoo away the inquisitive faerie, but it was a useless gesture. In this house, with Anna's presence to fuel their quenchless curiosity, it was like trying to catch the wind.

"I've made us some tea," Meran said. "It'll make you feel better."

Anna appeared docile now, her earlier anger fled as though it had never existed. Outside, rain pattered gently against the window panes. The face of a nosy hob was pressed against one lower pane, its breath clouding the glass, its large eyes glimmering with their own inner light.

"Can...can you make them go away?" Anna asked.

Meran shook her head. "But I can make you forget again."

"Forget." Anna's voice grew dreamy. "Is that what you did before? You made me forget?"

"No. You did that on your own. You didn't want to remember, so you simply forgot."

"And you...you didn't do a thing?"

"We do have a certain...aura," Meran admitted, "which accelerates the process. It's not even something we consciously work at. It just seems to happen when we're around those who'd rather not remember what they see."

"So I'll forget, but they'll all still be there?"

Meran nodded.

"I just won't be able to see them?"

"It'll be like it was before," Meran said.

"I...I don't think I'd like that..."

Her voice slurred. Meran leaned forward with a worried expression. Anna seemed to regard her through blurring vision.

"I think I'm going...away...now..." she said.

Her eyelids fluttered, then her head lolled to one side and she lay still. Meran called Anna's name and gave her a little shake, but there was no response. She put two fingers to Anna's throat and found her pulse. It was regular and strong, but try though she did, Meran couldn't rouse the woman.

Rising from the sofa, she went into the kitchen to phone for an ambulance. As she was dialing the number, she heard Cerin's harp begin to play by itself up in his study on the second floor.

⊢ ⊤ ⊣

Lesli's tears lasted until she thought she saw something moving in the rain on the other side of the window. It was a flicker of movement and colour, just above the outside windowsill, as though a pigeon had come in for a wet landing, but it had moved with far more grace and deftness than any pigeon she'd ever seen. And that memory of colour was all wrong, too. It hadn't been the blue/white/grey of a pigeon; it had been more like a butterfly—

doubtful, she thought, in the rain and this time of year

—or a hummingbird—

even more doubtful

—but then she remembered what the music had woken at her last flute lesson. She rubbed at her eyes with her sleeve to remove the blur of her tears and looked more closely into the rain. Face-on, she couldn't see anything, but as soon as she turned her head, there it was again, she could see it out of the corner of her eye, a dancing dervish of colour and movement that flickered out of her line of sight as soon as she concentrated on it.

After a few moments, she turned from the window. She gave the door a considering look and listened hard, but there was still no sound of Cutter's return.

Maybe, she thought, maybe magic can rescue me...

She dug out her flute from her knapsack and quickly put the pieces together. Turning back to the window, she sat on her haunches and tried to start up a tune, but to no avail. She was still too nervous, her chest felt too tight, and she couldn't get the air to come up properly from her diaphragm.

She brought the flute down from her lip and laid it across her knees. Trying not to think of the locked door, of why it was locked and who would be coming through it, she steadied her breathing.

In, slowly now, hold it, let it out, slowly. And again.

She pretended she was with Meran, just the two of them in the basement of the Old Firehall. There. She could almost hear the tune that Meran was playing, except it sounded more like the bell-like tones of a harp than the breathy timbre of a wooden flute. But still, it was there for her to follow, a path marked out on a roadmap of music.

Lifting the flute back up to her lip, she blew again, a narrow channel of air going down into the mouth hole at an angle, all her fingers down, the low D note ringing in the empty room, a deep rich sound, resonant and full. She played it again, then caught the music she heard, that particular path laid out on the roadmap of all tunes that are or yet could be, and followed where it led.

It was easier to do than she would have thought possible, easier than all those lessons with Meran. The music she followed seemed to allow her instrument to almost play itself. And as the tune woke from her flute, she fixed her gaze on the rain falling just outside the window where a flicker of colour appeared, a spin of movement.

Please, she thought. Oh please...

And then it was there, hummingbird wings vibrating in the rain, sending incandescent sprays of water arcing away from their movement; the tiny naked upper torso, the lower wrapped in tiny leaves and vines; the dark hair gathered wetly against her miniature cheeks and neck; the eyes, tiny and timeless, watching her as she watched back and all the while, the music played.

Help me, she thought to that little hovering figure. Won't you please—

She had been oblivious to anything but the music and the tiny faerie outside in the rain. She hadn't heard the footsteps on the stairs, nor heard them crossing the apartment. But she heard the door open.

The tune faltered, the faerie flickered out of sight as though it had never been there. She brought the flute down from her lip and turned, her heart drumming wildly in her chest, but she refused to be scared. That's what all guys like Cutter wanted. They wanted to see you scared of them. They wanted to be in control. But no more.

I'm not going to go without a fight, she thought. I'll break my flute over his stupid head. I'll...

The stranger standing in the doorway brought her train of thought to a scurrying halt. And then she realized that the harping she'd heard, the tune that had led her flute to join it, had grown in volume, rather than diminished.

"Who...who are you?" she asked.

Her hands had begun to perspire, making her flute slippery and hard to hold. The stranger had longer hair than Cutter. It was drawn back in a braid that hung down one side of his head and dangled halfway down his chest. He had a full beard and wore clothes that though they were simple jeans, shirt and jacket, seemed to have a timeless cut to them, as though they could have been worn at any point in history and not seemed out of place. Meran dressed like that as well, she realized.

But it was his eyes that held her—not their startling brightness, but the fire that seemed to flicker in their depths, a rhythmic movement that seemed to keep time to the harping she heard.

"Have you come to...rescue me?" she found herself asking before the stranger had time to reply to her first question.

"I'd think," he said, "with a spirit so brave as yours, that you'd simply rescue yourself."

Lesli shook her head. "I'm not really brave at all."

"Braver than you know, fluting here while a darkness stalked you through the storm. My name's Cerin Kelledy; I'm Meran's husband and I've come to take you home."

He waited for her to disassemble her flute and stow it away, then offered her a hand up from the floor. As she stood up, he took the knapsack and slung it over his shoulder and led her towards the door. The sound of the harping was very faint now, Lesli realized.

When they walked by the hall, she stopped in the doorway leading to the living room and looked at the two men that were huddled against the far wall, their eyes wild with terror. One was Cutter; the other a business man in suit and raincoat whom she'd never seen before. She hesitated, fingers tightening on Cerin's hand, as she turned to see what was frightening them so much. There was nothing at all in the spot that their frightened gazes were fixed upon.

"What...what's the matter with them?" she asked her companion. "What are they looking at?"

"Night fears," Cerin replied. "Somehow the darkness that lies in their hearts has given those fears substance and made them real."

The way he said "somehow" let Lesli know that he'd been responsible for what the two men were undergoing.

"Are they going to die?" she asked.

She didn't think she was the first girl to fall prey to Cutter so she wasn't exactly feeling sorry for him at that point.

Cerin shook his head. "But they will always have the *sight*. Unless they change their ways, it will show them only the dark side of Faerie."

Lesli shivered.

"There are no happy endings," Cerin told her. "There are no real endings ever—happy or otherwise. We all have our own stories which are just a part of the one Story that binds both this world and Faerie. Sometimes we step into each others' stories—perhaps just for a few minutes, perhaps for years—and then we step out of them again. But all the while, the Story just goes on."

That day, his explanation only served to confuse her.

ⴹ Ⲧ ⴹ

From Lesli's diary, entry dated November 24th:

Nothing turned out the way I thought it would.

Something happened to Mom. Everybody tells me it's not my fault, but it happened when I ran away, so I can't help but feel that I'm to blame. Daddy says she had a nervous breakdown and that's why she's in the sanitarium. It happened to her before and it had been coming again for a long time. But that's not the way Mom tells it.

I go by to see her every day after school. Sometimes she's pretty spaced from the drugs they give her to keep her calm, but on one of her good days, she told me about Granny Nell and the Kelledys and Faerie. She says the world's just like I said it was in that essay I did for English. Faerie's real and it didn't go away; it just got freed from people's preconceptions of it and now it's just whatever it wants to be.

And that's what scares her.

She also thinks the Kelledys are some kind of earth spirits.

"I can't forget this time," she told me.

"But if you know," I asked her, "if you believe, then why are you in this place? Maybe I should be in here, too."

And you know what she told me? "I don't want to believe in any of it; it just makes me feel sick. But at the same time, I can't stop knowing it's all out there: every kind of magic being and nightmare. They're all real."

I remember thinking of Cutter and that other guy in his apartment and what Cerin said about them. Did that make my Mom a bad person? I couldn't believe that.

"But they're not supposed to be real," Mom said. "That's what's got me feeling so crazy. In a sane world, in the world that was the way I'd grown up believing it to be, that wouldn't

be real. The Kelledys could fix it so that I'd forget again, but then I'd be back to going through life always feeling like there was something important that I couldn't remember. And that just leaves you with another kind of craziness — an ache that you can't explain and it doesn't ever go away. It's better this way, and my medicine keeps me from feeling too crazy."

She looked away then, out the window of her room. I looked, too, and saw the little monkey-man that was crossing the lawn of the sanitarium, pulling a pig behind him. The pig had a load of gear on its back like it was a pack horse.

"Could you...could you ask the nurse to bring my medicine," Mom said.

I tried to tell her that all she had to do was accept it, but she wouldn't listen. She just kept asking for the nurse, so finally I went and got one.

I still think it's my fault.

⋏ ⋎ ⋏

I live with the Kelledys now. Daddy was going to send me away to a boarding school, because he felt that he couldn't be home enough to take care of me. I never really thought about it before, but when he said that, I realized that he didn't know me at all.

Meran offered to let me live at their place. I moved in on my birthday.

There's a book in their library — ha! There's like ten million books in there. But the one I'm thinking of is by a local writer, this guy named Christy Riddell.

In it, he talks about Faerie, how everybody just thinks of them as ghosts of wind and shadow.

"Faerie music is the wind," he says, "and their movement is the play of shadow cast by moonlight, or starlight, or no light at all. Faerie lives like a ghost beside us, but only the city remembers. But then the city never forgets anything."

I don't know if the Kelledys are part of that ghostliness. What I do know is that, seeing how they live for each other, how they care so much about each other, I find myself feeling more hopeful about things. My parents and I didn't so much not get along, as lack interest in each other. It got to the point where I figured that's how everybody was in the world, because I never knew any different.

So I'm trying harder with Mom. I don't talk about things she doesn't want to hear, but I don't stop believing in them either. Like Cerin said, we're just two threads of the Story. Sometimes we come together for awhile and sometimes we're apart. And no matter how much one or the other of us might want it to be different, both our stories are true.

But I can't stop wishing for a happy ending.

1991

Desert Moments
Introduction

Something different this year.

In the latter part of October, MaryAnn and I had the great good fortune to spend a week and a half in Tucson, Arizona, staying with our friend Terri Windling in "Tapu'at House," a marvelous place that she shares with her roommate Ellen and three cats.

Tapu'at House sits on the edge of the desert. You have but to step out the door and the magic of the landscape swallows you whole. There is a little Fairy House, up on the ridge behind Terri and Ellen's house, where MaryAnn and I played tunes and from which we managed to watch the sunset at least a couple of times. I say "managed" because our time there was so happily filled with road trips and desert walks, good company and inspiring conversation, that it's a wonder we got up there at all.

What follows is a series of images and memories that grew out of our stay. They're told in verse, partly because their nature seemed to call for the language of poetry, but more importantly, because MaryAnn has long wanted to see a collection of my verse in print. This seemed the perfect opportunity to do so, since what these verses describe are experiences that we were able to share at the time, and can now look back on together.

MaryAnn and I would especially like to offer them to Terri and Ellen, for their wonderful spirits and warm hospitality, and to Charles Vess and Karen Shaffer, with whom we had not nearly enough good times. We'll have to do it all again, and try not to compress it into such a short time when we do.

And, of course, we would also like to share these desert moments with all of you to whom we send this yearly chapbook. If "life's a beach," then the desert is a place of the spirit that we all carry within us. In that wilderness, may we never fail to recognize each other, and may we always prosper.

Ottawa,
Winter, 1991

Tapu'at House
(for Terri & Ellen)

In the Women's House,
spirits are speaking.

The women
are tapping word-hoards
until stories
jump like cholla thorns
from mind to pen,
burrowing deep beneath
the skin.

In the Fairy House,
Coyote sleeps.

All around him, in the desert,
saguaro dream like green giants
while Coyote juggles
mischief and luck in his sleep.
All around him, in the desert,
the uncles and aunts
teach us to remember
that we are still animals.

In the Women's House,
the otherworld is watching.

The women
are borrowing from the dry hills
shape and pigment,
vision and song,

allowing totems to guide them
through this pathless world.

In the Spirit House,
women are singing.

Their voices
are like the silent laughter
of cats.
With every day's work
they move closer to the
vanishing ghost of a wilderness
that now exists only
in peripheral vision.

What you and I no longer remember,
the women in this house
have never forgotten.

Sacred Land

From this ridge
I can see the Catalinas,
their sharp dark crest lines
cutting jaggedly across the sky.
Behind me are the Rincon Mountains
where we went
skidding and slipping down
a winding path to the bottom
of an arroyo
and met the afternoon
with quiet conversation
that would have been lost
in waterfall thunder
had the rains come this year.

Visions seem to quicken in this dry air,
in the wide vistas;
possibilities unfold
not just in the magic times
—twilight,
deep night—
but day and night.
In this place
I can believe in desert fairies
and shaman,
trickster coyote, fetishes
and kachinas that represent
figures from history
rather than myth.

The *yei*
in their masks,
the sacred spirits,
must live here—

I'toi and Coyote,
Changing Woman and Kokopelli,
all.

I can understand
why the Tohono O'odham believe
that all the land within view
of Elder Brother
is sacred land,
why the Hopi believe
that their mesas
center the world,
why the Dineh remain
within the boundaries
of their four sacred mountains,
but not why the Anasazi
abandoned Chaco Canyon
in mid-meal,
stoneware dishes
still on their tables.

Thousands of miles north,
in the midst of a different Beauty,
I realize that
a finger of my soul
remained behind
when I left that vast land
to return to these
dark, enclosing woods.

Apollo, Arizona and Oliver Twist

Here in this desert house
I meet
three feline muses,
but untraditionally,
only one is female.

Why do so many
artists and writers
live with cats?

Not just for the companionship,
I decide,
but also for the presence
of the animal spirit
that cats invest
in their surroundings.
They are particularly
primal muses,
and yes,
particular, too.

But no matter how calmly
they lie a-lapped,
purrs rumbling in their chests
and Cheshire-grinning,
under the thin veneer
of civilized behaviour
that they have learned to wear
with such aplomb,
they remain forever feral
and untamed.

The Fairy House

He meant well,
the landlord,
when he first built it
on the ridge
up behind the house—
the perfect place
from which to watch the sunset.

But it was
no more than a bunker:
ugly stone, cemented together,
all sharp angles
and discomfort;
plain wooden supports
to hold its netted roof.

It took loose stones
set against the bunker walls
in happy disarray;
saguaro ribs to roof it,
cholla-cactus skeletons
like oversized honeycombs
and driftwood gathered
from the dry washes
to break the symmetry;
perfect pebbles,
carefully chosen,
laid out in random
by an old oil lamp
holding dried flowers;
fimo fairy faces
cunningly concealed
in twist of wood
and sheltered stone shadow.

It took all this
and heart,

great heart,
to make the magic hold.

But now when sunset pads
across the distant view,
the lights of Tucson disappear
and the Fairy House
becomes a fetish
that defines the enchantment
of mountain crests
haloed with impossible pigments.
To its shelter come
the ghostwalking *alo*
of the jumping cholla and the ricegrass,
of the palo verde and the barrel cacti,
of the sleeping fairy dusters
and the desert holly.
To its shelter come
coyote cries and the westering wind,
the hoarse chirp of the Mormon cricket
and the cackling calls of quail.
To its shelter come
the kit fox and the mourning dove,
the tree lizard and the desert cottontail.
To its shelter come
all the spirits of the desert,
called by the shaman hand
that gathered the stones from the field,
driftwood from the wash,
harvest from the hills,
faces from clay,
and made what was silent
into a song.

The steep incline,
up behind the house,
stones slipping underfoot,
mesquite tugging at our sleeves,
becomes a benediction

when we finally reach
the Fairy House.

To its shelter
we come
to partake of a simple view,
only to be drawn into
the persuasive tangle
of its witcheries.

And there,
when we are still,
when we allow our spirits to see
what is hidden from the eye,
we are forever
transformed.

The Fairy House Jig

brightly

Mission San Xavier del Bac

An astonishing vision,
the Mission rises from the desert,
a gleaming white church
that pays tribute to the faith
of the Spanish missionaries
and the Tohono O'odham
who built it.

This "White Dove of the Desert"
took its name from
Padre Kino's patron saint,
to which the Tohono O'odham
added Bac,
"where the waters gathered."
There's little water
here now.

We see food stalls where
Navajo women sell flatbread and chili,
a small plaza across the parking lot
housing Native American arts,
a hill to the east
on the side of which
a replica of the Grotto of Lourdes
is festooned with small ribbons
and photos of the healed grateful.

The first time we come,
it's almost dusk.
Tourists mingle with a wedding party,
though whether it's an actual wedding,
or merely a rehearsal,
we can't tell.
The bridesmaids are in blood-red dresses,
the men in black, Spanish-styled suits;

the bride,
of course,
in white.
Part of the wedding party,
a covey of teenage girls
with dark complexions and in tight dresses
linger by the gates, giggling.

We return another day
to go inside.
As we walk through the dimly-lit interior,
I marvel at the candles,
hundreds of candles,
so many prayers burning,
faith flickering in a multitude
of hopeful light.
There was a shortage of building materials
and skilled artisans
at the time the Mission was built,
so the altar is painted
to look like marble,
the dados painted to look like glazed tiles,
there are even chandeliers
painted on the walls.
It seems the more welcoming for that.

A bus unloads a tourist group
and suddenly the interior is filled
with camera flashbulbs going off
and the shuffling of feet.
The tourists settle in pews
as a voice comes from hidden speakers
and begins to give the history
of the Mission.
I find that I can't pay attention.
Instead,
I watch a man with skin the colour of the desert,
hair black, clothes plain,
as he slowly walks down the aisle,

genuflects before the nave,
then sits in a free pew.
He holds a candle that he will light
and set to join the others.
His head is bowed in prayer
and I wonder how he can ignore
the tourists,
or the droning voice of the narrator
that comes from the speakers.
I am embarrassed to be intruding
upon this private moment.
When MaryAnn touches my arm,
I am grateful for her wordless suggestion
that we quietly withdraw.

Flatbread & Chili

At her stall,
standing by the west walls
of the San Xavier Mission,
the Navajo woman
has skin the colour
of the Sonora hills,
eyes dark as a desert night.
She cooks chili and flatbread
over a mesquite fire
—a familiar collection of ingredients
made exotic
by the locale
and the cook's hand.

We fold the flatbread over the chili
and eat it in the shadow of the Mission,
sitting in the wind.
It's easy to imagine
that the parking lot is gone,
the cars,
the sign that reads, "Gift shop."
It's easy to imagine
that we are a hundred years,
two hundred years,
timeless years
in the past.

Then the woman's
eleven-year-old daughter
points out to her mother
an item she wants
from a mail-order catalogue
and the spell is
not so much broken
as changed.

Bajada

Once
this was all ocean,
once.
Now stone fish float belly up,
their fossilized voices
silent.
Even the air is dry,
and the wind, too,
is silent.

But still I listen
for one moment.
For one long moment,
there among the smoke trees and jojoba,
I meet Mystery,
strangely unfamiliar
without her cloak of north wood leaves,
and she beckons to me.

I stand
in the shadow
of a towering saguaro
and look out to where
wave upon wave of dry hills
break against the distant mountains.
I find
what might be a piece
of ancient crockery
or merely an oddly-shaped stone.
I shift from one foot to another
and a lizard,
invisible before it moved,
skitters away.

I imagine a hawk floating high
in this cloudless sky

and see the ghost
of a giant longfin dace
swimming away from me—
swimming languorously,
away from me,
westward.

There the sun sinks,
holding a quarter moon
in its setting glory,
and all the world is ablaze
with an aura of colour
that leaves me speechless;
that I know I will never
again experience
in this same configuration.

I have no time for regret.
I can only be in this moment,
swallowing the experience—
a more precious treasure
than can be counted in coin.

For this one moment,
I have coyote eyes
and the blood of the desert
is dry poetry in my veins.

For this one moment
I can see that
with every tear,
born of sorrow, or born of joy,
we cry our own ancient seas.
I can see that
we carry deserts
within us: forbidding,
  forgotten,
  forlorn,
  forever.

But never was one of them
a wasteland.

The sun sets.
Darkness falls across the desert
and steals the day's warmth
from the shrouded hills.
Stars peer at me
from around the shadowed arms
of the saguaro.
Somewhere,
behind me,
a coyote calls.
Then there is only
the scratchy chirp
of the crickets.

But I can imagine
the sound of
humpbacked Kokopelli's flute,
echoing across these dark hills.
I can imagine
the spirits of the cholla,
of the mesquite and palo verde,
of the uncles and the aunts,
as they dance to secret music—
hollow wood, lipped,
wind on hills,
rainstick waterfall,
mingled,
mingling,
to the rhythm of my own
heartbeat.

And I will remember.
Long after the north woods reclaim me,
I will remember.

Tucson

It's a sprawling gridwork
of streets
laid out in an orderly pattern
and seemingly no different
from any other big city
except for the height
of its buildings,
one or two stories tall,
mostly,
and that wide, flat urban sprawl.
It takes at least twenty minutes
to get from any one part of town
to another,
and everyone drives.

Yes, there are galleries downtown
and the Mexican restaurants,
surprises like East 6th Street
with its adobe houses and cacti gardens,
and the funky charm
of North 4th Avenue's boutiques
—you can get your hair cut where
The Coyote Wore Sideburns,
buy a silver saguaro pin,
a bolo tie,
or an old cowboy shirt
in How Sweet It Was,
eat lunch at La Indita
and have your taste buds
continue tingling
for hours.

But it's big,
Tucson is,
and it's dusty—
overflowing with strips
of fast food outlets,

and warehouses,
billboards advertising
cigarettes and beer,
row upon row,
of shopping malls,
and the traffic,
always the traffic,
and one can't help but wonder:
why live here?

Until you remember the mountains,
one range for each compass point,
surrounding the city,
the Catalinas and the Tucsons,
the Rincon and the Santa Ritas,
one glorious range or another,
always in sight.

And then there is the desert,
the spirit of the desert...

I look again at Tucson
and see a saguaro
smiling at me from beside a Safeway;
in the suburbs
the aromatic scent of creosote bushes
follows the rain;
I hear coyote cry
in the wake of a pickup
that's speeding down Broadway.
And then I know that
no matter how much the city
encroaches upon the desert,
with its concrete and its lights,
the wilderness lingers here still.

Mount Lemmon

It seems so odd,
driving up
out of the desert,
8000 feet above sea level,
to suddenly find ourselves
in a Canadian forest,
the pine and maple
so familiar,
but the view—
there was never
such a view in our
Eastern woods.

Saguaro Dream

with feeling

Coyote

1.

Coyote's
all used up now,
some say.

His mystery has
been diminished
by too much attention:
a hundred times a hundred
times a hundred times over
he's sold as a memory
to tourists—
snout pointing moonward,
howl in throat;
his image has become
quick shorthand
to the apperception
of Trickster as myth
and every would-be shaman,
born of book
or New Age guru,
is on a first name basis with him.

Though, of course,
Coyote only ever had
the one given name.

The commercialization
is robbing Coyote
of his Trickster myth,
those same worriers go on.
It's not a recent phenomena;
he's already been swallowed by cartoons.
He's Bugs Bunny and Tweety Bird,
and even the Roadrunner
(where Wiley plays the fool

—but that's Trickster,too).
Now he's Bart Simpson,
they say,
Trickster for the nineties,
and the real magic's
all gone away.

2.

Here's Coyote
as we met him:

A raucous sound
cutting across the night's
comforting cricket chorus—
it's freshman week
at Desert U.
as a half-dozen coyote voices
mimic drunken students;
party animal, indeed.

MaryAnn calling me
to an early-morning window,
pointing, "There,"
as two reddish grey and buff shapes,
white-bellied and cock-eared,
continue on down the road,
disappearing finally
behind a stand of mesquite
and beavertail cacti:
calm ghosts,
not so much shy,
as cautious.

Terri and I driving
to Tappan and Beth's,
stopped a half-dozen yards
from the driveway
as two coyotes come

down the dry wash,
stand to watch us
as we watch them,
—curiosity on their part,
awe on ours—
then slip away into the brush.

Standing on the small hill
that holds a replica
of the Grotto of Lourdes
just east of the San Xavier Mission,
I point down the hill at a dog,
and joke, "There's a coyote,"
but it's no joke;
the lean shape ambles
in between the parked cars and buses,
and makes his brazen way
along the wall enclosing
the San Xavier Plaza,
set across the parking lot
from the Mission.
He's in sight a moment longer,
then he crosses the road
and saunters away,
into the scrub.

On the stones of a dry riverbed
at the bottom of an arroyo,
sitting with MaryAnn and Terri,
the slopes rising up on either side,
red stone and green cacti,
a secret place,
my gaze was caught
by a broken branch-stump
on the lower trunk
of a desert willow,
and there was Coyote,
rising from the wood,
head lifting out of the bark

nose pointed high,
ears cocked—
features pulled from the tree
by wind and stormy weather.

Driving back to Terri's
with Charles and Karen
in the backseat,
MaryAnn saying to them,
"I hope you'll get to see
a coyote before you go,"
and no sooner do the words leave her mouth,
than there he is,
a lean grey and brown form
caught in the headlights,
the reflection from
the tapetum layers behind his retinas
turning his gaze bright red.

3.

Coyote will survive
commercialism
and New Ageism
and tourism
and any other -isms
we care to throw his way.
He'll adapt to our intrusions,
into both myth and nature,
because he is Coyote.

It isn't mysticism
that sustains him,
but mystery.

4.

We brought home
Coyote in a photograph:

desert brush and cacti,
sun-bleached stone and faded dirt,
and somewhere in the picture,
hidden—
spot the coyote.

We brought home
Coyote on a T-shirt,
Bryer's coyote woman playing a flute
while all around her,
the coyotes are singing.

We brought home
Coyote as a Zuni fetish,
jet, inlaid with turquoise,
myth wise.

We brought home
Coyote in a pencil sketch
and another I did
with a ball point pen.

We brought home
Coyote and his mate,
in Terri's "Coyotes Mate for Life,"
brownprint and pastels,
an image that perfectly
steps the intuitive path
between coyote spirit
and human spirit.

The point is,
what we brought home
was the idea of Coyote,
the resonance of his presence
as it plays against my spirit,
but Coyote remains
as he always has been:
mythic spirit and desert predator,

cockily brazen and ghost shy,
Trickster and *Canis latrans*,
capable of adapting to
any environment or lifestyle,
and forever unconcerned
with how we perceive him.

5.

Coyote's
all used up now,
some will still insist.

Such a sentiment says more about
the one who holds it to be true
than it ever could about
Coyote.

At The Border

Coming back into Canada
after a seven-or-more-day visit abroad,
there's a $300 limit
as to what one can bring back,
duty-free.

The customs officer asks,
"What do you have to declare?"
I want to tell him,
memories
—desert moments
and coyote dreams
more precious than
the most intricate
turquoise and silver Navajo jewelry,
irreplaceable—
but I say only, "$298.45,"
show him a list of the items
I acquired,
and he waves me on through.

1992

The Bone Woman

No one really stops to think of Ellie Spink, and why should they?

She's no one.

She has nothing.

Homely as a child, all that the passing of years did was add to her unattractiveness. Face like a horse, jaw long and square, forehead broad; limpid eyes set bird-wide on either side of a gargantuan nose; hair a nondescript brown, greasy and matted, stuffed up under a woolen touque lined with a patchwork of metal foil scavenged from discarded cigarette packages. The angularity of her slight frame doesn't get its volume from her meager diet, but from the multiple layers of clothing she wears.

Raised in foster homes, she's been used, but she's never experienced a kiss. Institutionalized for most of her adult life, she's been medicated, but never treated. Pass her on the street and your gaze slides right on by, never pausing to register the difference between the old woman huddled in the doorway and a bag of garbage.

Old woman? Though she doesn't know it, Monday, two weeks past, was her thirty-seventh birthday. She looks twice her age.

There's no point in trying to talk to her. Usually no one's home. When there is, the words spill out in a disjointed mumble, a rambling, one-sided dialogue itemizing a litany of misperceived conspiracies and ills that soon leave you feeling as confused as she herself must be.

Normal conversation is impossible and not many bother to try it. The exceptions are few: The odd pitying passerby. A concerned social worker, fresh out of college and new to the streets. Maybe one of the other street people who happens to stumble into her particular haunts.

They talk and she listens or she doesn't—she never makes any sort of a relevant response, so who can tell? Few push the matter. Fewer still, however well-intentioned, have the stamina to make the attempt to do so more than once or twice. It's easier to just walk away; to bury your guilt, or laugh off her confused ranting as the excessive rhetoric it can only be.

I've done it myself.

I used to try to talk to her when I first started seeing her around, but I didn't get far. Angel told me a little about her, but even knowing her name and some of her history didn't help.

"Hey, Ellie. How're you doing?"

Pale eyes, almost translucent, turn towards me, set so far apart it's as though she can only see me with one eye at a time.

"They should test for aliens," she tells me. "You know, like in the Olympics."

"Aliens?"

"I mean, who cares who killed Kennedy? Dead's dead, right?"

"What's Kennedy got to do with aliens?"

"I don't even know why they took down the Berlin wall. What about the one in China? Shouldn't they have worked on that one first?"

It's like trying to have a conversation with a game of Trivial Pursuits that specializes in information garnered from supermarket tabloids. After awhile I'd just pack an extra sandwich whenever I was busking in her neighbourhood. I'd sit beside her, share my lunch and let her talk if she wanted to, but I wouldn't say all that much myself.

That all changed the day I saw her with the Bone Woman.

⪜ ⪛ ⪜

I didn't call her the Bone Woman at first; the adjective that came more immediately to mind was fat. She couldn't have been much more than five-foot-one, but she had to weigh in at two-fifty, leaving me with the impression that she was wider than she was tall. But she was light on her feet—peculiarly graceful for all her squat bulk.

She had a round face like a full moon, framed by thick black hair that hung in two long braids to her waist. Her eyes were small, almost lost in that expanse of face, and so dark they seemed all pupil. She went barefoot in a shapeless black dress, her only accessory an equally shapeless shoulder-bag made of some kind of animal skin and festooned with dangling thongs from which hung various feathers, beads, bottle-caps and other found objects.

I paused at the far end of the street when I saw the two of them together. I had a sandwich for Ellie in my knapsack, but I hesitated in approaching them. They seemed deep in conversation, real conversation, give and take, and Ellie was—knitting? Talking *and* knitting? The pair of them looked like a couple of old gossips, sitting on the back porch of their building. The sight of Ellie acting so normal was something I didn't want to interrupt.

I sat down on a nearby stoop and watched until Ellie put away her knitting and stood up. She looked down at her companion with an expression in her features that I'd never seen before. It was awareness, I realized. She was completely *here* for a change.

As she came up the street, I stood up and called a greeting to her, but by the time she reached me she wore her usual vacuous expression.

"It's the newspapers," she told me. "They use radiation to print them and that's what makes the news seem so bad."

Before I could take the sandwich I'd brought her out of my knapsack, she'd shuffled off, around the corner, and was gone. I glanced back down the street to where the fat woman was still sitting, and decided to find Ellie later. Right now I wanted to know what the woman had done to get such a positive reaction out of Ellie.

When I approached, the fat woman was sifting through the refuse where the two of them had been sitting. As I watched, she picked up a good-sized bone. What kind, I don't know, but it was as long as my forearm and as big around as the neck of my fiddle. Brushing dirt and a sticky candy-wrapper from it, she gave it a quick polish on the sleeve of her dress and stuffed it away in her shoulder-bag. Then she looked up at me.

My question died stillborn in my throat under the sudden scrutiny of those small dark eyes. She looked right through me—not the drifting, unfocused gaze of so many of the street people, but a cold far-off seeing that weighed my presence, dismissed it, and gazed further off at something far more important.

I stood back as she rose easily to her feet. That was when I realized how graceful she was. She moved down the sidewalk as daintily as a doe, as though her bulk was filled with helium, rather than flesh, and weighed nothing. I watched her until she reached the far end of the street, turned her own corner and then, just like Ellie, was gone as well.

I ended up giving Ellie's sandwich to Johnny Rew, an old wino who's taught me a fiddle tune or two, the odd time I've run into him sober.

⅄ Y ⅄

I started to see the Bone Woman everywhere after that day. I wasn't sure if she was just new to town, or if it was one of those cases where you see something or someone you've never noticed before and after that you see them all the time. Everybody I talked to about her seemed to know her, but no one was quite sure how long she'd been in the city, or where she lived, or even her name.

I still wasn't calling her the Bone Woman, though I knew by then that bones was all she collected. Old bones, found bones, rattling around together in her shoulder-bag until she went off at the end of the day and showed up the next morning, ready to start filling her bag again.

When she wasn't hunting bones, she spent her time with the street's worst cases—people like Ellie that no one else could talk to. She'd get them making things—little pictures or carvings or beadwork, keeping their hands busy. And talking. Someone like Ellie still made no sense to anybody else, but you could tell when she was with the Bone Woman that they were sharing a real dialogue. Which was a good thing, I suppose, but I couldn't shake the feeling that there was something more going on, something if not exactly sinister, then still strange.

It was the bones, I suppose. There were so many. How could she keep finding them the way she did? And what did she do with them?

My brother Christy collects urban legends, the way the Bone Woman collects her bones, rooting them out where you'd never think they could be. But when I told him about her, he just shrugged.

"Who knows why any of them do anything?" he said.

Christy doesn't live on the streets, for all that he haunts them. He's just an observer—always has been, ever since we were kids. To him, the street people can be pretty well evenly divided between the sad cases and the crazies. Their stories are too human for him.

"Some of these are big," I told him. "The size of a human thigh-bone."

"So point her out to the cops."

"And tell them what?"

A smile touched his lips with just enough superiority in it to get under my skin. He's always been able to do that. Usually, it makes me do something I regret later which I sometimes think is half his intention. It's not that he wants to see me hurt. It's just part and parcel of that air of authority that all older siblings seem to wear. You know, a raised eyebrow, a way of smiling that says "you have so much to learn, little brother."

"If you really want to know what she does with those bones," he said, "why don't you follow her home and find out?"

"Maybe I will."

⟞ ⟟ ⟜

It turned out that the Bone Woman had a squat on the roof of an abandoned factory building in the Tombs. She'd built herself some kind of a shed up there—just a leaning, ramshackle affair of cast-off lumber and sheet metal, but it kept out the weather and could easily be heated with a woodstove in the spring and fall. Come winter, she'd need warmer quarters, but the snows were still a month or so away.

I followed her home one afternoon, then came back the next day when she was out to finally put to rest my fear about these bones she was collecting. The thought that had stuck in my mind was that she was taking something away from the street people like Ellie, people who were already at the bottom rung and deserved to be helped, or at least just left alone. I'd gotten this weird idea that the bones were tied up with the last remnants of vitality that someone like Ellie might have, and the Bone Woman was stealing it from them.

What I found was more innocuous, and at the same time creepier, than I'd expected.

The inside of her squat was littered with bones and wire and dog-shaped skeletons that appeared to be made from the two. Bones held in place by wire, half-connected ribs and skulls and limbs. A pack of bone dogs. Some of the figures were almost complete, others were merely suggestions, but everywhere I looked, the half-finished wire-and-bone skeletons sat or stood or hung suspended from the ceiling. There had to be more than a dozen in various states of creation.

I stood in the doorway, not willing to venture any further, and just stared at them all. I don't know how long I was there, but finally I turned away and made my way back down through the abandoned building and out onto the street.

So now I knew what she did with the bones. But it didn't tell me how she could find so many of them. Surely that many stray dogs didn't die, their bones scattered the length and breadth of the city like so much autumn residue?

ⳕ Ⲧ ⳕ

Amy and I had a gig opening for the Kelledys that night. It didn't take me long to set up. I just adjusted my microphone, laid out my fiddle and whistles on a small table to one side, and then kicked my heels while Amy fussed with her pipes and the complicated tangle of electronics that she used to amplify them.

I've heard it said that all Uillean pipers are a little crazy—that they have to be to play an instrument that looks more like what you'd find in the back of a plumber's truck than an instrument—but I think of them as perfectionists. Every one I've ever met spends more time fiddling with their reeds and adjusting the tuning of their various chanters, drones and regulators than would seem humanly possible.

Amy's no exception. After awhile I left her there on the stage, with her red hair falling in her face as she poked and prodded at a new reed she'd made for one of her drones, and wandered into the back where the Kelledys were making their own preparations for the show, which consisted of drinking tea and looking beatific. At least that's the way I always think of the two of them. I don't think I've ever met calmer people.

Jilly likes to think of them as mysterious, attributing all kinds of fairy tale traits to them. Meran, she's convinced, with the green highlights in her nut-brown hair and her wise brown eyes, is definitely dryad material—the spirit of an oak tree come to life— while Cerin is some sort of wizard figure, a combination of adept and bard. I think the idea amuses them and they play it up to Jilly. Nothing you can put your finger on, but they seem to get a kick out of spinning a mysterious air about themselves whenever she's around.

I'm far more practical than Jilly—actually, just about anybody's more practical than Jilly, God bless her, but that's another story. I think if you find yourself using the word magic to describe the Kelledys, what you're really talking about is their musical talent. They may seem preternaturally calm off-stage, but as soon as they begin to play, that calmness is transformed into a bonfire of energy. There's enchantment then, burning on stage, but it comes from their instrumental skill.

"Geordie," Meran said after I'd paced back and forth for a few minutes. "You look a little edgy. Have some tea."

I had to smile. If the Kelledys had originated from some mysterious elsewhere, then I'd lean more towards them having come from a fiddle tune than Jilly's fairy tales.

"When sick is it tea you want?" I said, quoting the title of an old Irish jig that we all knew in common.

Meran returned my smile. "It can't hurt. Here," she added, rummaging around in a bag that was lying by her chair. "Let me see if I have something that'll ease your nervousness."

"I'm not nervous."

"No, of course not," Cerin put in. "Geordie just likes to pace, don't you?"

He was smiling as he spoke, but without a hint of Christy's sometimes annoying demeanor.

"No, really. It's just..."

"Just what?" Meran asked as my voice trailed off.

Well, here was the perfect opportunity to put Jilly's theories to the test, I decided. If the Kelledys were in fact as fey as she made them out to be, then they'd be able to explain this business with the bones, wouldn't they?

So I told them about the fat woman and her bones and what I'd found in her squat. They listened with far more reasonableness than I would have if someone had been telling the story to me—especially when I went on to explain the weird feeling I'd been getting from the whole business.

"It's giving me the creeps," I said, finishing up, "and I can't even say why."

"*La Huesera*," Cerin said when I was done.

Meran nodded. "The Bone Woman," she said, translating it for me. "It does sound like her."

"So you know her."

"No," Meran said. "It just reminds us of a story we heard when we were playing in Phoenix a few years ago. There was a young Apache man opening for us and he and I started comparing flutes. We got on to one of the Native courting flutes which used to be made from human bone and somehow from there John started telling me about a legend they have in the Southwest about this old fat woman who wanders through the mountains and arroyos, collecting bones from the desert that she brings back to her cave."

"What does she collect them for?"

"To preserve the things that are in danger of being lost to the world," Cerin said.

"I don't get it."

"I'm not sure of the exact details," Cerin went on, "but it had something to do with the spirits of endangered species."

"Giving them a new life," Meran said.

"Or a second chance."

"But there's no desert around here," I said. "What would this Bone Woman being doing up here?"

Meran smiled. "I remember John saying that she's been seen as often riding shotgun in an eighteen-wheeler as walking down a dry wash."

"And besides," Cerin added. "Any place is a desert when there's more going on underground than on the surface."

That described Newford perfectly. And who lived a more hidden life than the street people? They were right in front of us every day, but most people didn't even see them anymore. And who was more deserving of a second chance than someone like Ellie, who'd never even gotten a fair first chance?

"Too many of us live desert lives," Cerin said, and I knew just what he meant.

⋋ ⊀ ⋌

The gig went well. I was a little bemused, but I didn't make any major mistakes. Amy complained that her regulators had sounded too buzzy in the monitors, but that was just Amy. They'd sounded great to me, their counterpointing chords giving the tunes a real punch whenever they came in.

The Kelledys' set was pure magic. Amy and I watched them from the stage wings and felt higher as they took their final bow than we had when the applause had been directed at us.

I begged off getting together with them after the show, regretfully pleading tiredness. I *was* tired, but leaving the theatre, I headed for an abandoned factory in the Tombs instead of home. When I got up on the roof of the building, the moon was full. It looked like a saucer of buttery gold, bathing everything in a warm yellow light. I heard a soft voice on the far side of the roof near the Bone Woman's squat. It wasn't exactly singing, but not chanting either. A murmuring, sliding sound that raised the hairs at the nape of my neck.

I walked a little nearer, staying in the shadows of the cornices, until I could see the Bone Woman. I paused then, laying my fiddlecase quietly on the roof and sliding down so that I was sitting with my back against the cornice.

The Bone Woman had one of her skeleton sculptures set out in front of her and she was singing over it. The dog shape was complete now, all the bones wired in place and gleaming in the moonlight. I couldn't make out the words of her song. Either there were none, or she was using a language I'd never heard before. As I watched, she stood, raising her arms up above the wired skeleton, and her voice grew louder.

The scene was peaceful—soothing, in the same way that the Kelledys' company could be—but eerie as well. The Bone Woman's voice had the cadence of one of the medicine chants I'd heard at a powwow up on the Kickaha rez—the same nasal tones and ringing quality. But that powwow hadn't prepared me for what came next.

At first I wasn't sure that I was really seeing it. The empty spaces between the skeleton's bones seemed to gather volume and fill out, as though flesh were forming on the bones. Then there was fur, highlit by the moonlight, and I couldn't deny it any more. I saw a bewhiskered muzzle lift skyward, ears twitch, a tail curl up, thick-haired and strong. The powerful chest began to move rhythmically, at first in time to the Bone Woman's song, then breathing of its own accord.

The Bone Woman hadn't been making dogs in her squat, I realized as I watched the miraculous change occur. She'd been making wolves.

The newly-animated creature's eyes snapped open and it leapt up, running to the edge of the roof. There it stood with its forelegs on the cornice. Arcing its neck, the wolf pointed its nose at the moon and howled.

I sat there, already stunned, but the transformation still wasn't complete. As the wolf howled, it began to change again. Fur to human skin. Lupine shape, to that of a young woman. Howl to merry laughter. And as she turned, I recognized her features.

"Ellie," I breathed.

She still had the same horsey-features, the same skinny body, all bones and angles, but she was beautiful. She blazed with the fire of a spirit that had never been hurt, never been abused, never been degraded. She gave me a radiant smile and then leapt from the edge of the roof.

I held my breath, but she didn't fall. She walked out across the city's skyline, out across the urban desert of rooftops and chimneys, off and away, running now, laughter trailing behind her until she was swallowed by the horizon.

I stared out at the night sky long after she had disappeared, then slowly stood up and walked across the roof to where the Bone Woman was sitting outside the door of her squat. She tracked my approach, but there was neither welcome nor dismissal in those small dark eyes. It was like the first time I'd come up to her; as far as she was concerned, I wasn't there at all.

"How did you do that?" I asked.

She looked through, past me.

"Can you teach me that song? I want to help, too."

Still no response.

"Why won't you *talk* to me?"

Finally her gaze focused on me.

"You don't have their need," she said.

Her voice was thick with an accent I couldn't place. I waited for her to go on, to explain what she meant, but once again, she ignored me. The pinpoints of black that passed for eyes in that round moon face looked away into a place where I didn't belong.

Finally, I did the only thing left for me to do. I collected my fiddlecase and went on home.

ᛉ Ⴤ ᛈ

Some things haven't changed. Ellie's still living on the streets and I still share my lunch with her when I'm down in her part of town. There's nothing the Bone Woman can do to change what this life has done to the Ellie Spinks of the world.

But what I saw that night gives me hope for the next turn of the wheel. I know now that no matter how downtrodden someone like Ellie might be, at least somewhere a piece of her is running free. Somewhere that wild and innocent part of her spirit is being preserved with those of the wolf and the rattlesnake and all the other creatures whose spirit-bones *la Huesera* collects from the desert—deserts natural, and of our own making.

Spirit-bones. Collected and preserved, nurtured in the belly of the Bone Woman's song, until we learn to welcome them upon their terms, rather than our own.

Author's note: The idea of *la Huesera* comes from the folklore of the American Southwest. My thanks to Clarissa Pinkola Estés for making me aware of the tale.

Mr. Truepenny's
Book Emporium and Gallery

The constellations were consulted
for advice, but no one understood
them.

Elias Canetti

My name's Sophie and my friend Jilly says I have faerie blood. Maybe she's right.

Faerie are supposed to have problems dealing with modern technology and I certainly have trouble with anything technological. The simplest appliances develop horrendous problems when I'm around. I can't wear a watch because they start to run backwards, unless they're digital; then they just flash random numbers as though the watch's inner workings have taken to measuring fractals instead of time. If I take a subway or bus, it's sure to be late. Or it'll have a new driver who takes a wrong turn and we all get lost.

This kind of thing actually happens to me. Once I got on the #3 at the Kelly Street Bridge and somehow, instead of going downtown on Lee, we ended up heading north into Foxville.

I also have strange dreams.

I used to think they were the place that my art came from, that my subconscious was playing around with images, tossing them up in my sleep before I put them down on canvas or paper. But then a few months ago I had this serial dream that ran on for a half dozen nights in a row, a kind of fairy tale that was either me stepping into Faerie and therefore real within its own parameters—which is what Jilly would like me to believe— or it was just my subconscious making another attempt to deal with the way my mother abandoned my father and me when I was a kid. I don't really know which I believe anymore, because I still find myself going back to that dream world from time to time and meeting the people I first met there.

I even have a boyfriend in that place, which probably tells you more about my ongoing social states than it does my state of mind.

Rationally, I know it's just a continuation of that serial dream. And I'd let it go at that, except it feels so damn real. Every morning when I wake up from the latest installment, my head's filled with memories of what I've done that seem as real as anything I do during the day—sometimes more so.

But I'm getting off on a tangent. I started off meaning to just introduce myself, and here I am, giving you my life story. What I really wanted to tell you about was Mr. Truepenny.

The thing you have to understand is that I made him up. He was like one of those invisible childhood friends, except I deliberately created him.

We weren't exactly well-off when I was growing up. When my mother left us, I ended up being one of those latch-key kids. We didn't live in the best part of town; Upper Foxville is a rough part of the city and it could be a scary place for a little girl who loved art and books and got teased for that love by the other neighbourhood kids who couldn't even be bothered to learn how to read. When I got home from school, I went straight in and locked the door.

I'd get supper ready for my dad, but there were always a couple of hours to kill in between my arriving home and when he finished work— longer if he had to work late. We didn't have a TV, so I read a lot, but we couldn't afford to buy books. On Saturday mornings, we'd go to the library and I'd take out my limit—five books—which I'd finish by Tuesday, even if I tried to stretch them out.

To fill the rest of the time, I'd draw on shopping bags or the pads of paper that dad brought me home from work, but that never seemed to occupy enough hours. So one day I made up Mr. Truepenny.

I'd daydream about going to his shop. It was the most perfect place that I could imagine: all dark wood and leaded glass, thick carpets and club chairs with carved wooden-based reading lamps strategically placed throughout. The shelves were filled with leather-bound books and folios, and there was a small art gallery in the back.

The special thing about Mr. Truepenny's shop was that all of its contents only existed within its walls. Shakespeare's *The Storm of Winter*. *The Chapman's Tale* by Chaucer. *The Blissful Stream* by William Morris. Steinbeck's companion collection to *The Long Valley*, *Salinas*. *North Country Stoic* by Emily Bronte.

None of these books existed, of course, but being the dreamy sort of kid that I was, not only could I daydream of visiting Mr. Truepenny's shop, but I could actually read these unwritten stories. The gallery in the back of the shop was much the same. There hung works by the masters that saw the light of day only in my imagination. Van Goghs and Monets and Da Vincis. Rossettis and Homers and Cézannes.

Mr. Truepenny himself was a wonderfully eccentric individual who never once chased me out for being unable to make a purchase. He had a Don Quixote air about him, a sense that he was forever tilting at windmills. He was tall and thin with a thatch of mouse-brown hair and round spectacles, a rumpled tweed suit and a huge briar pipe that he continually fussed with but never actually lit. He always greeted me with genuine affection and seemed disappointed when it was time for me to go.

My imagination was so vivid that my daydream visits to his shop were as real to me as when my dad took me to the library or the Newford Gallery of Fine Art. But it didn't last. I grew up, went to Butler University on student loans and the money from far too many menial jobs—"got a life," as the old saying goes. I made friends, I was so busy, there was no time, no need to visit the shop anymore. Eventually I simply forgot all about it.

Until I met Janice Petrie.

Wendy and I were in the Market after a late night at her place the previous evening. I was on my way home, but we'd decided to shop for groceries together before I left. Trying to make up my mind between green beans and a head of broccoli, my gaze lifted above the vegetable stand and met that of a little girl standing nearby with her parents. Her eyes widened with recognition, though I'd never seen her before.

"You're the woman!" she cried. "You're the woman who's evicting Mr. Truepenny. I think it's a horrible thing to do. You're a horrible woman!"

And then she started to cry. Her mother shushed her and apologized to me for the outburst before bustling the little girl away.

"What was all *that* about, Sophie?" Wendy asked me.

"I have no idea," I said.

But of course I did. I was just so astonished by the encounter that I didn't know what to say. I changed the subject and that was the end of it until I got home. I dug out an old cardboard box from the back of my hall closet and rooted about in it until I came up with a folder of drawings I'd done when I still lived with my dad. Near the back I found the ones I was looking for.

They were studies of Mr. Truepenny and his amazing shop.

God, I thought, looking at these awkward drawings, pencil on brown grocery bag paper, ball-point on foolscap. The things we forget.

I took them out onto my balcony and lay down on the old sofa, studying them, one by one. There was Mr. Truepenny, writing something in his big leather-bound ledger. Here was another of him, holding his cat Dodger, the two of them looking out the leaded glass windows of the shop. There was a view of the main aisle of the shop, leading down to the gallery, the perspective slightly askew, but not half bad considering I was no older when I did them than was the little girl in the Market today.

How could she have known? I found myself thinking. Mr. Truepenny and his shop was something I'd made up. I couldn't remember ever telling anyone else about it—not even Jilly. And what did she mean about my evicting him from the shop?

I could think of no rational response. After awhile, I just set the drawings aside and tried to forget about it. Exhaustion from the late night before soon had me nodding off and I fell asleep only to find myself, not in my boyfriend's faerie dream world, but on the streets of Mabon, the made-up city in which I'd put Mr. Truepenny's Book Emporium and Gallery.

⊱ ⋎ ⊰

I'm half a block from the shop. The area's changed. The once-neat cobblestones are thick with grime. Refuse lies everywhere. Most of the storefronts are boarded up, their walls festooned with graffiti. When I reach Mr. Truepenny's shop, I see a sign in the window that reads, "Closing soon due to lease expiration."

Half-dreading what I'll find, I open the door and hear the familiar little bell tinkle as I step inside. The shop's dusty and dim, and much smaller than I remember it. The shelves are almost bare. The door leading to the gallery is shut and has a "Closed" sign tacked onto it.

"Ah, Miss Etoile. It's been so very long."

I turn to find Mr. Truepenny at his usual station behind the front counter. He's smaller than I remember as well and looks a little shabby now. Hair thinning, tweed suit threadbare and more shapeless than ever.

"What...what's happened to the shop?" I ask.

I've forgotten that I'm asleep on the sofa out on my balcony. All I know is this awful feeling I have inside as I look at what's become of my old childhood haunt.

"Well, times change," he says. "The world moves on."

"This—is this my doing?"

His eyebrows rise quizzically.

"I met this little girl and she said I was evicting you."

"I don't blame you," Mr. Truepenny says and I can see in his sad eyes that it's true. "You've no more need for me or my wares, so it's only fair that you let us fade."

"But you...that is...well, you're not real."

I feel weird saying this because while I remember now that I'm dreaming, this place is like one of my faerie dreams that feels as real as the waking world.

"That's not strictly true," he tells me. "You did conceive of the city and this shop, but we were drawn to fit the blueprint of your plan from...elsewhere."

"What elsewhere?"

He frowns, brow furrowing as he thinks.

"I'm not really sure myself," he tells me.

"You're saying I didn't make you up, I just drew you here from somewhere else?"

He nods.

"And now you have to go back?"

"So it would seem."

"And this little girl—how can she know about you?"

"Once a reputable establishment is open for business, it really can't deny any customer access, regardless of their age or station in life."

"She's visiting my daydream?" I ask. This is too much to accept, even for a dream.

Mr. Truepenny shakes his head. "You brought this world into being through your single-minded desire, but now it has a life of its own."

"Until I forgot about it."

"You had a very strong will," he says. "You made us so real that we've been able to hang on for decades. But now we really have to go."

There's a very twisty sort of logic involved here, I can see. It doesn't make sense by way of the waking world's logic, but I think there are different rules in a dreamscape. After all, my faerie boyfriend can turn into a crow.

"Do you have more customers than that little girl?" I ask.

"Oh yes. Or at least, we did." He waves a hand to encompass the shop. "Not much stock left, I'm afraid. That was the first to go."

"Why doesn't their desire keep things running?"

"Well, they don't have faerie blood, now do they? They can visit, but they haven't the magic to bring us across or keep us here."

It figures. I think. We're back to that faerie blood thing again. Jilly would love this.

I'm about to ask him to explain it all a little more clearly when I get this odd jangling sound in my ears and wake up back on the sofa. My doorbell's ringing. I go inside the apartment to accept what turns out to be a FedEx package.

"Can dreams be real?" I ask the courier. "Can we invent something in a dream and have it turn out to be a real place?"

"Beats me, lady," he replies, never blinking an eye. "Just sign here."

I guess he gets all kinds.

ᚹ Y ᚸ

So now I visit Mr. Truepenny's shop on a regular basis again. The area's vastly improved. There's a café nearby where Jeck—that's my boyfriend that I've been telling you about—and I go for tea after we've browsed through Mr. Truepenny's latest wares. Jeck likes this part of Mabon so much that he's now got an apartment on the same street as the shop. I think I might set up a studio nearby.

I've even run into Janice—the little girl who brought me back here in the first place. She's forgiven me, of course, now that she knows it was all a misunderstanding, and lets me buy her an ice cream from the soda fountain sometimes before she goes home.

I'm very accepting of it all—you get that way after awhile. The thing that worries me now is, what happens to Mabon when I die? Will the city get run down again and eventually disappear? And what about its residents? There's all these people here; they've got family, friends, lives. I get the feeling it wouldn't be the same for them if they have to go back to that elsewhere place Mr. Truepenny was so vague about.

So that's the reason I've written all this down and had it printed up into a little folio by one of Mr. Truepenny's friends in the waking world. I'm hoping somebody out there's like me. Someone's got enough faerie blood to not only visit, but keep the place going. Naturally, not just anyone will do. It has to be the right sort of person, a book-lover, a lover of old places and tradition, as well as the new.

If you think you're the person for the position, please send a résumé to me care of Mr. Truepenny's Book Emporium and Gallery, Mabon. I'll get back to you as soon as I can.

1993

Coyote Stories

Four directions blow the sacred winds
We are standing at the center
Every morning wakes another chance
To make our lives a little better

Kiya Heartwood,
from "Wishing Well"

 This day Coyote is feeling pretty thirsty, so he goes into Joey's Bar, you know, on the corner of Palm and Grasso, across from the Men's Mission, and he lays a nugget of gold down on the counter, but Joey he won't serve him.

"So you don't serve skins no more?" Coyote he asks him.

"Last time you gave me gold, it turned to shit on me," is what Joey says. He points to the Rolex on Coyote's wrist. "But I'll take that. Give you change and everything."

Coyote scratches his muzzle and pretends he has to think about it. "Cost me twenty-five dollars," he says. "It looks better than the real thing."

"I'll give you fifteen, cash, and a beer."

"How about a bottle of whiskey?"

So Coyote comes out of Joey's Bar and he's missing his Rolex now, but he's got a bottle of Jack in his hand and that's when he sees Albert, just around the corner, sitting on the ground with his back against the

385

brick wall and his legs stuck out across the sidewalk so you have to step over them, you want to get by.

"Hey, Albert," Coyote says. "What's your problem?"

"Joey won't serve me no more."

"That because you're indigenous?"

"Naw. I got no money."

So Coyote offers him some of his whiskey. "Have yourself a swallow," he says, feeling generous, because he only paid two dollars for the Rolex and it never worked anyway.

"Thanks, but I don't think so," is what Albert tells him. "Seems to me I've been given a sign. Got no money means I should stop drinking."

Coyote shakes his head and takes a sip of his Jack. "You are one crazy skin," he says.

That Coyote he likes his whiskey. It goes down smooth and puts a gleam in his eye. Maybe, he drinks enough, he'll remember some good time and smile, maybe he'll get mean and pick himself a fight with a lamp post like he's done before. But one thing he knows, whether he's got money or not's got nothing to do with omens. Not for him, anyway.

Å Y ⊣

But a lack of money isn't really an omen for Albert either; it's a way of life. Albert, he's like the rest of us skins. Left the reserve, and we don't know why. Come to the city, and we don't know why. Still alive, and we don't know why. But Albert, he remembers it being different. He used to listen to his grandmother's stories, soaked them up like the dirt will rain, thirsty after a long drought. And he tells stories himself, too, or pieces of stories, talk to you all night long if you want to listen to him.

It's always Coyote in Albert's stories, doesn't matter if he's making them up or just passing along gossip. Sometimes Coyote's himself, sometimes he's Albert, sometimes he's somebody else. Like it wasn't Coyote sold his Rolex and ran into him outside Joey's Bar that day, it was Billy Yazhie. Maybe ten years ago now, Billy he's standing under a turquoise sky beside Spider Rock one day, looking up, looking up for a long time, before he turns away and walks to the nearest highway, sticks out his thumb and he doesn't look back till it's too late. Wakes up one morning and everything he knew is gone and he can't find his way back.

Oh that Billy he's a dark skin, he's like leather. You shake his hand and it's like you took hold of a cowboy boot. He knows some of the old songs and he's got himself a good voice, strong, ask anyone. He used to drum for the dancers back home, but his hands shake too much now, he says. He doesn't sing much anymore, either. He's got to be like the rest of us, hanging out in Fitzhenry Park, walking the streets, sleeping in an alleyway because the Men's Mission it's out of beds. We've got the stoic faces down real good, but you look in our eyes, maybe catch us off guard, you'll see we don't forget anything. It's just most times we don't want to remember.

⊱ ⅄ ⊰

This Coyote he's not too smart sometimes. One day he gets into a fight with a biker, says he going to count coup like his plains brothers, knock that biker all over the street, only the biker's got himself a big hickory-handled hunting knife and he cuts Coyote's head right off. Puts a quick end to that fight, I'll tell you. Coyote he spends the rest of the afternoon running around, trying to find somebody to sew his head back on again.

"That Coyote," Jimmy Coldwater says, "he's always losing his head over one thing or another."

I tell you we laughed.

⊱ ⅄ ⊰

But Albert he takes that omen seriously. You see him drinking still, but he's drinking coffee now, black as a raven's wing, or some kind of tea he brews for himself in a tin can, makes it from weeds he picks in the empty lots and dries in the sun. He's living in an abandoned factory these days, and he's got this one wall, he's gluing feathers and bones to it, nothing fancy, no eagles' wings, no bear's jaw, wolf skull, just what he can find lying around, pigeon feathers and crows', rat bones, bird bones, a necklace of mouse skulls strung on a wire. Twigs and bundles of weeds, rattles he makes from tin cans and bottles and jars. He paints figures on the wall, in between all the junk. Thunderbird. Bear. Turtle. Raven.

Everybody's starting to agree, that Albert he's one crazy skin.

Now when he's got money, he buys food with it and shares it out. Sometimes he walks over to Palm Street where the skin girls are working the trade and he gives them money, asks them to take a night off. Sometimes they take the money and just laugh, getting into the next car that pulls up. But sometimes they take the money and they sit in a coffee shop, sit there by the window, drinking their coffee and look out at where they don't have to be for one night.

And he never stops telling stories.

"That's what we are," he tells me one time. Albert he's smiling, his lips are smiling, his eyes are smiling, but I know he's not joking when he tells me that. "Just stories. You and me, everybody, we're a set of stories, and what those stories are is what makes us what we are. Same thing for whites as skins. Same thing for a tribe and a city and a nation and the world. It's all these stories and how they braid together that tells us who and what and where we are.

"We got to stop forgetting and get back to remembering. We got to stop asking for things, stop waiting for people to give us the things we think we need. All we really need is the stories. We have the stories and they'll give us the one thing nobody else can, the thing we can only take for ourselves, because there's nobody can give you back your pride. You've got to take it back yourself.

"You lose your pride and you lose everything. We don't want to know the stories, because we don't want to remember. But we've got to take the good with the bad and make ourselves whole again, be proud again. A proud people can never be defeated. They lose battles, but they'll never lose the war, because for them to lose the war you've got to go out and kill each and every one of them, everybody with even a drop of the blood. And even then, the stories will go on. There just won't be any skins left to hear them."

ⲗ Ⲩ ⲗ

This Coyote he's always getting in trouble. One day he's sitting at a park bench, reading a newspaper, and this cop starts to talk big to one of the skin girls, starts talking mean, starts pushing her around. Coyote's feeling chivalrous that day, like he's in a white man's movie, and he gets into a fight with the cop. He gets beat up bad and then more cops come and they take him away, put him in jail.

The judge he turns Coyote into a mouse for a year so that there's Coyote, got that same lopsided grin, got that sharp muzzle and those long ears and the big bushy tail, but he's so small now you can hold him in the palm of your hand.

"Doesn't matter how small you make me," Coyote he says to the judge. "I'm still Coyote."

⊢ ⋎ ⊣

Albert he's so serious now. He gets out of jail and he goes back to living in the factory. Kids've torn down that wall of his, so he gets back to fixing it right, gets back to sharing food and brewing tea and helping the skin girls out when he can, gets back to telling stories. Some people they start thinking of him as a shaman and call him by an old Kickaha name.

Dan Whiteduck he translates the name for Billy Yazhie, but Billy he's not quite sure what he's heard. Know-more-truth, or No-more-truth?

"You spell that with a 'K' or what?" Billy he asks Albert.

"You take your pick how you want to spell it," Albert he says.

Billy he learns how to pronounce that old name and that's what he uses when he's talking about Albert. Lots of people do. But most of us we just keep on calling him Albert.

⊢ ⋎ ⊣

One day this Coyote decides he wants to have a powwow, so he clears the trash from this empty lot, makes the circle, makes the fire. The people come but no one knows the songs anymore, no one knows the drumming that the dancers need, no one knows the steps. Everybody they're just standing around, looking at each other, feeling sort of stupid, until Coyote he starts singing, *ya-ha-hey*, *ya-ha-hey*, and he's stomping around the circle, kicking up dirt and dust.

People they start to laugh, then, seeing Coyote playing the fool.

"You are one crazy skin!" Angie Crow calls to him and people laugh some more, nodding in agreement, pointing at Coyote as he dances round and round the circle.

But Jimmy Coldwater he picks up a stick and he walks over to the drum Coyote made. It's this big metal tub, salvaged from a junkyard, that Coyote's covered with a skin and who knows where he got that skin, nobody's asking. Jimmy he hits the skin of the drum and everybody they stop laughing and look at him, so Jimmy he hits the skin again. Pretty soon he's got the rhythm to Coyote's dance and then Dan Whiteduck he picks up a stick, too, and joins Jimmy at the drum.

Billy Yazhie he starts up to singing then, takes Coyote's song and turns it around so that he's singing about Spider Rock and turquoise skies, except everybody hears it their own way, hears the stories they want to hear in it. There's more people drumming and there's people dancing and before anyone knows it, the night's over and there's the dawn poking over the roof of an abandoned factory, thinking, these are some crazy skins. People they're lying around and sitting around, eating the flatbread and drinking the tea that Coyote provided, and they're all tired, but there's something in their hearts that feels very full.

"This was one fine powwow," Coyote he says.

Angie she nods her head. She's sitting beside Coyote all sweaty and hot and she'd never looked quite so good before.

"Yeah," she says. "We got to do it again."

Ⲗ Ⲩ Ⲗ

We start having regular powwows after that night, once, sometimes twice a month. Some of the skins they start to making dancing outfits, going back up to the reserve for visits and asking about steps and songs from the old folks. Gets to be we feel like a community, a small skin nation living here in exile with the ruins of broken-down tenements and abandoned buildings all around us. Gets to be we start remembering some of our stories and sharing them with each other instead of sharing bottles. Gets to be we have something to feel proud about.

Some of us we find jobs. Some of us we try to climb up the side of the wagon but we keep falling off. Some of us we go back to homes we can hardly remember. Some of us we come from homes where we can't live, can't even breathe, and drift here and there until we join this tribe that Albert he helped us find.

And even if Albert he's not here anymore, the stories go on. They have to go on, I know that much. I tell them every chance I get.

Ⲗ Ⲩ Ⲗ

See, this Coyote he got in trouble again, this Coyote he's always getting in trouble, you know that by now, same as me. And when he's in jail this time he sees that it's all tribes inside, the same as it is outside. White tribes, black tribes, yellow tribes, skin tribes. He finally understands, finally realizes that maybe there can't ever be just one tribe, but that doesn't mean we should stop trying.

But even in jail this Coyote he can't stay out of trouble and one day he gets into another fight and he gets cut again, but this time he thinks maybe he's going to die.

"Albert," Coyote he says, "I am one crazy skin. I am never going to learn, am I?"

"Maybe not this time," Albert says, and he's holding Coyote's head and he's wiping the dribble of blood that comes out of the side of Coyote's mouth and is trickling down his chin. "But that's why you're Coyote. The wheel goes round and you'll get another chance."

Coyote he's trying to be brave, but he's feeling weaker and it hurts, it hurts, this wound in his chest that cuts to the bone, that cuts the thread that binds him to this story.

"There's a thing I have to remember," Coyote he says, "but I can't find it. I can't find its story…"

"Doesn't matter how small they try to make you," Albert he reminds Coyote. "You're still Coyote."

"*Ya-ha-hey*," Coyote he says. "Now I remember."

Then Coyote he grins and he lets the pain take him away into another story.

1994

Heartfires

1

Nobody tells you the really important stuff, so in the end you have to imagine it for yourself. It's like how things connect. A thing is just a thing until you have the story that goes with it. Without the story, there's nothing to hold on to, nothing to relate this mysterious new thing to who you are—you know, to make it a part of your own history. So if you're like me, you make something up and the funny thing is, lots of times, once you tell the story, it comes true. Not *poof*, hocus-pocus, magic it comes true, but sure, why not, and after it gets repeated often enough, you and everybody else end up believing it.

It's like quarks. They're neither positive nor negative until the research scientists look at them. Right up until that moment of observation they hold the possibility of being one or the other. It's the *looking* that makes them what they are. Which is like making up a story for them, right?

The world's full of riddles like that.

The lady or the tiger.

Did she jump, or was she pushed?

The door standing by itself in the middle of the field—does it lead to somewhere, or from somewhere?

Or the locked room we found one night down in Old City, the part of it that runs under the Tombs. A ten-by-ten foot room, stone walls, stone floor and ceiling, with a door in one wall that fits so snugly you wouldn't even know it was there except for the bolts—a set on either side of the door, big old iron fittings, rusted, but still solid. The air in that room is dry, touched with the taste of old spices and sagegrass. And the place is clean. No dust. No dirt. Only these scratches on that weird door, long gouges cut into the stone like something was clawing at it, both sides of the door, inside and out.

So what was it for? Before the 'quake dropped the building into the ground, that room was still below street level. Somebody from the long ago built that room, hid it away in the cellar of what must have been a seriously tall building in those days—seven stories high. Except for the top floor, it's all underground now. We didn't even know the building was there until Bear fell through a hole in the roof, landing on his ass in a pile of rubble which, luckily for him, was only a few feet down. Most of that top floor was filled with broken stone and crap, like someone had bulldozed another tumbled-down building inside it and overtop of it, pretty much blocking any way in and turning that top floor into a small mountain covered with metal junk and weeds and every kind of trash you can imagine. It was a fluke we ever found our way in, it was that well hidden.

But why was it hidden? Because the building couldn't be salvaged, so cover it up, make it safe? Or because of that room?

That room. Was it to lock something in? Or keep something out?

Did our going into it make it be one or the other? Or was it the story we found in its stone confines?

We told that story to each other, taking turns like we usually do, and when we were done, we remembered what that room was. We'd never been in it before, not that room, in that place, but we remembered.

2

Devil's Night, October 30th. It's not even nine o'clock and they've already got fires burning all over the Tombs: sparks flying, grass fires in the empty lots, trash fires in metal drums, the guts of derelict tenements and factory buildings going up like so much kindling. The sky overhead fills with an evil glow, like an aura gone bad, gone way bad. The smoke from the fires rises in streaming columns. It cuts through the orange glare hanging over that square mile or so of lost hopes and despair the way ink spreads in water.

The streets are choked with refuse and abandoned cars, but that doesn't stop the revelers from their fun, the flickering light of the fires playing across their features as they lift their heads and howl at the devil's glow. Does stop the fire department, though. This year they don't even bother to try to get their trucks in. You can almost hear the mayor telling the chiefs: "Let it burn."

Hell, it's only the Tombs. Nobody living here but squatters and hoboes, junkies and bikers. These are the inhabitants of the night side of the city—the side you only see out of the corner of your eye until the sun goes down and suddenly they're all over the streets, in your face, instead of back in the shadows where they belong. They're not citizens. They don't even vote.

And they're having some fun tonight. Not the kind of recreation you or I might look for, but a desperate fun, the kind that's born out of knowing you've got nowhere to go but down and you're already at the bottom. I'm not making excuses for them. I just understand them a little better than most citizens might.

See, I've run with them. I've slept in those abandoned buildings, scrabbled for food in dumpsters over by Williamson Street, trying to get there before the rats and feral dogs. I've looked for oblivion in the bottom of a bottle or at the end of a needle.

No, don't go feeling sorry for me. I had me some hard times, sure. Everybody does. But I'll tell you, I never torched buildings. Even in the long ago. When I'm looking to set a fire, I want it to burn in the heart.

3

I'm an old crow, but I still know a few tricks. I'm looking rough, maybe even used up, but I'm not yet so old I'm useless. You can't fool me, but I fool most everyone, wearing clothes, hiding my feathers, walking around on my hind legs like a man, upright, not hunched over, moving pretty fast, considering.

There were four of us in those days, ran together from time to time. Old spirits, wandering the world, stopped awhile in this place before we went on. We're always moving on, restless, looking for change so that things'll stay the same. There was me, Crazy Crow, looking sharp with my flat-brimmed hat and pointy-toed boots. Alberta the Dancer with those antlers poking up out of her red hair, you know how to look, you can see them. Bear, he was so big you felt like the sky had gone dark when he stood by you. And then there was Jolene.

She was just a kid that Devil's Night. She gets like that. One year she's about knee-high to a skinny moment and you can't stop her from tomfooling around, another year she's so fat even Bear feels small around her. We go way back, Jolene and me, knew each other pretty good, we met so often.

Me and Alberta were together that year. We took Jolene in like she was our daughter, Bear her uncle. Moving on the wheel like a family. We're dark-skinned—we're old spirits, got to be the way we are before the European look got so popular—but not so dark as fur and feathers. Crow, grizzly, deer. We lose some colour when we wear clothes, walking on our hind legs all the time.

Sometimes we lose other things, too. Like who we really are and what we're doing here.

4

"Hey, 'bo."

I look up to see it's a brother calling to me. We're standing around an oil drum, warming our hands, and he comes walking out of the shadows like he's a piece of them, got free somehow, comes walking right up to me like he thinks I'm in charge. Alberta smiles. Bear lights a smoke, takes a couple of drags, then offers it to the brother.

"Bad night for fires," he says after he takes a drag. He gives the cigarette a funny look, tasting the sweetgrass mixed in with the tobacco. Not much, just enough.

"Devil's Night," Jolene says, grinning like it's a good thing. She's a little too fond of fires this year for my taste. Next thing you know she'll be wanting to tame metal, build herself a machine and wouldn't that be something?

"Nothing to smile about," the brother tells her. "Lot of people get hurt, Devil's Night. Gets out of hand. Gets to where people think it's funny, maybe set a few of us 'boes on fire, you hear what I'm saying?"

"Times are always hard," I say.

He shrugs, takes another drag of the cigarette, then hands it back to Bear.

"Good night for a walk," he says finally. "A body might walk clear out of the Tombs on a night like this, come back when things are a little more settled down."

We all just look at him.

"Got my boy waiting on me," he says. "Going for that walk. You all take care of yourselves now."

We never saw the boy, standing there in the shadows, waiting on his pa, except maybe Jolene. There's not much she misses. I wait until the shadow's almost swallowed the brother before I call after him.

"Appreciate the caution," I tell him.

He looks back, tips a finger to his brow, then he's gone, part of the shadows again.

"Are we looking for trouble?" Bear asks.

"Uh-huh," Jolene pipes up, but I shake my head.

"Like he said," I tell them, jerking a thumb to where the brother walked away.

Bear leads the way out, heading east, taking a direct route and avoiding the fires we can see springing up all around us now. The dark doesn't bother us, we can see pretty much the same, doesn't matter if it's night or day. We follow Bear up a hillside of rubble. He gets to the top before us and starts dancing around, stamping his feet, singing, "Wa-hey, look at me. I'm the king of the mountain."

And then he disappears between one stamp and the next, and that's how we find the room.

5

I don't know why we slide down to where Bear's standing instead of him climbing back up. Curious, I guess. Smelling spirit mischief and we just have to see where it leads us, down, down, till we're standing on a dark street, way underground.

"Old City," Alberta says.

"Walked right out of the Tombs we did," Jolene says, then she shoots Bear a look and giggles. "Or maybe slid right out of it on our asses'd be a better way to put it."

Bear gives her a friendly whack on the back of the head but it doesn't budge a hair. Jolene's not looking like much this year, standing about halfway to nothing, but she's always solidly built, doesn't much matter what skin she's wearing.

"Let's take that walk," I say, but Bear catches hold of my arm.

"I smell something old," he tells me.

"It's an old place," I tell him. "Fell down here a long time ago and stood above ground even longer."

Bear shakes his head. "No. I'm smelling something older than that. And lower down."

We're on an underground street, I'm thinking. Way down. Can't get much lower than this. But Bear's looking back at the building we just came out of and I know what's on his mind. Basements. They're too much like caves for him to pass one by, especially when it's got an old smell. I look at the others. Jolene's game, but then she's always game when she's wearing this skin. Alberta shrugs.

"When I want to dance," she says, "you all dance with me, so I'm going to say no when Bear wants to try out a new step?"

I can't remember the last time we all danced, but I can't find any argument with what she's saying.

"What about you, Crazy Crow?" Bear asks.

"You know me," I tell him. "I'm like Jolene, I'm always game."

So we go back inside, following Bear who's following his nose, and he leads us right up to the door of that empty stone room down in the cellar. He grabs hold of the iron bolt, shoves it to one side, hauls the door open, rubs his hand on his jeans to brush off the specks of rust that got caught up on his palm.

"Something tried hard to get out," Alberta says.

I'm thinking of the other side of the door. "And in," I add.

Jolene's spinning around in the middle of the room, arms spread wide. "Old, old, old," she sings.

We can all smell it now. I get the feeling that the building grew out of this room, that it was built to hold it. Or hide it.

"No ghosts," Bear says. "No spirits here."

Jolene stops spinning. "Just us," she says.

"Just us," Bear agrees.

He sits down on the clean stone floor, cross-legged, rolls himself a smoke. We all join him, sitting in a circle, like we're dancing, except it's only our breathing that's making the steps. We each take a drag of the cigarette, then Bear sets the butt down in the middle of the circle. We watch the smoke curl up from it, tobacco with that pinch of sweetgrass. It makes a long curling journey up to the ceiling, thickens there like a small storm cloud, pregnant with grandfather thunders.

Somewhere up above us, where the moon can see it, there's smoke rising, too, Devil's Night fires filling the hollow of the sky with pillars of silent thunder.

Bear takes a shotgun cartridge out of his pocket, brass and red cardboard, twelve-gauge, and puts it down on the stone beside the smoldering butt, stands it on end, brass side down.

"Guess we need a story," he says. He looks at me. "So we can understand this place."

We all nod. We'll take turns, talking until one of us gets it right.

"Me first," Jolene says.

She picks up the cartridge and rolls it back and forth on that small dark palm of hers and we listen.

6

Jolene says:

It's like that pan-girl, always cooking something up, you know the one. You can smell the wild onion on her breath a mile away. She's got that box that she can't look in, tin box with a lock on it that rattles against the side of the box when she gives it a shake, trying to guess what's inside. There's all these scratches on the tin, inside and out, something trying to get out, something trying to get in.

That's this place, the pan-girl's box. You know she opened that box, let all that stuff out that makes the world more interesting. She can't get it back in, and I'm thinking why try?

Anyway, she throws that box away. It's a hollow now, a hollow place, can be any size you want it to be, any shape, any colour, same box. Now we're sitting in it, stone version. Close that door and maybe we can't get out. Got to wait until another pan-girl comes along, takes a break from all that cooking, takes a peek at what's inside. That big eye of hers'll fill the door and ya-hey, here we'll be, looking right back at her, rushing past her, she's swatting her hands at us trying to keep us in, but we're already gone, gone running back out into the world to make everything a little more interesting again.

7

Bear says:

Stone. You can't get much older than stone. First house was stone. Not like this room, not perfectly square, not flat, but stone all the same. Found places, those caves, just like we found this place. Old smell in them. Sometimes bear. Sometimes lion. Sometimes snake. Sometimes the ones that went before.

All gone when we come. All that's left is their messages painted or scratched on the walls. Stories. Information. Things they know we have to figure out, things that they could have told us if they were still around. Only way to tell us now is to leave the messages.

This place is a hollow, like Jolene said, but not why she said it. It's hollow because there's no messages. This is the place we have to leave our messages so that when we go on we'll know that the ones to follow will be able to figure things out.

8

Alberta says:

Inside and out, same thing. The wheel doesn't change, only the way we see it. Door opens either way. Both sides in, both sides out. Trouble is, we're always on the wrong side, always want the thing we haven't got, makes no difference who we are. Restless spirits want life, living people look for something better to come. Nobody *here*. Nobody content with what they got. And the reason for that's to keep the wheel turning. That simple. Wheel stops turning, there's nothing left.

It's like the woman who feels the cage of her bones, those ribs they're a prison for her. She's clawing, clawing at those bone bars, making herself sick. Inside, where you can't see it, but outside, too.

So she goes to see the Lady of the White Deer—looks just like you, Jolene, the way you were last year. Big woman. Big as a tree. Got dark, dark eyes you could get lost in. But she's smiling, always smiling. Smiling as she listens, smiling when she speaks. Like a mother smiles, seen it all, heard it all, but still patient, still kind, still understanding.

"That's just living," she tells the caged woman. "Those aren't bars, they're the bones that hold you together. You keep clawing at them, you make yourself so sick you're going to die for sure."

"I can't breathe in here," the caged woman says.

"You're not paying attention," the Lady of the White Deer says. "All you're doing is breathing. Stop breathing and you'll be clawing at those same bones, trying to get back in."

"You don't understand," the caged woman tells her and she walks away.

So she goes to see the Old Man of the Mountains—looks just like you, Bear. Same face, same hair. A big old bear, sitting up there on the top of the mountain, looking out at everything below. Doesn't smile so much, but understands how everybody's got a secret dark place sits way deep down there inside, hidden but wanting to get out. Understands how you can be happy but not happy at the same time. Understands that sometimes you feel you got to go all the way out to get back in, but if you do, you can't. There's no way back in.

So not smiling so much, but maybe understanding a little more, he lets the woman talk and he listens.

"We all got a place inside us, feels like a prison," he tells her. "It's darker in some people than others, that's all. Thing is, you got to balance what's there with what's around you or you'll find yourself on a road that's got no end. Got no beginning and goes nowhere. It's just always this same thing, never grows, never changes, only gets darker and darker, like that candle blowing in the wind. Looks real nice till the wind blows it out—you hear what I'm saying?"

"I can't breathe in here," the woman tells him.

That Old Man of the Mountain he shakes his head. "You're breathing," he says. "You're just not paying attention to it. You're looking inside, looking inside, forgetting what's outside. You're making friends with that darkness inside you and that's not good. You better stop your scratching and clawing or you're going to let it out."

"You don't understand either," the caged woman says and she walks away.

So finally she goes to see the Old Man of the Desert—looks like you, Crazy Crow. Got the same sharp features, the same laughing eyes. Likes to collect things. Keeps a pocket full of shiny mementos that used to belong to other people, things they threw away. Holds onto them until they want them back and then makes a trade. He'd give them away, but he knows what everybody thinks: all you get for nothing is nothing. Got to put a price on a thing to give it any worth.

He doesn't smile at all when he sees her coming. He puts his hand in his pocket and plays with something while she talks. Doesn't say anything when she's done, just sits there, looking at her.

"Aren't you going to help me?" she asks.

"You don't want my help," the Old man of the Desert says. "You just want me to agree with you. You just want me to say, aw, that's bad, really bad. You've got it bad. Everybody else in the world is doing fine, except for you, because you got it so hard and bad."

The caged woman looks at him. She's got tears starting in her eyes.

"Why are you being so mean to me?" she asks.

"The truth only sounds mean," he tells her. "You look at it from another side and maybe you see it as kindness. All depends where you're looking, what you want to see."

"But I can't breathe," she says.

"You're breathing just fine," he says right back to her. "The thing is, you're not thinking so good. Got clouds in your head. Makes it hard to see straight. Makes it hard to hear what you don't want to hear anyway. Makes it hard to accept that the rest of the world's not out of step on the wheel, only you are. Work on that and you'll start feeling a little better. Remember who you are instead of always crying after what you think you want to be."

"You don't understand either," she says.

But before she can walk away, the Old Man of the Desert takes that thing out of his pocket, that thing he's been playing with, and she sees it's her dancing. He's got it all rolled up in a ball of beads and cowrie shells and feathers and mud, wrapped around with a rope of braided sweetgrass. Her dancing. Been a long time since she's seen that dancing. She thought it was lost in the long ago. Thought it disappeared with her breathing.

"Where'd you get that dancing?" she asks.

"Found it in the trash. You'd be amazed what people will throw out—every kind of piece of themselves."

She puts her hand out to take it, but the Old Man of the Desert shakes his head and holds it out of her reach.

"That's mine," she says. "I lost that in the long ago."

"You never lost it," the Old Man of the Desert tells her. "You threw it away."

"But I want it back now."

"You got to trade for it," he says.

The caged woman lowers her head. "I got nothing to trade for it."

"Give me your prison," the Old Man of the Desert says.

She looks up at him. "Now you're making fun of me," she says. "I give you my prison, I'm going to die. Dancing's not much use to the dead."

"Depends," he says. "Dancing can honour the dead. Lets them breathe in the faraway. Puts a fire in their cold chests. Warms their bone prisons for a time."

"What are you saying?" the caged woman asks. "I give you my life and you'll dance for me?"

The Old Man of the Desert smiles and that smile scares her because it's not kind or understanding. It's sharp and cuts deep. It cuts like a knife, slips in through the skin, slips past the ribs of her bone prison.

"What you got caging you is the idea of a prison," he says. "That's what I want from you."

"You want some kind of...story?"

He shakes his head. "I'm not in a bartering mood—not about this kind of thing."

"I don't know how to give you my prison," she says. "I don't know if I can."

"All you got to do is say yes," he tells her.

She looks at that dancing in his hand and it's all she wants now. There's little sparks coming off it, the smell of smudge-sticks and licorice and gasoline. There's a warmth burning in it that she knows will drive the cold away. That cold. She's been holding that cold for so long she doesn't hardly remember what it feels like to be warm anymore.

She's looking, she's reaching. She says yes and the Old Man of the Desert gives her back her dancing. And it's warm and familiar, lying there in her hand, but she doesn't feel any different. She doesn't know what to do with it, now she's got it. She wants to ask him what to do, but he's not paying attention to her anymore.

What's he doing? He's picking up dirt and he's spitting on it, spitting and spitting and working the dirt until it's like clay. And he makes a box out of it and in one side of the box he puts a door. And he digs a hole in the dirt and he puts the box in it. And he covers it up again. And then he looks at her.

"One day you're going to find yourself in that box again," he says, "but this time you'll remember and you won't get locked up again."

She doesn't understand what he's talking about, doesn't care. She's got other things on her mind. She holds up her dancing, holds it in the air between them.

"I don't know what to do with this," she says. "I don't know how to make it work."

The Old Man of the Desert stands up. He gives her a hand up. He takes the dancing from her and throws it on the ground, throws it hard, throws it so hard it breaks. He starts shuffling his feet, keeping time with a clicking sound in the back of his throat. The dust rises up from the ground and she breathes it in and then she remembers what it was like and who she was and why she danced.

It was to honour the bone prison that holds her breathing for this turn of the wheel. It was to honour the gift of the world underfoot. It was to celebrate what's always changing: The stories. The dance of our lives. The wheel of the world and the sky spinning above it and our place in it.

The bones of her prison weren't there to keep her from getting out. They were there to keep her together.

9

I'm holding the cartridge now, but there's no need for me to speak. The story's done. Somewhere up above us, the skies over the Tombs are still full of smoke, the Devil's Night fires are still burning. Here in the hollow of this stone room, we've got a fire of our own.

Alberta looks across the circle at me.

"I remember," she says.

"That was the first time we met," Jolene says. "I remember, too. Not the end, but the beginning. I was there at the beginning and then later, too. For the dancing."

Bear nods. He takes the cartridge from my fingers and puts it back into his pocket. Out of another pocket he takes packets of colour, ground pigments. Red and yellow and blue. Black and white. He puts them on the floor, takes a pinch of colour out of one of the packets and lays it in the palm of his hand. Spits into his palm. Dips a finger in. He gets up, that Old Man of the Mountain, and he crosses over to one of the walls. Starts to painting. Starts to leave a message for the ones to follow.

Those colours, they're like dancing. Once someone starts, you can't help but twitch and turn and fidget until you're doing it, too. Next thing you know, we're all spitting into our palms, we're all dancing the colour across the walls.

Remembering.

Because that's what the stories are for.

Even for old spirits like us.

We lock ourselves up in bone prisons same as everybody else. Forget who we are, why we are, where we're going. Till one day we come across a story we left for ourselves and remember why we're wearing these skins. Remember why we're dancing.

1995

Crow Girls

*I remember what somebody said about nostalgia,
he said it's okay to look back, as long as you
don't stare.*

Tom Paxton, from an interview
with Ken Rockburn

People have a funny way of remembering where they've been, who they were. Facts fall by the wayside. Depending on their temperament they either remember a golden time when all was better than well, better than it can be again, better than it ever really was: a first love, the endless expanse of a summer vacation, youthful vigor, the sheer novelty of being alive that gets lost when the world starts wearing you down. Or they focus in on the bad, blow little incidents all out of proportion, hold grudges for years, or maybe they really did have some unlucky times, but now they're reliving them forever in their heads instead of moving on.

But the brain plays tricks on us all, doesn't it? We go by what it tells us, have to I suppose, because what else do we have to use as touchstones? Trouble is we don't ask for confirmation on what the brain tells us. Things don't have to be real, we just have to believe they're real, which pretty much explains politics and religion as much as it does what goes on inside our heads.

Don't get me wrong; I'm not pointing any fingers here. My people aren't guiltless either. The only difference is our memories go back a lot further than yours do.

⋌ Υ ⋋

"I don't get computers," Heather said.

Jilly laughed. "What's not to get? "

They were having cappuccinos in the Cyberbean Café, sitting at the long counter with computer terminals spaced along its length the way those little individual juke boxes used to be in highway diners. Jilly looked as though she'd been using the tips of her dark ringlets as paintbrushes, then cleaned them on the thighs of her jeans—in other words, she'd come straight from the studio without changing first. But however haphazardly messy she might allow herself or her studio to get, Heather knew she'd either cleaned her brushes, or left them soaking in turps before coming down to the café. Jilly might seem terminally easygoing, but some things she didn't blow off. No matter how the work was going—good, bad or indifferent—she treated her tools with respect.

As usual, Jilly's casual scruffiness made Heather feel overdressed, for all that she was only wearing cotton pants and a blouse, nothing fancy. But she always felt a little like that around Jilly, ever since she'd first taken a class from her at the Newford School of Art a couple of winters ago. No matter how hard she tried, she hadn't been able to shake the feeling that she looked so typical: the suburban working mother, the happy wife. The differences since she and Jilly had first met weren't great. Her blonde hair had been long then, while now it was cropped short. She was wearing glasses now instead of her contacts.

And two years ago she hadn't been carrying an empty wasteland around inside her chest.

"Besides," Jilly added. "You use a computer at work, don't you?"

"Sure, but that's work," Heather said. "Not games and computer screen romances and stumbling around the Internet, looking for information you're never going to find a use for outside of Trivial Pursuits."

"I think it's bringing back a sense of community," Jilly said.

"Oh, right."

"No, think about it. All these people who might have been just vegging out in front of a TV are chatting with each other in cyberspace instead—hanging out, so to speak, with kindred spirits that they might never have otherwise met."

Heather sighed. "But it's not real, human contact."

"No. But at least it's contact."

"I suppose."

Jilly regarded her over the brim of her glass coffee mug. It was a mild gaze, not in the least probing, but Heather couldn't help but feel as though Jilly was seeing right inside her head, all the way down to where desert winds blew through the empty space where her heart had been.

"So what's the real issue?" Jilly asked.

Heather shrugged. "There's no issue." She took a sip of her own coffee, then tried on a smile. "I'm thinking of moving downtown."

"Really?"

"Well, you know. I already work here. There's a good school for the kids. It just seems to make sense."

"How does Peter feel about it?"

Heather hesitated for a long moment, then sighed again. "Peter's not really got anything to say about it."

"Oh, no. You guys always seemed so..." Jilly's voice trailed off. "Well, I guess you weren't really happy, were you?"

"I don't know what we were anymore. I just know we're not together. There wasn't a big blow up or anything. He wasn't cheating on me and I certainly wasn't cheating on him. We're just...not together."

"It must be so weird."

Heather nodded. "Very weird. It's a real shock, suddenly discovering after all these years, that we really don't have much in common at all."

Jilly's eyes were warm with sympathy. "How are you holding up?"

"Okay, I suppose. But it's so confusing. I don't know what to think, who I am, what I thought I was doing with the last fifteen years of my life. I mean, I don't regret the girls—I'd have had more children if we could have had them—but everything else..."

She didn't know how to begin to explain.

"I married Peter when I was eighteen and I'm forty-one now. I've been a part of a couple for longer than I've been anything else, but except for the girls, I don't know what any of it meant anymore. I don't know who I am. I thought we'd be together forever, that we'd grow old together, you know? But now it's just me. Casey's fifteen and Janice is twelve. I've got another few years of being a mother, but after that, who am I? What am I going to do with myself?"

"You're still young," Jilly said. "And you look gorgeous."

"Right."

"Okay. A little pale today, but still."

Heather shook her head. "I don't know why I'm telling you this. I haven't told anybody."

"Not even your mom or your sister?"

"Nobody. It's..."

She could feel tears welling up, the vision blurring, but she made herself take a deep breath. It seemed to help. Not a lot, but some. Enough to carry on. How to explain why she wanted to keep it a secret? It wasn't as though it was something she could keep hidden forever.

"I think I feel like a failure," she said.

Her voice was so soft she almost couldn't hear herself, but Jilly reached over and took her hand.

"You're not a failure. Things didn't work out, but that doesn't mean it was your fault. It takes two people to make or break a relationship."

"I suppose. But to have put in all those years..."

Jilly smiled. "If nothing else, you've got two beautiful daughters to show for them."

Heather nodded. The girls did a lot to keep the emptiness at bay, but once they were in bed, asleep, and she was by herself, alone in the dark, sitting on the couch by the picture window, staring down the street at all those other houses just like her own, that desolate place inside her seemed to go on forever.

She took another sip of her coffee and looked past Jilly to where two young women were sitting at a corner table, heads bent together, whispering. It was hard to place their ages—anywhere from late teens to early twenties, sisters, perhaps, with their small builds and similar dark looks, their black clothing and short blue-black hair. For no reason she could explain, simply seeing them made her feel a little better.

"Remember what it was like to be so young?" she said.

Jilly turned, following her gaze, then looked back at Heather.

"You never think about stuff like this at that age," Heather went on.

"I don't know," Jilly said. "Maybe not. But you have a thousand other anxieties that probably feel way more catastrophic."

"You think?"

Jilly nodded. "I know. We all like to remember it as a perfect time, but most of us were such bundles of messed-up hormones and nerves I'm surprised we ever managed to reach twenty."

"I suppose. But still, looking at those girls..."

Jilly turned again, leaning her head on her arm. "I know what you mean. They're like a piece of summer on a cold winter's morning."

It was a perfect analogy, Heather thought, especially considering the winter they'd been having. Not even the middle of December and the snowbanks were already higher than her chest, the temperature a seriously cold minus-fifteen.

"I have to remember their faces," Jilly went on. "For when I get back to the studio. The way they're leaning so close to each other—like confidantes, sisters in their hearts, if not by blood. And look at the fine bones in their features...how dark their eyes are."

Heather nodded. "It'd make a great picture."

It would, but the thought of it depressed her. She found herself yearning desperately in that one moment to have had an entirely different life, it almost didn't matter what. Perhaps one that had no responsibility but to draw great art from the world around her the way Jilly did. If she hadn't had to support Peter while he was going through law school, maybe she would have stuck with her art...

Jilly swiveled in her chair, the sparkle in her eyes deepening into concern once more.

"Anything you need, anytime," she said. "Don't be afraid to call me."

Heather tried another smile. "We could chat on the Internet."

"I think I agree with what you said earlier: I like this better."

"Me, too," Heather said. Looking out the window, she added, "It's snowing again."

↳ ⅄ ↲

Maida and Zia are forever friends. Crow girls with spiky blue-black hair and eyes so dark it's easy to lose your way in them. A little raggedy and never quiet, you can't miss this pair: small and wild and easy in their skins, living on Zen time. Sometimes they forget they're crows, left their feathers behind in the long ago, and sometimes they forget they're girls. But they never forget that they're friends.

People stop and stare at them wherever they go, borrowing a taste of them, drawn by they don't know what, they just have to look, try to get close, but keeping their distance, too, because there's something scary/craving about seeing animal spirits so pure walking around on a city street. It's a shock, like plunging into cold water at dawn, waking up from the comfortable familiarity of warm dreams to find, if only for a moment, that everything's changed. And then, just before the way you know the world to be comes rolling back in on you, maybe you hear giddy laughter, or the slow flap of crows' wings. Maybe you see a couple of dark-haired girls sitting together in the corner of a café, heads bent together, pretending you can't see them, or could be they're perched on a tree branch, looking down at you looking up, working hard at putting on serious faces but they can't stop smiling.

It's like that rhyme, "two for mirth." They can't stop smiling and neither can you. But you've got to watch out for crow girls. Sometimes they wake a yearning you'll be hard-pressed to put back to sleep. Sometimes only a glimpse of them can start up a familiar ache deep in your chest, an ache you can't name, but you've felt it before, early mornings, lying alone in your bed, trying to hold onto the fading tatters of a perfect dream. Sometimes they blow bright the coals of a longing that can't ever be eased.

⅄ Ⴗ ⅃

Heather couldn't stop thinking of the two girls she'd seen in the café earlier in the evening. It was as though they'd lodged pieces of themselves inside her, feathery slivers winging dreamily across the wasteland. Long after she'd played a board game with Janice, then watched the end of a Barbara Walters special with Casey, she found herself sitting up by the big picture window in the living room when she should be in bed herself. She regarded the street through a veil of falling snow, but this time she wasn't looking at the houses, so alike, except for the varying heights of their snowbanks, they might as well all be the same one. Instead, she was looking for two small women with spiky black hair, dark shapes against the white snow.

There was no question but that they knew exactly who they were, she thought when she realized what she was doing. Maybe they could tell her who she was. Maybe they could come up with an exotic past for her so that she could reinvent herself, be someone like them, free, sure of herself. Maybe they could at least tell her where she was going.

But there were no thin, dark-haired girls out on the snowy street, and why should there be? It was too cold. Snow was falling thick with another severe winter storm warning in effect tonight. Those girls were safe at home. She knew that. But she kept looking for them all the same, because in her chest she could feel the beat of dark wings—not the sudden panic that came out of nowhere when once again the truth of her situation reared without warning in her mind, but a strange, alien feeling. A sense that some otherness was calling to her.

The voice of that otherness scared her almost more than the grey landscape lodged in her chest.

She felt she needed a safety net, to be able to let herself go and not have to worry about where she fell. Somewhere where she didn't have to think, be responsible, to do anything. Not forever. Just for a time.

She knew Jilly was right about nostalgia. The memories she carried forward weren't necessarily the way things had really happened. But she yearned, if only for a moment, to be able to relive some of those simpler times, those years in high school before she'd met Peter, before they were married, before her emotions got so complicated.

And then what?

You couldn't live in the past. At some point you had to come up for air and then the present would be waiting for you, unchanged. The wasteland in her chest would still stretch on forever. She'd still be trying to understand what had happened. Had Peter changed? Had she changed? Had they both changed? And when did it happen? How much of their life together had been a lie?

It was enough to drive her mad.

It was enough to make her want to step into the otherness calling to her from out there in the storm and snow, step out and simply let it swallow her whole.

Λ Υ ⅃

Jilly couldn't put the girls from the café out of her mind either, but for a different reason. As soon as she'd gotten back to the studio, she'd taken her current work-in-progress down from the easel and replaced it with a fresh canvas. For a long moment she stared at the texture of the pale ground, a mix of gesso and a light burnt ochre acrylic wash, then she took up a stick of charcoal and began to sketch the faces of the two dark-haired girls before the memory of them left her mind.

She was working on their bodies, trying to capture the loose splay of their limbs and the curve of their backs as they'd slouched in towards each other over the café table, when there came a knock at her door.

"It's open," she called over her shoulder, too intent on what she was doing to look away.

"I could've been some mad, psychotic killer," Geordie said as he came in.

He stamped his feet on the mat, brushed the snow from his shoulders and hat. Setting his fiddlecase down by the door, he went over to the kitchen counter to see if Jilly had any coffee on.

"But instead," Jilly said, "it's only a mad, psychotic fiddler, so I'm entirely safe."

"There's no coffee."

"Sure there is. It's just waiting for you to make it."

Geordie put on the kettle, then rummaged around in the fridge, trying to find which tin Jilly was keeping her coffee beans in this week. He found them in one that claimed to hold Scottish shortbreads.

"You want some?" he asked.

Jilly shook her head. "How's Tanya?"

"Heading back to L.A. I just saw her off at the airport. The driving's horrendous. There were cars in the ditch every couple of hundred feet and I thought the bus would never make it back."

"And yet, it did," Jilly said.

Geordie smiled.

"And then," she went on, "because you were feeling bored and lonely, you decided to come visit me at two o'clock in the morning."

"Actually, I was out of coffee and I saw your light was on." He crossed the loft and came around behind the easel so that he could see what she was working on. "Hey, you're doing the crow girls."

"You know them?"

Geordie nodded. "Maida and Zia. You've caught a good likeness of them—especially Zia. I love that crinkly smile of hers."

"You can tell them apart?"

"You can't?"

"I never saw them before tonight. Heather and I were in the Cyberbean and there they were, just asking to be drawn." She added a bit of shading to the underside of a jaw, then turned to look at Geordie. "Why do you call them the crow girls?"

Geordie shrugged. "I don't. Or at least I didn't until I was talking to Jack Daw and that's what he called them when they came sauntering by. The next time I saw them I was busking in front of St. Paul's, so I started to play 'The Blackbird,' just to see what would happen, and sure enough, they came over to talk to me."

"Crow girls," Jilly repeated. The name certainly fit.

"They're some kind of relation to Jack," Geordie explained, "but I didn't quite get it. Cousins, maybe."

Jilly was suddenly struck with the memory of a long conversation she'd had with Jack one afternoon. She was working up sketches of the Crowsea Public Library for a commission when he came and sat beside her on the grass. With his long legs folded under him, black brimmed hat set at a jaunty angle, he'd regaled her with a long, rambling discourse on what he called the continent's real first nations.

"Animal people," she said softly.

Geordie smiled. "I see he fed you that line, too."

But Jilly wasn't really listening—not to Geordie. She was remembering another part of that old conversation, something else Jack had told her.

"The thing we really don't get," he'd said, leaning back in the grass, "is these contracted families you have. The mother, the father, the children, all living alone in some big house. Our families extend as far as our bloodlines and friendship can reach."

"I don't know much about bloodlines," Jilly said. "But I know about friends."

He'd nodded. "That's why I'm talking to you."

Jilly blinked and looked at Geordie. "It made sense what he said."

Geordie smiled. "Of course it did. Immortal animal people."

"That, too. But I was talking about the weird way we think about families and children. Most people don't even like kids—don't want to see, hear, or hear about them. But when you look at other cultures, even close to home...up on the rez, in Chinatown, Little Italy...it's these big rambling extended families, everybody taking care of everybody else."

Geordie cleared his throat. Jilly waited for him to speak but he went instead to unplug the kettle and finish making the coffee. He ground up some beans and the noise of the hand-cranked machine seemed to reach out and fill every corner of the loft. When he stopped, the sudden silence was profound, as though the city outside was holding its breath along with the inheld breath of the room. Jilly was still watching him when he looked over at her.

"We don't come from that kind of family," he said finally.

"I know. That's why we had to make our own."

⊱ Υ ⊰

It's late at night, snow whirling in dervishing gusts, and the crow girls are perched on the top of the wooden fence that's been erected around a work site on Williamson Street. Used to be a parking lot there, now it's a big hole in the ground on its way to being one more office complex that nobody except the contractors want. The top of the fence is barely an inch wide at the top and slippery with snow, but they have no trouble balancing there.

Zia has a ring with a small spinning disc on it. Painted on the disc is a psychedelic coil that goes spiraling down into infinity. She keeps spinning it and the two of them stare down into the faraway place at the center of the spiral until the disc slows down, almost stops. Then Zia gives it another flick with her fingernail, and the coil goes spiraling down again.

"Where'd you get this anyway?" Maida asks.

Zia shrugs. "Can't remember. Found it somewhere."

"In someone's pocket."

"And you never did?"

Maida grins. "Just wish I'd seen it first, that's all."

They watch the disc some more, content.

"What do you think it's like down there?" Zia says after awhile. "On the other side of the spiral."

Maida has to think about that for a moment. "Same as here," she finally announces, then winks. "Only dizzier."

They giggle, leaning into each other, tottering back and forth on their perch, crow girls, can't be touched, can't hardly be seen, except someone's standing down there on the sidewalk, looking up through the falling snow, his worried expression so comical it sets them off on a new round of giggles.

"Careful now!" he calls up to them. He thinks they're on drugs—they can tell. "You don't want to—"

Before he can finish, they hold hands and let themselves fall backwards, off the fence.

"Oh, Christ!"

He jumps, gets a handhold on the top of the fence and hauls himself up. But when he looks over, over and down, way down, there's nothing to be seen. No girls lying at the bottom of that big hole in the ground, nothing at all. Only the falling snow. It's like they were never there.

His arms start to ache and he lowers himself back down the fence, lets go, bending his knees slightly to absorb the impact of the last couple of feet. He slips, catches his balance. It seems very still for a moment, so still he can hear an odd rhythmical whispering sound. Like wings. He looks up, but there's too much snow coming down to see anything. A cab comes by, skidding on the slick street, and he blinks. The street's full of city sounds again, muffled, but present. He hears the murmuring conversation of a couple approaching him, their shoulders and hair white with snow. A snowplow a few streets over. A distant siren.

He continues along his way, but he's walking slowly now, trudging through the drifts, not thinking so much of two girls sitting on top of a fence as remembering how, when he was a boy, he used to dream that he could fly.

⊁ ⋎ ⊰

After fiddling a little more with her sketch, Jilly finally put her charcoal down. She made herself a cup of herbal tea with the leftover hot water in the kettle and joined Geordie where he was sitting on the sofa, watching the snow come down. It was warm in the loft, almost cozy compared to the storm on the other side of the windowpanes, or maybe because of the storm. Jilly leaned back on the sofa, enjoying the companionable silence for awhile before she finally spoke.

"How do you feel after seeing the crow girls?" she asked.

Geordie turned to look at her. "What do you mean, how do I feel?"

"You know, good, bad...different..."

Geordie smiled. "Don't you mean 'indifferent?'"

"Maybe." She picked up her tea from the crate where she'd set it and took a sip. "Well?" she asked when he didn't continue.

"Okay. How do I feel? Good, I suppose. They're fun, they make me smile. In fact, just thinking of them now makes me feel good."

Jilly nodded thoughtfully as he spoke. "Me, too. And something else as well."

"The different," Geordie began. He didn't quite sigh. "You believe those stories of Jack's, don't you?"

"Of course. And you don't?"

"I'm not sure," he replied, surprising her.

"Well, I think these crow girls were in the Cyberbean for a purpose," Jilly said. "Like in that rhyme about crows."

Geordie got it right away. "Two for mirth."

Jilly nodded. "Heather needed some serious cheering up. Maybe even something more. You know how when you start feeling low, you can get on this descending spiral of depression...everything goes wrong, things get worse, because you expect them to?"

"Fight it with the power of positive thinking, I always say."

"Easier said than done when you're feeling that low. What you really need at a time like that is something completely unexpected to kick you out of it and remind you that there's more to life than the hopeless, grey expanse you think is stretching in every direction. What Colin Wilson calls absurd good news."

"You've been talking to my brother."

"It doesn't matter where I got it from—it's still true."

Geordie shook his head. "I don't buy the idea that Maida and Zia showed up just to put your friend in a better mood. Even bird people can get a craving for a cup of coffee, can't they?"

"Well, yes," Jilly said. "But that doesn't preclude their being there for Heather as well. Sometimes when a person needs something badly enough, it just comes to them. A personal kind of steam engine time. You might not be able to articulate what it is you need, you might not even know you need something—at least, not at a conscious level—but the need's still there, calling out to whatever's willing to listen."

Geordie smiled. "Like animal spirits."

"Crow girls."

Geordie shook his head. "Drink your tea and go to bed," he told her. "I think you need a good night's sleep."

"But—"

"It was only a coincidence. Things don't always have a meaning. Sometimes they just happen. And besides, how do you even know they had any effect on Heather?"

"I could just tell. And don't change the subject."

"I'm not."

"Okay," Jilly said. "But don't you see? It doesn't matter if it was a coincidence or not. They still showed up when Heather needed them. It's more of that 'small world, spooky world' stuff Professor Dapple's goes on about. Everything's connected. It doesn't matter if we can't see how, it's still all connected. You know, chaos theory and all that."

Geordie shook his head, but he was smiling. "Does it ever strike you as weird when something Bramley's talked up for years suddenly becomes an acceptable element of scientific study?"

"Nothing strikes me as truly weird," Jilly told him. "There's only stuff I haven't figured out yet."

ㅏ Υ ㅓ

Heather barely slept that night. For the longest time she simply couldn't sleep, and then when she finally did, she was awake by dawn. Wide awake, but heavy with an exhaustion that came more from heartache than lack of sleep.

Sitting up against the headboard, she tried to resist the sudden tightness in her chest, but that sad, cold wasteland swelled inside her. The bed seemed depressingly huge. She didn't so much miss Peter's presence as feel adrift in the bed's expanse of blankets and sheets. Adrift in her life. Why was it he seemed to have no trouble carrying on when the simple act of getting up in the morning felt as though it would require far more energy than she could ever hope to muster?

She stared at the snow swirling against her window, not at all relishing the drive into town on a morning like this. If anything, it was coming down harder than it had been last night. All it took was the suggestion of snow and everybody in the city seemed to forget how to drive, never mind common courtesy or traffic laws. A blizzard like this would snarl traffic and back it up as far as the mountains.

She sighed, supposing it was just as well she'd woken so early since it would take her at least an extra hour to get downtown today.

Up, she told herself, and forced herself to swing her feet to the floor and rise. A shower helped. It didn't really ease the heartache, but the hiss of the water made it easier to ignore her thoughts. Coffee, when she was dressed and had brewed a pot, helped more, though she still winced when Janice came bounding into the kitchen.

"It's a snow day!" she cried. "No school. They just announced it on the radio. The school's closed, closed, closed!"

She danced about in her flannel nightie, pirouetting in the small space between the counter and the table.

"Just yours," Heather asked, "or Casey's, too?"

"Mine, too," Casey replied, following her sister into the room.

Unlike Janice, she was maintaining her cool, but Heather could tell she was just as excited. Too old to allow herself to take part in Janice's spontaneous celebration, but young enough to be feeling giddy with the unexpected holiday.

"Good," Heather said. "You can look after your sister."

"*Mom*!" Janice protested. "I'm not a baby."

"I know. It's just good to have someone older in the house when—"

"You can't be thinking of going in to work today," Casey said.

"We could do all kinds of stuff," Janice added. "Finish decorating the house. Baking."

"Yeah," Casey said, "all the things we don't seem to have time for anymore."

Heather sighed. "The trouble is," she explained, "the real world doesn't work like school. We don't get snow days."

Casey shook her head. "That is *so* unfair."

The phone rang before Heather could agree.

"I'll bet it's your boss," Janice said as Heather picked up the phone. "Calling to tell you it's a snow day for you, too."

Don't I wish, Heather thought. But then what would she do at home all day? It was so hard being here, even with the girls and much as she loved them. Everywhere she turned, something reminded her of how the promises of a good life had turned into so much ash. At least work kept her from brooding.

She brought the receiver up to her ear and spoke into the mouthpiece. "Hello?"

"I've been thinking," the voice on the other end of the line said. "About last night."

Heather had to smile. Wasn't that so Jilly, calling up first thing in the morning as though they were still in the middle of last night's conversation.

"What about last night?" she said.

"Well, all sorts of stuff. Like remembering a perfect moment in the past and letting it carry you through a hard time now."

If only, Heather thought. "I don't have a moment that perfect," she said.

"I sort of got that feeling," Jilly told her. "That's why I think they were a message—a kind of perfect moment now that you can use the same way."

"What *are* you talking about?"

"The crow girls. In the café last night."

"The crow…" It took her a moment to realize what Jilly meant. Their complexions had been dark enough, so she supposed they could have been Indians. "How do you know what tribe they belonged to?"

"Not crow, Native American," Jilly said, "but crow, bird people."

Heather shook her head as she listened to what Jilly went on to say, for all that only her daughters were here to see the movement. Glum looks had replaced their earlier excitement when they realized the call wasn't from her boss.

"Do you have any idea how improbable all of this sounds?" she asked when Jilly finished. "Life's not like your paintings."

"Says who?"

"How about common sense?"

"Tell me," Jilly said. "Where did common sense ever get you?"

Heather sighed. "Things don't happen just because we want them to," she said.

"Sometimes that's *exactly* why they happen," Jilly replied. "They happen because we need them to."

"I don't live in that kind of a world."

"But you could."

Heather looked across the kitchen at her daughters once more. The girls were watching her, trying to make sense out of the one-sided conversation they were hearing. Heather wished them luck. She was hearing both sides and that didn't seem to help at all. You couldn't simply reinvent your world because you wanted to. Things just were how they were.

"Just think about it," Jilly added. "Will you do that much?"

"I..."

That bleak landscape inside Heather seemed to expand, growing so large there was no way she could contain it. She focused on the faces of her daughters. She remembered the crow girls in the café. There was so much innocence in them all, daughters and crow girls. She'd been just like them once and she knew it wasn't simply nostalgia colouring her memory. She knew there'd been a time when she lived inside each particular day, on its own and by itself, instead of trying to deal with all the days of her life at once, futilely attempting to reconcile the discrepancies and mistakes.

"I'll try," she said into the phone.

They said their goodbyes and Heather slowly cradled the receiver.

"Who was that, mom?" Casey asked.

Heather looked out the window. The snow was still falling, muffling the world. Covering its complexities with a blanket as innocent as the hope she saw in her daughters' eyes.

"Jilly," she said. She took a deep breath, then smiled at them. "She was calling to tell me that today really is a snow day."

The happiness that flowered on their faces helped ease the tightness in her chest. The grey landscape waiting for her there didn't go away, but for some reason, it felt less profound. She wasn't even worried about what her boss would say when she called to tell him she wouldn't be in today.

⤙ Υ ⤚

Crow girls can move like ghosts. They'll slip into your house when you're not home, sometimes when you're only sleeping, go walking spirit-soft through your rooms and hallways, sit in your favorite chair, help themselves to cookies and beer, borrow a trinket or two which they'll mean to return and usually do. It's not break & enter so much as simple curiosity. They're worse than cats.

Privacy isn't in their nature. They don't seek it and barely understand the concept. Personal property is even more alien. The idea of owner-ship—that one can lay proprietary claim to a piece of land, an object, another person or creature—doesn't even register.

"Whatcha looking at?" Zia asks.

They don't know whose house they're in. Walking along on the street, trying to catch snowflakes on their tongues, one or the other of them suddenly got the urge to come inside. Upstairs, the family sleeps.

Maida shows her the photo album. "Look," she says. "It's the same people, but they keep changing. See, here she's a baby, then she's a little girl, then a teenager."

"Everything changes," Zia says. "Even we get old. Look at Crazy Crow."

"But it happens so fast with them."

Zia sits down beside her and they pore over the pictures, munching on apples they found earlier in a cold cellar in the basement.

Upstairs, a father wakes in his bed. He stares at the ceiling, wonder-ing what woke him. Nervous energy crackles inside him like static elec-tricity, a sudden spill of adrenaline, but he doesn't know why. He gets up and checks the children's rooms. They're both asleep. He listens for in-truders, but the house is silent.

Stepping back into the hall, he walks to the head of the stairs and looks down. He thinks he sees something in the gloom, two dark-haired girls sitting on the sofa, looking through a photo album. Their gazes lift to meet his and hold it. The next thing he knows, he's on the sofa himself, holding the photo album in his hand. There are no strange girls sitting there with him. The house seems quieter than it's ever been, as though the fridge, the furnace and every clock the family owns are holding their breath along with him.

He sets the album down on the coffee table, walks slowly back up the stairs and returns to his bed. He feels like a stranger, misplaced. He doesn't know this room, doesn't know the woman beside him. All he can think about is the first girl he ever loved and his heart swells with a bittersweet sorrow. An ache pushes against his ribs, makes it almost impossible to breathe.

What if, what if...

He turns on his side and looks at his wife. For one moment her face blurs, becomes a morphing image that encompasses both her features and those of his first true love. For one moment it seems as though anything is possible, that for all these years he could have been married to another woman, to that girl who first held, then unwittingly, broke his heart.

"No," he says.

His wife stirs, her features her own again. She blinks sleepily at him. "Wha...?" she mumbles.

He holds her close, heartbeat drumming, more in love with her for being who she is than he has ever been before.

Outside, the crow girls are lying on their backs, making snow angels on his lawn, scissoring their arms and legs, shaping skirts and wings. They break their apple cores in two and give their angels eyes, then run off down the street, holding hands. The snow drifts are undisturbed by their weight. It's as though they, too, like the angels they've just made, also have wings.

⊁ Υ ⊀

"This is so cool," Casey tells her mother. "It really feels like Christmas. I mean, not like Christmases we've had, but, you know, like really being part of Christmas."

Heather nods. She's glad she brought the girls down to the soup kitchen to help Jilly and her friends serve a Christmas dinner to those less fortunate than themselves. She's been worried about how her daughters would take the break from tradition, but then realizes, with Peter gone, tradition is already broken. Better to begin all over again.

The girls had been dubious when she first broached the subject with them—"I don't want to spend Christmas with *losers*," had been Casey's first comment. Heather hadn't argued with her. All she'd said was, "I want you to think about what you just said."

Casey's response had been a sullen look—there were more and more of these lately—but Heather knew her own daughter well enough. Casey had stomped off to her room, but then come back half an hour later and helped her explain to Janice why it might not be the worst idea in the world.

She watches them now, Casey having rejoined her sister where they are playing with the homeless children, and knows a swell of pride. They're such good kids, she thinks as she takes another sip of her cider. After a couple of hours serving coffee, tea and hot cider, she'd really needed to get off her feet for a moment.

"Got something for you," Jilly says, sitting down on the bench beside her.

Heather accepts the small, brightly-wrapped parcel with reluctance. "I thought we said we weren't doing Christmas presents."

"It's not really a Christmas present. It's more an everyday sort of a present that I just happen to be giving you today."

"Right."

"So aren't you going to open it?"

Heather peels back the paper and opens the small box. Inside, nestled in a piece of folded Kleenex, are two small silver earrings cast in the shapes of crows. Heather lifts her gaze.

"They're beautiful."

"Got them at the craft show from a local jeweler. Rory Crowther. See, his name's on the card in the bottom of the box. They're to remind you—"

Heather smiles. "Of crow girls?"

"Partly. But more to remember that this—" Jilly waves a hand that could be taking in the basement of St. Vincent's, could be taking in the whole world. "It's not all we get. There's more. We can't always see it, but it's there."

For a moment, Heather thinks she sees two dark-haired slim figures standing on the far side of the basement, but when she looks more closely they're only a baglady and Geordie's friend Tanya, talking.

For a moment, she thinks she hears the sound of wings, but it's only the murmur of conversation. Probably.

What she knows for sure is that the grey landscape inside her chest is shrinking a little more, every day.

"Thank you," she says.

She isn't sure if she's speaking to Jilly or to crow girls she's only ever seen once, but whose presence keeps echoing through her life. Her new life. It isn't necessarily a better one. Not yet. But at least it's on the way up from wherever she'd been going, not down into a darker despair.

"Here," Jilly says. "Let me help you put them on."

1996

My Life as a Bird

From the August, 1996 issue of the
Spar Distributions catalogue:

THE GIRL ZONE, No. 10. Written &
illustrated by Mona Morgan. Latest issue
features new chapters of The True Life
Adventures of Rockit Grrl, Jupiter Jewel
& My Life As A Bird. Includes a one-page
jam with Charles Vess.
My Own Comix Co., $2.75
Back issues available.

ᐳ ᐩ ᐊ

"My Life As A Bird"
Mona's monologue from chapter three:

The thing is, we spend too much time looking outside ourselves for what we should really be trying to find inside. But we can't seem to trust what we find in ourselves—maybe because that's where we find it. I suppose it's all a part of how we ignore who we really are. We're so quick to cut away pieces of ourselves to suit a particular relationship, a job, a circle of friends, incessantly editing who we are until we fit in. Or we do it to someone else. We try to edit the people around us.

I don't know which is worse.

Most people would say it's when we do it to someone else, but I don't think either one's a very healthy option.

Why do we love ourselves so little? Why are we suspect for trying to love ourselves, for being true to who and what we are rather than what someone else thinks we should be? We're so ready to betray ourselves, but we never call it that. We have all these other terms to describe it: Fitting in. Doing the right thing. Getting along.

I'm not proposing a world solely ruled by rank self-interest; I know that there have to be some limits of politeness and compromise or all we'll have left is anarchy. And anyone who expects the entire world to adjust to them is obviously a little too full of their own self-importance.

But how can we expect others to respect or care for us, if we don't respect and care for ourselves? And how come no one asks, "If you're so ready to betray yourself, why should I believe that you won't betray me as well?"

ᐳ ᐩ ᐊ

"And then he dumped you—just like that?"

Mona nodded. "I suppose I should've seen it coming. All it seems we've been doing lately is arguing. But I've been so busy trying to get the new issue out and dealing with the people at Spar who are still being such pricks..."

She let her voice trail off. Tonight the plan had been to get away from her problems, not focus on them. She often thought that too many people used Jilly as a combination den mother/emotional junkyard and she'd promised herself a long time ago that she wouldn't be one of them. But here she was anyway, dumping her problems all over the table between them.

The trouble was, Jilly drew confidences from you as easily as she did a smile. You couldn't not open up to her.

"I guess what it boils down to," she said, "is I wish I was more like Rockit Grrl than Mona."

Jilly smiled. "Which Mona?"

"Good point."

The real-life Mona wrote and drew three ongoing strips for her own bi-monthly comic book, *The Girl Zone*. Rockit Grrl was featured in "The True Life Adventures of Rockit Grrl," the pen & ink-Mona in a semi-autobiographical strip called "My Life As A Bird." Rounding out each issue was "Jupiter Jewel."

Rockit Grrl, AKA "The Menace from Venice"—Venice Avenue, Crowsea, that is, not the Italian city or the California beach—was an in-your-face punkette with an athletic body and excellent fashion sense, strong and unafraid; a little too opinionated for her own good, perhaps, but that only allowed the plots to pretty much write themselves. She spent her time righting wrongs and combating heinous villains like "Didn't-Phone-When-He-Said-He-Would Man" and "Honest-My-Wife-and-I-Are-As-Good-As-Separated Man."

The Mona in "My Life As A Bird" had spiky blonde hair and jean overalls just as her creator did, though the real life Mona wore a T-shirt under her overalls and she usually had an inch or so of dark roots show-ing. They both had a quirky sense of humour and tended to expound at length on what they considered the mainstays of interesting conversa-tion—love and death, sex and art—though the strip's monologues were far more coherent. The stories invariably took place in the character's apart-ment, or the local English-styled pub down the street from it, which was based on the same pub where she and Jilly were currently sharing a pitcher of draught.

Jupiter Jewel had yet to make an appearance in her own strip, but the readers all felt as though they already knew her since her friends—who did appear—were always talking about her.

"The Mona in the strip, I guess," Mona said. "Maybe life's not a smooth ride for her either, but at least she's usually got some snappy come-back line."

"That's only because you have the time to think them out for her."

"This is true."

"But then," Jilly added, "that must be half the fun. Everybody thinks of what they should have said after the fact, but you actually get to use those lines."

"Even more true."

Jilly refilled their glasses. When she set the pitcher back down on the table there was only froth left in the bottom.

"So did you come back with a good line?" she asked.

Mona shook her head. "What could I say? I was so stunned to find out that he'd never taken what I do seriously that all I could do was look at him and try to figure out how I ever thought we really knew each other."

She'd tried to put it out of her mind, but the phrase "that pathetic little comic book of yours" still stung in her memory.

"He used to like the fact that I was so different from the people where he works," she said, "but I guess he just got tired of parading his cute little Bohemian girlfriend around to office parties and the like."

Jilly gave a vigorous nod which made her curls fall down into her eyes. She pushed them back from her face with a hand that still had the inevitable paint lodged under the nails. Ultramarine blue. A vibrant coral.

"See," she said. "That's what infuriates me about the corporate world. The whole idea that if you're doing something creative that doesn't earn big bucks, you should consider it a hobby and put your real time and effort into something serious. Like your art isn't serious enough."

Mona took a swallow of beer. "Don't get me started on that."

Spar Distributions had recently decided to cut back on the non-superhero titles they carried and *The Girl Zone* had been one of the casualties. That was bad enough, but then they also wouldn't cough up her back issues or the money they owed her from what they had sold.

"You got a lousy break," Jilly told her. "They've got no right to let things drag on the way they have."

Mona shrugged. "You'd think I'd have had some clue before this," she said, more willing to talk about Pete. At least she could deal with him. "But he always seemed to like the strips. He'd laugh in all the right places and he even cried when Jamaica almost died."

"Well, who didn't?"

"I guess. There sure was enough mail on that story."

Jamaica was the pet cat in "My Life As A Bird"—Mona's one concession to fantasy in the strip, since Pete was allergic to cats. She'd thought that she was only in between cats when Crumb ran away and she first met

Pete, but once their relationship began to get serious she gave up on the idea of getting another one.

"Maybe he didn't like being in the strip," she said.

"What wasn't to like?" Jilly asked. "I loved the time you put me in it, even though you made me look like I was having the bad hair day from hell."

Mona smiled. "See, that's what happens when you drop out of art school."

"You have bad hair days?"

"No, I mean—"

"Besides, I didn't drop out. You did."

"My point exactly," Mona said. "I can't draw hair for the life of me. It always looks all raggedy."

"Or like a helmet, when you were drawing Pete."

Mona couldn't suppress a giggle. "It wasn't very flattering, was it?"

"But you made up for it by giving him a much better butt," Jilly said.

That seemed uproariously funny to Mona. The beer, she decided, was making her giddy. At least she hoped it was the beer. She wondered if Jilly could hear the same hysterical edge in her laugh that she did. That made the momentary good humour she'd been feeling scurry off as quickly as Pete had left their apartment earlier in the day.

"I wonder when I stopped loving him," Mona said. "Because I did, you know, before we finally had it out today. Stop loving him, I mean."

Jilly leaned forward. "Are you going to be okay? You can stay with me tonight if you like. You know, just so you don't have to be alone your first night."

Mona shook her head. "Thanks, but I'll be fine. I'm actually a little relieved, if you want to know the truth. The past few months I've been wandering through a bit of a fog, but I couldn't quite figure out what it was. Now I know."

Jilly raised her eyebrows.

"Knowing's better," Mona said.

"Well, if you change your mind…"

"I'll be scratching at your window the way those stray cats you keep feeding do."

⅃ ⅄ ⅄

When they called it a night, an hour and another half pitcher of draught later, Mona took a longer route home than she normally would. She wanted to clear her head of the decided buzz that was making her stride less than steady, though considering the empty apartment she was going home to, maybe that wasn't the best idea, never mind her brave words to Jilly. Maybe, instead, she should go back to the pub and down a couple of whiskeys so that she'd really be too tipsy to mope.

"Oh damn him anyway," she muttered and kicked at a tangle of crumpled newspapers that were spilling out of the mouth of an alleyway she was passing.

"Hey, watch it!"

Mona stopped at the sound of the odd gruff voice, then backed away as the smallest man she'd ever seen crawled out of the nest of papers to glare at her. He couldn't have stood more than two feet high, a disagreeable and ugly little troll of a man with a face that seemed roughly carved and then left unfinished. His clothes were ragged and shabby, his face bristly with stubble. What hair she could see coming out from under his cloth cap was tangled and greasy.

Oh my, she thought. She was drunker than she'd realized.

She stood there swaying for a long moment, staring down at him and half-expecting him to simply drift apart like smoke, or vanish. But he did neither and she finally managed to find her voice.

"I'm sorry," she said. "I just didn't see you down…there." This was coming out all wrong. "I mean…"

His glare deepened. "I suppose you think I'm too small to be noticed?"

"No. It's not that. I…"

She knew that his size was only some quirk of genetics, an unusual enough trait to find in someone out and about on a Crowsea street at midnight, but at the same time her imagination or, more likely, all the beer she'd had, was telling her that the little man scowling up at her had a more exotic origin.

"Are you a leprechaun?" she found herself asking.

"If I had a pot of gold, do you think I'd be sleeping on the street?"

She shrugged. "No, of course not. It's just…"

He put a finger to the side of his nose and blew a stream of snot onto the pavement. Mona's stomach did a flip and a sour taste rose up in her throat. Trust her that, when she finally did have some curious encounter like the kind Jilly had so often, it had to be with a grotty little dwarf such as this.

The little man wiped his nose on the sleeve of his jacket and grinned at her.

"What's the matter, princess?" he asked. "If I can't afford a bed for the night, what makes you think I'd go out and buy a handkerchief just to avoid offending your sensibilities?"

It took her a moment to digest that. Then digging in the bib pocket of her overalls, she found a couple of crumpled dollar bills and offered them to him. He regarded the money with suspicion and made no move to take it from her.

"What's this?" he said.

"I just...I thought maybe you could use a couple of dollars."

"Freely given?" he asked. "No strings, no ties?"

"Well, it's not a loan," she told him. Like she was ever going to see him again.

He took the money with obvious reluctance and a muttered "Damn."

Mona couldn't help herself. "Most people would say thank you," she said.

"Most people wouldn't be beholden to you because of it," he replied.

"I'm sorry?"

"What for?"

Mona blinked. "I meant, I don't understand why you're indebted to me now. It was just a couple of dollars."

"Then why apologize?"

"I didn't. Or I suppose I did, but—" This was getting far too confusing. "What I'm trying to say is that I don't want anything in return."

"Too late for that." He stuffed the money in his pocket. "Because your gift was freely given, it means I owe you now." He offered her his hand. "Nacky Wilde, at your service."

Seeing it was the same one he'd used to blow his nose, Mona decided to forgo the social amenities. She stuck her own hands in the side pockets of her overalls.

"Mona Morgan," she told him.

"Alliterative parents?"

"What?"

"You really should see a doctor about your hearing problem."

"I don't have a hearing problem," she said.

"It's nothing to be ashamed of. Well, lead on. Where are we going?"

"*We're* not going anywhere. I'm going home and you can go back to doing whatever it was you were doing before we started this conversation."

He shook his head. "Doesn't work that way. I have to stick with you until I can repay my debt."

"I don't think so."

"Oh, it's very much so. What's the matter? Ashamed to be seen in my company? I'm too short for you? Too grubby? I can be invisible, if you like, but I get the feeling that'd only upset you more."

She had to be way more drunk than she thought she was. This wasn't even remotely a normal conversation.

"Invisible," she repeated.

He gave her an irritated look. "As in, not perceptible by the human eye. You do understand the concept, don't you?"

"You can't be serious."

"No, of course not. I'm making it up just to appear more interesting to you. Great big, semi-deaf women like you feature prominently in my daydreams, so naturally I'll say anything to try to win you over."

Working all day at her drawing desk didn't give Mona as much chance to exercise as she'd like, so she was a bit touchy about the few extra pounds she was carrying.

"I'm not big."

He craned his neck. "Depends on the perspective, sweetheart."

"And I'm not deaf."

"I was being polite. I thought it was kinder than saying you were mentally disadvantaged."

"And you're *certainly* not coming home with me."

"Whatever you say," he said.

And then he vanished.

One moment he was there, two feet of unsavoury rudeness, and the next she was alone on the street. The abruptness of his disappearance, the very weirdness of it, made her legs go all watery and she had to put a hand against the wall until the weak feeling went away.

I am *way* too drunk, she thought as she pushed off from the wall.

She peered into the alleyway, then looked up and down the street. Nothing. Gave the nest of newspapers a poke with her foot. Still nothing. Finally she started walking again, but nervously now, listening for footsteps, unable to shake the feeling that someone was watching her. She was almost back at her apartment when she remembered what he'd said about how he could be invisible.

Impossible.

But what if...?

In the end she found a phonebooth and gave Jilly a call.

"Is it too late to change my mind?" she asked.

"Not at all. Come on over."

Mona leaned against the glass of the booth and watched the street all around her. Occasional cabs went by. She saw a couple at the far end of the block and followed them with her gaze until they turned a corner. So far as she could tell, there was no little man, grotty or otherwise, anywhere in view.

"Is it okay if I bring my invisible friend?" she said.

Jilly laughed. "Sure. I'll put the kettle on. Does your invisible friend drink coffee?"

"I haven't asked him."

"Well," Jilly said, "if either of you are feeling as woozy as I am, I'm sure you could use a mug."

"I could use something," Mona said after she'd hung up.

⅄ ⅄ ⅄

"My Life As A Bird"
Mona's monologue from chapter eight:

Sometimes I think of God as this little man sitting on a café patio somewhere, bewildered at how it's all gotten so out of his control. He had such good intentions, but everything he made had a mind of its own and, right from the first, he found himself unable to contain their conflicting impulses. He tried to create paradise, but he soon discovered that free will and paradise were incompatible because everybody has a different idea as to what paradise should be like.

But usually when I think of him, I think of a cat: a little mysterious, a little aloof, never coming when he's called. And in my mind, God's always a he. *The Bible* makes it pretty clear that men are the doers; women can only be virgins or whores. In God's eyes, we can only exist somewhere in between the two Marys, the Mother of Jesus and the Magdalene.

What kind of a religion is that? What kind of religion ignores the rights of half the world's population just because they're supposed to have envy instead of a penis? One run by men. The strong, the brave, the true. The old boys' club that wrote the book and made the laws.

I'd like to find him and ask him, "Is that it, God? Did we really get cloned from a rib and because we're hand-me-downs, you don't think we've got what it takes to be strong and brave and true?"

But that's only part of what's wrong with the world. You also have to ask, what's the rationale behind wars and sickness and suffering?

Or is there no point? Is God just as bewildered as the rest of the us? Has he finally given up, spending his days now on that café patio, sipping strong espresso, and watching the world go by, none of it his concern anymore? Has he washed his hands of it all?

I've got a thousand questions for God, but he never answers any of them. Maybe he's still trying to figure out where I fit on the scale between the two Marys and he can't reply until he does. Maybe he doesn't hear me, doesn't see me, doesn't think of me at all. Maybe in his version of the what the world is, I don't even exist.

Or if he's cat, then I'm a bird, and he's just waiting to pounce.

➤ ⊤ ⊰

"You actually believe me, don't you?" Mona said.

The two of them were sitting in the windowseat of Jilly's studio loft, sipping coffee from fat china mugs, piano music playing softly in the background, courtesy of a recording by Mitsuko Uchida. The studio was tidier than Mona had ever seen it. All the canvases that weren't hanging up had been neatly stacked against one wall. Books were in their shelves, paint brushes cleaned and lying out in rows on the worktable, tubes of paint organized by colour in wooden and cardboard boxes. The drop cloth under the easel even looked as though it had recently gone through a wash.

"Spring clean up and tidying," Jilly had said by way of explanation.

"Hello? It's September."

"So I'm late."

The coffee had been waiting for Mona when she arrived, as had been a willing ear as she related her curious encounter after leaving the pub. Jilly, of course, was enchanted with the story. Mona didn't know why she was surprised.

"Let's say I don't disbelieve you," Jilly said.

"I don't know if I believe me. It's easier to put it down to those two pitchers of beer we had."

Jilly touched a hand to her head. "Don't remind me."

"Besides," Mona went on. "Why doesn't he show himself now?" She looked around Jilly's disconcertingly tidy studio. "Well?" she said, aiming her question at the room in general. "What's the big secret, Mr. Nacky Wilde?"

"Well, it stands to reason," Jilly said. "He knows that I could just give him something as well, and then he'd be indebted to me, too."

"I don't *want* him indebted to me."

"It's kind of late for that."

"That's what he said."

"He'd probably know."

"Okay. I'll just get him to do my dishes for me or something."

Jilly shook her head. "I doubt it works that way. It probably has to be something that no one else can do for you except him."

"This is ridiculous. All I did was give him a couple of dollars. I didn't mean anything by it."

"Money doesn't mean anything to you?"

"Jilly. It was only two dollars."

"It doesn't matter. It's still money and no matter how much we'd like things to be different, the world revolves around our being able to pay the rent and buy art supplies and the like, so money's important in our lives. You freely gave him something that means something to you and now he has to return that in kind."

"But anybody could have given him the money."

Jilly nodded. "Anybody could have, but they didn't. You did."

"How do I get myself into these things?"

"More to the point, how do you get yourself out?"

"You're the expert. You tell me."

"Let me think about it."

⋋ ⋎ ⋌

Nacky Wilde didn't show himself again until Mona got back to her own apartment the next morning. She had just enough time to realize that Pete had been back to collect his things—there were gaps in the bookshelves and the stack of CDs on top of the stereo was only half the size it had been the previous night—when the little man reappeared. He was slouched on her sofa, even more disreputable looking in the daylight, his glower softened by what could only be the pleasure he took from her gasp at his sudden appearance.

She sat down on the stuffed chair across the table from him. There used to be two, but Pete had obviously taken one.

"So," she said. "I'm sober and you're here, so I guess you must be real."

"Does it always take you this long to accept the obvious?"

"Grubby little men who can appear out of thin air and then disappear back into it again aren't exactly a part of my everyday life."

"Ever been to Japan?" he asked.

"No. What's that got to—"

"But you believe it exists, don't you?"

"Oh, please. It's not at all the same thing. Next thing you'll be wanting me to believe in alien abductions and little green men from Mars."

He gave her a wicked grin. "They're not green and they don't come from—"

"I don't want to hear it," she told him, blocking her ears. When she saw he wasn't going to continue, she went on, "So was Jilly right? I'm stuck with you?"

"It doesn't make me any happier than it does you."

"Okay. Then we have to have some ground rules."

"You're taking this rather well," he said.

"I'm a practical person. Now listen up. No bothering me when I'm working. No sneaking around being invisible when I'm in the bathroom or having a shower. No watching me sleep—*or* getting into bed with me."

He looked disgusted at the idea. Yeah, me too, Mona thought.

"And you clean up after yourself," she finished. "Come to think of it, you could clean up yourself, too."

He glared at her. "Fine. Now for my rules. First—"

Mona shook her head. "Uh-uh. This is my place. The only rules that get made here are by me."

"That hardly seems fair."

"None of this is fair," she shot back. "Remember, nobody asked you to tag along after me."

"Nobody asked you to give me that money," he said and promptly disappeared.

"I *hate* it when you do that."

"Good," a disembodied voice replied.

Mona stared thoughtfully at the now-empty sofa cushions and found herself wondering what it would be like to be invisible, which got her thinking about all the ways one could be nonintrusive and still observe the world. After awhile, she got up and took down one of her old sketchbooks, flipping through it until she came to the notes she'd made when she'd first started planning her semi-autobiographical strip for *The Girl Zone*.

⊢ ⊤ ⊣

"My Life As A Bird"
Notes for chapter one:

(Mona and Hazel are sitting at the kitchen table in Mona's apartment having tea and muffins. Mona is watching Jamaica, asleep on the windowsill, only the tip of her tail twitching.)

MONA: Being invisible would be the coolest, but the next best thing would be, like, if you could be a bird or a cat—something that no one pays any attention to.

HAZEL: What kind of bird?

MONA: I don't know. A crow, all blue-black wings and shadowy. Or, no. Maybe something even less noticeable, like a pigeon or a sparrow.

(She gets a happy look on her face.)

MONA: Because you can tell. They pay attention to everything, but no one pays attention to them.

HAZEL: And the cat would be black, too, I suppose?

MONA: Mmm. Lean and slinky like Jamaica. Very Egyptian. But a bird would be better—more mobility—though I guess it wouldn't matter, really. The important thing is how you'd just be there, another piece of the landscape, but you'd be watching everything. You wouldn't miss a thing.

HAZEL: Bit of a voyeur, are we?

MONA: No, nothing like that. I'm not even interested in high drama, just the things that go on every day in our lives—the stuff most people don't pay attention to. That's the real magic.

HAZEL: Sounds boring.

MONA: No, it would be very Zen. Almost like meditating.

HAZEL: You've been drawing that comic of yours for too long.

⊢ ⊤ ⊣

The phone rang that evening while Mona was inking a new page for "Jupiter Jewel." The sudden sound startled her and a blob of ink fell from the end of her nib pen, right beside Cecil's head. At least it hadn't landed on his face.

I'll make that a shadow, she decided as she answered the phone.

"So do you still have an invisible friend?" Jilly asked.

Mona looked down the hall from the kitchen table where she was working. What she could see of the apartment appeared empty, but she didn't trust her eyesight when it came to her uninvited houseguest.

"I can't see him," she said, "but I have to assume he hasn't left."

"Well, I don't have any useful news. I've checked with all the usual sources and no one quite knows what to make of him."

"The usual sources being?"

"Christy. The professor. An old copy of *The Newford Examiner* with a special section on the fairy folk of Newford."

"You're kidding."

"I am," Jilly admitted. "But I did go to the library and had a wonderful time looking through all sorts of interesting books, from K.M. Briggs to *When the Desert Dreams* by Anne Bourke, neither of whom write about Newford, but I've always loved those fairy lore books Briggs compiled and Anne Bourke lived here, as I'm sure you knew, and I really liked the picture on the cover of her book. I know," she added, before Mona could break in. "Get to the point already."

"I'm serenely patient and would never have said such a thing," Mona told her.

"Humble, too. Anyway, apparently there are all sorts of tricksy fairy folk, from hobs to brownies. Some relatively nice, some decidedly nasty, but none of them quite fit the Nacky Wilde profile."

"You mean sarcastic, grubby and bad mannered, but potentially helpful?"

"In a nutshell."

Mona sighed. "So I'm stuck with him."

She realized that she'd been absently doodling on her art and set her pen aside before she completely ruined the page.

"It doesn't seem fair, does it?" she added. "I finally get the apartment to myself, but then some elfin squatter moves in."

"How *are* you doing?" Jilly asked. "I mean, aside from your invisible squatter?"

"I don't feel closure," Mona said. "I know how weird that sounds, considering what I told you yesterday. After all, Pete stomped out and then snuck back while I was with you last night to get his stuff—so I *know* it's over. And the more I think of it, I realize this had to work out the way it did. But I'm still stuck with all this emotional baggage, like trying to figure out why things ended up the way they did, and how come I never noticed."

"Would you take him back?"

"No."

"But you miss him?"

"I do," Mona said. "Weird, isn't it?"

"Perfectly normal, I'd say. Do you want a shoulder to commiserate on?"

"No, I need to get some work done. But thanks."

After she hung up, Mona stared down at the mess she'd made of the page she'd been working on. She supposed she could try to incorporate all the squiggles into the background, but it didn't seem worth the bother. Instead she picked up a bottle of white acrylic ink, gave it a shake and opened it. With a clean brush she began to paint over the doodles and the blob of ink she'd dropped by Cecil's head. It was obvious now that it wouldn't work as shadow, seeing how the light source was on the same side.

Waiting for the ink to dry, she wandered into the living room and looked around.

"Trouble with your love life?" a familiar, but still disembodied voice asked.

"If you're going to talk to me," she said, "at least show your face."

"Is this a new rule?"

Mona shook her head. "It's just disorienting to be talking into thin air—especially when the air answers back."

"Well, since you asked so politely..."

Nacky Wilde reappeared, slouching in the stuffed chair this time, a copy of one of Mona's comic books open on his lap.

"You're not actually reading that?" Mona said.

He looked down at the comic. "No, of course not. Dwarves can't read—their brains are much too small to learn such an obviously complex task."

"I didn't mean it that way."

"I know you didn't, but I can't help myself. I have a reputation to maintain."

"As a dwarf?" Mona asked. "Is that what you are?"

He shrugged and changed the subject. "I'm not surprised you and your boyfriend broke up."

"What's that supposed to mean?"

He stabbed the comic book with a short stubby finger. "The tension's so apparent—if this bird story holds any truth. One never gets the sense that any of the characters really like Pete."

Mona sat down on the sofa and swung her feet up onto the cushions. This was just what she needed—an uninvited, usually invisible squatter of a houseguest who was also a self-appointed analyst. Except, when she thought about it, he was right. "My Life As A Bird" was emotionally true, if not always a faithful account of actual events, and the Pete character in it had never been one of her favourites. Like the real Pete, there was an underlying tightness in his character; it was more noticeable in the strip because the rest of the cast was so Bohemian.

"He wasn't a bad person," she found herself saying.

"Of course not. Why would you let yourself be attracted to a bad person?"

Mona couldn't decide if he was being nice or sarcastic.

"They just wore him down," she said. "In the office. Won him over to their way of thinking, and there was no room for me in his life anymore."

"Or for him in yours," Nacky said.

Mona nodded. "It's weird, isn't it? Generosity of spirit seems to be so old-fashioned nowadays. We'd rather watch somebody trip on the sidewalk than help them climb the stairs to whatever it is they're reaching for."

"What is it you're reaching for?" Nacky asked.

"Oh, god." Mona laughed. "Who knows? Happiness, contentment. Some days all I want is for the lines to come together on the page and look like whatever it is that I'm trying to draw." She leaned back on the arm of the sofa and regarded the ceiling. "You know, that trick you do with invisibility is pretty cool." She turned her head to look at him. "Is it something that can be taught or do you have to be born magic?"

"Born to it, I'm afraid."

"I figured as much. But it's always been a fantasy of mine. That, or being able to change into something else."

"So I've gathered from reading this," Nacky said, giving the comic another tap with his finger. "Maybe you should try to be happy just being yourself. Look inside yourself for what you need—the way your character recommends in one of the earlier issues."

"You really have been reading it."

"That is why you write it, isn't it—to be read?"

She gave him a suspicious look. "Why are you being so nice all of a sudden?"

"Just setting you up for the big fall."

"Uh-huh."

"Thought of what I can do for you yet?" he asked.

She shook her head. "But I'm working on it."

⊢ ⅄ ⊣

"My Life As A Bird"
Notes for chapter seven:

(So after Mona meets Gregory, they go walking in Fitzhenry Park and sit on a bench from which they can see Wendy's Tree of Tales growing. Do I need to explain this, or can it just be something people who know will understand?)

GREGORY: Did you ever notice how we don't tell family stories anymore?

MONA: What do you mean?

GREGORY: Families used to be made up of stories—their history—and those stories were told down through the generations. It's where a family got its identity, the same way a neighbourhood or even a country did. Now the stories we share we get from television and the only thing we talk about is ourselves.

(Mona realizes this is true—maybe not for everybody, but it's true for her. Argh. How do I draw this???)

MONA: Maybe the family stories don't work anymore. Maybe they've lost their relevance.

GREGORY: They've lost nothing.

(He looks away from her, out across the park.)

GREGORY: But we have.

⊢ ⅄ ⊣

In the days that followed, Nacky Wilde alternated between the sarcastic grump Mona had first met and the surprisingly good company he could prove to be when he didn't, as she told him one night, "have a bee up his butt." Unfortunately, the good of the one didn't outweigh the frustration of having to put up with the other and there was no getting rid of him. When he was in one of his moods, she didn't know which was worse: having to look at his scowl and listen to his bad-tempered remarks, or telling him to vanish but know that he was still sulking around the apartment, invisible and watching her.

⤙ ⋎ ⤚

A week after Pete had moved out, Mona met up with Jilly at the Cyberbean Café. They were planing to attend the opening of Sophie's latest show at The Green Man Gallery and Mona had once again promised herself not to dump her problems on Jilly, but there was no one else she could talk to.

"It's so typical," she found herself saying. "Out of all the hundreds of magical beings that populate folk tales and legends, I had to get stuck with the one that has a multiple personality disorder. He's driving me crazy."

"Is he with us now?" Jilly asked.

"Who knows? Who cares?" Then Mona had to laugh. "God, listen to me. It's like I'm complaining about a bad relationship."

"Well, it is a bad relationship."

"I know. And isn't it pathetic?" Mona shook her head. "If this is what I rebounded to from Pete, I don't want to know what I'll end up with when I finally get this nasty little man out of my life. At least the sex was good with Pete."

Jilly's eyes went wide. "You're not...?"

"Oh, please. That'd be like sleeping with the eighth dwarf, Snotty—the one Disney kept out of his movie and with good reason."

Jilly had to laugh. "I'm sorry, but it's just so—"

Mona wagged a finger at her. "Don't say it. You wouldn't be laughing if it was happening to you." She looked at her watch. "We should get going."

Jilly took a last sip of her coffee. Wrapping what she hadn't finished of her cookie in a napkin, she stuck it in her pocket.

"What are you going to do?" she asked as they left the café.

"Well, I looked in The Yellow Pages, but none of the exterminators have cranky dwarves listed among the household pests they'll get rid of, so I guess I'm stuck with him for now. Though I haven't looked under exorcists yet."

"Is he Catholic?" Jilly asked.

"I didn't think it mattered. They just get rid of evil spirits, don't they?"

"Why not just ask him to leave? That's something no one else but he can do for you."

"I already thought of that," Mona told her.

"And?"

"Apparently it doesn't work that way."

"Maybe you should ask him what he can do for you."

Mona nodded thoughtfully. "You know, I never thought of that. I just assumed this whole business was one of those Rumpelstiltskin kind of things—that I had to come up with it on my own."

⊱ Ⲧ ⊰

"What?" Nacky said later that night when Mona returned from the gallery and asked him to show himself. "You want me to list my services like on a menu? I'm not a restaurant."

"Or computer software," Mona agreed, "though it might be easier if you were either, because then at least I'd know what you can do without having to go through a song and dance to get the information out of you."

"No one's ever asked this kind of thing before."

"So what?" she asked. "Is it against the rules?"

Nacky scowled. "What makes you think there are rules?"

"There are always rules. So come on. Give."

"Fine," Nacky said. "We'll start with the most popular items." He began to count the items off on his fingers. "Potions, charms, spells, incantations—"

Mona held up a hand. "Hold on there. Let's back up a bit. What are these potions and charms and stuff."

"Well, take your ex-boyfriend," Nacky said.

Please do, Mona thought.

"I could put a spell on him so that every time he looked at a woman that he was attracted to, he'd break out in hives."

"You could do that?"

Nacky nodded. "Or it could just be a minor irritation—an itch that will never go away."

"How long would it last?"

"Your choice. For the rest of his life, if you want."

Wouldn't that serve Pete right, Mona thought. Talk about a serious payback for all those mean things he'd said about her and *The Girl Zone*.

"This is so tempting," she said.

"So what will it be?" Nacky asked, briskly rubbing his hands together. "Hives? An itch? Perhaps a nervous tic under his eye so that people will always think he's winking at them. Seems harmless, but it's good for any number of face slaps and more serious altercations."

"Hang on," Mona told him. "What's the big hurry?"

"I'm in no hurry. I thought you were. I thought the sooner you got rid of Snotty, the eighth dwarf, the happier you'd be."

So he had been in the café.

"Okay," Mona said. "But first I have to ask you. These charms and things of yours—do they only do negative stuff?"

Nacky shook his head. "No. They can teach you the language of birds, choose your dreams before you go to sleep, make you appear to not be somewhere when you really are—"

"Wait a sec'. You told me I had to be born magic to do that."

"No. You asked about, and I quote, 'the trick *you* do with invisibility,' the emphasis being mine. How I do it, you have to be born magic. An invisibility charm is something else."

"But it does the same thing?"

"For all intents and purposes."

God, but he could be infuriating.

"So why didn't you tell me that?"

Nacky smirked. "You didn't ask."

I will not get angry, she told herself. I am calmness incarnate.

"Okay," she said. "What else?"

He went back to counting the items on his fingers, starting again with a tap of his right index finger onto his left. "Potions to fall in love, to fall out of love. To make hair longer, or thicker. To make one taller, or shorter, or—" he gave her a wicked grin "—slimmer. To speak with the recent dead, to heal the sick—"

"Heal them of what?" Mona wanted to know.

"Whatever ails them," he said, then went on in a bored voice. "To turn kettles into foxes, and vice versa. To—"

Mona was beginning to suffer overload.

"Enough already," she said. "I get the point."

"But you—"

"Shh. Let me think."

She laid her head back in her chair and closed her eyes. Basically, what it boiled down to was she could have whatever she wanted. She could have revenge on Pete—not for leaving her, but for being so mean-spirited about it. She could be invisible, or understand the language of birds and animals. And though he'd claimed not to have a pot of gold when they first met, she could probably have fame and fortune, too.

But she didn't really want revenge on Pete. And being invisible probably wasn't such a good idea since she already spent far too much time on her own as it was. What she should really do is get out more, meet more people, make more friends of her own, instead of all the people she knew through Pete. As for fame and fortune…corny as it might sound, she really did believe that the process was what was important, the journey her art and stories took her on, not the place where they all ended up.

She opened her eyes and looked at Nacky.

"Well?" he said.

She stood up and picked up her coat where she'd dropped it on the end of the sofa.

"Come on," she said as she put it on.

"Where are we going?"

"To hail a cab."

⊱ ⊤ ⊰

She had the taxi take them to the children's hospital. After paying the fare, she got out and stood on the lawn. Nacky, invisible in the vehicle, popped back into view. Leaves crackled underfoot as he joined her.

"There," Mona said, pointing at the long square block of a building. "I want you to heal all the kids in there."

There was a long moment of silence. When Mona turned to look at her companion, it was to find him regarding her with a thoughtful expression.

"I can't do that," he said.

Mona shook her head. "Like you couldn't make me invisible?"

"No semantics this time," he said. "I can't heal them all."

"But that's what I want."

Nacky sighed. "It's like asking for world peace. It's too big a task. But I could heal one of them."

"Just one?"

Nacky nodded.

Mona turned to look at the building again. "Then heal the sickest one."

She watched him cross the lawn. When he reached the front doors, his figure shimmered and he seemed to flow through the glass rather than step through the actual doors.

He was gone a long time. When he finally returned, his pace was much slower and there was a haunted look in his eyes.

"There was a little girl with cancer," he said. "She would have died later tonight. Her name—"

"I don't want to know her name," Mona told him. "I just want to know, will she be all right?"

He nodded.

I could have had anything, she found herself thinking.

"Do you regret giving the gift away?" Nacky asked her.

She shook her head. "No. I only wish I had more of them." She eyed him for a long moment. "I don't suppose I could freely give you another couple of dollars...?"

"No. It doesn't—"

"Work that way," she finished. "I kind of figured as much." She knelt down so that she wasn't towering over him. "So now what? Where will you go?"

"I have a question for you," he said.

"Shoot."

"If I asked, would you let me stay on with you?"

Mona laughed.

"I'm serious," he told her.

"And what? Things would be different now, or would you still be snarly more often than not?"

He shook his head. "No different."

"You know I can't afford to keep that apartment," she said. "I'm probably going to have to get a bachelor somewhere."

"I wouldn't mind."

Mona knew she'd be insane to agree. All she'd been doing for the past week was trying to get him out of her life. But then she thought of the look in his eyes when he'd come back from the hospital and knew that he wasn't all bad. Maybe he was a little magic man, but he was still stuck living on the street and how happy could that make a person? Could be, all he needed was what everybody needed—a fair break. Could be, if he was treated fairly, he wouldn't glower so much, or be so bad-tempered.

But could she put up with it?

"I can't believe I'm saying this," she told him, "but, yeah. You can come back with me."

456

She'd never seen him smile before, she realized. It transformed his features.

"You've broken the curse," he said.

"Say what?"

"You don't know how long I've had to wait to find someone both selfless and willing to take me in as I was."

"I don't know about the selfless—"

He leaned forward and kissed her.

"Thank you," he said.

And then he went whirling off across the lawn, spinning like a dervishing top. His squatness melted from him and he grew tall and lean, fluid as a willow sapling, dancing in the wind. From the far side of the lawn he waved at her. For a long moment, all she could do was stare, open-mouthed. When she finally lifted her hand to wave back, he winked out of existence, like a spark leaping from a fire, glowing brightly before it vanished into the darkness.

This time she knew he was gone for good.

⅄ ⅄ ⅃

"My Life As A Bird"
Mona's closing monologue from chapter eleven:

The weird thing is I actually miss him. Oh, not his crankiness, or his serious lack of personal hygiene. What I miss is the kindness that occasionally slipped through—the piece of him that survived the curse.

Jilly says that was why he was so bad-tempered and gross. He had to make himself unlikable, or it wouldn't have been so hard to find someone who would accept him for who he seemed to be. She says I stumbled into a fairy tale, which is pretty cool when you think about it, because how many people can say that?

Though I suppose if this really were a fairy tale, there'd be some kind of "happily ever after" wrap up, or I'd at least have come away with a fairy gift of one sort or another. That invisibility charm, say, or the ability to change into a bird or a cat.

But I don't really need anything like that.

I've got *The Girl Zone*. I can be anything I want in its pages. Rockit Grrl, saving the day. Jupiter, who can't seem to physically show up in her own life. Or just me.

I've got my dreams. I had a fun one last night. I was walking downtown and I was a birdwoman, spindly legs, beak where my nose should be, long wings hanging down from my shoulders like a ragged cloak. Or maybe I was just wearing a bird costume. Nobody recognized me, but they knew me all the same and thought it was way cool.

And I've touched a piece of real magic. Now, no matter how grey and bland and pointless the world might seem sometimes, I just have to remember that there really is more to everything than what we can see. Everything has a spirit that's so much bigger and brighter than you think it could hold.

Everything has one.

Me, too.

1997

The Fields Beyond the Fields

I just see my life better in ink.

Jewel Kilcher,
from an interview
on MuchMusic, 1997

Saskia is sleeping, but I can't. I sit up at my rolltop desk, writing. It's late, closer to dawn than midnight, but I'm not tired. Writing can be good for keeping sleep at bay. It also helps me make sense of things where simply thinking about them can't. It's too easy to get distracted by a wayward digression when the ink's not holding the thoughts to paper. By focusing on the page, I can step outside myself and look at the puzzle with a clearer eye.

Earlier this evening Saskia and I were talking about magic and wonder, about how it can come and go in your life, or more particularly, how it comes and goes in my life. That's the side of me that people don't get to see when all they can access is the published page. I'm as often a skeptic as a believer. I'm not the one who experiences those oddities that appear in the stories; I'm the one who chronicles the mystery of them, trying to make sense out what they can impart about us, our world, our preconceptions of how things should be.

The trouble is, mostly life seems to be exactly what it is. I can't find the hidden card waiting to be played because it seems too apparent that the whole hand is already laid out on the table. What you see is what you get, thanks, and do come again.

I want there to be more.

Even my friends assume I'm the knowledgeable expert who writes the books. None of them knows how much of a hypocrite I really am. I listen well and I know exactly what to say to keep the narrative flowing. I can accept everything that's happened to them—the oddest and most absurd stories they tell me don't make me blink an eye—but all the while there's a small voice chanting in the back of my head.

As if, as if, as if...

I wasn't always like this, but I'm good at hiding how I've changed, from those around me, as well as from myself.

But Saskia knows me too well.

"You used to live with a simple acceptance of the hidden world," she said when the conversation finally turned into a circle and there was nothing new to add. "You used to live with magic and mystery, but now you only write about it."

I didn't know how to reply.

I wanted to tell her that it's easy to believe in magic when you're young. Anything you couldn't explain was magic then. It didn't matter if it was science or a fairy tale. Electricity and elves were both infinitely mysterious and equally possible—elves probably more so. It didn't seem particularly odd to believe that actors lived inside your TV set. That there was a repertory company inside the radio, producing its chorus of voices and music. That a fat, bearded man lived at the North Pole and kept tabs on your behaviour.

I wanted to tell her that I used to believe she was born in a forest that only exists inside the nexus of a connection of computers, entangled with one another where they meet on the World Wide Web. A wordwood that appears in pixels on the screen, but has another, deeper existence somewhere out there in the mystery that exists concurrent to the Internet, the way religion exists in the gathering of like minds.

But not believing in any of it now, I wasn't sure that I ever had.

The problem is that even when you have firsthand experience with a piece of magic, it immediately begins to slip away. Whether it's a part of the enchantment, or some inexplicable defense mechanism that's been wired into us either by society or genetics, it doesn't make any difference. The magic still slips away, sliding like a melted icicle along the slick surface of our memories.

That's why some people need to talk about it—the ones who want to hold on to the marvel of what they've seen or heard or felt. And that's why I'm willing to listen, to validate their experience and help them keep it alive. But there's no one around to validate mine. They think my surname Riddell is a happy coincidence, that it means I've solved the riddles of the world instead of being as puzzled by them as they are. Everybody assumes that I'm already in that state of grace where enchantment lies thick in every waking moment, and one's dreams—by way of recompense, perhaps?—are mundane.

As if, as if, as if...

The sigh that escapes me seems self-indulgent in the quiet that holds the apartment. I pick up my pen, put it down when I hear a rustle of fabric, the creak of a spring as the sofa takes someone's weight. The voice of my shadow speaks then, a disembodied voice coming to me from the darkness beyond the spill of the desk's lamplight, but tonight I don't listen to her. Instead I take down volumes of my old journals from where they're lined up on top of my desk. I page through the entries, trying to see if I've really changed. And if so, when.

I don't know what makes sense anymore; I just seem to know what doesn't.

⊢ ⊤ ⊣

When I was young, I liked to walk in the hills behind our house, looking at animals. Whether they were big or small, it made no difference to me. Everything they did was absorbing. The crow's lazy flight. A red squirrel scolding me from the safety of a hemlock branch, high overhead. The motionless spider in a corner of its patient web. A quick russet glimpse of a fox before it vanishes in the high weeds. The water rat making its daily journeys across Jackson's Pond and back. A tree full of cedar waxwings, gorging on berries. The constantly shifting pattern of a gnat ballet.

I've never been able to learn what I want about animals from books or nature specials on television. I have to walk in their territories, see the world as they might see it. Walk along the edges of the stories they know.

The stories are the key, because for them, for the animals, everything that clutters our lives, they keep in their heads. History, names, culture, gossip, art. Even their winter and summer coats are only ideas, genetic imprints memorized by their DNA, coming into existence only when the seasons change.

I think their stories are what got me writing. First in journals, accounts as truthful as I could make them, then as stories where actuality is stretched and manipulated, because the lies in fiction are such an effective way to tell emotional truths. I took great comfort in how the lines of words marched from left to right and down the page, building up into a meaningful structure like rows of knitting. Sweater stories. Mitten poems. Long, rambling journal entries like the scarves we used to have when we were kids, scarves that seemed to go on forever.

I never could hold the stories in my head, though in those days I could absorb them for hours, stretched out in a field, my gaze lost in the expanse of forever sky above. I existed in a timeless place then, probably as close to Zen as I'll ever get again. Every sense alert, all existence focused on the present moment. The closest I can come to recapturing that feeling now is when I set pen to paper. For those brief moments when the words flow unimpeded, everything I am is simultaneously focused into one perfect detail and expanded to encompass everything that is. I own the stories in those moments, I am the stories, though, of course, none of them really belong to me. I only get to borrow them. I hold them for awhile, set them down on paper, and then let them go.

I can own them again, when I reread them, but then so can anyone.

ⲁ Ⲧ ⲁ

According to Jung, at around the age of six or seven we separate and then hide away the parts of ourselves that don't seem acceptable, that don't fit in the world around us. Those unacceptable parts that we secret away become our shadow.

I remember reading somewhere that it can be a useful exercise to visualize the person our shadow would be if it could step out into the light. So I tried it. It didn't work immediately. For a long time, I was simply talking to myself. Then, when I did get a response, it was only a spirit voice I heard in my head. It could just as easily have been my own. But over time, my shadow took on more physical attributes, in the way that a story grows clearer and more pertinent as you add and take away words, molding its final shape

Not surprisingly, my shadow proved to be the opposite of who I am in so many ways. Bolder, wiser, with a better memory and a penchant for dressing up with costumes, masks, or simply formal wear. A cocktail dress in a raspberry patch. A green man mask in a winter field. She's short, where I'm tall. Dark-skinned, where I'm light. Red-haired, where mine's dark. A girl to my boy, and now a woman as I'm a man.

If she has a name, she's never told me it. If she has an existence outside the times we're together, she has yet to divulge it either. Naturally I'm curious about where she goes, but she doesn't like being asked questions and I've learned not to press her because when I do, she simply goes away.

Sometimes I worry about her existence. I get anxieties about schizophrenia and carefully study myself for other symptoms. But if she's a delusion, it's singular, and otherwise I seem to be as normal as anyone else, which is to say, confused by the barrage of input and stimuli with which the modern world besets us, and trying to make do. Who was it that said she's always trying to understand the big picture, but the trouble is, the picture just keeps getting bigger? Ani DiFranco, I think.

Mostly I don't get too analytical about it—something I picked up from her, I suppose, since left to my own devices, I can worry the smallest detail to death.

We have long conversations, usually late at night, when the badgering clouds swallow the stars and the darkness is most profound. Most of the time I can't see her, but I can hear her voice. I like to think we're friends; even if we don't agree about details, we can usually find common ground on how we'd like things to be.

⊢ ⅄ ⊣

There are animals in the city, but I can't read their stories the same as I did the ones that lived in the wild. In the forested hills of my childhood.

⊢ ⅄ ⊣

I don't know when exactly it was that I got so interested in the supernatural, you know, fairy tales and all. I mean, I was always interested in them, the way kids are, but I didn't let them go. I collected unusual and odd facts, read the Brothers Grimm, Lady Gregory, Katharine Briggs, but *Famous Monsters* and ghost stories, too. They gave me something the animals couldn't—or didn't—but I needed it all the same.

Animal stories connected me to the landscape we inhabited—to their world, to my world, to all the wonder that can exist around us. They grounded me, but were no relief from unhappiness and strife. But fairy tales let me escape. Not away from something, but *to* something. To hope. To a world beyond this world where other ways of seeing were possible. Where other ways of treating each other were possible.

An Irish writer, Lord Dunsany, coined the phrase "Beyond the Fields We Know" to describe fairyland, and that's always appealed to me. First there's the comfort of the fields we do know, the idea that it's familiar and friendly. Home. Then there's the otherness of what lies beyond them that so aptly describes what I imagine the alien topography of fairyland to be. The grass is always greener in the next field over, the old saying goes. More appealing, more vibrant. But perhaps it's more dangerous as well. No reason not to explore it, but it's worthwhile to keep in mind that one should perhaps take care.

⊱ Υ ⊰

If I'd thought that I had any aptitude as an artist, I don't think I'd ever have become a writer. All I ever wanted to capture was moments. The trouble is, most people want narrative, so I tuck those moments away in the pages of a story. If I could draw or paint the way I see those moments in my head, I wouldn't have to write about them.

It's scarcely an original thought, but a good painting really can hold all the narrative and emotional impact of a novel—the viewer simply has to work a little harder than a reader does with a book. There are fewer clues. Less taking the viewer by the hand and leading him or her through all the possible events that had to occur to create this visualized moment before them.

I remember something Jilly once said about how everyone should learn to draw competently at an early age, because drawing, she maintains, is one of the first intuitive gestures we make to satisfy our appetites for beauty and communication. If we could acknowledge those hungers, and do so from an early age, our culture would be very different from the way it is today. We would understand how images are used to compel us, in the same way that most of us understand the subtleties of language.

Because, think of it. As children, we come into the world with a natural desire to both speak and draw. Society makes sure that we learn language properly, right from the beginning, but art is treated as a gift of innate genius, something we either have or don't. Most children are given far too much praise for their early drawings, so much so that they rarely learn the ability to refine their first crude efforts the way their early attempts at language are corrected.

How hard would it be to ask a child what they see in their head? How big should the house be in comparison to the family standing in front of it? What is it about the anatomy of the people that doesn't look right? Then let them try it again. Teach them to learn how to see and ask questions. You don't have to be Michelangelo to teach basic art, just as you don't have to be Shakespeare to be able to teach the correct use of language.

Not to be dogmatic about it, because you wouldn't want any creative process to lose its sense of fun and adventure. But that doesn't mean you can't take it seriously as well.

Because children know when they're being patronized. I remember, so clearly I can remember, having the picture in my head and it didn't look at all like what I managed to scribble down on paper. When I was given no direction, in the same way that my grammar and sentence structure and the like were corrected, I lost interest and gave up. Now it seems too late.

I had a desk I made as a teenager—a wide board laid across a couple of wooden fruit crates. I'd set out my pens and ink, my paper, sit cross-legged on a pillow in front of it and write for hours. I carried that board around with me for years, from rooming house to apartments. I still have it, only now it serves as a shelf that holds plants underneath a window in the dining room. Saskia finds it odd that I remain so attached to it, but I can't let it go. It's too big a piece of my past—one of the tools that helped free me from a reality that had no room for the magic I needed the world to hold, but could only make real with words.

I didn't just like to look at animals. I'd pretend to be them, too. I'd scrabble around all day on my hands and knees through the bush to get an understanding of that alternate viewpoint. Or I'd run for miles, the horse in me effortlessly carrying me through fields, over fences, across streams. Remember when you'd never walk, when you could run? It never made any *sense* to go so slow.

And even at home, or at school, or when we'd go into town, the animals would stay with me. I'd carry them secreted in my chest. That horse, a mole, an owl, a wolf. Nobody knew they were there, but I did. Their secret presence both comforted and thrilled me.

≻ Y ≺

I write differently depending on the pen I use. Ballpoints are only good for business scribbles, or for making shopping lists, and even then, I'll often use a fountain pen. When I first wrote, I did so with a dip pen and ink. Coloured inks, sometimes—sepia, gold, and a forest green were the most popular choices—but usually India ink. I used a mapping nib, writing on cream-coloured paper with deckled edges and more tooth than might be recommended for that sort of nib. The dip pen made me take my time, think about every word before I committed to it.

But fountain pens grew to be my writing implement of choice. A fat, thick-nibbed, deep-green Cross from which the ink flowed as though sliding across ice, or a black Waterman with a fine point that made tiny, bird track-like marks across the page.

When I began marketing my work, I typed it up—now I use a computer—but the life of my first drafts depends on the smooth flow of a fountain pen. I can, and did, and do, write anywhere with them. All I need is the pen and my notebook. I've written standing up, leaning my notebook on the cast-iron balustrade of the Kelly Street Bridge, watching the dark water flow beneath me, my page lit by the light cast from a streetlamp. I've written by moonlight and in cafés. In the corner of a pub and sitting at a bus stop.

I can use other implements, but those pens are best. Pencil smears, pen and ink gets too complicated to carry about, Rapidographs and rollerballs don't have enough character, and ballpoints have no soul. My fountains pens have plenty of both. Their nibs are worn down to the style of my hand, the shafts fit into my fingers with the comfort of the voice of a long-time friend, met unexpectedly on a street corner, but no less happily for the surprise of the meeting.

≻ Y ≺

Time passes oddly. Though I know the actual contrast is vast, I don't feel much different now from when I was fifteen. I still feel as clumsy and awkward and insecure about interacting with others, about how the world sees me, though intellectually, I understand that others don't perceive me in the same way at all. I'm middle-aged, not a boy. I'm at that age when the boy I was thought that life would pretty much be over, yet now I insist it's only begun. I have to. To think otherwise is to give up, to actually *be* old.

That's disconcerting enough. But when a year seems to pass in what was only a season for the boy, a dreamy summer that would never end, the long cold days of winter when simply stepping outside made you feel completely alive, you begin to fear the ever-increasing momentum of time's passage. Does it simply accelerate forever, or is there a point when it begins to slow down once again? Is that the real meaning of "over the hill"? You start up slow, then speed up to make the incline. Reach the top and gravity has you speeding once more. But eventually your momentum decreases, as even a rolling stone eventually runs out of steam.

I don't know. What I do know is that the antidote for me is to immerse myself in something like my writing, though simply puttering around the apartment can be as effective. There's something about familiar tasks that keeps at bay the unsettling sense of everything being out of my control. Engaging in the mundane, whether it be watching the light change in the sky at dusk, playing with my neighbour's cat, enjoying the smell of freshly brewed coffee, serves to alter time. It doesn't so much stop the express, as allow you to forget it for awhile. To recoup, catch your breath.

But writing is best, especially the kind that pulls you out of yourself, off the page, and takes you into a moment of clarity, an instant of happy wonder, so perfect that words, stumbling through the human mind, are inadequate to express.

The writer's impossible task is to illuminate such moments, yes, but also the routines, the things we do or feel or simply appreciate, that happen so regularly that they fade away into the background the way street noise and traffic become inaudible when you've lived in the city long enough. It's the writer's job to illuminate such moments as well, to bring them back into awareness, to acknowledge the gift of their existence and share that acknowledgment with others.

By doing this, we are showing deference to the small joys of our lives, giving them meaning. Not simply for ourselves, but for others as well, to remind them of the significance to be found in their lives. And what we all discover, is that nothing is really ordinary or familiar after all. Our small worlds are more surprising and interesting than we perceive them to be.

⊢ Υ ⊣

But we still need enchantment in our lives. We still need mystery. Something to connect us to what lies beyond the obvious, to what, perhaps, *is* the obvious, only seen from another, or better-informed, perspective.

Mystery.

I love that word. I love how, phonetically, it seems to hold both "myth" and "history." The Kickaha use it to refer to God, the Great Mystery. But they also ascribe to animism, paying respect to small, mischievous spirits that didn't create the world, but rather, are *of* the world. They call them mysteries, too. *Manitou.* The little mysteries.

We call them faerie.

We don't believe in them.

Our loss.

⊢ Υ ⊣

Saskia is still sleeping. I look in on her, then slowly close the bedroom door. I put on my boots and jacket and go downstairs, out onto the pre-dawn streets. It's my favorite time of day. It's so quiet, but everything seems filled with potential. The whole world appears to hold its breath, waiting for the first streak of light to lift out of the waking eastern skies.

After a few blocks, I hear footsteps and my shadow falls in beside me.

"Still soul searching?" she asks.

I nod, expecting a lecture on how worrying about "what if" only makes you miss out on "what is," but she doesn't say anything. We walk up Lee Street to Kelly, past the pub and up onto the bridge. Halfway across, I lean my forearms on the balustrade and look out across the water. She puts her back to the rail. I can feel her gaze on me. There's no traffic. Give it another few hours and the bridge will be choked with commuters.

"Why can't I believe in magic?" I finally say.

When there's no immediate response, I look over to find her smiling.

"What do you think I am?" she asks.

"I don't know," I tell her honestly. "A piece of me. Pieces of me. But you must be more than that now, because you've had experiences I haven't shared since you...left."

"As have you."

"I suppose." I turn my attention back to the water flowing under us. "Unless I'm delusional."

She laughs. "Yes, there's always the risk of that, isn't there?"

"So which is it?"

She shrugs.

"At least tell me your name," I say.

Her only response is another one of those enigmatic smiles of hers that would have done Leonardo proud. I sigh, and try one more time.

"Then tell me this," I say. "Where do you go when you're not with me?"

She surprises me with an answer.

"To the fields beyond the fields," she says.

"Can you take me with you some time?" I ask, keeping my voice casual. I feel like Wendy, waiting at the windowsill for Peter Pan.

"But you already know the way."

I give her a blank look.

"It's all around you," she says. "It's here." She touches her eyes, her ears. "And here." She moves her hand to her temple. "And here." She lays a hand upon her breast.

I look away. The sun's rising now and all the skyscrapers of midtown have a haloing glow, an aura of morning promise. A pair of crows lift from the roof of the pub and their blue-black wings have more colour in them than I ever imagined would be possible. I watch them glide over the river, dip down, out of the sunlight, and become shadow shapes once more.

I feel something shift inside me. A lifting of...I'm not sure what. An unaccountable easing of tension—not in my neck, or shoulders, but in my spirit. As though I've just received what Colin Wilson calls "absurd good news."

When I turn back, my companion is gone. But I understand. The place where mystery lives doesn't necessarily have to make sense. It's not that it's nonsense, so much, as beyond sense.

My shadow is the parts of me I'd hidden away—some because they didn't fit who I thought I was supposed to be, some that I just didn't understand.

Her name is Mystery.

St. John of the Cross wrote, "If a man wants to be sure of his road he must close his eyes and walk in the dark."

Into his shadow.

Into mystery.

I think I can do that.

Or at least I can try.

I pause there a moment longer, breathing deep the morning air, drawing the sun's light down into my skin, then I turn, and head for home and Saskia. I think I have an answer for her now. She'll still be sleeping, but even asleep, I know she's waiting for me. Waiting for who I was to catch up with who I'll be. Waiting for me to remember who I am and all I've seen.

I think I'll take the plants off that board in the dining room and reclaim the desk it was.

I think I'll buy a sketchbook when the stores open and take one of those courses that Jilly teaches at the Newford School of Art. Maybe it's not too late.

I think I'll reacquaint myself with the animals that used to live in my chest.

I think I'll stop listening to that voice whispering "as if," and hold onto what I experience, no matter how far it strays from what's supposed to be.

I'm going to live here, in the Fields We Know, fully, but I'm not going to let myself forget how to visit the fields beyond these fields. I'll go there with words on the page, but without them, too. Because it's long past time to stop letting pen and ink be the experience, instead of merely recording it.

1998

Second Chances

There was a time, long ago, when speaking was a ceremony. This was before written laws and books and all the other little boxes we've got to put words in now. Back then, everything had a voice. The land, people, animals. It was all tribes, and words were a tribe of their own, a ceremony we could share with each other, an allowance that cut across species, connecting crow and woman and cedar and stream. Because everything was connected in those days. Still is, I guess, but we don't see the pattern of it so clearly anymore. What we said had weight in those days because its effects could carry on for generations. We didn't speak about the world, we spoke the world into being.

Those times are gone now. But every once in awhile something stirs that old tribe and some of those words wake up. And then, for a moment, anything can happen.

➤ ➤ ➤

I found myself in the Harp one night at the tail end of the year. It was a music night—not a session; they'd set up a little stage in one corner of the bar and the Kelledys were playing, harp and flute, a few songs, a lot of stories. I'd planned to stop in for a pint and then go, but the tunes got my foot tapping and the stories held me to the barstool. There are people that need stories, that can't exist without them. I'm one of those people, always have been. Nose in a book, ear cocked for gossip, wouldn't go to bed without a story and that lasted a lot longer for me than it does for most kids. I still read for an hour or so before I go to sleep.

I didn't recognize a lot of the tunes. They seemed to be mostly original, though in the tradition. But I picked out "Eliz Iza" not long after I got there, and later the flute player sang a haunting, wordless version of "Airde Cuan," the harp backing her up with rich, resonating chords. I remembered both airs from this album by Alan Stivell that I played to death in the seventies. I hadn't heard either of them, or the rest of the album for that matter, in years.

When the harper finished a story that he attributed to Seamus Ennis, about the origins of a piece called "The Gold Ring," and the pair launched into the actual tune, I turned to the bar and ordered another Caffrey's from the barman. A woman sat down beside me, but I barely noticed her. I had a sip of the beer, foam moustaching my upper lip, and returned my attention to the band.

"Joey?" she said. "Joey Straw?"

A closer look told me that I knew her, but it still took me a moment to figure out from where. When I did, I couldn't believe that it had taken any time at all. The black-rimmed glasses were what threw me off. The last time I'd seen Annie Ledford she'd been wearing contacts. I decided I liked the glasses. Combined with her short blonde hair and black jeans, they gave her a funky look.

"How've you been, Annie?" I said. "You're looking great."

She could still blush like a schoolgirl. I remember how that used to drive her crazy. I guess it still did, because she bent her head for a moment like she was checking out our footwear. Her eyes were bright behind the glasses when she looked up at me again. I wondered if it was the beer, or loneliness, or if she really was that happy to see me. Time's a funny thing. Sometimes it exaggerates a memory; sometimes it just lets it fade away.

"I've been good," she said. "It's been forever, hasn't it? What have you been up to?"

Nothing I could be proud of, but I figured this wasn't show and tell. I didn't have to go into details.

"Nothing much," I told her. "I've been keeping a low profile. And you?"

Turned out she was a booking agent now. The reason she was here tonight was that she was the one who brought the Kelledys in for the weekend.

"Good choice," I said.

She smiled. "Like it was a hard sell. They always draw a good crowd."

Our conversation died then. I don't get out much, and when I do, I usually keep to myself. But I felt I owed her something. An explanation, if nothing else.

"Look," I said. "About the way I just walked out on you..."

"It's okay," she said. "It's not like I didn't hear about your brother."

Yeah, Nicky had been a piece of work all right. He'd still be serving a life sentence in a federal pen for all the things he'd done if he hadn't taken his own life in an NPD jail cell. He was finally arrested for killing a man in Fitzhenry Park, but that came after a lot of years on the run for the murder of his own family. I'll never forget getting the call that night, my father's choked voice as he told me what had happened.

"Everything changed that night," I said, surprised to hear the words coming out of my mouth. "It wasn't just finding out that Nicky was this monster, but the way everybody treated the rest of us. Like we were responsible. Like it was in our blood and we could snap any moment, just like he did. It broke my mother's heart and my father's spirit. My sister's still not talking to any of us. I don't know where she moved, I just know it was far."

"And you?" she asked.

I shrugged.

"I tried calling you," she said. "A lot."

"I went away. I had to. I stopped answering the phone after the first reporter called. Just packed up and left the city."

She didn't say anything for a long moment. On the stage, the harper was announcing the last piece for this set. I had some more of my Caffrey's. The room seemed awfully hot to me.

"I told myself you weren't running away from me," Annie said as the harp began to play a syncopated intro. "From us."

"I wasn't. In the end I realized I was just running away from myself."

"So you came back."

I nodded. "I got tired of drifting, doing piecework. But it hasn't been much better since I got back."

"Were you going to call me?"

I shook my head. "And say what? I figured you had a new life by now, a better one. The last thing you'd need was Nicky Straw's brother back in it again."

"So you're still running," she said.

I gave her a humourless smile. "Only this time I'm doing it standing still."

She gave me a sad nod. "I have to go to the ladies' room. Watch my seat for me, would you?"

"Sure."

"You'll still be here when I get back?"

"I'm not going anywhere," I said.

Though to tell you the truth, I didn't expect her to come back. What was there to come back for?

There was a deep ache in my chest as I watched her go. I guess I always knew that by returning to the city, this day would come. I just thought I'd be better prepared for it.

I was only half aware that the Kelledys had finished their set and some canned music was playing. Generic Irish. Fiddles and pipes, a guitar hammering out the rhythm. A woman sat down in Annie's seat. I started to say something, then realized it was the flute player. She caught me off guard with a warm smile. Up close, I was surprised to see that the green tints in her hair hadn't been put there by the stage lights.

"Are you a friend of Annie's?" she asked.

"We go back awhile."

"I'm Meran," she said and offered me her hand.

"Joey Straw," I said as I shook.

Her handclasp took me off guard. Her hand was soft, but the grip showed steel.

"Annie's talked about you," she said.

My heart sank. I live for stories, but I don't like the idea of my life being one for others. Still, what can you do? I looked around for her husband, the harper, thinking he'd come by and our conversation could focus on safer ground. We could talk about their music, maybe. Even the weather. But he was sitting at a table near the stage, chatting with a couple who didn't seem to be old enough to be up this late, never mind ordering a beer. I remember feeling so mature at their age; now they looked like infants to me.

"It's not what you're thinking," Meran went on. "Annie's never blamed you. She talked about you because she missed you."

"I missed her, too," I said, turning back to look at her. "But it's old history now."

"Is it?"

"What do you mean?"

"What is it you're so afraid of?"

"That they were right. That what happened to Nicky could happen to me."

I didn't know why I was telling her this. I should have been saying, look, you seem like a nice lady, but this is really none of your business. But there was something about her that inspired confidences. That called them forth before you could even stop to think about what you were saying, what secrets you were revealing that were better left unspoken.

"Do you really believe that?" she asked.

"Hell, Nicky was a choirboy," I tell her. "What he did—it came out of nowhere. There was no history of, you know, hurting animals and stuff. He wasn't abused—at least not so's I ever knew. Anybody hurt my little brother, I'd have had a piece of him. So you tell me: what happened?"

"Let me tell you a story instead," she said.

That's when she told me about how words had their own tribe, back in some long ago. How when you spoke, you weren't just talking about the world, you were remaking it.

"I don't understand," I said. "Why are you telling me this?"

"Annie's a dear friend of ours. I'd like her to be happy."

"Don't worry. I'm not going to mess up her life again."

Meran shook her head. "I never thought you would."

"How can you say that? You don't even know me."

"The Joey she told me about would never hurt her."

"But I did."

"Yes. But you wouldn't hurt her again, would you?"

"Of course not, but..."

This conversation was making my head spin. I felt like I'd been walking forever with my shoes on the wrong feet and my coat on backwards.

"Annie's got her own life now," I said. "And what could I offer her anyway?"

"Truth. Trust. Love."

I felt a strange sense of disassociation. I wondered when Annie was coming back from the ladies' room, if she was coming back at all. But then I realized that time didn't seem to be moving the way it should. It was as though the inside of the pub had turned into a pocket world where everything was different from the world outside its doors, as though I was looking at everything from the corner of my eye. The air swayed. Every minute held the potential of an eternity.

"I can wake up that old tribe of words for you," she said. "Not for long, but for long enough. Tell me which ones you need."

I understood what she was saying, but it didn't make any sense. Things just don't work in the real world the way they do in a story. Strangers only offered magical assistance in fairy tales.

"Look—"

"Don't question it," she said. "You know it can happen."

The weird thing is, I believed her. I can't even begin to explain why. It really did feel like we were sideways to the world at that moment. That anything could happen.

"Magic words," I said. "Can they change the past?"

She shook her head. "They can only change the present."

"But everything we say or do changes the present."

She shook her head again. "Not like this. The words I can wake for you will bring about true transformation. Which will you choose?"

There was no contest. Until I'd seen Annie tonight I hadn't realized what it was that had really brought me back to the city.

"Trust enough for a second chance," I said.

"Done," Meran told me and she smiled.

I heard a rumbling deep underground, like distant thunder reverberating in the belly of the world. The vibration of it rose up, shivering the floor, rattling the glasses and liquor bottles behind the bar. Something swelled inside me, something too big and old and weighty to fit in my body, in my head, in my soul. Then it was gone, like a cat shaking water from its fur.

I looked around, but no one in the pub seemed to have noticed. Only the harper, Meran's husband. He lifted his head and slowly studied the room until his gaze reached us. Then he nodded and returned to his conversation.

"What..?" I began.

"Here she comes," Meran said. She squeezed my elbow before she stepped away. "Now you have to do your part. Earn your second chance."

I turned to see Annie coming towards me and didn't worry about the explanation I'd thought I needed so desperately a moment ago. Everything seemed out of focus right then, except for her. I didn't know where I was going to begin. But I knew I had to try.

"What was Meran talking to you about?" she asked as she sat back down on her stool. "The pair of you looked positively conspiratorial."

"Second chances," I said.

Annie's eyes went bright behind her glasses again.

"I've got a lot to tell you," I said.

She studied me for a long moment, swallowed a couple of times. I knew what she was thinking. Once burned, twice shy. Who could blame her? I just prayed the magic words would do their stuff.

"I'm listening," she said.

➤ ❮ ◀

It's funny the difference a month can make.

I managed to get a job at a garage a couple of days after that night. I've always been good with cars and my boss is helping me work out a schedule so that I can take the courses I need to get my mechanic's license.

Annie and I are taking it slow. We go on dates, we talk incessantly— on the phone if we're not together. We don't make promises, but we keep them all the same.

I didn't see Meran again until I went to a gallery opening with Annie at the end of January. It was a group show by some friends of hers. The Kelledys were there. Cerin was playing his harp in a corner of the gallery while Meran mingled with the other guests. I waited until I had the chance to talk to her on her own. She was studying a canvas that depicted a flood of wildflowers growing in a junkyard. It was only when you looked close that you saw these little people peeking out at you from among the flowers. They looked like they were made of nuts and twigs, held together with vines, but you could tell they were alive.

"Lovely, isn't it?" Meran said.

I nodded. I liked the way it looked both realistic and like a painting, if you know what I mean. All the information was there, but you could still see the brush strokes. Art like this tells a real story; you just have to work out the details on your own.

"I want to thank you for helping me," I told her.

Meran turned to look at me and smiled.

"I didn't do anything you couldn't have done for yourself," she said. "Except maybe give you the courage to try. Everything else was already inside you, just waiting for the chance to come out." She waited a beat, then added, "But you're most welcome all the same."

I felt so disappointed, the way you do when you finally figure out there isn't a Santa Claus, an Easter Bunny, a Tooth Fairy.

"So…the words…" I said. "There was no magic in them?"

Of course there wasn't. How could there have been?

Meran kept smiling, but now there was an enigmatic look in her eyes.

"Oh, there's always magic," she said.

1999

The Buffalo Man

1

The oaks were full of crows, as plentiful as leaves, more of the raucous black-winged birds than Jilly had ever seen together in one place. She kept glancing out the living room window at them, expecting some further marvel, though their enormous gathering was marvel enough all on its own. The leaded panes framed group after group of them in perfect compositions that made her itch to draw them in the sketchbook she hadn't thought to bring along.

"There are an awful lot of crows out there this evening," she said after her hundredth inspection of them.

"You'll have to forgive her," the professor told their hosts with a smile. "Sometimes I think she's altogether too concerned with crows and what they're up to. For some people it's the stock market, others it's the weather. It's a fairly new preoccupation, but it does keep her off the streets."

"As if."

"Before this it was fruit faeries," the professor added, leaning forward from the sofa where he was sitting, his tone confidential.

"Wasn't."

The professor tched. "As good as was."

"Well, we all need a hobby," Cerin said.

"This is, of course, true," Jilly allowed, after first sticking out her tongue at the pair of them. "It's so sad that neither of you have one."

She'd been visiting with Professor Dapple, involved in a long, meandering conversation concerning Kickaha mountain ballads vis-à-vis their relationship to British folktales, when he suddenly announced that he was due for tea at the Kelledys' that afternoon and did she care to join them? Was the Pope Catholic? Did the moon have wings? Well, one out of two wasn't bad, and of course she had to come.

The Kelledys' rambling house on McKennitt Street was a place of endless fascination for her with its old-fashioned architecture, all gables and gingerbread, with climbing vines and curious rooflines. The rooms were full of great solid pieces of furniture that crouched on Persian carpets and the hardwood floors like sleeping animals, not to mention any number of wonderfully bright and mysterious things perched on the shelves and sideboards, on the windowsills and meeting rails, like so many half-hidden lizards and birds. And then there were the oak trees that surrounded the building, a regular forest of them larger and taller than anywhere else in the city, each one easily a hundred years old.

The house was magic in her eyes, as much as the couple who inhabited it, and she loved any excuse to come by for a visit. On a very lucky day, Cerin would bring out his harp, Meran her flute, and they would play a haunting, heart-lifting music that Jilly never heard except from them.

"I didn't know fruit had their own faeries," Meran said. "The trees, yes, but not the individual fruit itself."

"I wonder if there are such things as acorn faeries," Cerin said.

"I must ask my father."

Jilly gave a theatrical sigh. "We're having far too long a conversation about fruit and nuts, and whether or not they have faeries, and not nearly enough about great, huge, cryptic parliaments of crows."

"It would be a murder, actually," the professor put in.

"Whatever. I think it's wonderfully mysterious."

"At this time of the day," Meran said, "they'd be gathering together to return to their roosts."

Jilly shook her head. "I'm not so sure. But if that *is* the case, then they've decided to roost in your yard."

She turned back to look out over the leaf-covered lawn that lay under the trees, planning some witty observation that would make them see just how supremely marvelous it all was, but the words died unborn in her throat as she watched a large, bald-headed Buddha of a man step onto the Kelledys' walk. He was easily the largest human being she'd ever seen—

she couldn't guess how many hundreds of pounds he must weigh—but oddly enough he moved with the supple grace of a dancer a fraction his size. His dark suit was obviously expensive and beautifully tailored, and his skin was as black as a raven's wing. As he came up the walk, the crows became agitated and flew around him, filling the air with their hoarse cries—growing so loud that the noise resounded inside the house with the windows closed.

But neither the enormous man, nor the actions of the crows, were what had dried up the words in Jilly's throat. It was the limp figure of a slender man that the dapper Buddha carried in his arms. In sharp contrast, he was poorly dressed for the brisk weather, wearing only a raggedy shirt and jeans so worn they had almost no colour left in them. His face and arms were pale as alabaster, even his braided hair was white—yet another striking contrast to the man carrying him. She experienced something familiar, yet strange when she gazed on his features, like taking out a favourite, old sweater she hadn't worn in years and feeling at once quite unacquainted with it and affectionately comfortable when she put it on.

"That's no crow," Cerin said, having stepped up to the window to stand beside Jilly's chair.

Meran joined him, then quickly went to the door to let the new visitor in. The professor rose from the sofa when she ushered the man and his burden into the room, waving a hand towards the seat he'd just quit.

"Put him down here," he said.

The black man nodded his thanks. Stepping gracefully across the room, he knelt and carefully laid the man out on the sofa.

"It's been a long time, Lucius," the professor said as the man straightened up. "You look different."

"I woke up."

"Just like that?"

Lucius gave him a slow smile. "No. A red-haired storyteller gave me a lecture about responsibility and I realized she was right. It had been far too long since I'd assumed any."

He turned his attention to the Kelledys then.

"I need a healing," he said.

There was something formal in the way he spoke the words, the way a subject might speak to his ruler, though there was nothing remotely submissive in his manner.

"There are no debts between us," Cerin said.

"But now—"

"Nonsense," Meran told him. "We've never turned away someone in need of help before and we don't mean to start now. But you'll have to tell us how he was injured."

She knelt down on the floor beside the sofa as she spoke. Reaching out, she touched her middle finger to the centre of his brow, then lifted her hand and moved it down his torso, her palm hovering about an inch above him.

"I know little more than you, at this point," Lucius said.

"Do you at least know who he is?" Cerin asked.

Lucius shook his head. "The crow girls found him lying by a dumpster out behind the Williamson Street Mall. They tried to heal him, but all they could manage was to keep him from slipping further away. Maida said he was laid low by ill-will."

Jilly's ears perked up at the mention of the crow girls. They were the real reason for her current interest in all things corvid, a pair of punky, black-haired young women who seemed to have the ability to change your entire perception of the world simply by stepping into the periphery of your life. Ever since she'd first seen them in a café, she kept spotting them in the most unlikely places, hearing the most wonderful stories about them. Whenever she saw a crow now, she'd peer closely at it, wondering if this was one of the pair in avian form.

"That makes it more complicated," Meran said.

Sitting back on her heels, she glanced at Lucius. He gave her an apologetic look.

"I know he has buffalo blood," he told her.

"Yes, I see that."

"What did Maida mean by ill-will?" Cerin asked. "He doesn't appear to have any obvious physical injuries."

Lucius shrugged. "You know how they can be. The more they tried to explain it to me, the less I understood."

Jilly had her own questions as she listened to them talk, such as why hadn't someone immediately called for an ambulance, or why had this Lucius brought the injured man here, rather than to a hospital? But there was a swaying, eddying sensation in the air, a feeling that the world had turned a step from the one everyone knew and they now had half a foot in some other, perhaps more perilous, realm. She decided to be prudent for a change and listen until she understood better what was going on.

She wasn't the only one puzzled, it seemed.

"We need to know more," Meran said.

Lucius nodded. "I'll see if I can find them."

"I'll come with you," Cerin said.

Lucius hesitated for a long moment, then gave another nod and the two men left the house. Jilly half expected them to fly away, but when she looked out the window she saw them walking under the oaks towards the street like an ordinary, if rather mismatched, pair, Lucius so broad and large that the tall harper at his side appeared slender to the point of skinniness. The crows remained in the trees this time, studying the progress of the two men until they were lost from sight.

"I have some things to fetch," Meran said. "Remedies to try. Will you watch over our patient until I get back?"

Jilly glanced at the professor.

"Um, sure," she said.

And then the two of them were alone with the mysteriously stricken man. Laid low by ill-will. What did *that* mean?

Jilly pulled a footstool over to the sofa where Meran had been kneeling and sat down. Looking at the man, she found herself wishing for pencil and sketchbook again. He was so handsome, like a figure from a Pre-Raphaelite painting. Except for the braids and raggedy clothes, of course. Then she felt guilty for where her thoughts had taken her. Here was the poor man, half dead on the sofa, and all she could think about was drawing him.

"He doesn't look very happy, does he?" she said.

"Not very."

"Where do you know Lucius from?"

The professor took off his wire-rimmed glasses and gave them a polish they didn't need before replacing them.

"I can't remember where or when I first met him," he said. "But it was a long time ago—before the war, certainly. Not long after that he became somewhat of a recluse. At first I'd go visit him at his house—he lives close by—but then it came to the point where he grew so withdrawn that one might as well have been visiting a sideboard or a chair. Finally I stopped going 'round."

"What happened to him, do you think?"

The professor shrugged. "Hard to tell with someone like him."

"You're being deliberately mysterious, aren't you?"

"Not at all. There just isn't much to say. I know he's related to the crow girls. Their grandfather, or an uncle or something. I never did quite find out which."

"So that's why all the crows are out there."

"I doubt it," the professor said. "He's corbæ, all right, but raven not crow."

Jilly felt a thrill of excitement. A raven uncle, crow girls, the man on the sofa with his buffalo blood. She was in the middle of some magical story for once, rather than on the edges of it, looking in, and her proximity made everything feel bright and clear and very much in focus. Then she felt guilty again because it had taken someone getting hurt to draw her into this story. Considering the unfortunate circumstances, it didn't seem right to be so excited by it.

She turned back to look at the pale man, lying there so still.

"I wonder if he can turn into a buffalo," she said.

"I believe it's more of a metaphorical designation," the professor told her, "rather than an actual shapeshifting option."

Jilly shook her head. She could remember the night in Old Market when she'd first seen the crow girls slip from crow to girl and back again. It wasn't exactly something you forgot, though oddly enough the memory did have a tendency to try to slip away from her. To make sure it didn't, she'd fixed the moment in pigment and hung the finished painting on the wall of her studio as a reminder.

"I don't think so," she said. "I think it's a piece of real magic."

She leaned closer to the man and reached forward to push aside a few long white hairs that had come to lie across his lashes. When she touched him, that swaying, eddying sensation returned, stronger than ever. She had long enough to say, "Oh, my," then the world slipped away and she was somewhere else entirely.

2

"I *have* resumed my responsibilities," Lucius said as the two men walked to his house a few blocks further away.

Cerin gave him a sidelong glance. "Guilt's a terrible thing, isn't it?"

"What do you mean?"

The harper shrugged. "It makes you question people's motives, even when they're as straightforward as my wanting to help you find a pair of somewhat wayward and certainly mischievous relatives."

"They can be a handful," Lucius said. "It's possible we'll find them more quickly with your help."

Cerin hid a smile. He knew that was about as much of an apology as he'd be getting, but he didn't mind. He hadn't really wanted one. He'd only wanted Lucius to understand that no one was holding him to blame for withdrawing from the world the way he had—at least no one in the Kelledy household was. Responsibility was a sharp-edged sword that sometimes cut too deep, even for an old spirit such as Lucius Portsmouth.

So all he said was, "Um-hmm," then added, "Odd winter we've been having, isn't it? So close to Christmas and still no snow. I wonder whose fault *that* is."

Lucius sighed. "You can be insufferable."

This time Cerin didn't hide his smile. "As Jilly would say, it's just this gift I have."

"But I appreciate your confidence."

"Apology accepted," Cerin told him, unable to resist.

"You wouldn't have any crow blood in you, would you?"

"Nary a drop."

Lucius harrumphed and muttered, "I'd still like to see the results of a DNA test."

"What was that?"

"I said, I wonder where they keep their nest."

Stanton Street was lined with oaks, not so old as those that grew around the Kelledy house, but they were stately monarchs nonetheless. Having reached the Rookery where Lucius lived, the two men paused to look up where the bare branches of the trees laid their pattern against the sky above. Twilight had given way to night and they could see stars peeking down from amongst the boughs. Stars, but no black-haired, giggling crow girls. Lucius called, his voice ringing up into the trees like a raven's cry.

Kaark. Kaark. Tok.

There was no reply.

"They weren't so happy with this foundling of theirs," Lucius said, turning to his companion. "At first I thought it was because their healing didn't take, but when I carried him to your house, I began to understand their uneasiness."

He called again, but there was still no response.

"What do you find so troubling about him?" Cerin asked.

Though he had an idea. There were people and places that were like doors to other realms, to the spiritworld and to worlds deeper and older than that. In their presence, you could feel the world shift uneasily underfoot, the ties binding you to it loosening their grip—an unsettling sensation for anyone, but more so for those who could normally control where they walked.

The still, pale man with his white braids had been like that.

Lucius said as much, then added, "The trouble with such doors isn't so much what they open into, as what they can close you from."

Cerin nodded. To be denied access to the spiritworld would be like losing a sense. One's hearing, one's taste.

"So you don't think they'll come," he said.

Lucius shrugged. "They can be willful...not so responsible as some."

"Let me try."

"Never let it be said I turned down someone's help."

Cerin smiled. He closed his eyes and reached back to his home, back to a room on the second floor. A harp stood there with a rose carved into the wood where curving neck met forepillar. His fingers twitched at his sides and the sound of that roseharp was suddenly in the air all around them, a calling-on song that rose up as though from the ground and spun itself out against the branches above, then higher still, as though reaching for the stars.

"A good trick," Lucius said. "Cousin Brandon does much the same with his instrument, though in his case, he's the only one to hear its tones."

"Perhaps you're not listening hard enough," Cerin said.

"Perhaps."

He might have said more, but there came a rustling in the boughs above them and what appeared to be two small girls were suddenly there, hanging upside down from the lowest branch by their hooked knees, laughter crinkling in the corners of their eyes while they tried to look solemn.

"Oh, that was veryvery mean," Maida said.

Zia gave an upside down nod. "Calling us with magic music."

"We'd give you a good bang on the ear."

"Reallyreally we would."

"Except the music's so pretty."

"Ever so truly pretty."

"And magic, of course."

Cerin let the harping fall silent.

"We need you to tell us more about the man you found," he said.

The crow girls exchanged glances.

"Surely such wise and clever people as you don't need help from us," Maida said.

"That would be all too very silly," Zia agreed.

"And yet we do," Cerin told them. "Will you help us?"

There was another exchange of glances between the pair, then they dropped lightly to the ground.

"Are there sweets in your house?" Zia asked.

"Mountains of them."

"Oh, good," Maida said. She gave Lucius a sad look. "Old Raven never has any sweets for us."

Zia nodded. "It's veryvery sad. What kind do you have?"

"I'm not sure."

"Well, come on," Maida said, taking Cerin's hand. "We'd better hurry up and find out."

Zia nodded, looking a little anxious. "Before someone else eats them all."

In this mood, Cerin didn't know that they'd get anything useful out of the pair, but at least they'd agreed to come. He'd let Meran sort out how to handle them once he got them home.

Zia took his other hand and with the pair of them tugging on his hands, they started back up Stanton Street. Lucius taking the rear, a smile on his face as the crow girls chattered away to Cerin about exactly what their favourite sweets were.

3

Jilly was no stranger to the impossible, so she wasn't as surprised as some might have been to find herself transported from the Kelledys' living room, full of friendly shadows and known corners, to an alleyway that could have been anywhere. Still, she wasn't entirely immune to the surprise of it all and couldn't ignore the vague, unsettled feeling that was tiptoeing up and down the length of her spine.

Because that was the thing about the impossible, wasn't it? When you did experience it, well, first of all, hello, it proved to be all too possible, and secondly, it made you rethink all sorts of things that you'd blindly agreed to up to this point. Things like the world being round—was gravity really so clever that it kept people on the upside down part of the world from falling off into the sky? That Elvis was dead—if he was, then why did *so* many people still see him? That UFOs were actually weather balloons or swamp gas—never mind the improbability of so many balloons going AWOL, how did a swamp get indigestion in the first place?

So being somewhere she shouldn't be didn't render Jilly helpless, stunned, or much more than curiously surprised. By looking up at the skyline, she placed herself in an alleyway behind the Williamson Street Mall, right where the crow girls had found—

Her gaze dropped to the mound of litter beside the closest dumpster, and there he was, Meran's comatose patient, except here, in this wherever she was, he was sitting on top of the garbage, knees drawn up to his chin, and regarding her with a gloomy gaze. She focused on the startling green of his eyes. Odd, she thought. Weren't albinos supposed to have red, or at least pink eyes?

She waited a moment to give him the opportunity to speak first. When he didn't, she cleared her throat.

"Hello," she said. "Did you bring me here?"

He frowned at the question. "I don't know you...do I?"

"Well, we haven't been formally introduced or anything, and while you weren't exactly the life of the party when I first met you, right now we're sharing the same space somewhere else as well as here, which is sort of like us knowing each other, or at least me knowing you."

He gave her a confused look.

"Oh, that's right. You wouldn't remember, being unconscious and all. I'm not sure of all the details myself, but you're supposed to have been, and I quote, 'laid low by ill-will,' and when I went to brush some hair out of your eyes, I found myself here. With you again, except you're awake this time. How were you laid low by this ill-will? I'm assuming someone hit you, which would be ill-willish enough so far as I can see, but somehow I think it's more than that."

She paused and gave him a rueful smile. "I guess I'm not doing a very good job with this explanation, am I?"

"How can you be so cheerful?" he asked her.

Jilly drew a battered wooden fruit crate over to where he was sitting and sat down herself.

"What do you mean?" she asked.

"The world is a terrible place," he said. "Every day, every moment,

494

its tragedies deepen, the mean-spiritedness of its inhabitants quickens and escalates until one can't imagine a kindness existing anywhere for more than an instant before being suffocated."

"Well, it's not perfect," Jilly agreed. "But that doesn't mean we have to—"

"I can see that you've been hurt and disappointed by it—cruelly so, when you were much younger. Yet here you sit before me, relatively trusting, certainly cheerful, optimism bubbling in you like a fountain. How can this be?"

Jilly was about to make some lighthearted response, speaking without thinking as she did too often, but then part of what he'd said really registered.

"How would you know what my life was like when I was a kid?"

He shrugged. "Our histories are written on our skin—how can you be surprised that I wouldn't know?"

"It's not something I've ever heard of before."

"Perhaps you have to know how to look for the stories."

Well, that made a certain kind of sense, Jilly thought. There were so many hidden things in the world that only came into focus when you learned how to pay attention to them, so why not stories on people's skin?

"So," she said. "I guess nobody could lie to you, could they?"

"Why do you think the world depresses me the way it does?"

"Except it's not all bad. You can't tell me that the only stories people have are bad ones."

"They certainly outweigh the good."

"Maybe *you're* not looking in the right place."

"I understand thinking the best of people," he said. "Looking for the good in them, rather than the wrongs they've done. But ignoring the wrongs is almost like condoning them, don't you think?"

"I don't ignore them," Jilly told him. "But I don't dwell on them either."

"Even when you've been hurt as much as you have?"

"Maybe especially because of that," she said. "What I try to do is make people feel better. It's hard to be mean, when you're smiling, or when a laugh's building up inside you."

"That's a child's view of the world."

Jilly shook her head. "A child lives in the now, and they're usually pretty self-absorbed. Which is what can make them unaware of other people's feelings at times."

"I meant simplistic."

Jilly wouldn't accept that either. "I'm aware of what's wrong. I just try to balance it with something good. I know I can't solve every problem in the world, but if I try to help the ones I come upon as I come upon them, I think it makes a difference. And you know, most people aren't really bad. They're just kind of thoughtless at times."

"How can you believe that? Listen to them and then tell me again how they're really kind at heart."

Jilly's head suddenly filled with conversation.

...why I have to buy anything for that old bag, anyway...

...hello, can't we leave the kids at home for one afternoon...the miserable, squalling monsters...

...hear that damn song one more time, I'll kill...

No, they were thoughts, she realized, stolen from the shoppers in the mall that lay on the other side of the alley's wall. It was impossible to tell their age or gender, except by inference.

...damn bells...oh, it's the Sally Ann, doing their annual beg-a-thon...hey, nice rack on her...wonder why a looker like her's collecting money for losers...

...doesn't get me what I want this year, I'll show him what being miserable is all about...

Jilly blinked when the voices were suddenly gone again.

"Now do you see?" her companion said.

"Those thoughts are taken out of context with the rest of their lives," Jilly told him. "Just because someone has an ugly thought, it doesn't make them a bad person."

"Oh no?"

"And being kind oneself does make a difference."

"Against the great swell of indifferent unkindnesses that threaten to wash us completely away with the force of a tsunami?"

"Is this what they meant with the ill-will that laid you low?"

"What who meant?"

"The crow girls. They're the ones who found you and brought you to the Kelledys' house because they couldn't heal you themselves."

A small smile touched his features. "I remember some crow girls I saw once. Their good humour could make yours seem like grumbling, but they carried the capacity for large angers as well."

"Was that when you were a buffalo?"

"What do you know about buffalo?"

"You're supposed to have buffalo blood," Jilly explained.

He gave her a slow nod.

"Those-who-came," he said. "They slaughtered the buffalo. Then, when the People danced and called the buffalo spirit back, they slaughtered the People as well. That's the history I read on the skin of the world—not only here, but everywhere. Blood and pain and hunger and hatred. It's an old story that has no end. How can a smile, a laugh, a good deed, stand up against the weight of such a history?"

"I…I guess it can't," Jilly said. "But you still have to try."

"Why?"

"Because that's all you can do. If you don't try to stand up against the darkness, it swallows you up."

"And if in the end, there is only darkness? If the world is meant to end in darkness?"

Jilly shook her head. She refused to believe it.

"How can you deny it?" he asked.

"It's just…if there's only supposed to be darkness, then why were we given light?"

For a long moment, he sat there, shoulders drooped, staring down at his hands. When he finally looked up, there was something in his eyes that Jilly couldn't read.

"Why indeed?" he said softly.

4

When Meran returned to the living room, it was to find Jilly slumped across the body of her patient, Professor Dapple standing over the pair of them, hands fluttering nervously in front of him.

"What's happened?" she said, quickly crossing the room.

"I don't know. One moment she was talking to me, then she leaned over and touched his cheek and she simply collapsed."

He moved aside as Meran knelt down by the sofa once more. Before she could study the problem more closely, the roseharp began to play upstairs.

The professor looked surprised, his gaze lifting to the ceiling.

"I thought Cerin had gone with Lucius," he said.

"He did," Meran told him. "That's only his harp playing."

The professor regarded her for a long slow moment.

"Of course," he finally said.

Meran smiled. "It's nothing to be nervous about. Really. I'm more worried about what's happened to Jilly."

The sofa was wide enough that, with the professor's help, she was able to lay Jilly out beside the stranger. Whatever had struck Jilly down was as much of a mystery to Meran as the stranger's original ailment. In her mind, she began to run through a list of other healers she could contact to ask for help when there was a sudden commotion at the front door. A moment later the crow girls trooped in with Cerin and Lucius following behind them.

"Jilly...?" Cerin began.

Meran briefly explained what little she knew of what had happened since they'd been gone.

"We can't help him," Zia said before anyone else could speak.

"We tried," Maida added, "but we weren't so very useful, were we?"

Zia shook her head.

"Not very useful at all," Maida said.

"But," Zia offered, "we could maybe help her."

Maida nodded and leaned closer to peer at Jilly. "She's very pretty, isn't she? I think we know her."

"She's Geordie's friend," Zia said.

"Oh, yes." Zia looked at Cerin. "But he plays much nicer music."

"Ever so very much more."

"It's for listening to, you see. Not for making you do things."

"I'm sorry," Cerin said. "But we needed to get your attention."

"Well, we're ever so very attentive now," Maida told him.

Whereupon the pair of them went very still and fixed Cerin with expectant gazes. He turned helplessly to his wife.

"How can you help Jilly?" she asked.

"Jilly," Maida repeated. "Is that her name?"

"Silly Jilly."

"Willy-nilly."

"Up down dilly."

"I'm sure making fun of her name's helpful," Lucius said.

"Oh, poo," Maida said. "Old Raven never gets a joke."

"That's the trouble with this raven, all right," Zia agreed.

"We've seen jokes fly right out the window when they see he's in the room."

"About Jilly," Meran tried again.

"Well, you see," Maida said, suddenly serious. "The buffalo man is a piece of the Grace."

"And we can't help the Grace—she has to help herself."

Maida nodded. "But Jilly—"

Zia giggled, then quickly put a hand over her mouth.

"—only needs to be shown the way back to her being all of one piece again," Maida finished.

"You mean her spirit has gone somewhere?" Cerin asked.

"Duh."

"How can we bring her back?" Meran asked.

The crow girls looked at Cerin.

"Well," Zia said. "If you know her calling-on song as well as you do ours, that would maybe work."

"I'll get the roseharp," Cerin said, standing up.

"Now he needs it in hand," Lucius said.

Cerin started to frame a reply, but then he looked at Meran and left the room.

"We were promised sweets," Maida said.

Zia nodded. "The actual promise was that there'd be mountains of them."

"Do you mind if we finish up here first?" Meran asked.

"Oh, no," Maida said. "We love to wait."

Zia gave Meran a bright smile. "Honestly."

"Anticipation is so much better than being attentive."

"Though they're much the same, in some ways."

"Because they both involve waiting, you see," Maida explained, her smile as bright as her companion's.

Meran stifled a sigh and returned their smile. She'd forgotten how maddening the crow girls could be. Normally she enjoyed bantering with their tricksy kind, but at the moment she was too worried about Jilly to join the fun. And then there was the stranger whose appearance who had started it all. They hadn't even *begun* to deal with him.

When Cerin returned with the roseharp, he sat down on a footstool and drew the instrument onto his lap.

"Play something Jilly," Maida suggested.

"Did you say silly?" Zia asked. "Because that's not being serious at all, you know, making jokes about very serious things."

"I didn't say silly."

"I think maybe you did."

Cerin ignored the pair of them and turned to his wife. "I might not be able to bring her back," he said. "Because of him. Because of the doors he can close."

"I know," Meran said. "You can only try."

5

"I think I know now what the crow girls meant," Jilly said.

The buffalo man raised his eyebrows questioningly.

"About this ill-will business," Jilly explained. "Every ugly thought or bad deed you come into contact with steals away a piece of your vitality, doesn't it? It's like erosion. The pieces keep falling away until finally you get so worn away that you slip into a kind of coma."

"Something like that."

"Has this happened before?"

He nodded.

"So what happens next?"

"I die."

Jilly stared at him, not sure she'd heard him right.

"You...die."

He nodded. "And then I come back and the cycle begins all over again."

Neither of them spoke for a long moment then. It was quiet in the alley where they sat, but Jilly could hear the traffic go by down the block where the alley opened into the street. There was a repetitive pattern to the sound, bus, bus, a car horn, a number of vehicles in a group, then the buses again.

"I guess what I don't understand," Jilly finally said, "is why all the good things in the world don't balance it out—you know, recharge your vitality."

"They're completely overshadowed," he said.

Jilly shook her head. "I don't believe that. I know there are awful things in the world, but I also know there's more that's good."

"Then why am I so weak right now—in this, your season of good-will?"

"I think it's because you don't let the good in anymore. You don't trust there to be any good left, so you've put up these protective walls that keep it out."

"And the bad? Why does it continue to affect me?"

"Because you concentrate on it," Jilly said. "And by doing that, you let it get in. It's like you're doing the exact opposite to what you should be doing."

"If only it could be so simple."

"But it is," she said. "In the end, it always comes down to small, simple things, because that's the way the world really works. We're the ones who make it so complicated. I mean, think about it. If everybody really and truly treated each other the way they'd want to be treated, all the problems of the world would be solved. Nobody'd starve, because nobody'd want to go hungry themselves. Nobody'd steal, or kill, or hurt each other, because they wouldn't want that to happen to themselves."

"So what stops them from doing so?" he asked.

"Trust. Or rather a lack of it. Too many people don't trust the other person to treat them right, so they just dig in, accumulating stuff, thinking only of themselves or their own small group—you know, family, com-pany, community, whatever. A tribal thing." She hesitated a moment, then added, "And that's what's holding you back, too. You don't trust the good to outweigh the bad."

"I don't know that I even can."

"No one can help you with that," Jilly told him. "That's something that can only come from inside you."

He gave her a slow nod. "Maybe I will try harder, the next time."

"What next time? What's wrong with right now?"

He held out his arms. "If you could read the history written on my skin, you would not need to ask that question."

Jilly pushed up her sleeves and held out her own arms.

"Look," she said. "You read what I went through as a kid. I'm no better or stronger or braver than you are. But I am determined to leave things a little better than they were before I got here. That's what gets me through. And I have to admit there's a certain selfishness involved. You see, I want to live in that better world. I know it's not going to happen unless we all clean up our act and I know I can't make anybody else do that. But I'll be damned if I don't do it myself. You know, like a Kickaha friend of mine says, live large and walk in Beauty."

"You are very...persuasive."

Jilly grinned. "It's just this gift I have."

She stood up and offered him a hand.

"So what do you say, buffalo man? You want to give this life another shot?"

He allowed her to help him up to his feet.

"There's a problem," he said.

"No, no, no. Ignore the negatives, if only for now."

"You don't understand. The door that brought us here—it only opens one way."

"What door?"

"My old life was finished and I was on my way to the new. All of this—" He made a motion with his hand to encompass everything around them. "Is only a memory."

"Whose memory?" Jilly asked, getting a bad feeling.

"Mine. The memory of a dying man."

She smiled brightly. "So live. I thought we'd already been through this earlier."

"I would. You've convinced me enough of that. Only there's no way back."

"There's always a way back...isn't there?"

He didn't answer. He didn't have to.

"Oh, great. I get to be in a magical adventure only it turns out to be like a train on a one-way track and we left the happy ending station miles back."

"I'm sorry."

She took his hand and gave it a squeeze. "Me, too."

6

"Nothing's happening," Maida said.

Zia peered at the two still bodies on the sofa. She gave Jilly a gentle poke with her finger.

"She's still veryvery far away," she agreed.

Cerin sighed and let his fingers fall from the strings of the roseharp. The music echoed on for a few moments, then all was still.

"I tried to put all the things she loves into the calling-on," he said. "Painting and friendship and crows and whimsy, but it's not working. Wherever she's gone, it's further than I can reach."

"How did it happen anyway?" the professor asked. "All she did was touch him. Meran did the same and she wasn't taken away."

"Jilly's too open and trusting," Meran said. "She didn't think to guard herself from the man's spirit. When we fall away into death, most of us will grab hold of anything we can to stay our fall. That's what happened to her—he grabbed her and held on hard."

"He's dying?"

Meran glanced at the professor and nodded.

"I should never have brought him here," Lucius said.

"You couldn't have known."

"It's our fault," Zia said.

Maida nodded glumly. "Oh, we're the most miserably bad girls, we are."

"Let's worry about whose fault it was some other time," Meran said. "Right now I want to concentrate on where he could have taken her."

"I've never died," Lucius said, "so I can't say where a dying man would draw another's soul, but I've withdrawn from the world..."

"And?" Meran prompted him.

"I went into my own mind. I lived in my memories. I didn't *remember*. I lived in them."

"So if we knew who he was," Cerin said. "Then perhaps we could—"

"We don't need to know who he is," Meran broke in. "All we need to know is what he was thinking."

"Would the proverbial life flashing before one's eyes be relevant here?" the professor asked. "Because that could touch on anything."

"We need something more specific," Cerin said.

Meran nodded. "Such as...where the crow girls found him. Wouldn't he be thinking of his surroundings at some point?"

"It's still a one-way door," Cerin pointed out.

"But if we can open it even a crack," Lucius said.

Cerin smiled. "Then maybe we can pull them out before it closes on us again."

"We can do that," Maida said.

Zia nodded. "We're very good at opening things."

"Even better when there's sweets inside."

Zia rapped on the man's head with a knuckle.

"Hello, hello in there," she said. "Can you hear me?"

"Zia!" Lucius said.

"Well, how else am I supposed to get his attention?"

"Hold on," Meran said. "Perhaps we're going about this all wrong. Instead of concentrating on the door he is, we should be concentrating on the door Jilly is."

"Oh, good idea," Maida said.

The crow girls immediately turned their attention to Jilly. They leaned close, one on either side, and began whispering in her ears.

7

"So I guess this is sort of like a recording," Jilly said, "except instead of being on pause, we're in a tape loop."

Which was why the traffic noise she heard was so repetitive. Being part of his memory, it, too, was in a loop.

"You have such an interesting way of looking at things," the buffalo man said.

"No, humour me in this. We're in a loop of your memory, right? Well, what's to stop you from thinking of something else? Or concentrating and getting us past the loop."

"To what purpose?"

"To whatever comes next."

"We know what comes next," he said.

"No. You assume we do. The last thing you seem to remember is lying here in this alleyway. You must have passed out at that point, which is the loop we're in. Except, I showed up and you're conscious and we've been talking—none of this is memory. We're already somewhere else than your memory. So what's to stop you from taking us further?"

"I have no memory beyond the point where I closed my eyes."

But Jilly was on a roll.

"Of course not," she said. "So we'll have to use our imaginations."

"And imagine what?"

"Well, crows would be good for starters. The crow girls would have been flying above, and then they noticed you and..." She paused, cocking her head. "Listen. Can you hear that?"

At first he shook his head, but then his gaze lifted and the strip of sky above the alley went dark with crows. A cloud of them blocked the sun, circling just above the rooftops and filling the air with their raucous cries.

"Wow," Jilly said. "You've got a great imagination."

"This isn't my doing," he said.

They watched as two of the birds left the flock and came spiralling down on their black wings. Just before they reached the pavement, they changed into a pair of girls with spiky black hair and big grins.

"Hello, hello!" they cried.

"Hello, yourselves," Jilly said.

She couldn't help but grin back at them.

"We've come to take you home," one of them said.

"You can't say no."

"Everyone will think it's our fault if you don't come."

"And then we won't get any sweets."

"Not that we're doing this for sweets."

"No, we're just very kindhearted girls, we are."

"Ask anyone."

"Except for Raven."

They were tugging on her hands now, each holding one of hers with two of their own.

"Don't dawdle," the one on her right said.

Jilly looked back at the buffalo man.

"Go on," he said.

She shook her head. "Don't be silly."

For some reason that made the crow girls giggle.

"There's no reason you can't come, too," she said. She turned to look at the crow girls. "There isn't, is there?"

"Well..." one of them said.

"I suppose not."

"The door's closed," the buffalo man told them. "I can feel it inside, shut tight."

"Your door's closed," one of the girls agreed.

"But hers is still open."

Still he hesitated. Jilly pulled away from the crow girls and walked over to him.

"Half the trick to living large," she said, "is the living part."

He let her take him by the hand and walk him back to where the crow girls waited. Holding hands, with one of the spiky-haired girls on either side of them, they walked towards the mouth of the alleyway. But before they could get halfway there...

⅃ Y ⅂

Jilly blinked and opened her eyes to a ring of concerned faces.

"We did it, we did it, we did it!" the crow girls cried.

They jumped up from Jilly's side and danced around in a circle, banging into furniture, stepping on toes and generally raising more of a hullabaloo than would seem possible for two such small figures. It lasted only a moment before Lucius put a hand on each of their shoulders and held them firmly in place.

"And very clever you were, too," he said as they squirmed in his grip. "We're most grateful."

Jilly turned to look at the man lying next to her on the sofa.

"How are you feeling?" she asked.

His gaze made a slow survey of the room, taking in the Kelledys, the professor, Lucius and the wriggling crow girls.

"Confused," he said finally. "But in a good way."

The two of them sat up.

"So you'll stay?" Jilly asked. "You'll see it through this time?"

"You're giving me a choice?"

Jilly grinned. "Not likely."

8

Long after midnight, the Kelledys sat in their living room, looking out at the dark expanse of their lawn. The crows were still roosting in the oaks, quiet now except for the odd rustle of feathers, or a soft, querulous croak. Lucius and the crow girls had gone back to the Rookery on Stanton Street, but not before the two girls had happily consumed more cookies, chocolates and soda pop than seemed humanly possible. But then, they weren't human, they were corbæ. The professor and Jilly had returned to their respective homes as well, leaving only a preoccupied buffalo man who'd finally fallen asleep in one of the extra rooms upstairs.

"Only a few more days until Christmas," Cerin said.

"Mmm."

"And still no snow."

"Mmm."

"I'm thinking of adopting the crow girls."

Meran gave him a sharp look.

He smiled. "Just seeing if you were paying attention. What were you thinking of?"

"If there's a word for a thing because it happens, or if it happens because there's a word for it."

"I'm not sure I'm following you."

Meran shrugged. "Life, death. Good, bad. Kind, cruel. What was the world like before we had language?"

"Mercurial, I'd think. Like the crow girls. One thing would flow into another. Nothing would have really been separate from anything else because everything would have been made up of pieces of everything else."

"It's like that now."

Cerin nodded. "Except we don't think of it that way. We have the words to say this is one thing, this is another."

"So we've lost...what? A kind of harmony?"

"Perhaps. But we gained free will."

Meran sighed. "Why did we have to give up the one to gain the other?"

"I don't know for sure, but I'd guess it's because we need to be individuals. Without our differences, without our needing to communicate with one another, we'd lose our ability to create art, to love, to dream..."

"To hate. To destroy."

"But most of us strive for harmony. The fact that we can fall into the darkness is what makes our choice to reach for the light such a precious thing."

Meran leaned her head on his shoulder.

"When did you become so wise?" she asked.

"When you chose me to be your companion on your journey into the light."

Pixel Pixies

Only when Mistress Holly had retired to her apartment above the store would Dick Bobbins peep out from behind the furnace where he'd spent the day dreaming and drowsing and reading the books he borrowed from the shelves upstairs. He would carefully check the basement for unexpected visitors and listen for a telltale floorboard to creak from above. Only when he was very very sure that the mistress, and especially her little dog, had both, indeed, gone upstairs, would he creep all the way out of his hidden hobhole.

Every night, he followed the same routine.

Standing on the cement floor, he brushed the sleeves of his drab little jacket and combed his curly brown hair with his fingers. Rubbing his palms briskly together, he plucked last night's borrowed book from his hidey-hole and made his way up the steep basement steps to the store. Standing only two feet high, this might have been an arduous process all on its own, but he was quick and agile, as a hob should be, and in no time at all he'd be standing in amongst the books, considering where to begin the night's work.

There was dusting and sweeping to do, books to be put away. Lovely books. It didn't matter to Dick if they were serious leather-bound tomes or paperbacks with garish covers. He loved them all, for they were filled with words, and words were magic to this hob. Wise and clever humans had used some marvelous spell to imbue each book with every kind of story and character you could imagine, and many you couldn't. If you knew the key to unlock the words, you could experience them all.

Sometimes Dick would remember a time when he hadn't been able to read. All he could do then was riffle the pages and try to smell the stories out of them. But now, oh now, he was a magician, too, for he could unearth the hidden enchantment in the books any time he wanted to. They were his nourishment and his joy, weren't they just.

So first he worked, earning his keep. Then he would choose a new book from those that had come into the store while he was in his hobhole, drowsing away the day. Sitting on top of one of the bookcases, he'd read until it got light outside and it was time to return to his hiding place behind the furnace, the book under his arm in case he woke early and wanted to finish the story while he waited for the mistress to go to bed once more.

➤ ⅄ ◄

I hate computers.

Not when they do what they're supposed to. Not even when I'm the one who's made some stupid mistake, like deleting a file I didn't intend to, or exiting one without saving it. I've still got a few of those old war-horse programs on my machine that doesn't pop up a reminder asking if I want to save the file I was working on.

No, it's when they seem to have a mind of their own. The keyboard freezing for no apparent reason. Getting an error message that you're out of disc space when you know you've got at least a couple of gigs free. Passwords becoming temporarily, and certainly arbitrarily, obsolete. Those and a hundred other, usually minor, but always annoying, irritations.

Sometimes it's enough to make you want to pick up the nearest component of the machine and fling it against the wall.

For all the effort they save, the little tasks that they automate and their wonderful storage capacity, at times like this—when everything's going as wrong as it can go—their benefits can't come close to outweighing their annoyances.

My present situation was partly my own fault. I'd been updating my inventory all afternoon and before saving the file and backing it up, I'd decided to go on the Internet to check some of my competitors' prices. The used book business, which is what I'm in, has probably the most arbitrary pricing in the world. Though I suppose that can be expanded to include any business specializing in collectibles.

I logged on without any trouble and went merrily browsing through listings on the various book search pages, making notes on the particu-larly interesting items, a few of which I actually had in stock. It wasn't

until I tried to exit my browser that the trouble started. My browser wouldn't close and I couldn't switch to another window. Nor could I log off the Internet.

Deciding it had something to do with the page I was on—I know that doesn't make much sense, but I make no pretence to being more than vaguely competent when it comes to knowing how the software actually interfaces with the hardware—I called up the drop-down menu of "My Favourites" and clicked on my own home page. What I got was a fan shrine to pro wrestling star Steve Austin.

I tried again and ended up at a commercial software site.

The third time I was taken to the site of someone named Cindy Margolis—the most downloaded woman on the Internet, according to the *Guinness Book of World Records*. Not on this computer, my dear.

I made another attempt to get off-line, then tried to access my home page again. Each time I found myself in some new outlandish and unrelated site.

Finally I tried one of the links on the last page I'd reached. It was supposed to bring me to Netscape's home page. Instead I found myself on the web site of a real estate company in Santa Fe, looking at a cluster of pictures of the vaguely Spanish-styled houses that they were selling.

I sighed, tried to break my Internet connection for what felt like the hundredth time, but the "Connect To" window still wouldn't come up.

I could have rebooted, of course. That would have gotten me off-line. But it would also mean that I'd lose the whole afternoon's work because, being the stupid woman I was, I hadn't had the foresight to save the stupid file before I went gadding about on the stupid Internet.

"Oh, you stupid machine," I muttered.

From the front window display where she was napping, I heard Snippet, my Jack Russell terrier stir. I turned to reassure her that, no, she was still my perfect little dog. When I swiveled my chair to face the computer again, I realized that there was a woman standing on the other side of the counter.

I'd seen her come into the store earlier, but I'd lost track of everything in my one-sided battle of wits with the computer—it having the wits, of course. She was a very striking woman, her dark brown hair falling in Pre-Raphaelite curls that were streaked with green, her eyes both warm and distant, like an odd mix of a perfect summer's day and the mystery you can feel swell up inside you when you look up into the stars on a crisp, clear autumn night. There was something familiar about her, but I couldn't quite place it. She wasn't one of my regulars.

She gave me a sympathetic smile.

"I suppose it was only a matter of time before they got into the computers," she said.

I blinked. "What?"

"Try putting your sweater on inside out."

My face had to be registering the confusion I was feeling, but she simply continued to smile.

"I know it sounds silly," she said. "But humour me. Give it a try."

Anyone in retail knows, you get all kinds. And the second-hand market gets more than its fair share, trust me on that. If there's a loopy person anywhere within a hundred blocks of my store, you can bet they'll eventually find their way inside. The woman standing on the other side of my counter looked harmless enough, if somewhat exotic, but you just never know anymore, do you?

"What have you got to lose?" she asked.

I was about to lose an afternoon's work as things stood, so what was a little pride on top of that.

I stood up and took my sweater off, turned it inside out, and put it back on again.

"Now give it a try," the woman said.

I called up the "Connected to" window and this time it came up. When I put the cursor on the "Disconnect" button and clicked, I was logged off. I quickly shut down my browser and saved the file I'd been working on all afternoon.

"You're a life-saver," I told the woman. "How did you know that would work?" I paused, thought about what I'd just said, what had just happened. "*Why* would that work?"

"I've had some experience with pixies and their like," she said.

"Pixies," I repeated. "You think there are pixies in my computer?"

"Hopefully, not. If you're lucky, they're still on the Internet and didn't follow you home."

I gave her a curious look. "You're serious, aren't you?"

"At times," she said, smiling again. "And this is one of them."

I thought about one of my friends, an electronic pen pal in Arizona, who has this theory that the first atom bomb detonation forever changed the way that magic would appear in the world. According to him, the spirits live in the wires now instead of the trees. They travel through phone and modem lines, take up residence in computers and appliances where they live on electricity and lord knows what else.

It looked like Richard wasn't alone in his theories, not that I pooh-poohed them myself. I'm part of a collective that originated this electronic database called the Wordwood. After it took on a life of its own, I pretty much keep an open mind about things that most people would consider preposterous.

"I'd like to buy this," the woman went on.

She held up a trade paperback copy of *The Beggars' Shore* by Zak Mucha.

"Good choice," I said.

It never surprises me how many truly excellent books end up in the secondary market. Not that I'm complaining—it's what keeps me in business.

"Please take it as thanks for your advice," I added.

"You're sure?"

I looked down at my computer where my afternoon's work was now safely saved in its file.

"Oh, yes," I told her.

"Thank you," she said. Reaching into her pocket, she took out a business card and gave it to me. "Call me if you ever need any other advice along the same lines."

The business card simply said "The Kelledys" in a large script. Under it were the names "Meran and Cerin" and a phone number. Now I knew why, earlier, she'd seemed familiar. It had just been seeing her here in the store, out of context, that had thrown me.

"I love your music," I told her. "I've seen you and your husband play several times."

She gave me another of those kind smiles of hers.

"You can probably turn your sweater around again now," she said as she left.

Snippet and I watched her walk by the window. I took off my sweater and put it back on properly.

"Time for your walk," I told Snippet. "But first let me back up this file to a zip disk."

➤ ⊤ ◄

That night, after the mistress and her little dog had gone upstairs, Dick Bobbins crept out of his hobhole and made his nightly journey up to the store. He replaced the copy of *The Woods Colt* that he'd been reading, putting it neatly back on the fiction shelf under "W" for Williamson, fetched the duster, and started his work. He finished the "History" and "Local Interest" sections, dusting and straightening the books, and was climbing up onto the "Poetry" shelves near the back of the store when he paused, hearing something from the front of the store.

Reflected in the front window, he could see the glow of the computer's monitor and realized that the machine had turned on by itself. That couldn't be good. A faint giggle spilled out of the computer's speakers, quickly followed by a chorus of other voices, tittering and snickering. That was even less good.

A male face appeared on the screen, looking for all the world as though it could see out of the machine. Behind him other faces appeared, a whole gaggle of little men in green clothes, good-naturedly pushing and shoving each other, whispering and giggling. They were red-haired like the mistress, but there the resemblance ended. Where she was pretty, they were ugly, with short faces, turned-up noses, squinting eyes and pointed ears.

This wasn't good at all, Dick thought, recognizing the pixies for what they were. Everybody knew how you spelled "trouble." It was "P-I-X-Y."

And then they started to clamber out of the screen, which shouldn't have been possible at all, but Dick was a hob and he understood that just because something shouldn't be able to happen, didn't mean it couldn't. Or wouldn't.

"Oh, this is bad," he said mournfully. "Bad bad bad."

He gave a quick look up to the ceiling. He had to warn the mistress. But it was already too late. Between one thought and the next, a dozen or more pixies had climbed out of the computer onto her desk, not the one of them taller than his own waist. They began riffling through her papers, using her pens and ruler as swords to poke at each other. Two of them started a pushing match that resulted in a small stack of books falling off the side of the desk. They landed with a bang on the floor.

The sound was so loud that Dick was sure the mistress would come down to investigate, her and her fierce little dog. The pixies all stood like little statues until first one, then another, started to giggle again. When they began to all shove at a bigger stack of books, Dick couldn't wait any longer.

Quick as a monkey, he scurried down to the floor.

"Stop!" he shouted as he ran to the front of the store.

And, "Here, you!"

And, "Don't!"

The pixies turned at the sound of his voice and Dick skidded to a stop.

"Oh, oh," he said.

The little men were still giggling and elbowing each other, but there was a wicked light in their eyes now, and they were all looking at him with those dark, considering gazes. Poor Dick realized that he hadn't thought any of this through in the least bit properly, for now that he had their attention, he had no idea what to do with it. They might only be a third his size, individually, but there were at least twenty of them and everybody knew just how mean a pixy could be, did he set his mind to it.

"Well, will you look at that," one of the pixies said. "It's a little hobberdy man." He looked at his companions. "What shall we do with him?"

"Smash him!"

"Whack him!"

"Find a puddle and drown him!"

Dick turned and fled, back the way he'd come. The pixies streamed from the top of Mistress Holly's desk, laughing wickedly and shouting threats as they chased him. Up the "Poetry" shelves Dick went, all the way to the very top. When he looked back down, he saw that the pixies weren't following the route he'd taken.

He allowed himself a moment's relief. Perhaps he was safe. Perhaps they couldn't climb. Perhaps they were afraid of heights.

Or, he realized with dismay, perhaps they meant to bring the whole bookcase crashing down, and him with it.

For the little men had gathered at the bottom of the bookcase and were putting their shoulders to its base. They might be small, but they were strong, and soon the tall stand of shelves was tottering unsteadily, swaying back and forth. A loose book fell out. Then another.

"No, no! You mustn't!" Dick cried down to them.

But he was too late.

With cries of "Hooray!" from the little men below, the bookcase came tumbling down, spraying books all around it. It smashed into its neighbour, bringing that stand of shelves down as well. By the time Dick hit the floor, hundreds of books were scattered all over the carpet and he was sitting on top of a tall, unsteady mountain of poetry, clutching his head, awaiting the worst.

The pixies came clambering up its slopes, the wicked lights in their eyes shining fierce and bright. He was, Dick realized, about to become an ex-hob. Except then he heard the door to Mistress Holly's apartment open at the top of the back stairs.

Rescued, he thought. And not a moment too soon. She would chase them off.

All the little men froze and Dick looked for a place to hide from the mistress's gaze.

But the pixies seemed unconcerned. Another soft round of giggles arose from them as, one by one, they transformed into soft, glittering lights no bigger than the mouth of a shot glass. The lights rose up from the floor where they'd been standing and went sailing towards the front of the store. When the mistress appeared at the foot of the stairs, her dog at her heels, she didn't even look at the fallen bookshelves. She saw only the lights, her eyes widening with happy delight.

Oh, no, Dick thought. They're pixy-leading her.

The little dog began to growl and bark and tug at the hem of her long flannel nightgown, but she paid no attention to it. Smiling a dreamy smile, she lifted her arms above her head like a ballerina and began to follow the dancing lights to the front of the store. Dick watched as pixy magic made the door pop open and a gust of chilly air burst in. Goosebumps popped up on the mistress's forearms but she never seemed to notice the cold. Her gaze was locked on the lights as they swooped, around and around in a gallitrap circle, then went shimmering out onto the street beyond. In moments she would follow them, out into the night and who knew what terrible danger.

Her little dog let go of her hem and ran ahead, barking at the lights. But it was no use. The pixies weren't frightened and the mistress wasn't roused.

It was up to him, Dick realized.

He ran up behind her and grabbed her ankle, bracing himself. Like the pixies, he was much stronger than his size might give him to appear. He held firm as the mistress tried to raise her foot. She lost her balance and down she went, down and down, toppling like some enormous tree. Dick jumped back, hands to his mouth, appalled at what he'd had to do. She banged her shoulder against a display at the front of the store, sending yet another mass of books cascading onto the floor.

Landing heavily on her arms, she stayed bent over for a long time before she finally looked up. She shook her head as though to clear it. The pixy lights had returned to the store, buzzing angrily about, but it was no use. The spell had been broken. One by one, they zoomed out of the store, down the street and were quickly lost from sight. The mistress's little dog ran back out onto the sidewalk and continued to bark at them, long after they were gone.

"Please let me be dreaming..." the mistress said.

Dick stooped quickly out of sight as she looked about at the sudden ruin of the store. He peeked at her from his hiding place, watched her rub at her face, then slowly stand up and massage her shoulder where it had hit the display. She called the dog back in, but stood in the doorway herself for a long time, staring out at the street, before she finally shut and locked the door behind her.

Oh, it was all such a horrible, terrible, awful mess.

"I'm sorry, I'm sorry, I'm sorry," Dick murmured, his voice barely a whisper, tears blurring his eyes.

The mistress couldn't hear him. She gave the store another survey, then shook her head.

"Come on, Snippet," she said to the dog. "We're going back to bed. Because this is just a dream."

She picked her way through the fallen books and shelves as she spoke.

"And when we wake up tomorrow everything will be back to normal."

But it wouldn't be. Dick knew. This was more of a mess than even the most industrious of hobs could clear up in just one night. But he did what he could until the morning came, one eye on the task at hand, the other on the windows in case the horrible pixies decided to return. Though what he'd do if they did, probably only the moon knew, and she wasn't telling.

►Υ◄

Did you ever wake up from the weirdest, most unpleasant dream, only to find that it wasn't a dream at all?

When I came down to the store that morning, I literally had to lean against the wall at the foot of the stairs and catch my breath. I felt all faint and woozy. Snippet walked daintily ahead of me, sniffing the fallen books and whining softly.

An earthquake, I told myself. That's what it had been. I must have woken up right after the main shock, come down half-asleep and seen the mess, and just gone right back to bed again, thinking I was dreaming.

Except there'd been those dancing lights. Like a dozen or more Tinkerbells. Or fireflies. Calling me to follow, follow, follow, out into the night, until I'd tripped and fallen...

I shook my head slowly, trying to clear it. My shoulder was still sore and I massaged it as I took in the damage.

Actually, the mess wasn't as bad as it had looked at first. Many of the books appeared to have toppled from the shelves and landed in relatively alphabetical order.

Snippet whined again, but this time it was her "I really have to go" whine, so I grabbed her leash and a plastic bag from behind the desk and out we went for her morning constitutional.

It was brisk outside, but warm for early December, and there still wasn't any snow. At first glance, the damage from the quake appeared to be fairly marginal, considering it had managed to topple a couple of the bookcases in my store. The worst I could see were that all garbage canisters on the block had been overturned, the wind picking up the paper litter and carrying it in eddying pools up and down the street. Other than that, everything seemed pretty much normal. At least it did until I stopped into Café Joe's down the street to get my morning latte.

Joe Lapegna had originally operated a sandwich bar at the same location, but with the coming of Starbucks to town, he'd quickly seen which way the wind was blowing and renovated his place into a café. He'd done a good job with the décor. His café was every bit as contemporary and urban as any of the other high-end coffee bars in the city, the only real difference being that, instead of young college kids with rings through their noses, you got Joe serving the lattes and espressos. Joe with his broad shoulders and meaty, tattooed forearms, a fat caterpillar of a black moustache perched on his upper lip.

Before I could mention the quake, Joe started to tell me how he'd opened up this morning to find every porcelain mug in the store broken. None of the other breakables, not the plates or coffee makers. Nothing else was even out of place.

"What a weird quake it was," I said.

"Quake?" Joe said. "What quake?"

I waved a hand at the broken china he was sweeping up.

"This was vandals," he said. "Some little bastards broke in and had themselves a laugh."

So I told him about the bookcases in my shop, but he only shook his head.

"You hear anything about a quake on the radio?" he asked.

"I wasn't listening to it."

"I was. There was nothing. And what kind of a quake only breaks mugs and knocks over a couple of bookcases?"

Now that I thought of it, it was odd that there hadn't been any other disruption in my own store. If those bookcases had come down, why hadn't the front window display? I'd noticed a few books had fallen off my desk, but that was about it.

"It's so weird," I repeated.

Joe shook his head. "Nothing weird about it. Just some punks out having their idea of fun."

By the time I got back to my own store, I didn't know what to think. Snippet and I stopped in at a few other places along the strip and while everyone had damage to report, none of it was what could be put down to a quake. In the bakery, all the pies had been thrown against the front windows. In the hardware store, each and every electrical bulb was smashed—though they looked as though they'd simply exploded. All the rolls of paper towels and toilet paper from the grocery store had been tossed up into the trees behind their shipping and receiving bays, turning the bare-branched oaks and elms into bizarre mummy-like versions of themselves. And on it went.

The police arrived not long after I returned to the store. I felt like such a fool when one of the detectives came by to interview me. Yes, I'd heard the crash and come down to investigate. No, I hadn't seen anything.

I couldn't bring myself to mention the dancing lights.

No, I hadn't thought to phone it in.

"I thought I was dreaming," I told him. "I was half-asleep when I came downstairs and didn't think it had really happened. It wasn't until I came back down in the morning..."

The detective was of the opinion that it had been gang-related, kids out on the prowl, egging each other on until it had gotten out of control.

I thought about it when he left and knew he had to be right. The damage we'd sustained was all on the level of pranks—mean-spirited, to be sure, but pranks nonetheless. I didn't like the idea of our little area being the sudden target of vandals, but there really wasn't any other logical explanation. At least none occurred to me until I stepped back into the store and glanced at my computer. That's when I remembered Meran

Kelledy, how she'd gotten me to turn my sweater inside out and the odd things she'd been saying about pixies on the web.

If you're lucky, they're still on the Internet and didn't follow you home.

Of course that wasn't even remotely logical. But it made me think. After all, if the Wordwood database could take on a life of its own, who was to say that pixies on the Internet was any more improbable? As my friend Richard likes to point out, everyone has odd problems with their computers that could as easily be attributed to mischievous spirits as to software glitches. At least they could be if your mind was inclined to think along those lines, and mine certainly was.

I stood for a long moment, staring at the screen of my computer. I don't know exactly at what point I realized that the machine was on. I'd turned it off last night before Snippet and I went up to the apartment. And I hadn't stopped to turn it on this morning before we'd gone out. So either I was getting monumentally forgetful, or I'd turned it on while sleepwalking last night, or...

I glanced over at Snippet who was once again sniffing everything as though she'd never been in the store before. Or as if someone or something interesting and strange *had*.

"This is silly," I said.

But I dug out Meran's card and called the number on it all the same, staring at the computer screen as I did. I just hoped nobody had been tinkering with my files.

⊱ ⊤ ⊰

Bookstore hobs are a relatively recent phenomenon, dating back only a couple of hundred years. Dick knew hobs back home in the old country who'd lived in the same household for three times that length of time. He'd been a farm hob himself, once, living on a Devon steading for two hundred and twelve years until a new family moved in and began to take his services for granted. When one year they actually dared to complain about how poorly the harvest had been put away, he'd thrown every bit of it down into a nearby ravine and set off to find new habitation.

A cousin who lived in a shop had suggested to Dick that he try the same, but there were fewer commercial establishments in those days and they all had their own hob by the time he went looking, first up into Somerset, then back down through Devon, finally moving west to Cornwall.

In the end, he made his home in a small cubbyhole of a bookstore he found in Penzance. He lived there for years until the place went out of business, the owner setting sail for North America with plans to open another shop in the new land once he arrived.

Dick had followed, taking up residence in the new store when it was established. That was where he'd taught himself to read.

But he soon discovered that stores didn't have the longevity of a farm. They opened and closed up business seemingly on nothing more than a whim, which made it a hard life for a hob, always looking for a new place to live. By the latter part of this century, he had moved twelve times in the space of five years before finally settling into the place he now called home, the bookstore of his present mistress with its simple sign out front:

Holly Rue - Used Books

He'd discovered that a quality used book store was always the best. Libraries were good, too, but they were usually home to displaced gargoyles and the ghosts of writers and had no room for a hob as well. He'd tried new book stores, but the smaller ones couldn't keep him busy enough and the large ones were too bright, their hours of business too long. And he loved the wide and eclectic range of old and new books to be explored in a shop such as Mistress Holly's, titles that wandered far from the beaten path, or worthy books no longer in print, but nonetheless inspired. The stories he found in them sustained him in a way that nothing else could, for they fed the heart and the spirit.

But this morning, sitting behind the furnace, he only felt old and tired. There'd been no time to read at all last night, and he hadn't thought to bring a book down with him when he finally had to leave the store.

"I hate pixies," he said, his voice soft and lonely in the darkness. "I really really do."

Faerie and pixies had never gotten along, especially not since the last pitched battle between them in the old country when the faeries had been driven back across the River Parrett, leaving everything west of the Parrett as pixyland. For years, hobs such as Dick had lived a clandestine existence in their little steadings, avoiding the attention of pixies whenever they could.

Dick hadn't needed last night's experience to tell him why.

After awhile he heard the mistress and her dog leave the store so he crept out from behind the furnace to stand guard in case the pixies returned while the pair of them were gone. Though what he would do if the pixies did come back, he had no idea. He was an absolute failure when it came to protecting anything, that had been made all too clear last night.

Luckily the question never arose. Mistress Holly and the dog returned and he slipped back behind the furnace, morosely clutching his knees and rocking back and forth, waiting for the night to come. He could hear life go on upstairs. Someone came by to help the mistress right the fallen bookcases. Customers arrived and left with much discussion of the vandalism on the street. Most of the time he could hear only the mistress, replacing the books on their shelves.

"I should be doing that," Dick said. "That's my job."

But he was only an incompetent hob, concealed in his hidey-hole, of no use to anyone until they all went to bed and he could go about his business. And even then, any ruffian could come along and bully him and what could he do to stop them?

Dick's mood went from bad to worse, from sad to sadder still. It might have lasted all the day, growing unhappier with each passing hour, except at mid-morning he suddenly sat up, ears and nose quivering. A presence had come into the store above. A piece of an old mystery, walking about as plain as could be.

He realized that he'd sensed it yesterday as well, while he was dozing. Then he'd put it down to the dream he was wandering in, forgetting all about it when he woke. But today, wide awake, he couldn't ignore it. There was an oak king's daughter upstairs, an old and powerful spirit walking far from her woods. He began to shiver. Important faerie such as she wouldn't be out and about unless the need was great. His shiver deepened. Perhaps she'd come to reprimand him for the job so poorly done. She might turn him into a stick or a mouse.

Oh, this was very bad. First pixies, now this.

Whatever was he going to do? However could he even begin to explain that he'd meant to chase the pixies away, truly he had, but he simply wasn't big enough, nor strong enough. Perhaps not even brave enough.

He rocked back and forth, harder now, his face burrowed against his knees.

⊱ ⊻ ⊰

After I'd made my call to Meran, Samuel, who works at the deli down the street, came by and helped me stand the bookcases upright once more. The deli hadn't been spared a visit from the vandals either. He told me that they'd taken all the sausages out of the freezer and used them to spell out rude words on the floor.

"Remember when all we had to worry about was some graffiti on the walls outside?" he asked when he was leaving.

I was still replacing books on the shelves when Meran arrived. She looked around the store while I expanded on what I'd told her over the phone. Her brow furrowed thoughtfully and I was wondering if she was going to tell me to put my sweater on backwards again.

"You must have a hob in here," she said.

"A what?"

It was the last thing I expected her to say.

"A hobgoblin," she said. "A brownie. A little faerie man who dusts and tidies and keeps things neat."

"I just thought it didn't get all that dirty," I said, realizing as I spoke how ridiculous that sounded.

Because, when I thought about it, a helpful brownie living in the store explained a lot. While I certainly ran the vacuum cleaner over the carpets every other morning or so, and dusted when I could, the place never seemed to need much cleaning. My apartment upstairs required more and it didn't get a fraction of the traffic.

And it wasn't just the cleaning. The store, for all its clutter, was organized, though half the time I didn't know how. But I always seemed to be able to lay my hand on whatever I needed to find without having to root about too much. Books often got put away without my remembering I'd done it. Others mysteriously vanished, then reappeared a day or so later, properly filed in their appropriate section—even if they had originally disappeared from the top of my desk. I rarely needed to alphabetize my sections while my colleagues in other stores were constantly complaining of the mess their customers left behind.

"But aren't you supposed to leave cakes and cream out for them?" I found myself asking.

"You never leave a specific gift," Meran said. "Not unless you want him to leave. It's better to simply 'forget' a cake or a sweet treat on one of the shelves when you leave for the night."

"I haven't even done that. What could he be living on?"

Meran smiled as she looked around the store. "Maybe the books nourish him. Stranger things have been known to happen in Faerie."

"Faerie," I repeated slowly.

Bad enough I'd helped create a database on the Internet that had taken on a life of its own. Now my store was in Faerie. Or at least straddling the border, I supposed. Maybe the one had come about because of the other.

"Your hob will know what happened here last night," Meran said.

"But how would we even go about asking him?"

It seemed a logical question, since I'd never known I had one living with me in the first place. But Meran only smiled.

"Oh, I can usually get their attention," she told me.

She called out something in a foreign language, a handful of words that rang with great strength and appeared to linger and echo longer than they should. The poor little man who came sidling up from the basement in response looked absolutely terrified. He was all curly hair and raggedy clothes with a broad face that, I assumed from the laugh lines, normally didn't look so miserable. He was carrying a battered little leather carpet-bag and held a brown cloth cap in his hand. He couldn't have been more than two feet tall.

All I could do was stare at him, though I did have the foresight to pick up Snippet before she could lunge in his direction. I could feel the growl rumbling in her chest more than hear it. I think she was as surprised as me to find that he'd been living in our basement all this time.

Meran sat on her haunches, bringing her head down to the general level of the hob's. To put him at ease, I supposed, so I did the same myself. The little man didn't appear to lose any of his nervousness. I could see his knees knocking against each other, his cheek twitching.

"B-begging your pardon, your ladyship," he said to Meran. His gaze slid to me and I gave him a quick smile. He blinked, swallowed hard, and returned his attention to my companion. "Dick Bobbins," he added, giving a quick nod of his head. "At your service, as it were. I'll just be on my way, then, no harm done."

"Why are you so frightened of me?" Meran asked.

He looked at the floor. "Well, you're a king's daughter, aren't you just, and I'm only me."

A king's daughter? I thought.

Meran smiled. "We're all only who we are, no one of more importance than the other."

"Easy for you to say," he began. Then his eyes grew wide and he put a hand to his mouth. "Oh, that was a bad thing to say to such a great and wise lady such as yourself."

Meran glanced at me. "They think we're like movie stars," she explained. "Just because we were born in a court instead of a hobhole."

I was getting a bit of a case of the celebrity nerves myself. Court? King's daughter? Who exactly *was* this woman?

"But you know," she went on, returning her attention to the little man, "my father's court was only a glade, our palace no more than a tree."

He nodded quickly, giving her a thin smile that never reached his eyes.

"Well, wonderful to meet you," he said. "Must be on my way now."

He picked up his carpetbag and started to sidle towards the other aisle that wasn't blocked by what he must see as two great big hulking women and a dog.

"But we need your help," Meran told him.

Whereupon he burst into tears.

The mothering instinct that makes me such a sap for Snippet kicked into gear and I wanted to hold him in my arms and comfort him. But I had Snippet to consider, straining in my grip, the growl in her chest quite audible now. And I wasn't sure how the little man would have taken my sympathies. After all, he might be child-sized, but for all his tears, he was obviously an adult, not a child. And if the stories were anything to go by, he was probably older than me—by a few hundred years.

Meran had no such compunction. She slipped up to him and put her arms around him, cradling his face against the crook of her shoulder.

It took awhile before we coaxed the story out of him. I locked the front door and we went upstairs to my kitchen where I made tea for us all. Sitting at the table, raised up to the proper height by a stack of books, Dick told us about the pixies coming out of the computer screen, how they'd knocked down the bookcases and finally disappeared into the night. The small mug I'd given him looked enormous in his hands. He fell silent when he was done and stared glumly down at the steam rising from his tea.

"But none of what they did was your fault," I told him.

"Kind of you to say," he managed. He had to stop and sniff, wipe his nose on his sleeve. "But if I'd b-been braver—"

"They *would* have drowned you in a puddle," Meran said. "And I think you were brave, shouting at them the way you did and then rescuing your mistress from being pixy-led."

I remembered those dancing lights and shivered. I knew those stories as well. There weren't any swamps or marshes to be led into around here, but there were eighteen-wheelers out on the highway only a few blocks away. Entranced as I'd been, the pixies could easily have walked me right out in front of any one of them. I was lucky to only have a sore shoulder.

"Do you...really think so?" he asked, sitting up a little straighter.

We both nodded.

Snippet was lying under my chair, her curiosity having been satisfied that Dick was only one more visitor and therefore out-of-bounds in terms of biting and barking at. There'd been a nervous moment while she'd sniffed at his trembling hand and he'd looked as though he was ready to scurry up one of the bookcases, but they quickly made their peace. Now Snippet was only bored and had fallen asleep.

"Well," Meran said. "It's time we put our heads together and considered how we can put our unwanted visitors back where they came from and keep them there."

"Back onto the Internet?" I asked. "Do you really think we should?"

"Well, we could try to kill them..."

I shook my head. That seemed too extreme. I started to protest, only to see that she'd been teasing me.

"We could take a thousand of them out of the web," Meran said, "and still not have them all. Once tricksy folk like pixies have their foot in a place, you can't ever be completely rid of them." She smiled. "But if we can get them to go back in, there are measures we can take to stop them from troubling you again."

"And what about everybody else on-line?" I asked.

Meran shrugged. "They'll have to take their chances—just like they do when they go for a walk in the woods. The little people are everywhere."

I glanced across my kitchen table to where the hob was sitting and thought, no kidding.

"The trick, if you'll pardon my speaking out of turn," Dick said, "is to play on their curiosity."

Meran gave him an encouraging smile. "We want your help," she said. "Go on."

The little man sat up straighter still and put his shoulders back.

"We could use a book that's never been read," he said. "We could put it in the middle of the road, in front of the store. That would certainly make me curious."

"An excellent idea," Meran told him.

"And then we could use the old spell of bell, book and candle. The churchmen stole that one from us."

Even I'd heard of it. Bell, book and candle had once been another way of saying excommunication in the Catholic church. After pronouncing the sentence, the officiating cleric would close his book, extinguish the candle, and toll the bell as if for someone who had died. The book symbolized the book of life, the candle a man's soul, removed from the sight of God as the candle had been from the sight of men.

But I didn't get the unread book bit.

"Do you mean a brand new book?" I asked. "A particular copy that nobody might have opened yet, or one that's so bad that no one's actually made their way all the way through it?"

"Though someone would have had to," Dick said, "for it to have been published in the first place. I meant the way books were made in the old days, with the pages still sealed. You had to cut them apart as you read them."

"Oh, I remember those," Meran said.

Like she was there. I took another look at her and sighed. Maybe she had been.

"Do you have any like that?" she asked.

"Yes," I said slowly, unable to hide my reluctance.

I didn't particularly like the idea of putting a collector's item like that out in the middle of the road.

But in the end, that's what we did.

⊁ ⊤ ⊰

The only book I had that passed Dick's inspection was *The Trembling of the Veil* by William Butler Yeats, number seventy-one of a 1000-copy edition privately printed by T. Werner Laurie, Ltd. in 1922. All the pages were still sealed at the top. It was currently listing on the Internet in the $450 to $500 range and I kept it safely stowed away in the glass-doored bookcase that held my first editions.

The other two items were easier to deal with. I had a lovely brass bell that my friend Tatiana had given me for Christmas last year and a whole box of fat white candles just because I liked to burn them. But it broke my heart to go out onto the street around two a.m., and place the Yeats on the pavement.

We left the front door to the store ajar, the computer on. I wasn't entirely sure how we were supposed to lure the pixies back into the store and then onto the Internet once more, but Meran took a flute out of her bag and fit the wooden pieces of it together. She spoke of a calling-on music and Dick nodded sagely, so I simply went along with their better experience. Mind you, I also wasn't all that sure that my Yeats would actually draw the pixies back in the first place, but what did I know?

We all hid in the alleyway running between my store and the futon shop, except for Snippet, who was locked up in my apartment. She hadn't been very pleased by that. After an hour of crouching in the cold in the alley, I wasn't feeling very pleased myself. What if the pixies didn't come? What if they did, but they approached from the fields behind the store and came traipsing up this very alleyway?

By three-thirty we all had a terrible chill. Looking up at my apartment, I could see Snippet lying in the window of the dining room, looking down at us. She didn't appear to have forgiven me yet and I would happily have changed places with her.

"Maybe we should just—"

I didn't get to finish with "call it a night." Meran put a finger to her lips and hugged the wall. I looked past her to the street.

At first I didn't see anything. There was just my Yeats, lying there on the pavement, waiting for a car to come and run over it. But then I saw the little man, not even half the size of Dick, come creeping up from the sewer grating. He was followed by two more. Another pair came down the brick wall of the temporary office help building across the street. Small dancing lights that I remembered too clearly from last night, dipped and wove their way from the other end of the block, descending to the pavement and becoming more of the little men when they drew near to the book. One of them poked at it with his foot and I had visions of them tearing it apart.

Meran glanced at Dick and he nodded, mouthing the words, "That's the lot of them."

She nodded back and took her flute out from under her coat where she'd been keeping it warm.

At this point I wasn't really thinking of how the calling music would work. I'm sure my mouth hung agape as I stared at the pixies. I felt light-headed, a big grin tugging at my lips. Yes, they were pranksters, and mean-spirited ones at that. But they were also magical. The way they'd changed from little lights to little men...I'd never seen anything like it before. The hob who lived in my bookstore was magical, too, of course, but somehow it wasn't the same thing. He was already familiar, so down-to-earth. Sitting around during the afternoon and evening while we waited, I'd had a delightful time talking books with him, as though he were an old friend. I'd completely forgotten that he was a little magic man himself.

The pixies were truly puzzled by the book. I suppose it would be odd from any perspective, a book that old, never once having been opened or read. It defeated the whole purpose of why it had been made.

I'm not sure when Meran began to play her flute. The soft breathy sound of it seemed to come from nowhere and everywhere, all at once, a resonant wave of slow, stately notes, one falling after the other, rolling into a melody that was at once hauntingly strange and heartachingly familiar.

The pixies lifted their heads at the sound. I wasn't sure what I'd expected, but when they began to dance, I almost clapped my hands. They were so funny. Their bodies kept perfect time to the music, but their little eyes glared at Meran as she stepped out of the alley and Pied Pipered them into the store.

Dick fetched the Yeats and then he and I followed after, arriving in time to see the music make the little men dance up onto my chair, onto the desk, until they began to vanish, one by one, into the screen of my monitor, a fat candle sitting on top of it, its flame flickering with their movement. Dick opened the book and I took the bell out of my pocket.

Meran took the flute from her lips.

"Now," she said.

Dick slapped the book closed, she leaned forward and blew out the candle while I began to chime the bell, the clear brass notes ringing in the silence left behind by the flute. We saw a horde of little faces staring out at us from the screen, eyes glaring. One of the little men actually popped back through, but Dick caught him by the leg and tossed him back into the screen.

Meran laid her flute down on the desk and brought out a garland she'd made earlier of rowan twigs, green leaves and red berry sprigs still attached in places. When she laid it on top of the monitor, we heard the modem dial up my Internet service. When the connection was made, the little men vanished from the screen. The last turned his bum towards us and let out a loud fart before he, too, was gone.

The three of us couldn't help it. We all broke up.

"That went rather well," Meran said when we finally caught our breath. "My husband Cerin is usually the one to handle this sort of thing, but it's nice to know I haven't forgotten how to deal with such rascals myself. And it's probably best he didn't come along this evening. He can seem rather fierce and I don't doubt poor Dick here would thought him far too menacing."

I looked around the store.

"Where *is* Dick?" I asked.

But the little man was gone. I couldn't believe it. Surely he hadn't just up and left us like in the stories.

"Hobs and brownies," Meran said when I asked, her voice gentle, "they tend to take their leave rather abruptly when the tale is done."

"I thought you had to leave them a suit of clothes or something."

Meran shrugged. "Sometimes simply being identified is enough to make them go."

"Why does it have to be like that?"

"I'm not really sure. I suppose it's a rule or something, or a geas—a thing that has to happen. Or perhaps it's no more than a simple habit they've handed down from one generation to the next."

"But I *loved* the idea of him living here," I said. "I thought it would be so much fun. With all the work he's been doing, I'd have been happy to make him a partner."

Meran smiled. "Faerie and commerce don't usually go hand in hand."

"But you and your husband play music for money."

Her smile grew wider, her eyes enigmatic, but also amused.

"What makes you think we're faerie?" she asked.

"Well, you...that is..."

"I'll tell you a secret," she said, relenting. "We're something else again, but what exactly that might be, even we have no idea anymore. Mostly we're the same as you. Where we differ is that Cerin and I always live with half a foot in the otherworld that you've only visited these past few days."

"And only the borders of it, I'm sure."

She shrugged. "Faerie is everywhere. It just *seems* closer at certain times, in certain places."

She began to take her flute apart and stow the wooden pieces away in the instrument's carrying case.

"Your hob will be fine," she said. "The kindly ones such as he always find a good household to live in."

"I hope so," I said. "But all the same, I was really looking forward to getting to know him better."

⊱ ⊤ ⊰

Dick Bobbins got an odd feeling listening to the two of them talk, his mistress and the oak king's daughter. Neither was quite what he'd expected. Mistress Holly was far kinder and not at all the brusque, rather self-centered human that figured in so many old hob fireside tales. And her ladyship...well, who would have thought that one of the highborn would treat a simple hob as though he stood on equal footing? It was all very unexpected.

But it was time for him to go. He could feel it in his blood and in his bones.

He waited while they said their goodbyes. Waited while Mistress Holly took the dog out for a last quick pee before the pair of them retired to their apartment. Then he had the store completely to himself, with no chance of unexpected company. He fetched his little leather carpetbag from his hobhole behind the furnace and came back upstairs to say goodbye to the books, to the store, to his home.

Finally all there was left to do was to spell the door open, step outside and go. He hesitated on the welcoming carpet, thinking of what Mistress Holly had asked, what her ladyship had answered. Was the leaving song that ran in his blood and rumbled in his bones truly a geas, or only habit? How was a poor hob to know? If it was a rule, then who had made it and what would happen if he broke it?

He took a step away from the door, back into the store and paused, waiting for he didn't know what. Some force to propel him out the door. A flash of light to burn down from the sky and strike him where he stood. Instead all he felt was the heaviness in his heart and the funny tingling warmth he'd known when he'd heard the mistress say how she'd been looking forward to getting to know him. That she wanted him to be a partner in her store. Him. Dick Bobbins, of all things.

He looked at the stairs leading up to her apartment.

Just as an experiment, he made his way over to them, then up the risers, one by one, until he stood at her door.

Oh, did he dare, did he dare?

He took a deep breath and squared his shoulders. Then setting down his carpetbag, he twisted his cloth cap in his hands for a long moment before he finally lifted an arm and rapped a knuckle against the wood panel of Mistress Holly's door.